Crossing the Line

Alan Swindell

Alan Swindell

Elemental Books

First published by Elemental Books, Great Britain.

10 9 8 7 6 5 4 3 2

A CIP catalogue record for the title is available from the British Library

ISBN 0-9539415-0-7

Printed and bound by Short Run Press, Exeter

Elemental Books
Lower Stretchford
Buckfastleigh
South Devon TQ11 OJY

For Dad, who kept the Wildside alive.

PART ONE

Now is the time for walking in
woods
by the cold stream come from the
waterfall
are you afraid?

Frances Horovitz
Journey

ONE

`Fetch it.`

The boy spoke through the side of his mouth; ferret eyes fixed on the scrap of latex halfway across the motorway. The others looked at Beth, certain she would obey, uncertain of what it would mean. Of course Beth would do it. They made her do other things, stupid or dangerous things for a laugh, unspeakable things, to see how far she would go, to make her cry or angry, things she had learned to hate them for, of course she would walk through four lanes of screaming traffic to fetch the burst balloon. Of course Sam would say nothing, her big brother, twelve years old but useless, struck dumb, mesmerised by the power of those who could speak through any part of their mouth. But they did not need to ask. Beth was already walking through the traffic, not running but walking, like a ten-year old Moses parting the Red Sea, as though the tons of metal hurtling past were in her imagination. Horns blared, tyres screeched but Beth just walked, eyes forwards, ghost-like. The rest of them waited, frozen, certain that one nick from a wing mirror, one brush from a side light would burst her as surely as the balloon had burst, as surely as a fruit tossed into the flight of a baseball bat would spray itself gloriously into the air. They saw her stop and bend down. A moment later she vanished, hidden from view by the gleaming thunder of a container lorry, behind it a second and a third and in between each one a moment's glimpse of Beth straightening, turning, walking back, vanishing, walking, vanishing again, the rest of them speechless with horror, manic cars and groaning lorries missing her by chance, by an inch, sucking at her hair, clawing at her clothes, jealous of her resolve, but diverting her purpose not for one second.

`Give it.`

This time he looked at her, slate-grey eyes colder than death. He held out his hand and waited, the rest feeding on his uncertainty, a new balance of power born in the instant Beth ignored him, did not even look at him. She held it up for them all to admire. A scrap of orange latex. Tied to it with a piece of thread was a feather, a beautiful feather. It was from the wing of a jay, brilliant metal blue against ink black. That was all. A piece of litter and a feather. But far more. Like a dream rising up from the subconscious, drifting into daytime, arriving as something meaningless, but a reminder all the same: there is something else out there, there is another world, there is another way of being. She ignored the boy and his followers and handed it to Sam. `Keep it safe,` she said.

He saw how large his sister's eyes had become, how the pale skin around her lips was touched with blue but also how a smile was hiding, ready to break the spell. She walked through the gang and he followed, safe in her aura of invincibility. `One day, Sam,` she whispered, `One day soon.`

TWO

Alfred and the Danes. Finn thought of them as the geese flew past, more than twenty to a skein. You could still hear it in the vowels, they said, guttural one side, rounded the other. He wondered if the geese changed their call as they crossed the line from east to west. He was certain they would have shown on a screen somewhere: *Branta canadensis*, twenty-three, unauthorized crossing, map reference SO970352. One line goes and another takes its place, he thought. Which seemed to be the way of the world. He watched the leading bird drop suddenly, the rest following as one before resuming their course. She was playing with them, keeping them alert. Finn was doing much the same, playing with the things he had learned, composing a song line to mark the journey, one he could relate back home and which would fix in his memory for ever. It was a way of reshaping the things he had learned in the soft clay and hard boulders of the map. Ah the map! Almost an acre in size, it had taken him a month to build, which was long enough to both love and hate it, long enough for him to both despise the need for sleep and its interruption to his work yet ache for rest, to drop exhausted at the close of each day. By the end he could crawl around it blindfolded, picking out the hills and valleys, naming every inlet of the sea, every bend of the forest against the knuckles of moorland, every settlement and routeway marked by sprays of gravel. It was gone now, returned to the forest floor like so much else, left only as a memory in his tanned limbs. Travelling like this, by boat, brought it all back. Geography: The Severn valley and its one thousand islands, the heart of the Wildside. Marsh, reed beds, open water, polders old and new, a labyrinth of canals and channel ways. History: King Alfred ruled from Wessex and kept the Danes beyond an ancient boundary now returned to haunt the modern age. Literature: Wessex and Thomas Hardy. Finn's favourite. There was a description early on in *Tess* of the Blackmore Vale that he knew word for word. Which led to Philosophy: Wessex as idealized west, conscious versus unconscious, the need to push into the unknown, the need to create the unknown when all is mapped and measured. Or was that Psychology? Creating the unknown was Myth and Legend: The link between Alfred and Arthur. Alfred was one of the seven Arthurs. Current Affairs: Wildside politics, social consensus within an agreed anarchy. Law in a lawless world. The new wild-west. Outlaw as folk hero. Finn cleared his head, watched egrets stalk for frogs, counted harriers above the reeds. He missed his horse. He missed her smell and the simple demands she made on him and the world, demands that had a rhythm of their own. He thought about his own smell, wood smoke and wild garlic, feral but clean. It might offend the girl. Or would it attract her? Probably not. Probably she was used to soap and cleansers, wax and lotion, gel and polish. Even in the glut of her prolific sex life there would be no room for smells like his. More likely she might offend him, and she might frighten the horses. Which led to *wergeld.* Alfred and the Danes had operated a law, the law of *wergeld.* Slaves escaping from one side to the other would always be returned. Even though they were at war with each other they agreed on that much. It was in every one's interest. Except the slaves. Smelling of soap might not protect her from *wergeld.*

There was red in her hair. He had argued it with Anna but it was certainly there. That was the Danes and Vikings. He had seen it in the photographs. People would say it was black but if you looked closely you could sense rather than see the tell-tale sheen. The black was Celt. And so were the eyes that seemed, in the photograph at least, all-seeing, ready to expose him, the world he belonged to and the Quest he was on. He looked down at his feet. Long and agile toes gripped the boat's decking, the half-tan half-dirt of many days travel climbed up his calves and shins. He might have to wash for her. He might even, God-forbid, have to comb his hair. Most of all he wished it was over, the task done.

Most of all he wished it was not even necessary, that the world could leave him alone with his horse.

`Toll.`

The voice was bored but insistent. Its Dutch owner stared down from the causeway and caught the bag of coin thrown in his direction. Immigrants had built the thing twenty years ago to link Dumbleton with Bredon but now a gap had been cut in it to allow small boats backwards and forwards. Behind him a sign read `Cash or Kind`, proof of the transition into No-Man's-Land. `No cards` some joker had scrawled beneath in red paint only to be outdone by the second and more ominous scribble. `Yet` it said, as though one day the revolution would be undone, as though one day this whole fragile world would be unstitched. The toll house was post-modern, thrown together carefully of drift wood, fishing nets, old rope, lobster pots and bright galvanized lengths of chimney flue. It's windows were compound, like an insect's eye, tiny green discs made of wine bottles, bottoms out to collect the sun, necks in to release warm claret-scented air into the building. Only yards away two grey seals were sunning themselves on rocks, baleful eyes, Danish vowels.

Approaching Bredon always made Finn quiet. It was the largest island in the valley and guarded the entrance to Evesham Water. Its lower slopes were wooded, its summit topped with a tower of some kind from which steel threads swept down to the water's edge. Plumes of smoke rose from hidden places in the woods, a climbing cable car caught the sun and flashed brightly for a second. History: Larsen B and Wilkins were ice no more. Vast wastelands of perfect white had crumbled to grey slush in the last fifty years. The West Antarctic Ice Sheet, stunned into action, had taken its time, had hinted its intent, sent ominous warnings north in the form of glacial dreadnoughts, each stoic as stone, each a vast and ice-white nightmare of possibilities, each a silent declaration of war by stealth. The Industrial World braced itself, talked treaties, shuffled alliances but waited in terror for the second front to open, for Arctic land ice to declare its allegiance. The dogs of war, let slip from the north, seized the Odden Feature. The Gulf Stream faltered. Nightmare futures swarmed down every TV cable and filled every front room with delighted panic. Insurance empires melted quicker than the ice had done. Capital migrated faster than any displaced nations. Great engineered barrages rose and fell with each new tide, with each new estimate and prediction. Prophets of doom talked up every temperature reading into holocaust numbers. The silent war, they called it. Not a shot fired in anger. Capitulation total. Behind the sand-bagged cities and the defaulting insurance companies a thousand different types of panic trampled the wetter, better world into being. Bredon was the Church of England's polite and muffled panic. Scores of its piles went under and many of their artifacts got stolen or sold abroad but just as many got saved and brought to Bredon for safe keeping. From Bredon, one day, a return invasion might be launched, but for now the fonts, the stained glass, the wooden screens, the candlesticks and gargoyles, thousands of them, decorated the parks and gardens and the hundreds of chapels that had been built here in the last forty years. The whole island had become a huge open-air church, then a place of pilgrimage and finally a hospice. Literature: Bredon as favourite retreat for poets, hosts an annual festival of the arts. Sociology: exit music, music for the terminally ill, a cultural phenomena unique to the Wildside.

The boat was drawing through the gap between the two islands. His parents had farmed close to here, just below Ogwell. It had broken their hearts to lose it. Their anger, like that of so many like them, had helped shape the Wildside, had turned the world of carbon suicide on its head. Sixty dairy cattle. Now look at it. Finn wished they could, they might have felt better. Water, reeds, sandbanks dense with waders, tall marking poles each with its resident cormorant, small flocks of spoonbill and flamingo. Every winter tens of thousands of geese grazed the fields his parents had lost to Antarctic ice. He looked back to the west.

Idealised or not, the great expanse of water reaching across to Malvern in various shades of blue and the smudge of hills beyond were vivid in the early evening sun. As though on cue a rainbow reached up from the water and resolved itself somewhere above hills to the north. `Here in the valley,` it said in *Tess,* `the world seems to be constructed upon a smaller and more delicate scale; the fields are mere paddocks, so reduced that from this height their hedgerows appear a network of dark green threads overspreading the paler green grass.` For now the islands of Dumbleton and Bredon closed in on the view, cut him even further off from his horse and the smell of wild garlic. He had read once that in the Comfort Zone people rushed to watch car wrecks being pulled apart, that a special TV channel gave up-to-the-minute pictures of who was being dragged out of which car, and told where and how to get the best view of the injured and, best of all, the bereaved. Looking ahead, to the east, to his destination, he felt himself to be like one of those people, drawn to the blue glare of disaster, feeling something unwholesome in his motives but captive to the fascination of it. Beth Savage being pulled from the wreck. A corpse? Body parts? Or red-tinted Celt with knowing eyes and Comfort Zone appetites? He looked at the crossbow for reassurance. He had checked its action a dozen times already and fought the urge to do so again. There were times, and now was one of them, that finding the weapon so wonderfully balanced, so precise and simple in its mechanism he wondered whether he used it or it him. There was something indecent about its perfection. Early in his training he had avoided the crossbow, at first unconsciously, but later by design, concentrating instead on horse skills and tracking. For the first three years of five he had chosen to live rough, always making his own shelters, always pitted against the teacher who had tracked and challenged him at every turn, stealing his bed-roll in the depths of winter and his water at the height of summer, daring him to give up, to return to a life of comfort. He had learned to withstand cold, heat, hunger and thirst, to sit or stand still for hours on end in the pursuit of game, to track boar in the woods, deer on the moor and people in the towns, even to follow a single eel from estuary to hedge bottom over weeks and months. From the teacher he had learned the deeper secrets of landscape and trees and food plants, how to roast a hedgehog in mud, how to identify an old Saxon field system in a dense forest, how to date and age a tree by studying the plants around it. For a long time after the training Finn had found it difficult to sleep indoors and even now favoured the open night to an enclosed room. But there were things nobody could teach him, things he had to learn for himself and for which the cold perfection of the crossbow would be necessary. And if he failed? If the bleak logic of chance turned against this huge gamble, what then? The tollhouse graffiti was warning enough. Yet. The tide might turn and swamp them all, flood every Vale of Blackmore, real and imagined, with something far worse than tarmac and cement.

THREE

There are rules about crossing it. They are unwritten and depend on word of mouth but you ignore them at your peril. Don't expect to come back is rule number one, or if you do return it will be on their terms; deconstructed, unborn, a refugee in your own street. Rule number two is be prepared. Not with knives and crossbow and the ability to ride a horse or skin a rabbit, but be prepared to be taken apart, from the inside out, to be unwound, like an old jumper, rolled into a ball and made into something completely and utterly new, burst like a fruit, broadcast as unknown seed on uncertain ground.

Sam used to ask her what it was like. Over and over again the same question. Over and over again the sacred mantra: `What's it like, Beth? What's it like? ` Until who could have blamed her for snapping at him or ignoring him or walking away? Though she never did, not once. `It's like you want it to be, Sam,` she would say, telling him her dream. `It's like Dad says. There are trees and birds, more trees than you could ever climb or count. And horses, they ride on horses.` The idea of horses terrified Sam as it did Beth, but the trees he could dream about for hours, the trees he could climb and enter, smell and touch, endlessly.

`And are there shadows, Beth? `he would want to ask but didn't, knowing it would annoy her, knowing that all those trees would cast dense shadows for him to slip between and hide amongst. He would wait, content in the silence, examining the tight barbs of the wing feather, delighting in the way they fell back together as he parted them with his thumb.

`It's the Wildside,` she would say, looking at him like no one else could. `What do you think it's like? This is the Comfort Zone, that's the Wildside.` She would tell him the little she knew, much more that she guessed, but mostly what she hoped for: the horses, the trees, the silence, his eyes growing bigger with each new dream. `And will we go there, Beth? `he would want to ask, but never did, Beth not waiting for him to struggle for the words.

`One day we'll go there, Sam, you and me, we'll cross the Line together.` This she would always say softly, like a whisper, though there was never anyone to listen, and Sam would smile, a smile only Beth had ever seen, and she would turn away so that he could not see her eyes fill with tears and her lips tighten with anger.

The sharp black barbs gave way to the beautiful radiant blue. How did one piece of feather know it was meant to be black and the one next to it blue? And was the one jealous of the other? He soaked her words up like a sponge. He willed it to be true. To have a place to confine every fantasy and every horror was a kind of salvation. Everything you longed to act out but never could, everything you dreamed of but could tell no one, everything you feared and loved, all were possible. And nobody could deny it, because nobody owned the truth about the Wildside and nobody ever would. But Beth and Sam owned the feather. They had seen children, first contact with an alien species, normal looking children, not especially dirty or under-nourished or ridden with disease but prepared, waving through the noise, launching the balloon, it was they who had enticed Beth through the traffic, for them she had risked death.

For hours Sam would study the map, his fingers tracing the curves of blue where the sea had claimed the low ground. He would scan the cramped names of Comfort Zone conurbation, the matted scrawl of roads, the endless tumour of city, each one feeding into the next, the same stale blood pumped endlessly around. And then his eye would slip across the Line into the pale green vagueness, so much of it unnamed, a conspiracy of Celtic and Saxon spaces, great voids of forest and marsh, small towns, aberrations, clinging to inlets, backing into hollow hills and deep green meadows. What's it like, Beth? What's it really like? He could have told her, made her listen, everything, his descriptions sick with longing, but accurate.

Their father once said you could sell the Line to Hollywood. There is a line in each of us, he said, Hollywood might like it simplified. It was certainly more than a motorway. It was a technology, a means of surveillance and control, a scar cut through the landscape as though by a blind surgeon trying to salvage a corpse. Hollywood sucks, Beth answered, Hollywood covers shit with candy. It was the kind of rant she tried to frighten friends away with, the kind of angry statement she used to mark her territory. Beth's line. Beyond this line lives Beth Savage, rabid, keep out. Cross this one only if you know the complex rules.

So Beth had walked through traffic, Beth was immortal, Beth had picked up the balloon and feather from another world, ignored the boys who thought they controlled her and so confirmed the rumours and made her a target. They waited almost a year. Danger turned them. More powerful than any drug, the antidote to the dull grind of security, Wildside Danger, a magnetic force pulling deep beneath the surface of a comfortable world, a pull that grew stronger through the years of childhood until, for teenagers, like an alternative puberty, it could turn north to south.

There were only three of them, though it must have seemed as though a dozen pairs of hands had lifted her from the ground, sat her first in the wash basin, where they ran the hot water, and then in the bowl they had blocked with toilet paper and pissed in. Stainless steel walls on three sides reflected them back, distorted, a huge and hostile tribe.

`Get your Dad to fix it.` one of them grunted. His face was only inches from Beth's but few details stuck, only that he smelled of cigarette and had lips which tried to glue together with little threads of saliva. Like a cave. Stalagmites and stalactites leading to a dark interior which smelled of tar. Cigarettes. Against school rules. He would be caught and punished. For some reason this consoled her, it offered her a saliva-thin strand of hope, even though his two friends and their thousand reflections were leering somewhere in the background, waiting their turn and keeping a look-out for security guards in the corridor.

Fix what? Beth was too scared to ask, too shocked by this latest taste of violence, still disbelieving, expecting to wake up or for them to apologize for the mistake. Sorry, Beth, we thought you were somebody else. The world is a good place, it really is. Go and wash yourself. We were only joking.

`On Saturday and Sunday,` Dry-Mouth said, `Both days. Just get him to fix it. We know he can. If you don't we'll break your fuckin` neck. If you do, you'll be our mate, we'll look after you. Got it?`

Beth would be their mate. They would look after her. The playground, the way to school, crossing the wasteland where the gangs hung out, she wouldn't have to worry anymore. She would have friends to watch her back. Anything was better than no friends at all.

Dry-lips had the final word. With one hand he gripped her hair so tight that her scalp started to bleed, with the other he forced open her jaw and spat into her throat, a gob of venom to infect her with his private evil.

Of course she promised. But she did not cry. She wanted to cry in the classroom where the teacher bawled at her for wetting herself, she wanted to cry all the way home, she wanted to cry herself to sleep and all the way to school the next day but she did not allow it. She had a control over such things. And then she told them that she had spoken to her father and that he had fixed it, they could go ahead with their plan. Perhaps that was the happiest day of Beth's life, she seemed to skip through it. She had discovered that even the worst of terrors could be tamed by telling people what they wanted to hear.

Four days later the school was gripped with a raw horror and a grim fascination. It was after the weekend that her father was to have `fixed` things for the three youths, Beth's new friends.

She had promised, even if it was under duress. They had crossed the Line. They had braved the wire and used the canal according to one rumour, they had bolted over the motorway in the early hours of Saturday was the other version. Either way they had gone exploring in No-Man's Land, looking for drugs, some said. They had girls waiting for them was an alternative. They had been caught. They had been handed back. They were in prison and would never be let out. They had been let out but would not be coming back to school. They were coming back to school and they were going to break Beth's fucking neck. Beth wondered how. She imagined it would be in the toilets again, her head in the urinal, a knee forcing down, a hand jerking up, a click like the slide of a door bolt, all because she had broken her promise. Even at eleven years of age Beth knew that telling them whatever they wanted to hear would not save her a second time.

Her father kept her off school for as long as he dared. It was during those weeks at home that she finally found the courage to ask him what it was those boys had wanted, was it true that he could fix things, that he knew how to bridge one world with the other? If it was true then he could do it for her. He could take her and Sam across the Line and into a better world.

`Can you? ` Beth asked, already old enough to sense some of the things her father had left unsaid, desperate for it to be true, `everyone at school says you can.`

He had smiled at that and lowered his voice to make it their secret. `As a matter of fact, Beth, I can! `

But she wasn't old enough to know when to stop and asked one question more, perhaps prompted by the shadow that lingered behind her father. `And they say something else. They say you killed Mum. Is that true?`

FOUR

And this is Clegg, Nathaniel Clegg. Take time for Clegg for he may prove worth it, even as he sits in a frail dinghy, ready to freeze for the price of a fix. Close-cropped Clegg with a sullen glare, stubble lost in the shadow of his drawn-up collar. Washed-up Clegg whose self-esteem is as thread bare as the combat jacket he wears. Clegg who has never broken a promise. Who has never made one.

A three-quarter moon hangs limply above the trees trying to turn its face away from Clegg and his accomplice, Jacobs. It may observe their noisy dash across open water to an unlikely looking island of willow and alder. It may watch as they leave their boat in reeds, tied to an old jetty, to walk the three miles along the disused railway line to their chosen spot. It may observe that Jacobs walks strangely, his toes turned inwards and his jeans brushing together. Clegg, moon-like, notices such things. Clegg moon-like, glares back his irritation.

They sit in silence. They have nothing to talk about, nothing in common but the need for money, nothing to share but their contempt for each other. They see the moon brighten slowly, though not the bats that flit and jerk across its face. They see the shadows deepen beneath the scrub though not the songbirds settling there for the night. They hear a blackbird startle though not the weasel that has disturbed it. Clegg should have done, he has been trained in these things. Clegg has been trained in many dark arts, all of little use to him now. Tonight he must fight off boredom, always the boredom. And disbelief. Is there no one to care for, Clegg? No one to weigh against the risks? No wife, no child, no promises? Jenny? Finished with, cast off, access to her son, Jo, formally denied. He is her son, Clegg, not yours. Has Clegg ever loved or only faked it? The tragedy may be that he no longer knows. And has it really come to this? The great Nathaniel

Clegg grubbing in the soil for easy money? Mixing on equal terms, at best, with a no-hoper like Jacobs?

Less than two years ago Clegg had a real job, security in a high security hospital, passwords and smart cards, increments and privilege. Now look. Mr.Almost in a fibreglass dinghy. Almost won a medal in the army. Almost got away with smuggling dope. Almost got a reprieve. Almost adapted well to civilian life. Almost persuaded Jenny, sweet Jenny, to move back in with him. Almost adopted little Jo, legally, step-dad Clegg. And he had almost told Jacobs where to stick this tacky business.

But don't blame Jacobs or his dogs. Clegg`s addiction has brought him to this, the need for money to buy his thrills, to indulge his habit more and more.

Blame yourself Clegg.

He does. He can be surprisingly honest.

Not that the two men aren't confident, perhaps even casual. This is not their first time and Jacobs is something of an expert, or at least his dogs are. They could probably do it blindfold now, which is why they don't see the nightjar scraping in the dusk nor the owl which emerges from its trunk not fifty yards away, nor the youth, barefooted, a branch or two lower, who has been watching them for the last hour. The two men know to within a handful of minutes when the boar badger will emerge, his alert head on his tough body listening, snuffling, sensing in ways for which there are not yet words. Clegg admires that. He respects the badger for its procedures. He would rather work with this badger than with a prick like Jacobs.

Of course the men have taken care not to crush the wild garlic. Badgers favour setts amongst garlic. Its strong odour tells them what and when things have passed through their woods. Fresh garlic on the air and the boar will duck back, wait an hour, perhaps even sleep for another night and a day. No garlic tonight. No tell-tell smells or twigs rustling. The boar's striped head emerges. He listens to the great muffled silence and whisper of the night forest. He hears a farm dog barking miles away. He hears the deer picking their way through bracken fronds. He hears a hedgehog grubbing for snails. He vanishes again, more out of habit than concern soon to reappear. He is hungry, but more urgent is his teat-heavy sow, now weary of her four cubs that must soon take the air and be free of her milk.

Clegg has endured months of `Clockwork Orange`, his head clamped in a vice with his eye-lids forced open, hours of brutal desensitizing in front of army videos, drunken games in the hospital mortuary to immunize him to the pain and suffering of those he might be asked to kill. He has sat through gruesome films and watched horrific simulations all in the interest of job efficiency, of returning the tax-payer's investment in combat. And he has done the business, brutally and often. But he has never quite come to terms with killing badgers. Something old nags in Clegg`s memory, something on the edge of respect.

The sow follows. She is larger than her mate, a perfect brute, but better still if they can bag her cubs, because if her cubs are close she will perform wonders of violence, she will exceed her already considerable strength three or four times over on their behalf, she will raven and lay waste a dozen dogs before she even begins to flag. For the sow and the cubs warped men in Clegg`s hometown will pay in gold. If you have no conviction or courage of your own buy a badger's, borrow its rage for a few blood-choked minutes.

They are out. Four of them. It is their first sight and smell of the upstairs world. Exact miniatures of their fussing parents, bumbling almost as one into the silver shade of April woods, twitching, sniffing, snuffling, rolling into each other, their mother and the leaf litter around them, white flashes of nose against their own and the night's black camouflage. No training video prepared Clegg for this.

In a second the sacks and muzzles are removed and the terriers leap towards the sett. The sow will not bolt until her cubs are to earth and by then the terrier will be on her. Quick and noisy it should have been, the men leaping forwards, crashing through the undergrowth, the terriers growling and yelping through blood, the badgers squealing like pigs.

It is certainly quick.

The men leap forwards, clubs and coats in hand, then freeze, nonplussed. The first terrier yelps midway to the sett and spins sideways for a second as though pulled violently by an invisible thread. The second is almost at the mouth of the sett before it too is hit, too beautifully and cleanly for even a whimper, the crossbow bolt straight through its skull.

A crossbow bolt. This is the Wildside, Clegg, the Dark Ages. He has seen it, he has noted it, he has assessed their chances. Kill rate per asset expended in the First World War was 10%. By the time of Vietnam it was 60%. Clegg`s training expected 90%. Whoever fired these bolts has done even better.

The badgers grunt and are gone. The men look to left and right, silent but for an indisciplined obscenity from Clegg, a gob of Anglo-Saxon realism spat into the dusk. Jacobs seems inclined to reach for the nearest dog but a third crossbow bolt decides them, thumping into the tree to the left. 66%. `Get the hell out of it`, one shouts as both turn, clomping through the woods in a panic, each shout massive in the stillness of late dusk. `The dogs, what about my dogs?`, whimpers Jacobs, wheezing to keep up with Clegg.

`Forget your bloody dogs and run`, is Clegg`s advice. At least he is still fit enough to escape with dignity. How somebody had crept up on them undetected, outcrafted the great Nathaniel Clegg is another matter. Clegg`s military training is a question of pride. He has been bettered. Sod the dogs. Sod the Wildside.

They have gone no more than fifty yards when the horse and its rider emerge from the woods and position themselves across the track.

A bare-footed rider. Observe him well, Clegg. He is about to change the course of your sordid little life, for better or for worse. His training leaves you in the nursery, takes him to a different universe of skills. The crossbow is pointed skywards, stark as a crucifix. In Hollywood the moon would be huge, full and behind the raised weapon. This is an English moon, thin, pale, awkward with the drama. Lower the crossbow and the men will be sent grovelling to the undergrowth. The youth knows this and with his work only half done he does no more than threaten.

`Strip`, Finn says. They hear a young voice but certain. It has spoken words Clegg will never use, it is a stranger to the kind of language Clegg lives by. He repeats himself only once and tilts the bow only a few degrees. Very soon the men resemble plucked chickens in this light.

`Everything.`

Around their ankles are electronic tags, not unlike wristwatches in size and weight but far cleverer than any timepiece. These men are slightly too old for the up-to-date implant forced upon the younger generation, but nor are they criminals to have such artifacts. All seventy million residents of the Comfort Zone wear one or the other. Credit, access, status, security all neatly packaged and assured. No need for cash, no need to be lost, no need to be late. Remove their ankle tags? Become a no one, with nothing, illegal, nameless? Does the deep-sea diver cut his air hose or the diabetic discard the insulin? In the privacy of bathroom or bedroom these tags might carefully be removed but never out of doors and away from home. The enormity of such an act is stranger than a crossbow bolt.

`Everything.` Finn repeats.

Like an amputee, Clegg stands, balance unstrapped, certainty unbuckled, poise pitched into the nettles. He and Jacobs wait for the bolt. `Place the tags with your clothes.` Finn says. `A mile down the line is an abandoned signal box, you passed it as you walked in. It contains clothes and tags and a letter of instruction. Put on the clothes and tags. Go home. Read the letter and do exactly as it says. Exactly. Neither more nor less. If you manage then your own tags will be returned tomorrow evening. Where you tied up your boat.`

Nothing else.

As they back away up the track Finn dismounts and bundles the clothes and tags into a shoulder bag. For some moments after he vanishes into the trees, the night's only sound is of chattering teeth.

FIVE

They went with their father to watch a puppet show. They went with him to watch lots of things. Which made them strange. Any excuse to escape the confines of brick and mortar, he would say, any excuse to see real people in a real world. As if such things still existed. He would take them to watch a man flying a kite, to see the first snowdrops of the year, to wait for a barge to pass through the lock. Every house they passed would be purple with hazed light, the sedative screen glowing in the corner. He would rage silently at the numbed state of his fellow men and draw the children closer, as though to deliver them from evil. At the show Sam looked at Beth sideways. She's still a girl, he thought, but one day, one day soon, she'll grow up, she'll need to know more than this world can ever teach her, the alien energy will invade her from within. He was still shocked by the question and by her need to ask it. Of course their Dad had killed their Mum, they both knew he had, they both knew there had been no other way and yet she had still asked, Beth had come right out and broken the spell and now Sam was confused, more confused than at any time in the nine years since his mother's death. Questions swarmed up in him but he lacked the courage to speak, to cast shadow words into the bright light of day that his sister and father inhabited. But she knew. Beth knew from his face and the deeper quality of his silence that he was annoyed with her. She looked back at him and smiled. Already his eyes were pale denials of life, their soul reflections turned back on themselves, but she could see beyond the vacancy. The smile was her reassurance. Separate we are less then nothing, she was telling him, together we are far more than our parts.

Sam noticed in the puppet show that the strings cast shadows on the backdrop. The strings held the puppets slightly off the ground and by a sleight of hand the legs moved, the arms twisted and a parody of life jerked onto the stage. But after a short time he wasn't watching the puppets or even their strings. He was watching the shadows. The shadow-strings moved by sleight of thought and then the shadow puppets moved, twisted, jerked into a parody of life. Who was to say that the movement of the shadows did not control the movements of the real puppets? The strings would never move ahead of the shadows. The eye could not separate them out and no amount of fancy camera could prove it one way or the other. By moving the shadows and not the strings, he realized, you could control whole galaxies of puppets. He knew even then that he would never control the strings. But the shadows? They were a different matter.

That night in their room he asked Beth to explain. He didn't use words, because they could be misunderstood, they cast shadows he was afraid of. Instead he used the crayons and drew the map, the one he always used, with the line down the middle, with trees and horses to the left and with buildings and cars to the right. The map was accurate, technically, because he had studied the reality for hours every day, learning the names of places, rivers and forests. It was the competent drawing of a thirteen-year-old. But right on the line, in the middle of the picture, the line right through her, he drew their mother, and not as they knew her from photographs but exactly as a four year old would draw a woman, face on, arms and legs stiff, face smiling, a triangle of skirt rooted to the ground by splayed feet. As he would have drawn her when she died, when he had last seen her.

`She's not on either side.` Beth answered. `I wish she was, Sam. She's neither here nor there.`

`She's in limbo.` he wanted to say, but instead he took the crayons and turned his mother into a tree, he spread her feet down into the land and water of the Wildside and Comfort Zone, he spread her arms out across Wales to the left, the North Sea to the right and in one hand, somewhere south of Scotland, he sketched in the bright detail of the jay's feather, mum waving it triumphantly above the brave new world. What's it like, Beth?

What's it really like? Wild with trees, Sam, deep with comfort, asleep with green forever, huge and mapless, no wires, no lines, no puppet strings. And trees. Beth took the drawing and pinned it above her bed. Where she couldn't see it. She kissed Sam on the forehead and went into the garden where she curled into a ball, like a fruit, the way she always slept.

A year later the police came for their father. Perhaps Sam already knew. Perhaps the silent eyes of the silent child could see the shadows move before the strings. They came at three in the morning. That is when the next world war will start. Responses are dull, witnesses are few and the newspapers have been put to bed. There were three police cars for John Savage, no sirens but plenty of flashing lights and no particular attempt to muffle their voices or radios or the slamming of doors. They read Savage his rights, body searched him, took away some files and discs and then, to the amazement of Sam and Beth, emerged from the garden shed with a crate of small gold ingots. They left the children with a cod-eyed policewoman, drinking tea, shivering, waiting for Savage's sister Kath to arrive from the next street. Nobody attempted to go back to bed. Kath replaced the policewoman. Beth started to make pop corn, Sam did the previous night's washing up and Kath began to install herself in the spare room, thankful for something to do and at the same time acknowledging that she was here to stay. And then it started again. It was exactly six o'clock because Sam had put the radio on for the news. This time there were sirens but only two cars. A brutal banging at the door and the wonderful flourish of a blackbird singing its heart out from the bottom of the garden to a background of barked radio commands and men in a hurry. Where was John Savage? they asked. It was pointless to lie. His ankle tag had gone `cold ` which could only mean he had removed it and was not in the same room. Why was their auntie with them? Had their father told them to expect trouble? The children's surprise was so genuine that the officer in charge was quick to lose confidence. He was used to people telling lies professionally and for that reason he must have known they were genuine. Her father had already been taken away, Beth told them, there must have been a mistake, the police had been for him three hours earlier. More crackling of radios, a great salvo of notes from the blackbird directly above the offending police cars and then the arrival, like royalty, of the third car, unmarked, the awkward deference of the other police officers as the car stopped, its back door was opened and a Presence emerged, long coat and polished head, cool blue eyes and a skin rich with skiing and vanity. He nodded politely to the duty sergeant whilst the blackbird seemed shocked into silence.

`You must be Sam.` he had said, voice soft as butter. `You're the quiet one, I remember now. I'm so sorry, I'm so terribly sorry.` Why was he sorry? Because Sam was quiet? Because Sam lived in a private world of lines and shadows? Or was he apologizing for something far greater, for something capable of silencing all the world's blackbirds? `We met at your mother's funeral, a long time ago. I don't suppose you remember. I'm an old friend of the family. My name is David Armstrong.` But Sam did remember, Sam forgot nothing. `I'm afraid there has been a terrible mistake.` Armstrong purred, apparently content with his role and power even in the midst of crisis. `A terrible mistake. Your father has been abducted, kidnapped if you prefer. Our friends from the Wildside have spirited him away.` He made the word `spirited` sound delightful, redolent of pantomime strings and Peter Pan sailing above the audience. `Don't worry. We'll get him back. I promise.`

This time there was nothing to fetch. No balloon, no feather. In the five years since that first sighting there had been nothing to console or excite from across the Line, only the bland silence of trees and shadows. Since the day Beth had waded through traffic there had been nothing to confirm or deny their daydreams.

Sam watched as the lorries thundered past, cars whining between them like flies scurrying around a huge and stampeding herd of awful animals. The quick rip of warm rubber on tar, the snatched air in the pocket of noise trailing each vehicle. This road was the Line. At least here surveillance had a physical boundary. Along the central reservation sensors at regular intervals sent data between themselves and up to the satellite, to God's Eye, to regulate the lives of the Comfort Zone many. Beyond was only shade and silence, a presence of warm dust settling on tired leaves, the Wildside watching with a quiet, vegetable intensity. There is another way of Being, the trees murmured, there is another world across here. Your father has gone, your mother is dead. Why wait?

The first step was the worst, like plunging into cold water. The rest followed easily. There was no question of dodging a route, of shimmying between the trucks and cars, it had to be a line, purposeful and without compromise, as straight as the one Beth had walked five years before. To deviate, to make allowance for the traffic, to mistrust the inevitable would be to betray the way she had walked, the way she had fetched the feather that wonderful day. The noises were the same: a scream of tyres, the whine of rubber, the bleat of horns. The angry heat of passing metal, the imagined faces, horrified behind tinted glass, all were the same. The Wildside appeared, vanished, reappeared, just as Beth had done, obscured, blurred, revealed between tons of polished steel, the trees patient, unflinching. `We're ready, Sam.` they might have said. `But are you? We've always been ready.` Over there you could do anything you wanted. You could ride a horse and sit naked by campfires, you could rub mud onto bare skin and worship trees. It had never been closer nor more distant, less likely. One nick of a wing mirror, one brush from a sidelight, burst like fruit, uncertain seed on ungrateful ground and it would be out of reach for all time.

Between one shadow and the next the truth hit Sam as violently as any amount of mindless metal, as brightly as the glance of sun on chrome. He could move these shadows at will. His brief lifetime of silence had prepared him to enter the minds and motives of others sweetly and stealthily, to shape unknown worlds to their appropriate course. And Beth was his to enter, to inhabit, to wear as a hand wears a glove. This was one Line they would cross together.

SIX

Arch removed the nail from his bleached dread-locks and drove it into the earth. Drove-it-into-the-earth. Penetration. `Joseph knew her not` it said in the bible, it meant he had never screwed her, never penetrated her, never stuck the nail in. It felt the same each time, thought Arch, like sex, like a mini crucifixion, except the thrill was even better, the thrill was like nothing he had ever known or even dreamed about, the thrill was the most amazing High conceivable because it delivered the earth, the entire earth and all its secrets, all *her* secrets, as feminine as breast and egg and inner-thigh combined.

Whither the nail? thought Arch, as he plunged it in, deep into her loins, as the hairs on his forearm stood erect and his breath came slow and heavy, whither the nail? `Suck it all out, honey`, he muttered to himself, `suck it all out, Arch is ready to suckle.` So what if they didn't believe him, so what if they thought he was nuts? Ahead of his time, that was all, waiting for the rest to catch up. If the fucking Wildside jammed the ether, if the half-baked ecolites banned wires and waves then Arch would tap the source the good-old-fashioned way, the way God had intended it, with a nail thrust deep into the flesh, with cold hard iron drawing out all that goodness and light. Penetration. He would give them pene-fucking-tration. With the certainty and animal cunning of the junky he wrapped a short length of copper wire around the nail and hooked it to the nib of a pen which, once tapped, shot out a paper-thin screen. The screen's back of bright foil would draw from the meanest of suns the energy needed to run itself. The front was a monitor, ready to transport Arch to an even stranger world than the one he now inhabited, but a monitor he chose to bypass by slipping on the apparently cheap plastic shades, the expensive inner-coating of which would hover endless new worlds less than a centimeter from his cornea. He fondled the head of the nail, felt its expectant cold and stoic purpose. It was so much more than an aerial. Arch disliked the comparison. An aerial reached hopefully into the air, always begging for attention, constantly displaying its frustration and unanswered needs. But a nail was discreet, saved for the moment, economical of itself, used only to thrust until fulfilled. And worst of all, an aerial could be jammed, the airwaves scrambled, its client cut off from the Great Invisible. But the secrets of the earth, the great deep-throated rumble of Earth Mother herself could never be silenced. Her fond mutterings, her deep arch-backed moans, her intense sighs and most animal wailing would seek out Arch's nail gleefully, would pour themselves through the strands of iron, copper and silicon until their chorus, like the endearments of a desperate lover, would make every part of Arch's body rigid with desire. So what if people thought he imagined the whole trip? So what if only a handful of initiates could tap into the subterranean wavelengths being explored by Comfort Zone technicians? He needed to convince no one. `Honey, I'm home,` Arch crooned to himself, `Arch's back, as horny as hell. Arch's missed you and you've missed Arch but its all right, my sweet heart, Archy is coming in loud and clear.` He popped the tiny phones in his ears, `Talk to me,` he said, `You know you want to, tell your Uncle Arch, tell it all.` A tap of the keyboard, a humming under his breath, a swaying of the body backwards and forwards and then a long, deep and satisfied sigh. Arch had succeeded where Joseph had failed. His penetration of the virgin was complete. His body thrilled to the rush and thrill of endless love and purified lust. He was immortal, cruising the veins and arteries of his vast lover, `Here she is!` he shouted. `Stay with it. Arch's got it taped, go, go, go with Arch, the Black Knight speaketh, what shit has he got me into now?` All the time his fingers were caressing the pen whilst his other hand gripped and rotated two large marbles which ground at each other like teeth. Smiles of recognition, frowns of discernment, the occasional raised eye-brow, all flickered across his face as he re-entered the Game, checked out the other players, visited his alter ego and his imaginary opponents.

The chaos he could cope with, the chaos was normal. What really rattled Arch's cage was the suggestion of order, the hint of a pattern, no matter how deeply hidden, no matter how slightly suggested, the hint of some pre-ordained and carefully controlled structure to things. The faces had come to him since childhood. Everything formless had the tendency to twist and swirl into mouthing faces, mouthing but always silent, always frustrated by his inability to hear or his refusal to listen. Wood grain was the favourite, or water in the drain or leaves caught by the wind, all were media in which the faces could create themselves from one second to the next. He had leaned to ignore them, because to mention them was to bring mockery or punishment down on his much-battered head. Before he found alcohol at the age of twelve or drugs the next year he had almost forgotten how the gargoyles would twist and writhe themselves into being. But with maturity came voices. The frustrated faces began to smile, began to let up, to share their secrets, to welcome Arch into their strange fraternity. And with the voices came the instruction: Penetration. Drive the nail into the earth. Become part of her body. Listen and watch, she wants to speak to you, she has chosen you as her lover, you are allowed.

But Arch was not stupid. He suspected a con right from the start. He knew how the wavelengths were used by the world order to sustain itself, he knew how countless little men were manipulated by the faceless few, but so what? It beat the shit out of boredom and he trusted in his own ability to discern the crap from the manna, to distil the essence from all the bilge they threw at him.

He had to hand it to them, though. The world ether was full of virtual violence, virtual porn, virtual power. The Fallen Beings of Light, he called them, the electric brotherhood, they had clogged every available space between the world's synapses with white noise and bleached light. But below their feet, in the earth, where only the hard iron could penetrate, in the breast of the Earth Mother herself, there all was still pure, still untouched, a universe of delights waiting to be scripted and explored. And her language was mythical. Her language was epic, the stuff of legend. Here, Arch was sure, the ancient folk memory had resided, here, he was convinced, every half-remembered story of dragons, faery, cauldrons, screaming stones and speaking eagles, Kings and their wizards, the lot, here in the Earth Mother they had had their birth and here they had hidden for the past electric-dark centuries, waiting for him, for Arch the Navigator, the Deep Space Explorer to bring them to the surface, to conduct them, as a rod conducts lightening, back into the affairs of men. Whoever controlled the faces and their voices, whoever thought they twitched Arch on their strings had made the right choice. The elemental correctness of the images, the raw, iron-boned clarity of it all was so perfect, so bloody appropriate. So when the Black Knight spoke Arch listened, not because he believed in either the Black Knight or his own madness, but out of respect for what seemed to fit so snugly, out of appreciation for the work of a great artist. Yes, oh great one, King Arthur will awaken and the dragon will stir and the voice of Merlin will rip through the dense valleys like the cry of an avenging angel. Whatever. He loved it. Courting such madness was what kept him sane.

Arch removed the shades, took out the earpiece, turned his pale eyes to the dark sky and allowed the pictures to live on without the input from the nail, without the suspicion of fraud that always accompanied the Black Knight. This, above all else, was Arch's safety valve. Off-line, his own man, unwired. He let the images live in his unconscious. He let the voices die away and he listened, as an owl waiting to hear its prey, for the after-image, the truth before the final silence. Somewhere out there in Arch's private void he saw a girl squatting high up in a tree. Or perhaps he felt her, there was something to her that invited penetration, something soft and vulnerable yet needing to be hurt, keen for the thrust of his nail. She was very naked, but daubed in black, lines zigzagged across her tight body like a code. Arch moved as though to touch her but she changed into a something delicate, breathing, translucent. It was a feather, a jay's wing feather, brilliant metal blue against ink black and Arch shivered and watched as the feather became huge, filled the sky and shattered into a thousand grey-green shards of metal.

SEVEN

As a child and for hours, Sam would sit and watch his sister play, fascinated by her fumbling toddler's movements, by her first attempts at speech, by her first tantrums and smiles. He would pile blocks, one on top of the other for her to knock down. And then one day she stopped, she left the pile untouched and Sam grew afraid, fearful of her strength and brightness, amazed by the words she used and the strings she made of them. She comforted him and they understood, without words, they made an agreement, silently: as she grew into the world, he would withdraw, as she mastered language, he would abandon it, until finally, with Sam in reserve, her hidden weapon, she would be unbeatable.

Look at her now. Long hair pinched back, Viking sheen through the Celtic black, large forehead, soft grey eyes usually set in a light frown, a perfect neck and already a woman's body, like a threat beneath tight clothing, but still the light step and quick movements of a child, the same movement to her head and face but coupled with a long and intense stare, an ability to concentrate a gaze on people to their discomfort, and a way of licking her lips for an almost invisible moment before speaking and then a voice soft, but firm, like a knife sheathed in velvet, so often used for questions, always questions. `Keep asking,` her father used to say, `No matter what they tell you, just-dare-to-ask.`

Look at her with the sun behind and then close your eyes. What after-image burns through the dark? What glow remains when certainty is removed? She is left as a question mark on an empty page. She is the answer to question no one has the wit to ask. Was it you who walked through the traffic, Beth? Was it you who stood, insensible, uncrying at your mother's funeral? She is not alone in this. Sam enters her, as a brother never should, he slides apart the dark secret of her soul to fill the void of her new womanhood. She does not resist, but welcomes it.

At the corner of the street she tries hard not to look out of place but fails. Across the road is the undertakers, its neon sign scalpel bright. Rain should fall to make the orange light slick and ugly but the night is dry, as the days have been dry. Devils of dust and litter flit past. Beth waits for courage. At her heel is the dog, poor Jet, baleful as only a collie can be, too knowing by far. Well-trained. Beth and Sam have cherished Jet for five years but tonight she is, in the words of the military, expendable. Like dust. Beth crosses the road, dead to traffic for the moment, she walks past the undertakers, glances down the side alley, continues, reassures herself that tonight is the night, that nothing can go wrong, that all will be worth-while. Past the undertaker's the road turns right and crosses the canal by way of an old bridge. She climbs the bridge and looks down. Two hearses are parked in a barbed-wired yard, backing on to the canal. There is no barge to be seen. The canal disappears in a straight line between the scruffy backyards of small factories and workshops, every inch of its route lined with razor wire. Jet follows, always to heel, one ear alert to muttered commands. Beth pets her dog. She whispers words it fails to understand. She walks back across the bridge. The last of the light is fading. She is certain that no one is watching. She ducks into the alleyway at the side of the undertaker's and Jet follows, excited, sensing a change of mood, the call to adventure. Beth takes out the blade and makes the sacramental cut, a celebration of a cut, deep into the ankle where the tiny implant lies hidden in her flesh like gristle. An implant means a coming of age. An implant means your body has stopped changing. You have arrived to the world of adult deception. Today all teenagers leave behind the ageing technology of the ankle strap; today all teenagers have the virus spat into their flesh. The pain screams at her for a second and the dog whines, confused, as though sharing the discomfort. Beth looks at the tiny blood-soaked implant that has chained her to their web of deceit and manipulation. Strange to feel nothing towards it, no anger, no elation at its removal. Not yet. `Good dog`, she mutters, as much for herself as for Jet, as much to stop from screaming as to gentle the collie. `Good dog, you know what to do. Go on home.` She has fixed her implant to the dense fur on the dog's back. Separate from her body warmth the implant will alert the sensors, it will cry out in indignation to the most powerful, the most inclusive data-base ever devised of Man, but fixed to the dog this clever System may yet be fooled into thinking that it is Beth who now trots dutifully home. Jet is not so sure. They have practised this many times and the dog always looks pained and ill-used at the moment of dismissal but tonight it is not just Beth's imagination, it is not the contrivance of Hollywood's shit sentimentality, it is the awareness in the dog that all is not right, that Beth is anxious. It can smell her fear and shares in it. Its instincts are to stay and fight, to protect her from whatever danger threatens. `Go on home.` she says again, more firmly, desperate not to cry, too afraid for any other emotion to worm its way upwards. `Home, Jet, go.` The dog turns, does not look back, its ears flush to its skull, its tail awkwardly between its legs. Five years. Go home, Jet. You are expended. Like dust. Beth is leaving this world. Beth is crossing over.

Half way down the alley is a recess for dustbins and above the dustbins the window has been left on the latch, as promised, and Beth is up and through before she can look around to check her retreat, to be certain no one has seen her. Inside she drops to the floor and sends a metal waste bin thundering through the silence. A dog barks some way off. Not Jet, now intent on obeying, carrying the invisible electronic Beth safely back to bed. No alarm rings out, no sirens scream; the silence is awful, the most awful silence ever because Beth is alone in an undertaker's morgue and she is in pain and now very illegal and there is no going back, no unthinking the unthinkable. Beyond these walls her untagged body heat will alert any sensor she approaches. She is trapped in a tiny island for now, an electronic blind spot from which she can only escape by acting out everyone's worst possible nightmare.

The smell of formaldehyde. Or is that only in books? Nowadays the smells should be High-Tec and have designer names to disguise their function. But formaldehyde it is. Crushed laurel leaf and the smell of forced cleanliness, an excess of scrubbing trying to hide a background scent which is disturbingly sweet. Ground cloves and lavender for death.

It takes no little courage to open a coffin in a dark room, remove its body and climb in yourself. Beth would say later that her courage had long since failed her and that the whole thing was conducted in a kind of numb panic, with no regard for the noise she made or the sounds she muttered or the scratches to her fingers and knuckles and shins. There were seven lidded coffins. Twelve would have been a better number, more monumental. Legendary. The sleeper awakes, that kind of thing, but seven it was, of which only three opened. Two of these, thankfully, were empty. The third, and by the light of an ailing torch the impression was not what she expected, contained the body of an old man who seemed unbelievably serene, unbelievably calm, as though intent, in death, on advising caution on Beth, of reassuring her from beyond the grave that it was all right, she should take a deep breath, she should not panic, she should trust the careful machinations of those who had worked on her behalf to get her thus far, to bring her within reach, in theory at least, of a crossing, the final escape to the Wildside.

One small error of procedure: she forgot to open the mortuary draw. She grappled with the corpse, light and frail but still horribly difficult, she laid it on a table and slid open the freezer into which she was to stow the thing. Of course the table was not clear and of course things fell to the floor and broke and made an awful noise and when she bent to pick them up she rose to find herself suddenly face to face with the body and the scream she swallowed would stay cramped inside her anger for a very long time, but the draw offered its white plastic anonymity, and with a feeling of immense relief she slid the dead man smoothly out of view, grateful beyond words that it was done, almost forgetting for a second that the worse was still to come.

Beth's frown deepened for a second, her dark hair fell, but then a smile through the refusal to sob and a quick flick of the tongue across dry lips as she reached for the pills and threw them back, as per instruction. She thought of a children's book she had read years ago, *Moonfleet,* of some boy wallowing around in the bones of rotting coffins beneath a church but then she remembered Jet, expendable, just as her mother had been. `Screw them!` she spat, always a way with words, but the smile stayed, the smile endured longer than the anger, the smile almost macabre as she climbed into the coffin, adjusted her position and eased the lid over her body.

EIGHT

Take you baggage, Jenny said.
I have no baggage, Clegg replied.
You are only baggage, Nat. Nothing but baggage
So what's the problem?
Start with money
I have no money
So there's the problem.
So money solves the problems, Jen?
Money hides the problems, Nat.
So you want to hide?
It would be nice to have the choice, Nat.
Then I'll get money. And you can hide.
You'll get money. And you'll spend it.
I'll spend it?
You'll spend it.
Do I drink, Jenny?

No, Nat, you do not drink. No, Nat, you do not smoke. No, Nat, you do not shoot up, or sleep around. Yes, Nat, we have been here before, you're fucking perfect and it's all my fault. So take your baggage and go.

This is my only habit, Jen, this is my only fix, it's my escape and apology for the bullshit, my only escape, my only apology. You should try it, you should see for yourself, there are no limits, Jen, no control, no gravity, just me, or it could be you. Or it could be Jo. It could be the boy.

No, Nat! Never! Don't touch the boy, do you hear? He is not yours, he is not of you, he never has been and never will be. He worships you already. What more do you want? He idolises every bit of your hand-crafted baggage, so don't go anywhere near him and don't even think about taking him up, about letting him see any of it. Because it might be true, it might just be true all this crap you come back with, all that anger you dump on us every time you come down. Little Jo stays on the ground, Nat, little Jo must never know, he must *never* know what you know. I'm his mother and it's my job to keep him in the dark. Okay?

Sure it was okay. From here. Clegg and the air and the comforting noise and the illusion of complete freedom. Chains broken, tethers left behind, screw the lot of them, Jenny most of all, and fly. Fly. Nathaniel Clegg, unique for an hour. One thousand feet above the streets and houses and hung on a filament of webbing and aluminium, hung from two great nylon wings and thrust by a crafty, sensuous engine throbbing like a vein, compulsive. I'm immortal, Jenny, like you always suspected, I can float on air, I can eat stones and fling myself from the heights. You should try it, Jen. This engine. It's an engine to sell your soul for, more satisfying than sex, Jen, sorry, it's not a complaint, it's just a fact. More satisfying than crime. Let them look up from their boxes and cages to the tiny speck of Nathaniel Clegg, airborne, indulged, let them gawp in jealous awe. And Jo would love it. Jo would become an addict. Hold on to him, Jen. Perhaps you're right.

But today is different, Jen. Today Clegg is angry. Today Clegg needs to change the world even more than usual. He needs an explanation for what had happened, he needs to unravel the mystery of the smug youth with the crossbow who has made a fool of him and he needs to chew over the extraordinary instructions that have directed him and Jacobs back to the Comfort Zone and to the tip of a bizarre conspiracy. Surely you understand that, Jenny, surely you can leave Clegg his anger?

But it was more than that. It was to do with excitement. Clegg's future might be open to offers. And Clegg was ready, as ready as he had ever been, to shake off the chains, to lift into the air and fly into a sunset, any sunset, anywhere, anytime. But soon.

Clegg watched the landscape roll beneath him. He was above the motorway, clogged as usual. He could see each driver for an instant as he mocked their immobility with his own fluid movement. Urbia, they called it, the United Cities and Affiliated Counties, the Comfort Zone, the largest, densest urban sprawl beyond Mexico City, home to millions of box-dwellers, land of a thousand theme parks, ten-thousand ring-roads, half a million shopping precincts, fifty two flavours of condom; all the cities and suburbs of England, all the endless rat-maze of tarmac, lifted by the rising tide and dumped in this endless wrack of offal, needles, plastic and oil. Countless cars and lorries, all static, all stuck but only one Clegg. Thousands and thousands of motorways all choked but only one huge and empty sky, which Clegg had to himself. To the right and away from the road were endless acres of houses, boxes, cubes, low-rise, middle-rise, high-rise, great swathes and cancers in all the gaps, growing even as Clegg watched to house the drivers if they ever made it home and then a flick, a twist, a pull of the throttle, upwards, blue, nothing, the blue and banking away, this time to the west where the cancer stopped, dissolved into trees, resolved again into the marshes and reeds and slate blue of the river and then nothing, just miles and miles of empty nothing. Hill after hill; hump after hump, fresh green forest, blue green meadow, dull brown uplands. Clee, Mendip, Wyre, Wenlock, Mynd, Radnor. Why name them? The peasants living there in huts and hovels probably didn't. The clown with his crossbow probably knew less than Clegg about the woods and wastes he romped in. Clegg had seen more than most from his expensive loft: the marshes of the Severn with their reeds and wildfowl, the communes and colonies of New-Bristol perched above the water, the self-satisfied islands to the east like Lincoln and the Wolds where the tax-exiles banked. Of course he had thought about it in his youth. Didn't they all? The adventure of escape, a fishing boat perhaps or even a glider, the old railway tunnels to the west of Sheffield, a night crawl over the moors above Burnley, there were still ways across, still the appeal of a new life better than the old. He knew there were ways to go backwards and forwards, for a price and a risk, not only through the kind of insider bribery that had brought for him and Jacobs a brief crossing. Clegg had never more than half believed the scare stories of disease, the in-breeding, the boredom, the cold and discomfort, the shortages, but he knew the prospects of return after capture, the lifetime status of unemployable, unbalanced, uncertain. But what was the difference now? Clegg was unemployed, uncertain and had no wish to be weighed in the balance by any side or system.

Down to the marshes. Break the law, why not? Put up a flock of birds; scare the shit out of a wayward swan. Risk some hobbit from the west taking a pot shot at Clegg`s avenging eagle. Low over the chopped-up water where Clegg only a week earlier had indulged his love of speed with the boat and its out-board motor. And in that week the strangest of feelings. Like being in the army again. Obeying orders you could not question. Following instructions that made no sense. For what? In the army they never told you but this time he meant to find out.

His next step must be Danny. His younger brother by two years, Danny worked within the System, Danny could surf forbidden lanes and corridors to tell Clegg what he needed to know about the youth with the crossbow and the farce he had been obliged to act out. He would talk to Danny and Danny would unravel the mysteries of the universe with the roll of his finger on a scrolling pad. But of Jo and Bonny they would say nothing, because behind every man is a shadow and behind Clegg was the shadow of step-son Jo, who he could no longer see, who he could no longer even half claim as his own. And behind Danny was the shadow of a daughter, Bonny, Clegg's niece, the apple of her uncle's eye. Bonny would cast a pale, gauze-like shadow, because Bonny was losing touch, Bonny was drifting far out to sea. She was down there somewhere, floating like exhaust fumes, disembodied, nebulous. Only a month ago she had slit her wrists in the bath and almost floated away to the Land of the Perfect Figure. She was a few weeks short of fifteen. How many Bonnies,

Clegg? Look down and count the possibilities, extrapolate to some obscene number, fight back the bile. How tempting it must have been to cut the thread between life and death. No doubt she was under special surveillance now, blood pressure and heart rate distantly monitored as certainly as her father's bank account, but what amount of electronic wizardry can prevent the razor blade cut in the warm bath? What amount of distraction and entertainment can lessen the desire to ebb away in your own tepid blood?

Clegg bit at the thought of Bonny and swore. He knew that if anybody else had put this idea to him he would have laughed at them. It was easy to cross over, there was nothing physical to prevent it. It was returning that was so difficult. Electronic surveillance stopped at the border. Effectively it was the border. Very fitting that your absence was noted, was a criminal offence, whilst your presence was irrelevant. When you returned, voluntarily or at the hands of bounty hunters, official or unofficial, your life was quietly but ruthlessly deconstructed. Work and credit were the first to go. Sanity was never far behind. You risked being born again, a stateless stigmatized refugee in your own home, like Bonny in her bath.

But if risk depended on how desperate you were then Clegg was ready for big risks, for something new, for a kick, for the money to fly, for some purpose. He would do it. Screw the lot of them, he would do it. Perhaps this is what they had trained him for; perhaps this was why the army had taught him inhuman skills that were of no use in any kind of real world. He would take them to an unreal one. Clegg the bounty hunter, negotiating his own fee. It had a good ring to it, a hard-edged romance. Little Jo would like that, worthy of a heroic step-dad. That was reason enough to throw everything to the wind, and if he wanted further justification, how about anger at being made a fool of? Bloody hobbits, bloody half-baked tree worshippers. He'd show them. One street-wise Clegg would soon teach those pixies.

To the South of Birmingham in the Likey Hills, in a small puddle of green, ringed by high-rise, the imagined Jenny and Jo might be waving, the ice thawed out, all made whole again.

No hard feelings, Jenny, he could have said, but never would.

No hard feelings, Nat, she might have answered.

I can swoop you down and pluck you up, like rabbits.

Whatever you say, Nat.

Jo'll love it. I'll take care of him

I know you will, Nat, I know you will

You can trust me

I always have done

No one else has

I trust you

That makes you the first

Maybe the last, Nat

I'll bring him back safe. I'll make a man of him, Jen.

Where, Nat? Where will you make a man of him?

Don't ask, Jen

I have to ask

Even though you know the answer?

Especially because I know the answer.

Over there. Where else? In the dark emptiness of the Wildside, thought Clegg, deep in everyone's unconscious, peopled with their demons, in the place he was set undoing. Best stay where you are Jo, Cleggy will come back, get rich, fix you and your mum up, finance any habit you want. Even bulimia.

He dipped towards the horizon. Heading south across the marshes he could make out Bredon Island, rising black against a ribcage of light. Pink cirrus clouds. There were lights to his left but almost nothing to his right until Malvern came into view, perched on its ancient coral reef and reaching out across the waters which began at its simple harbour. To the left of the town cruising in the shadow of the ridge Clegg headed for the patch of the alder and willow he had prospected high from the air a week earlier when badgers had been the prey. Cutting off the engine and gasping at the sudden silence and the controlled stall and lurch of the wings he began a steady glide towards trees and water. It would be so easy. The stillness and grace of one moment would become the clumsy and noisy stumble of the next. Easy and irreversible. With fifty feet still to go he engaged the engine, pulled back on the throttle and rose to skim the tips of threatening alders. He knew what he had to do. But first he needed to know why.

NINE

Finn knew so little about her. Finn knew so little about girls, full stop. And Finn knew nothing at all about girls from the Comfort Zone, girls who spoke in incomplete sentences, who started their periods at age ten or earlier, girls who could live in a dream-like vagueness and have no wish to wake and who smelled of soap and polish. What if she was like that? What if their hopes were unfounded, if she was crossing the Line because she had no choice or because they were using her to expose their secret routes and contacts? What if she was doped, high on the legal stuff they doled out to children and teenagers to keep them quiet, to keep them happy, to keep them thin or fat or whatever the fashion was? Would he see it in her eyes? Would he know how to react if she expected him to flirt, to make love, as girls over there were said to, claiming their rights, adding to their lists? He was afraid of appearing too shy. It had always been part of him, like being tall, but she may never have met a shy person before, they even had pills for that over there, she might even laugh at him, take him to be some kind of freak. Two men at night, with the crossbow, that was a different matter. He had been afraid, but not shy. The crossbow would give anyone confidence, the stupid dumbness of the men had done the rest. It had all gone according to the script. But with her there would be no script, no fall-back.

He would know soon enough. Assuming she understood the letter and had taken the bait. The letter had been sent two months earlier, addressed to the aunt, John Savage's sister. It had been disguised as a letter from an estranged relative in Ireland. The relative did not exist but the clues were written in clearly enough for the family to understand but to exclude any snooper on the lookout for contact between the children and their father. After each reference to the health and well being of similarly fictional relatives there was a sentence of instruction. Mixed with the rest they made very little sense but lifted out and written as a list they constituted a clear directive. `Aunt Gemma is recovering,` was followed by `travelling to Malvern seems to have done her the world of good.` `Uncle Bob has brought more land.` led on to `travelling north west from there is very much the thing to do.` As a further precaution the clue following north west from Malvern would have meant nothing to anyone but the family. `Cousin Billy still has the arthritis and is still searching for a cure. Go to where the crowds gather, I told him, look for the thing you have dreamed of all your life with the face of your worst nightmare.` Not even Finn knew what that meant, he could only assume that Beth would know. But if somebody had asked him what his best dream and worst nightmare were he might not have been able to answer. It seemed strangely appropriate that both would have to be confronted if she was to find her father and if Finn was to succeed on his Quest. The letter closed with another family reference: `Your grandmother is well. She is not afraid to approach strangers and tell them her flute has been stolen and that she needs money to buy a new one. Where this will lead her is anyone's guess!` Beth played the flute, that much Finn had worked out for himself. The fiction fitted. Her first steps were very cleverly laid down, but there was something else, unrelated to direction but still an order. `Our youngest is in fine form and very brave, but I warn her again and again, trust no one, trust no one, trust no one, because no one is worthy of following in her footsteps.` Which might well be true, thought Finn, but it would not make his job any easier.

He watched the barges shunting through the locks. He marvelled at their bright colours and the precision of the lettering and floral designs that decorated most. History: Two centuries earlier horses had pulled these barges loaded with coal or wood or clay. Here loads had been checked, weighed, bartered, bought and sold, barges had been built and repaired, tradesmen had peddled anything from bone china to opium amongst the bargees and the smell of coal had competed with that of damp horse. All that had been short-lived. Railways and roads had won the day, canals had been filled in, gates had rotted, kingfishers and grebes had nested in grain bins and coal silos. Now, after a gap of nearly two hundred years and a brief interlude for the leisure industry it was once more business and commerce that bossed the waterways. Constitutional Law: article six of the Wildside constitution; all trade, this particular law stated, between East and West, between Comfort Zone and Wildside was to be conducted by water. At our pace, on our terms, to our scale, could have been added but was not necessary. Smuggling there would always be and good luck to those on either side who tried it but all official, legal and sanctioned trade would be by water and water only. Finn loved the logic. There were twenty such laws, each as brilliantly conceived as the next, each brought to life by their far-flung and often-unpredictable consequences.

The Boswell was moored less than a mile away; a small but beautifully cared for long boat. Its owner, Ron Johnson, a florid man in his middle years, was expecting the approach but Finn held back and for the best part of an hour watched. The man's overalls betrayed all the years of care and devotion lavished on the boat. Finn observed the concentration with which he applied the brush to the fine details of his boat's woodwork, wondering how it would feel to Beth to make contact, to take the risk. Such things were simple enough when you felt at home and secure in your skills but Finn was afraid that even this might be too much for the girl, in which case the whole thing would be doomed from the start. Such things were best left unthought. At last Finn presented himself and was shown to a small room at the rear of the barge in which he slept fitfully, dreaming of geese.

TEN

Comfort Zone rain, slick and warm. Clots of neon choke the gutter. The night has cut its throat and nobody seems to care, nobody seems to notice. Clegg stands in the doorway of a shop and watches hunched up figures being admitted to the warehouse opposite. He avoids his own reflection in the shop windows. He has a habit at times like this of pulling up his collar, of perching shades on the top of his head and chewing gum in one corner of his mouth, a parody of some Hollywood gangster. It has worked before and it will work again. It is an image that annoys him but which he is afraid to outgrow, uncertain of what could take its place. People respond as he wants, deference tinged with fear, for which he despises them. There is a false confidence in his stride as he dodges the spray from passing cars and ducks into the entrance where a mirror traps him, exposes his posing. He looks away, angry with himself, contemptuous of those who accept his disguise, he shakes himself down, stomps rain from his shoes. He removes the useless sun-glasses from his head but twirls them fluidly in his right hand as though toting a gun, he catches himself in time, rams them in his pocket, spits out the gum.

Take time for Clegg? Invest in a man with no stake in the future? Give credit to an ex-squaddie who wouldn't lend himself the time of day? The army had tried. The army had taught him to fly, to track, to evade, to kill. The army had force-fed him the high-resolution images of modern warfare. The army had invested in his subhuman part and even elevated it to the rank of corporal. And not only the army. More than one good woman had invested enough to share his mistakes and aspirations, of which the former outnumber the latter by several. The soft grey eyes, he always said, that was what got them. Too modest, Clegg. Perhaps they see something you won't.

The warehouse is not his favourite nightspot. At twenty eight he is too old for the noise and the smoke; he has left it behind but not quite moved on. They will know him to nod to, they will remember his past, remember that he never touches the drink, never makes a habit of anything. He has come for answers, not entertainment, though both might be different forms of escape. Back there in the woods he and Jacobs had been caught with their pants down in more ways than one. They had been left with no choice but to take the clothes and, most disturbing of all, the ankle tags from the signal box. They had not been surprised at finding their outboard motor stolen and a paddle left in its place. And then the next day, as the letter had dictated, they had driven to Nottingham to carry out the absurd instructions.

In the days that followed Clegg had tried to kid himself with options. The very idea of options, of various responses, strategy and tactics was a comfortable game for a day or two. But there were no options. To do nothing was certainly not in his nature, to concede defeat to the crossbow virtuoso was unthinkable and, ultimately, to do anything without Danny was out of the question.

Danny was Clegg with fewer mistakes. Danny the winner. Danny of the suit and tie and salary. Danny of the connections, some even legal. No suit and tie for Clegg. No salary these last six months, but worse still was the unspoken hint of dependence. Clegg`s illegal crossing of the Line to hunt badgers was thanks to Danny's knowledge of the System, knowing who and what to bribe to produce the blind spot which had enabled Clegg and Jacobs to disappear for a night. Clegg was uncomfortable with dependence. It was not his style. He was having to learn it. Twenty-four hours after the trip to Nottingham, twenty-four hours in which the option game had lost its appeal, Clegg had asked his brother two questions. Tonight, in the noise of the warehouse, there might be answers.

The Pig Trough was illegal but tolerated. Police had raided once or twice in the last few years but it was of more use to them open than closed. Beyond HIV testing the management was free to run an open house. Young girls outside the entrance looked keenly at Clegg, hoping for free entry in return for a trick. Their eyes were like old glass, caked with boredom, their tiny breasts, bare to the rain, offered like sweet meats. He guessed their ages at between twelve or thirteen and sensed in his own disgust the beginnings of senility. He popped a Blocker and they lost interest. Without the drug it would be difficult to turn down at least one advance, with it he could concentrate on business. He paid his dues at the door and left the wet coat in a locker. He removed his ankle tag at the entrance proper. Here a huge indoor arena played host to scores of pigs that ran and squealed in the bright disco lights, a dog or two in amongst them to stir them up and keep them moving. The place had used chimps until ten years ago but now primates had rights of which pigs could only dream. The man who took Clegg`s tag scanned it for HIV. He had a row of pigs penned and at the ready, constricted into a queue by tubular railings. He fixed Clegg`s tag to the first in line, a large and listless sow, released it into the arena and nodded to Clegg. `Betty` he said, `Ask for Betty when you've done.` Betty was finding her stride, running with the others, caught in two minds whether to make for the feed trough or dodge the dogs.

Above and all around the arena was a deep balcony lit in various colours. Recesses of dark, wells of bright red or cold blue, parlours of pulsating orange and green all had their place around the perimeter of the Pig Trough, the city's premier night club. The colour coding was an accepted convention, although fashion changed quickly. Green for gay, purple for speed, red for ambience and other men's wives. There were separate areas for more specialized tastes: older women and younger boys, tantric stuff, S&M, whatever sold. The toilets filled the entire basement. They were uni-sex, tastefully lit and padded. There were exactly as many punters spread around the vast complex as there were pigs charging around the arena. A couple of hundred was Clegg`s guess which made this a quiet night. At the weekend they had ways of spicing up the pork, as they called it, prompting the pigs to perform and to offer a spectacle. The pigs were the alter egos of the customers. Their metabolisms, being conveniently close to that of humans, allowed them to run and eat and rut in the arena whilst freeing their various clients. With your tag fixed to one of these simple beasts you could pursue your own indulgence free from the fear of electronic detection whilst satisfying the nightclub's obligation to monitor its clientele electronically. Clegg's generation had missed the implants. How tomorrow's youth would buy anonymity was not his concern but it would certainly see the slow demise of places like this.

Danny was in the blue room. A synthesizer played with itself fondly but the tables and chairs were mostly empty and there was more dark than blue available to the clients. One couple fondled each other in the corner before heading for the toilets, another sat at the bar, locked together in boredom.

A stranger might not have guessed these men as brothers. Their differences were obvious, their similarities subtle. Clegg, the older by two years, had close-cropped hair, his brother wore his long. They both had the same fair skin and long noses but only Clegg had the slate-grey eyes, made deeper by the light. Both had the same way of looking around before speaking. Danny looked around as though to invite people in. With Clegg it was a question of training, of institutionalized mistrust.

Wife, children, cars, football. What else was safe? They went through the list of small talk, Danny already cautious, wary of his brother, shades of the playground pecking order warning him to go easy. Yes, Clegg had split with Jenny. Yes it was a shame, stepson Jo was a good kid. No, there was no going back. Without knowing it Danny was confirming his worse fears. Once again his brother Nat had nothing and no one to hold him down, to make any sense of things.

Danny bought himself a whiskey and an orange juice for his brother. A hundred different types of intoxication were available in the Pig Trough but Danny knew his brother would touch not one of them.

Clegg watched as his brother fingered the glass nervously and rolled its contents around. It was the kind of thing that would have irritated him in others but in Danny he could forgive it, for Danny he would find any number of excuses. `Any luck?` Clegg asked after a sufficient pause, giving a cursory nod to the Danny's breast pocket, to where his palm top would most certainly be.

But it was never a question of luck, was it? Luck and data theft never went together. It was a question of risks and how many Danny had been willing to take for his brother. Danny worked in the System. He was touched with the glow of importance, the delicate perfume that clung exclusively to insiders. He was unique amongst present company in having something to lose. Perhaps that was what made him so nervous. His job was to turn junk information into sales. When a man smashed his car up a swarm of services and suppliers were happy to know. If a doctor diagnosed cancer then Danny was the immediate link to a dozen hospices and as many undertakers. If your birthday was approaching then rest assured that Danny and his type would have reminded your wife as she walked past the flower shop window. Wiping a computer's arse, Clegg called it, a description Danny never denied. But it bought contacts. If you were selling information then you must have access to it yourself or at least to the harvesters, the army of men and women whose job it was to programme and debrief the System's all-knowing search engines. Information was money, as Danny's job proved. It was also power, which was why he seemed uneasy. Entering the System, as Danny was fond of saying, was like entering a dragon's mouth for the pickings between its teeth; sifting through the turds, was Clegg's version, siphoning off the piss.

He drew his chair forwards and glanced at the couples, at the man on the fruit machines, at the bar staff. They could hardly hear themselves speak but caution seemed appropriate. He went straight for the personal angle. `Nat, you in trouble?'

`Not yet. Confused. You got answers for me?` Clegg fought the urge to chew non-existent gum. He pulled down his collar and tried woefully to look open and honest.

A puffing of cheeks from Danny. A fiddling with drink, beer mat, cuffs. `I'm just worried Nat, that's all. Don't want you in trouble.`

`Leave that to me, Dan. I usually get out, right?`

`It's not just you. If I get you started and it goes wrong, you know what I mean.`

`Then don't give me anything traceable. Like always.` Without knowing it Clegg had removed the sunglasses from his pocket and was fiddling with them on the tabletop, staring at the pattern they made of the lights. `You're old enough to look after yourself, Dan, and so am I. Now just tell me what you know.`

But Danny had a surprise for his brother. He also had the salesman's skill of knowing when to change tack. A sudden flash of honesty, a shift of body language towards the informal. `I'm more than worried, Nat`, he admitted. `More than worried, since you ask. Maybe I'm jealous.`

No, Clegg had not expected that from Danny. He was impressed. `Jealous?`

Danny shrunk a few inches into his drink and chair. `Why not? Why should you have all the fun, Nat? You know what I was pushing today? You don't want to know. Iron supplements to the anemic? Padded underwear for people with piles? What does it matter? We know it before they do, right? Straight from the hospital lab, straight down the hot line to Danny, Danny makes the link, Bingo! straight up another. Welcome home, your test results will arrive tomorrow, in the meantime, seeing as how it is cancer, why not try these pills? Last week it was abortion clinics to girls who didn't know they were pregnant.`

`It's a job.` Clegg made no attempt to sound sympathetic.

`So the contract says. Would it keep you smiling for long?`

`Are we supposed to?`

`What?`

`Keep smiling?`

Danny shrugged.

`No one told me.` said Clegg.

`So I noticed, Nat. So we all noticed. In the meantime, what the hell? You're onto something, kid, and I'm jealous. You going to share it or not?`

Before Clegg could answer they were both distracted by a roar from several of the bars around the balcony. The noise and the lights and the drugs were taking their effect on the pigs and one of the boars was misbehaving, attempting to mount one of the dogs. An electronic scoreboard above the bar kept up an inane commentary. Your porcine alter ego could get laid, keel over and die or spend all night eating. The seriously bored amongst the clientele identified closely with the pigs, put bets on them, spent the night watching them rooting around in the sawdust and beer slops.

`Share what, kid? No answers and there's nothing to share.`

`It's all right,` said Danny, `You'll get your answers. But I'm warning you, it's right out of your depth. Deeper than this does not exist. But I need something from you, Nat, I need to know your side of things.`

The sunglasses had stopped moving. Clegg looked at them with annoyance, as though they had betrayed something of his private thoughts and for the second time this evening stuffed them in a pocket. Until this very moment Clegg had assumed he would tell nothing to his brother of what had happened first on the Wildside and later in Nottingham but to his own surprise he found the story spilling out, Danny a ready listener. The only bit he found difficult to relate was the conclusion, but he was skilled in masking his feelings.

`We went to a place between Nottingham and Derby,` Clegg said, trying to keep his hands still, setting them carefully together. `There was a canal, all wired off, the usual security, but running into the canal was a river, or it might have been the other way around. The details don't matter. There was a weir. You could reach it from the towpath. It was noisy, fenced off, but there were holes in the wire and an unofficial path over the river on a black pipe. Jacobs stayed in the car. That's what the letter said, Jacobs in the car, me by the weir. There was nobody around until suddenly, across the river, there was a woman. I can't tell you anything about her, she only came to about fifty yards from me. She stopped and then sent the dog across.`

`Across?`

`Across the pipe.` Clegg spoke deliberately, spelling it out as much for himself as for Danny. `It must have been trained to do it but it didn't look too happy. It whined a bit, it looked back at the woman, but she just stood there, didn't say a thing. Couldn't have done really, the noise of the weir would have drowned her out.` Clegg suddenly laughed, genuinely amused at how awkward he found this. `I picked the dog up. There was an implant strapped to its collar, one of the tiny ones. It wasn't happy about being picked up. Ears back, big eyes, the lot. As though it knew what was coming.`

`And what was coming?`

`Can't you guess?`

`I hope I'm wrong.`

Danny often was. His instinct for human action and motives was somehow blunted, less keen by far than Clegg's. But not this time. `Well you're not, Dan. It struggled as we got close, of course, but it would never have bitten me, not in a million years. I heaved it over, straight into the weir. It never stood a chance.`

`And the woman?` Danny was genuinely shocked.

`Gone. As you'd expect. That was someone's well-trained pet. She wasn't going to hang around and watch it drown.`

Danny was shaking his head, staring at Clegg but not focused. He was matching this story to what his pickings between the teeth had revealed.

`Which one are you?` he suddenly asked, nodding at the electronic notice board.

Clegg took a moment to focus. In recalling the dog and the weir he had almost forgotten where they were. `Betty.` he answered.

Betty was having a quiet night. `I'm Bill` Danny said, shaking his head. `Bill's a loser. Gets picked on by the sows. I'm always Bill. Now Bruiser, there's a boar and a half. Give me a night as Bruiser any time.`

Bruiser was the number one. They pumped him full of viagra some nights to warm things up. You paid extra to have Bruiser drag your ankle tag through the shit.

Clegg knew his brother too well to rush him, he was shaping up for something.

`We live in strange times, Nat.` Danny continued, `comfortable, safe, but very strange. No crime, no terrorist bombs, no nonses, no shortages, wall-to-wall supermarkets, shop `till you crap yourself. Back to like it was before the millennium. Everyone's happy. Everyone's Bruiser all the time.`

`So how is Bonny?` Clegg asked, always a nose for the hidden agenda

Danny reached for his pocket screen, punched a few numbers, held it up for Clegg to see. Bonny was at home watching a film. Channel six. Danny turned its volume down but the beached figure on the sofa didn't notice or react. The floor was covered with cans and wrappers. He shook his head, shrugged, put his daughter back in his pocket. He looked at Clegg apologetically, half hoping for help, half desperate to talk. `Bulimia`, he said. `You know, bulimia, the eating disorder? It's official. Not that it helps. The thing is, I reckon we've all got it. Entertainment bulimia, white-knuckle bulimia, information bulimia. You can't get enough because there's always more so you drown in the stuff.`

`I just asked how she was.`

But Danny had embarked on his theory. It was less painful than talk of Bonny directly. `The point is it's the same with us, with the System. There is more information and there are more ways of accessing it than there are grains of sand in the desert.`

`So?`

`So everyone's terrified, because nobody knows how it works any more. That's why there's a Wildside. If we were masters of the System we would have tidied up their little hippy camp twenty years ago.`

`Somebody must know how it works.`

Danny nodded and took a long drink. He liked the dramatic pause but this was not deliberate. He was caught up in his own speculation. Mention of his daughter had set him back. He had prepared an angle and now his brother had changed the rules. Bonny might be one of millions of chronically unhappy individuals in their tinsel-wrapped world but she was his only daughter. When it reached the point where exceptions were in the majority you had to lie in more sophisticated ways. `So what's wrong with a bit of comfort?` he asked, almost of himself. `Why shouldn't we sit back and screw the world?`

`I thought we were. I thought that's what makes us all tick.`

With perfect timing a roar went up from around the balcony. Bruiser had covered his third sow of the night. Betty was in the news.

`On this side, maybe.`

The confirmation Clegg was waiting for. Danny's inquiries had led him across the Line, to the Wildside.

Danny glanced around the bar before continuing, he looked carefully at the barman, the petting couples, the loner on the fruit machine. `The name John Savage mean anything to you?`

Clegg was a long time in answering. He had come to Danny because there was no alternative but it may have been a mistake. Every time you asked a question you lost a little bit of control. Too much and you were quickly in free fall, being shafted by some super-stud boar. He was half inclined to get up and walk out, to forget the whole thing, to admit himself bettered by the crossbow freak. But something else kept him seated. He found himself sinking into his collar, lowering his voice. He would not have been surprised to hear himself drawling with an American accent. `Of course it does, I'm not stupid. The last I heard they arrested him for computer fraud. Lived where we grew up. Just down the road in fact. We were neighbours once. Some said there was more to it.`

`Oh there was more to it all right, more than grunts like us would be told. Ever wondered why he lived on that estate in that boarded-up house, a man who won a Nobel Prize for science? Ever wondered how his wife died, or why he never held down a proper job?`

`I remember them.` said Clegg, flatly. `I remember that day in the park. Him and the two kids. We pelted them with stones.`

`Everyone did, Nat. The newspapers told us to, till we got bored. Well let me remind you of how strange the world is, Nat. The man you stoned, the man who legged it through the park with two kids in tow was the great John Savage, and John Savage, dear brother is the only man on this planet who understands the computer system which runs our tiny little lives. John Savage devised the thing over twenty years ago. It wasn't computer fraud as we know it brother. It was treason, the kind they hang you for if they catch you.`

`They did catch him.` Clegg stated, thoughtfully, waiting for the catch.

`They didn't even arrest him. He pegged it to his pixie friends on the Wildside. Engineered some scam to make it look like the police.`

`So where is he now?`

Danny shrugged.

`Maybe he's happy.` suggested Clegg.

Danny laughed nervously, `Oh, he's happy all right. But there's the problem. A few wild-eyed academics can go and dig themselves a plot on the Wildside, milk their goats before breakfast, make eye contact with pebbles, talk to trees, but not John Savage. Not him, he is number one bad man, number one most wanted criminal.`

`So what's this got to do with me throwing a dog into a river?`

`I'm coming to it. Savage's wife died thirteen years ago. One son and one daughter. If they so much as fart we know it. Every book and magazine they've read, every film they've seen, every radio programme they've listened to we, know. The boy is size 8, the girl size 6. Got the idea?` Clegg nodded. `If we are to find Savage it'll be through his children. If you want to find God, follow Jesus, right? A close family you see, and closely watched, even more than most. The son tried to reach dad last year. Went badly wrong apparently. As for the daughter…`

Danny paused dramatically, but Clegg had been quiet for too long and quickly stole his brother's punch line. `Don't tell me. Let me guess. She disappeared last week.` He looked Danny up and down. `She jumped into a weir. Body not been found.`

Danny nodded, chilled by his brother's knowledge and what it might imply. `Jumped, Nat? Is that how it was? Or was she pushed?`

Clegg was silent, his eyes fixed somewhere on the shadows, pictures behind his eyes. Of a dog struggling against water, of a boar badger confident and assured, of a family walking through the park, being stoned by the local punks, of Bonny in pink bath water, shadows cast by invisible strings.

`If she was pushed, Dan,` he said, making ready to leave, `Maybe we should offer to pull her out?`

ELEVEN

Dear Sam,

You can't hear me, I can't post this, you wouldn't be able to read it but it doesn't matter, I'm going to write it anyway, I'm going to tell you as much as I can. I promised and it's only fair. No its not obligation, don't worry. I want to. It might help me understand it all. I'll write down as much as I can and then read it back to myself as though I were a stranger, as though I had found somebody's secret diary. Then I'll burn it. I'll burn it all and when the smoke rises up then its yours, then its for you. You can read it in the smoke, like Father Christmas used to. There was a tree, like the one at home, growing out of the mist. It was the first thing I saw, the last thing I'll forget. Just imagine how it must have seemed, just imagine if anyone had been watching, if anyone had seen it all happen, just imagine it had been you, out fishing, walking the dog, early, mist, there has to be mist, and then you see the coffin next to the canal. I didn't think any of this at the time. I felt like shit, like a hangover must feel. I forgot where I was or what had happened and then thought of Jet and wanted to cry. But I didn't. You know I didn't and never will. I looked away from the water, though. I imagined that Jet might have been washed down to the place where they left me but of course that is stupid. So there you are, walking the dog, in the mist, by a canal when you see this coffin and the lid opens and this girl sits up, looking like death. I knew you'd like that! There was no one around, of course. They made sure of that. They. It seems strange not to have seen them, not to be able to talk to them and thank them. It's as though it didn't really happen until I can thank them, whoever they are, whatever the risks they took. They must have been scared. They ditched me and the coffin at the first opportunity. If someone had found me before the drugs had worn off it could have been very different. They might have tipped me in, or called the sheriff, or adopted me, like Moses in the bulrushes. No, perhaps not. It was like being born again. Everything before that morning was a life before birth, a preparation for a new and real life. And there was the hawthorn tree, like ours would have been in another twenty years, waiting for me.

My ankle hurts, Sam! I'm not complaining, I know you'd swap and you have to put up with far worse, but it still hurts, all the other things don't take the pain away. At least it wasn't in one of my fillings, like in the spy films; at least I didn't have to pull a tooth out. I suppose they'll think of that next. I don't have any fillings. But that wouldn't stop them. Think of the Lady of Shallot. Or Ophelia in Hamlet. Or something from an old horror film. Black and white mist. Gothic, that's it. Grey make-up. So there I am in No-Man's -Land. I was scared. In the undertakers, doing that thing with the coffin and the body, all that time, do you think I was scared? I wasn't scared, because I was angry, I was in a kind of frenzy that stopped me from thinking too much about what I was doing, but now the frenzy is over I've got time to be frightened, which I suppose is a good thing because it makes me cautious. You know how we used to tell ghost stories at night until we were too scared to sleep? This is like living them. I didn't see any packs of wild dogs but that doesn't mean they weren't out there or that I wasn't scared of them. I love dogs, you know I do, but the thought, just the thought that packs of the things roam wild and attack people. It's all lies probably but it doesn't make it less scary. Yes, I know, like the ankle. Stop complaining. And don't mention Jet. Don't even think about Jet. And never ever compare what we did to Jet to what happened to Mum. There, I've said it and its finished.

First there was a shantytown of strange houses. I expected caravans and skips and old containers all cobbled together with corrugated iron and sheets of plastic but it wasn't like that. The houses were made of strawbales covered in mud. The roofs were of that fibre matting stuff that sprouts grass and they were all funny shapes: round, oval, oblong, built around frames of tree trunk, stripped of bark, but stained bright colours and decorated, carved, like totem poles. They had dogs but they kept themselves to themselves. I saw it all from a good distance and stayed well clear. I half wanted to go down and be part of it, to talk to the children and look at their horses but I was too scared. Can you understand that? Of course you can. You better than anyone. Aren't they drug smugglers? You know all those urban myths? Stories with a horrible twist? This must be where they come from. You find yourself imagining them when you skulk through the woods or hear voices in the distance. But you would love it, Sam, I know you would. Trees and birds and horses. But you don't need me to tell you that. You want some details. The Evesham valley? I think so; you'll have to be patient with me. You showed me the names but that doesn't mean it sank in. Then there was the canal, just like it was supposed to be. It was busy in a quiet sort of way. It was nice to watch it from the side. Just a shame I had to sleep through it all when it was me being transported. I wondered if one of the boats I saw was the one that had carried me, if there were men down there who had lifted me around in the coffin. Did you ever think why Dad's friends, his helpers, had to be undertakers? Did you ever think how strange that was? As though you have to pass through something like near-death to enter his world? The canal led to Stratford and even I'm not that stupid. Busy and dangerous Dad said. Bounty hunters, that kind of thing. I went as close as I dared because I had to make the first step to Malvern, otherwise I would be in limbo. Sorry. You know what I mean. I thought about stealing a canoe. You can do that over here, don't forget. You can steal anything. It's not even locked up most of it, stuff just lying around waiting to be nicked. Except that no one nicks it, at least I don't think so. I've spent the last six weeks practising on the lake at home, messing around in a canoe ready for this and when it came to it I just couldn't do it, I couldn't bring myself to steal the canoe. Stupid? Start as you mean to continue, I say. Something like that. It just seemed the wrong way to start,

that's all, like making this place dirty. I've not come here to do that. I don't want to be just a different kind of dirt because that would be horrible, that would seem like betraying something. What else? Woodsmoke, Sam. It smells sweet and bitter at the same time, its everywhere and its very nice. And quiet. Lots of quiet. You wouldn't believe how quiet it was down by the water, a little bit of wind in the reeds, a few birds, but nothing else. I've never heard quiet like that. They should bottle it. And spoonbills. Very white and very stupid looking with that blob on the end of their beaks, but I know you would have liked to see them so I mention them and then I burn them, in the letter, and perhaps share them a little bit with you. Because that's what I want Sam, just to share it with you. That's what I want more than anything in the world and that's exactly what I can't have, but you don't like it when I moan, so I won't. I am going to read Dad's letter one last time, even though I know it by heart and then burn it and this. Goodnight, Sam. Wish me luck.
PS The ankle still hurts like shit but to stop you from worrying I'll tell you its fine. It's fine.

Your best ever sister,

Beth.

TWELVE

Arch also saw a tree. At first he thought the vision was below ground in the great web of roots his nail could visit, the huge reservoir of osmosis and decay in which he could conjure up millions of talking heads. It was like Hades down there, he sometimes said, it was as though he had reached Hades by mistake and all the lost souls of history had been waiting, centuries some of them, to pour out their complaints, to make their requests, to explain the error that brought them there in the first place, and would Arch please do something about it, and soon, at the risk, otherwise, of being haunted through his next ten incarnations and having the curse of God-knows which Nordic slut brought down upon his children's children's children's children millennia hence? Whatever, Arch told them, usually with a shrug. You're no more real than I am, which really freaked them out, which really set the tent shaking with venom and anger. It's a conspiracy, he told them, sorry. I buy into some, I shit on the rest. Keep trying.

But this was above ground and burning. It came with a clarity that made him reach for his shades as though to take them off but he checked himself long enough, breathed deeply, eased back into the nail's rhythm. It was one and many trees, vague but specific. The Tree of Knowledge, the Tree of Life, the World Tree, all in one, a holy trinity, a hawthorn, two metres high and the same wide, plump with berries in the autumn, huge with blossom in the spring, all this he could smell or taste, or something between, the tang of old iron overlaid with the revelation of living green. It filled a tiny back garden, it glowed with bees and birdsong for much of the year and was the only one in its street, a real street with real people. A father, his son, his daughter. No mother. Arch could taste the mother's absence like blood on his tongue. No mother, but a tree, filling the garden, a notice to the world that the family was odd, outsiders, lost. Next door's washing, taken by the wind, caught in its branches, a sheet got shredded on its thorns. Words were exchanged. Silence one week, shouting the next. `Why can't you be like other people?` somebody asked. A neighbour? `Cover it with tarmac, buy some slabs.` Then the leaves dropped, just as they dropped every October, but this time the inconvenience of it all, the sheer uncontrolled and irresponsible mess of it all must have been too much. Arch was with the neighbour, he could relate to this stuff, but he knew the show was for the girl's sake, or the girl was for him, whatever. He also knew that the girl should not have seen what followed next, that the girl was in someway the victim. He had seen her before, naked, daubed, beautiful, but now she was even younger. Perhaps the neighbour timed it that way, knowing how she loved the tree, how she had played around its roots since before she could walk, how she strung nuts and rind to attract the verminous birds. Perhaps it was chance, a moment set-aside for the girl's future in ways no one could predict. The man squirted lighter fluid over the fence then tossed over a fire work and within seconds the burning bush was raging in the back garden, seething with heat, scorching the fascia boards, melting the window frames, calling the fire-brigade and setting fire to the girl. Setting fire to the girl? Arch flinched. Something was wrong here, someone had played around with the programme, rescripted the ending. Then he remembered, this was the land of images, where ideas had arms and legs and a life of their own. The girl was on fire with a blaze white hot in its intensity but invisible to the untrained eye, though Arch could see it, like a star turned in on itself, or a black hole, dense with rage. She waited a month. Arch admired her for that; he was on her side now. She waited until all the best washing was on the line: sheets, towels, shirts, trousers. She squirted lighter fluid over the fence, just like the neighbour. The whole lot burnt in seconds, the girl watching silently from the roof of the shed, no response to the abuse, no answers for the police, just a menacing silence.

Arch thought he was finished with the trip and was ready to move on, access the Black Knight, play the Game, score virtual points. But he couldn't. Something kept moving him back to the scar of the tree; something was nudging him to recognize, to remember, even though these were not his memories but the Earth Mother's. He realized there was no sadness. He had been here before at the death of a tree, drawn by lightening or a chain saw or a cry for help. All hell would rant and rail through the soil and stone and nag Arch for his inactivity but now, though the tree had died a dramatic death, there was no pain or sadness seeping through the humus and into the sub-soil. Strange. It was winter. In winter the earth was awake, it made the nail hum, it could overload the whole network in seconds, just as in summer the earth was asleep, its dreams above ground, in summer the nail could probe for hours and stir little more than gnomic laughter. But now he was in winter, suddenly, the earth was buzzing and the skeleton of the tree stood black and accusing in the garden as a kind of shrine devoted to the girl's anger. She snapped at her father when he suggested felling it, she scraped off the black from its trunk to daub herself and the neighbour's fence with, as an extra barrier between herself and the world. And then she cut it down. She went outside and cut it down with a blunt axe and a rusty saw. She cut it down in the same week her bleeding started. She was thirteen, Arch thought, although in real time, who could know? She was thirteen and her bleeding released the tree's pain until it shot through Arch like cramp, so much pain that he pulled off the shades and yanked the nail from the earth with a yelp, as though the thing was hot and for a second he was too scared to let the after-image form itself and reassure him. `Not my shit,` he muttered, rising up from the ground, `Not for me.` but he was not surprised to see a jay fly up from the scrub, settle briefly in a hawthorn and glare at him. `She's coming, Arch.` he told himself, `and chaos will never be the same again.`

THIRTEEN

Clegg, being in a good mood, allowed himself the shades, the Italian ones with light frames and tinted lenses. There was a weak sunshine to justify their use and a contented shuffle of shoppers to suggest wealth at leisure. He was less certain about the brown leather jacket and the scuffed cowboy boots and suspected that soon he would be too old for such things. He was smiling, shaking his head but smiling. `Who pushed her?` he asked lazily, the tension of the Pig Trough left far behind. `Who was with her next to the river?`

The two brothers had met by arrangement in the city centre. Danny, playing the spy, had bread with which to feed the pigeons. Clegg was less concerned. He sprawled on the seat, apparently at ease, watching with amusement the way the birds strutted and argued over crumbs. Since his last meeting with Danny his suspicions had grown into a near certainty. It almost made no difference what his brother had or had not extracted from between the System's teeth. Cometh the hour, cometh the man, wasn't there a saying to that effect? And Clegg was determined that the hour would be soon and that he would be the man. He also knew but might not admit it that he had been waiting for an excuse for years, biding his time with varying degrees of patience. He watched the public shuffling about its business and failed to prevent a feeling of smug superiority creep up on him. He was destined for big things. He had always known it and now Danny was here to confirm it.

Danny looked around anxiously. He ran thin fingers through his shoulder length hair and looked enviously at Clegg's pose, his sunglasses and comfortable leather. His anxiety was well founded. The machine in his breast pocket could access the world, it could unpick any lock, it could foretell any future but it could also betray its user. Finding the information had been easy, covering his tracks subsequently had taken hours. `John Savage  has a shepherd.` he muttered, following the progress of a one-legged pigeon, which seemed especially aggressive and determined. `One man who harvests everything that comes up about dad, sister, two kids, the lot, it all goes through him. No name, only a code number. That put me on my guard. They code them so that snoopers set off the alarms. But I found a way. Assume you know the name then check the Income Tax returns, using the code. Switch to tax reference number, refer back to personal records then up comes the name. Simple. They lock the front door, wait for you to climb in the window but forget the back way in. Anyway, the result is the same. The man whose job it is to find Savage. According to the System, according to the full stats. on who did what, where, when and to whom, he was next to that weir on the bridge with Savage's daughter. He threw her in.` Danny expected some response from his brother but got none.

To Clegg it made sense. The dog must have been carrying Beth Savage's tag, keeping it warm, just as the pigs kept tags warm in the nightclub. Savage and his cronies on the Wildside had used Clegg to carry the false tag and to throw the girl, or at least her dog and tag, to their death. A dangerous game to play by any standards. It would have given the girl more chance of a clean escape and up to this point could all have been guessed. The surprise was that Savage's shepherd was somehow implicated in the `death`. Whoever had dreamed up the scam, loaded the tags and juggled the data obviously had a sense of humour. But it raised more questions than it answered. Where was Beth Savage? Clegg would bet good money on her being alive and well. And why had they picked on him to carry out the messy errand? Was that planned, or just bad luck?

`What's it like, Nat?` Danny asked, breaking the silence. `What's it like? You've seen it. Is it like they say?`

`It's what you want.` said Clegg, not keen to be diverted, `It still rains. A tree's still a tree. What do you want?`

`I don't know what I want,` said Danny, sighing, `I want it to be different I suppose. The girls...`

`It was dark.` Clegg laughed. `I went in the dark, remember? Badgers. I wasn't looking for action.`

`A man once told me they don't live in families. Or houses. They move around in tribes, like in those nature films. And they don't have sex, not like we do. They still have marriage and rules, they stick to their own, that kind of crap. And they don't have money.

`They have money.`

`So what do they do with it?`

`Same as you or I.`

`But they don't work for it, everyone knows that, Nat.`

`So it grows on trees? Maybe that's why they plant so many.`

`Sure, they work, Nat, but not for money. They work for love. Be afraid. They work for love and the money is just a side issue. A kind of waste product.`

`It's crap.` Clegg said. `Golden pisspot land. Utopia. Isn't that it? The world turned on its head? Don't believe everything they tell you, Dan, please, never. Of course they live in families. And houses. Of course they need money. How else can they rip each other off?`

`How do you know? It was dark, you said yourself.`

`Look, Dan, they're not a different *species,* okay. Different rules, that's all.`

`No rules.`

`Okay, no rules, that's a kind of rule itself. No rules and don't mess with the livestock. Certainly not the badgers. Screw them, Danny Boy. Live and let live, right? Unless we can make a profit somewhere. What about the code?` Clegg saw his brother flinch as the questions moved to their conclusion, `The guy who is supposed to have thrown her into the weir. We know he was John Savage's shepherd. What about a name? Who was I?`

`I've got a name.` Danny lowered his voice even further. He might have been announcing the death of a loved one to judge by the awkwardness of his tone.

`Go on then.`

`You don't want to know, Nat.`

`*You* don't want to know, Danny. That's a different thing. But this is not about what you want, kid, this is about me. Go on! Who was I?`

`You were Bruiser for the night, Nat. You remember, at the Pig-Trough, number one sow-shagger?`

`In plain English, Dan,` Clegg said, moving forwards as he spoke, conceding to his brothers need to whisper. `We don't want any mistakes.`

`You should leave it, Nat. Walk away from it now. You've done your bit. You're a pawn in some one else's game. Just leave it. Please`

But Clegg was in no mood for caution. He took his brother firmly by the arm and pressed hard. `Done that, Dan. Been a pawn. Black, white, carved or ivory, been every kind of fucking pawn you can think of. It's time to move on. Cleggy senior is ready for a step up.` He let go of Danny, flicked the shades onto the top of his head and pinned his brother to the bench with a gaze ice-cold in its intensity. `Funny game chess, Danny Boy. Very funny game. Thing called endplay. Pawns can turn nasty you see, pushed around for hours on end, sacrificed without a care in the world, then suddenly they can turn, they can decide the game, when the big bastards have shot their load. Must be very satisfying to be that kind of pawn. Go on, Dan, who was I? Who chucked the girl in the river? `

`You were David Armstrong.` Danny said, defeated, hurling his last crust at the one-legged pigeon, expecting the whole flock to explode in a blind panic and flee the market square. `Sir David Armstrong.`

Clegg was staring up at the clock tower. Nobody ever referred to its hands or consulted it for the time. Most people had forgotten how. Your day was paged and measured by the certain pulse in your ankle, never too late and never too early.

`I told you, Nat, you're out of your depth. We both are.`

But Clegg was enjoying it. He allowed a smile to advance from ear to ear. For a few brief hours, courtesy of an illicit tag, he had been a VIP, Sir David Armstrong, Chief Commissioner of Police, no less, the Comfort Zone's answer to God.

`And for John Savage,` he asked, stroking his cow boy boot, certain now that he had dressed just right for the occasion, `Is there any reward?`

`A reward? Nat, you could negotiate your own. You're talking millions. Millions. If you deliver Savage you also deliver the Wildside. The whole farce. They have methods now, they have ways of picking the brains of these cyber terrorists. Get Savage and you get control of the System, complete control, even across the Line. There would be no Line. They'd be finished. The experts would crawl around Savage's head for a few hours and the army would move into the Wildside the next day. There would be nothing to stop them. End of experiment.`

Danny was ready to stand up, assuming their talk to be nearing its end, but Clegg had stretched himself even more comfortably on the bench. `Experiment.` he said, playing with the word. `Is that what it is, Dan? The Wildside's an experiment?`

`Call it what you want. Savage's toy train set. The postindustrial Nirvana. It can't last. Can it?` A long pause. Clegg miles away and Danny very anxious, sitting again. `Tell me, Nat. Tell me. What's the idea? Now what? You could just forget it all. They've used you and that's it, that's an end to it. There's nothing to tie you in with it. I checked. They covered your ass. Just leave it.`

But Clegg wasn't listening. He was playing with his brother's earlier question. What was it like? No wires, no cars, no rules. How would it be to go untagged through the world, unwatched, unmarked unmeasured? How would it be to follow the horses, the salmon, the season? The unboxed, they were called, the Wildsiders were unboxed. They didn't fit. No more than Clegg did.

`Sure, Dan.` Clegg smiled, enjoying his final flourish. `But why me? Why did they pick on me to carry the tag, to throw the dog in the river?`

`Chance. What else? Anyone would have done just as well.`

`And could anyone else have found out what you just told me? Could anyone else pick up a microlight and hop over to the Land that Time Forgot? Think about it, Dan. It's destiny, or a stitch up.`

`Which means?`

But Clegg did not answer. He reached inside Danny's breast pocket and took out the screen. `Bonny.` he said. `Now. Please.`

His brother obliged. A tapping of numbers followed by bright colours on a high-resolution thumb-nail screen. Deja vu. An immobile Bonny, wrappers and cans on the floor. Only the film was different. Channel fifteen. `Give her my love.` he said, standing up. He slipped his shades casually back into place, patted his brother on the shoulder and picked his way briskly through the clutter of shoppers and one-legged pigeons.

FOURTEEN

`It's a love letter, ` the man said, `it must be a love letter. Or a poem. Same thing in the end. Learn from it Timbo, learn from it. `

But the boy said nothing. He was watching how Beth twisted her hair with one hand whilst writing with the other. He was watching the way she half sat and half squatted at the water's edge, perfectly balanced, as though ready to jump up and run. She's an athlete, he thought, or a mermaid come to claim me. He tried to see her reflection in the water, as though that might reveal more of her. He turned to the old man for instructions.

`It's enough for one day, Timbo. Let's call it enough. ` He gestured to the flotsam at his feet. A car number plate, a street sign, a pump handle from a pub bar. `And you're sure about the phone box? `

The boy nodded, only half listening.

`A red one? `

The boy shrugged. `It was too dark. ` He said.

`And too long ago. ` the old man conceded. It had been a stupid question. It was enough that the boy had found the submerged pub and come back with the pump handle. The old maps said there had been a phone box outside, but whether it was the right kind was too early to tell.

The two of them looked back to the girl. She was less than a hundred paces away, but the wind and her concentration hid their voices. They had watched as she tried to light a fire and had smiled at her failure. The old man imagined he could see her swearing under her breath. From this distance they could not be certain about her ankle, the hint of blood on a bandage, but her movements were strange, her look overly anxious. But the sight of her drew them, as a magnet draws pins. The boy is too young for her, the man thought, and I'm too old

`So it's a poem.` the boy said. `What's to learn? ` He was fifteen or sixteen years of age, old enough to resent Beth. He was naked but for a diver's mask and snorkel perched on the top of his head. His chest was tattooed with an enormous dolphin which appeared to leap from his groin to his throat.

The old man sighed. He was quite bald and the polish of his skin caught the light off the water. He tried to smile but a lack of teeth took his face in on itself in a grimace. `Some are worth a lot. ` he said.

`Some what? `

`Poems. Some poems are worth a lot. `

The boy looked towards the girl differently, as though she might have discovered a nugget of gold in his claim of water. `More than this? ` he asked, pointing to the car number plate.

`Far more.` The old man shifted from his fisherman's stool and picked the rectangle of metal from amongst the slime and weed of the morning's salvage. He made as though to hurl it in the girl's direction but thought better of it. Instead he shouted. `You want to get across? `

Water birds flew up from the reeds close by. As they had expected, the girl startled and looked in their direction.

`She's going to run.` the boy muttered. `You shouldn't have done that. She's going to run. You want me to catch her? I don't want her to run. I can catch her and bring her back. ` His tone suddenly changed. `There's two of her.`

`What?`

`I said there's two of her. It's like I can see two people.`

`You're a fool.'

`So you always say.`

`And I'm always right.`

`Not this time. She's two in one.`

Before the old man could react Beth caught them both off guard. Instead of running she walked towards them, casually, as though she had nothing to fear. The anxiety they had seen in her private movements was well hidden. As she approached they took in the details: the tangled hair, pale skin, tired eyes, mermaid beauty. And the ankle.

`I might. ` Beth did not speak until she was within a few feet of them. She was angry with herself for being caught off guard and was struggling to hide it. There was no hint of fear, which fooled neither man nor boy but impressed both. Unwatched she had appeared as nervous as a sparrow. Now she was challenging them.

`She wants to get across.` the man said, addressing Timbo matter-of-factly.

Beth was trying hard to ignore the boy's nudity. She chose her favorite means of defense. `What are you doing? she asked, sure that her questions would prove safer than theirs.

`It's legal.` said the man, with another smile that screwed his face up like a paper bag. `We're both legal. Which is more than can be said for everyone around here.`

`I'm Timbo.` the boy said suddenly. `I get stuff from under the water. I'm a diver. Have you ever dived?`

Beth thought he might be simple, so unabashed was he by standing naked. But his eyes were calm. `I'm Beth.` she said, `No, I've never dived.` She tried not to stare at the dolphin as she spoke.

He smiled, shrugged and was gone, slipping on the mask and plunging into the dark water.

`He likes you,` the old man said. `He'll bring you a present. My name is Moses. It's biblical, you know. Of course you know. They found me in the rushes and I've been in the wilderness ever since. Timbo and I have been watching you this last hour. Writing a poem were you?`

She contained her anger but her voice rang flat, like cold metal. `A letter. And what's it got to do with you?` She tried to run through her actions of the last hour and wondered if the man was telling the truth. Why had she not seen or heard them? She had known the need for caution. Had she been so caught up in the letter that she had taken unacceptable risks?

`A letter.` he nodded to himself sagely. `I thought so. One you'll never send?`

`What do you mean by that?`

`What do I mean by that? Nothing! Nothing at all. Don't be so touchy. I'm a romantic that's all. I see a beautiful young lady writing, so I think love poem, I think love letter, I think two hearts yearning for each other across an ocean of time. Or across this slab of water. Just because I'm old it doesn't mean I can't dream.`

`You're full of bullshit.` Beth said.

The man burst out laughing. `You're not wrong there, pale face. Pity Timbo didn't hear that one. He'd love that one would Timbo. And love you even more. I'm full of bullshit and you've got blood soaking through your sock.` he nodded to her ankle.

`What if I have?`

`What if it gets infected? What if it enters the bone? What if you lose a leg?` He reached into a leather bag next to his stool and taking out a bottle. `Iodine.` he said. `You should have come prepared. Didn't they tell you that? Or have you come without help? Some still do, you know. Here, clean it up. I would do it for you but its not appropriate for a man of my age to touch a young girl like you. Besides,` he waved his wet and mud-stained hands in the air. `we're looking for salvage.` he said. `Antiques, bits of nostalgia. What are you looking for?`

`Who says I'm looking for anything?`

`I do.` This time he dispensed with the smile, tilted his head forwards to peer down his nose and looked at her as though to challenge any attempt at denial. He gave it several seconds but could not help himself from smiling again.

`So I want to get across.` she conceded. She had looked up the path to left and right. The boy was out in the water somewhere and there was nothing to stop her from walking away from the conversation but something told her she would only succeed in walking into the same or worse.

`Then I was right. Do you know what this is?` he held the object up for Beth to examine. She shook her head. `A pub tap.` he said. `Worth a couple of hundred. They used to pull on this to get the beer out of the barrels and into the glass.`

`A good day's work.` Beth suggested. She had found a place to sit on the edge of the path, safely away from the man but close enough to talk. She had taken the iodine and some cotton wool and was attending to the cut.

The man's eyes seemed to have fixed themselves on her bare foot. He fell vacant as he stared at it for several seconds and then seemed to shake himself awake. `I'm sorry.` he said. `It's not what you think. I'm not dirty. It's just that a foot like that, your foot. It's beautiful. So young. And it can still go so many places. Have you ever thought of that? All those places it can still go. Look at mine!` he plucked one out of the mud and waved it at Beth. It was as long and as lean as the hands that were exploring the pub tap.

`Who are you?` she asked.

`Moses, I told you. My parents were good Zionists once. Perhaps I can part the waters for you. Perhaps I'm your ferryman.` he looked across the water to where the boy had emerged onto a small wooden platform about one hundred yards from the shore. `There used to be a pub there.` he said. `I don't know why I'm telling you that, it's a trade secret. It's our little gold mine. If we can find a pub sign that would set us up for the year, pub signs are all the rage nowadays. But of course best would be a telephone box.`

`A telephone box?`

`Yes. Sometimes they had them outside the pub. The old red ones. Mostly rusted away and difficult to move, but you fill it with balloons and float it out, worth thousands they are.`

Beth looked at the pile of bric-a-brac next to the old man's stool. She recognized an old-fashioned traffic sign and a small metal plate with the number `24` still visible. A house number she guessed. The ferryman nodded to a car number plate. `They can trace them back, you know. Your great-grandfather might have driven that one. They sell. Everything sells these days. I'm not sure why.`

`What do you mean, the `ferryman`?` Beth asked.

He looked from her face to her ankle, as though searching for clues. `The ferryman. There is always a ferryman, you know. Its part of the ritual. I should come to you out of the mist, really, some kind of hood over my head. Offer to take you across in return for your soul or your first- born.`

`I don't know what you're talking about.`

`Don't you?` He looked sad for a moment, as though Beth had denied the faith by which he had lived a devout life. `Don't you really? Didn't they teach you anything at school? No, I don't suppose they did.` he concluded a little sadly. `Let's talk about this over food.` he said. `Are you hungry? They usually are.`

Beth's drugged sleep had lasted three days and three nights. Now the feeling of sickness was wearing off the very mention of food made her alert and tense. The man gathered his things together. He climbed stiffly from out of the mud and reeds and surprised Beth by the formality of his offered handshake. They turned away from the water just as the boy emerged. He shook water from himself as a dog might and then handed Beth a rusted object. It was some kind of metal tankard, its handle of bone. He offered it to her, grinning, but said nothing.

Half a mile away, in a small wooden hut suspended above the reeds on stilts Beth tore into warm soup and soft bread whilst the old man and Timbo attended outside to the artifacts they had reclaimed that day. Moses returned three times to refill her bowl and only after half an hour of devoted eating did it occur to Beth that he had left her alone with the food deliberately. With their work finished, Timbo lit a fire in the wood stove and Moses came to sit with Beth. He offered her a pipe, which she declined. She was waiting for the difficult questions. Where had she come from? How had she managed to cross the Line? And hardest of all, where was she going? But the old man took his time, chose his angle, cast obliquely.

`Its not nice,` he said, after a long and not uncomfortable silence, `being an outsider, its not nice. Me and Timbo, we're outsiders. Neither one thing nor the other really, neither fish nor foul. We're licensed to be here.` he reminded her, `but not to be insiders. Not anywhere.`

`Why are you telling me this?` she asked.

`Now the art of conversation,` he added thoughtfully, `There's a dying art. In some parts at least. A conversation is like a building, see, I lay a stone, you lay one on top. Try it. You might be amazed.`

He was telling her off very gently but she got the point. Don't jump down my throat, he might have said. The war is over. Some old instinct told her to try and please the man. `It must be difficult,` she suggested, laying a stone on his, `being neither fish nor foul.`

Moses chuckled, as though pleased with her progress. `Well it has its compensations if you must know.` He smiled thoughtfully. `Sometimes it's just how we want it, isn't that true, Timbo?` The boy did not answer. He was next to the stove, his back towards them, whittling with a knife at a piece of wood.

Beth caught sight of herself in a small mirror beyond the boy. She could not be certain but it seemed very likely that he had been watching her reflection all the time. She stared at the mirror, judging the right angle at which to confront him whilst appearing to answer Moses. `So you can't help me across?` she asked, `neither of you?`

`Oh, but I didn't say that. I didn't say that, Beth. I said you need a ferryman. And once you've got a ferryman you'll need a story.`

`An alibi?`

He laughed. `Like in the police films? No, paleface, not like in the police films. I mean a story, like in real life. Listen. You want to cross over, right? You've been told it's different? Well it is, take my word for it. It's more different than people realize. It couldn't be more different.`

`Don't start him off.` the boy said, `He'll talk all night.` He called Beth's bluff by looking straight into the mirror. Beth looked back, but this time differently. She imagined sex with him and the distraction of the dolphin, there was something beautiful about the way it leapt up from his groin. He would expect it, she assumed, and the brief feeling of power she felt at the thought was a reassurance.

`Its not like things were a hundred years ago,` Moses said, ignoring the interruption. `They're living a possible future. They're ahead of their time, not behind it. There's more over there than meets the eye, that is for sure. It's like under the water. Some people say there's nothing down there any more, its all been salvaged, its all been pulled up. But they're wrong. There's stuff buried so deep that a lifetime of nightmares wouldn't bring it to the surface. Lots of sadness gets buried, you know. Lots. You never find much joy down there. Even a child's toy is sad when it's under three feet of silt. Well it's the same over the Line. And I'll tell you another riddle. Some people cross over the Line but don't see anything different. Which is sad. Very sad. Okay, they see the horses instead of cars and they see the trees and they might notice that children don't start school till they're twelve and all that kind of thing, but that's all on the surface, its all on the surface, paleface, believe me. It's what's underneath all that, they don't see what's underneath all that because they don't cross over with a story. Life hasn't given them one. Oh no! That's not true.` he suddenly corrected himself. `That is certainly not true. Life has given them one, its just that no one has ever told them about it.`

`I told you not to get him started,` the boy said, `You wouldn't believe how many times I've listened to this crap.`

But Beth wasn't listening. Ask questions, her father had said, never be afraid to ask, but now the questions were stuck, they choked on her uncertainty. Part of her knew exactly what the old man was saying, but part of her was drowning in a sea of salvage. She wanted to play by his rules, add stone to stone, build a conversation that led somewhere but it was all too new and too strange.

`I've got a story.` she said, ignoring them both, `I've got a story. And it's secret.`

In the silence that followed the boy turned to face her and looked to his grandfather as though awaiting a command or permission. But nothing was forthcoming. Beth imagined she saw sadness in the boy's face, or pity. She had flattened any building that might have been taking shape. She had excluded them both from her conspiracy.

Later that evening the dolphin got up from his whittling and nodded to Beth to follow. He wore shorts embroidered with stars but his top was still bare. By the water's edge he showed her old salvage he had brought to the surface, but Beth was not interested. She could not see its relevance to either of her lives, past or future. When she was certain they would not be disturbed she gave him the look, the one that asserted her power, the one that never failed, the one that kept her and Sam safe and always put her in control. He was caught instantly. Helplessly unaware of what she had done to him she let him flounder in silence for several minutes. Unusually she could find no contempt for the boy's desire or the extent of his surrender, only pity. At last she undressed for him and peeled off his shorts. The dolphin she enjoyed. She followed its curves down into the groin and laughed at how eager he was and how he dissolved almost instantly in her hand. The usual feelings followed: anger, triumph, boredom; but this time there was something more. A sadness tried to come over her and a threat of emptiness that made her desperate for sleep and to be away from these people, to be away from all people as soon as possible.

When Beth had gone to bed and the boy was certain she was asleep he allowed himself a closer look, examining her closed eyes, her hair on the pillow, the lines of her body under the sheet. He was still shocked by the memory of her touch, uncertain that it had even happened. He felt through the pocket of her jacket that was draped over the chair next to the bed. He was not sure what he was looking for but after a few seconds he found a watch. It had no strap but a kind of ribbon and pin. On its back was an inscription. The boy read it and seemed confused. He turned to his grandfather and whispered. `She's two people. I told you, she's two people. We should get paid double.` He shook his head, sighed, and with a knife eased off the watch's back plate.

`She's as many people as she wants to be,` the old man said, fighting back a sigh, `they all are, all of then, though never ever themselves.`

FIFTEEN

Sir David Armstrong in his office, dreaming of the chase, trapped in the amber of his own melancholy. He had changed very little in the two years since the farce of John Savage's failed arrest. His high and gloriously domed forehead still gleamed with good health and his soft blue eyes still belied the quiet force with which he had been known to wield both his and unofficial powers. Here was a man frequently alone even in a crowded room. Here was a man often bored even in the presence of the nation's greatest minds. He could appear as trivial and skittish in cabinet as he could be profound and inward over tea and biscuits. He could be urbane and humorous with cleaners and chauffeurs within minutes of being rude and aloof towards royalty and politicians. His office was a vast wasteland of polished wood, its walls bare since he had confined the Lowry, Bacon and Hilton master-pieces to storage. In their place the breath-taking view across the Thames informed his wiser moments. Moments of lesser quality owed much to the demons with which he had peopled the empty spaces of his authority.

`He's a very clever man, Watson, John Savage is a very, very clever man. Allow me to warn you. I have said it before and I will, no doubt, say it again. Cleverer than John Savage? Not many, good friend Watson, not many that I am aware of.` Even the voice was lightly tanned, somewhere between waxed walnut and plate glass. He did not look at Watson as he spoke. Baleful eyes bathed themselves on the expensive view. An expression of the tortured mystic, great secrets hidden beneath the dome, stared fondly back from the window. Long pianist's fingers toyed with an ancient and useless fountain pen.

Today a single sheet of paper defiled Sir David's desk, the charge sheet that Watson had delivered so diligently only minutes earlier. The charge sheet that stated, in theory at least, that Sir David Armstrong was under arrest. The charge sheet that claimed he had journeyed to the Notts-Derby border and there disposed of one Beth Savage in the turbulent and filthy waters of the Erewash river. Although a half-hearted search had been instigated there was no real hope of finding the body in the Erewash, the Trent, or out in the Humber estuary. This particular body, they were quite sure, was alive and kicking in very different waters. But the charge sheet had brought with it far more. Echoes of the past settled in each corner of the room, squatted like polite undertakers ready to process death. The air, though bright and filtered was made heavy with them. Sadness tinged with the hope of redemption curled the charge sheet's edges.

`A very, very clever man,` he repeated, `Wouldn't you agree, Watson?`

`Most certainly, Sir.`

`Wouldn't you agree, Watson?`

`I'm sure you're right, Sir.

`Wouldn't you agree, Watson?`

The triple-whammy. Sir David loved to toy with Watson in his more stressful moments, it gave him the slight illusion of control. If he asked the same question three times Watson's repertoire was exhausted. Watson's answer was always the same after the third question and Sir David could enjoy the feeling of having taken things once more to the brink. `Are you feeling unwell, Sir?` Watson replied, ready to alert whoever or whatever lurked in the wings of Sir David's department. What message would Watson send if Sir David answered in the affirmative and how discreet would be the response was something the domed head often mused over.

`I'm feeling just fine thankyou, Watson,` he lied, `just fine.`

`I'm very glad to hear it, Sir.`

`I'm sure you are, Watson. Or might I call you Hal today?` One reason Sir David had aged so well, at least such was his theory, owed much to his passion for play. Games were an essential part of his regime of mental hygiene. Man is only free when at play, he often stated, quoting Schiller or some other German mystic. Keep the bastards on their toes, was how it translated, keep the buggers guessing, show them who is boss but never, ever, take them seriously. He had programmed Watson to respond in various ways to various names. Upon being called Hal, the computer always answered Sir David's next statement with the same reply. `I'm going to kill myself, Hal, I'm going to send out for coffee, Hal, I'm going to put a call through to the Home Secretary, Hal, I'm going to organize a *coup d'etat* , Hal.` It made no difference, Watson was stuck in a perpetual parody of the *2001* film computer, `I wouldn't do that if I were you, Dave.` the machine would reply, the slightly nasal and very American drawl synthesized perfectly by its voice card.

Sir David looked at the monitor. A strange symbiosis. The screen saver was an image of Doctor Watson from one of the old black and white Sherlock Holmes classics of the previous century. Watson's reassuring face was welcome and his plummy 19th century voice strangely soothing. The computer was a combination of police search-engines, data-base and psychotherapy loops, the latter set to affirmation mode. It repeated what its operator said but in a form that might stimulate the development of ideas and often with the addition of relevant information. Sir David sometimes went for days, even weeks without consultation. He had taught it to sulk at the end of such periods of neglect. `A very, very clever man,` Sir David repeated, `but rather selfish.`

`Rather selfish, Sir?`

`Certainly. He let his own wife die, you know, Watson, he let his own wife die. What do you have to say about that?`

Nothing. There was only one thing that could silence Watson and that was reference to Emma Savage. Sir David occasionally took the poor machine to the brink in order to explore and better understand the parameters employed by its programmers. They had assumed to know and understand the complexities of the last twenty years and had taught their simple machine a clumsy kind of tact.

`Tell me about John Savage's wife, Hal.`

`I wouldn't do that if I were you Dave.` It was as though one of the undertaker demons had stepped forward, doffed a cap, offered sympathies.

`No I'm sure you wouldn't, dear friend, I'm sure you wouldn't. But can you imagine being so fanatic that you would allow such a thing to happen? I wouldn't doubt he could throw his own daughter in the river.`

`He could not throw his own daughter in the river, Sir, not physically.`

`Because?`

`We understand him to be unwell. And we understand him to be in Narnia.`

Sir David had long since taught Watson a different vocabulary to that used by normal men in what passed for the normal world. The Wildside he had re-named Narnia, their own home was Airstrip One. It seemed appropriate that the Wildside should borrow a name from foolish children's literature whilst the Comfort Zone was served by one of George Orwell's more accurate predictions. Watson's ignorance to the humour of his statements still amused Sir David and inspired him to further mischief. But now he was in need of serious help. `What is going on, Watson, please, take the burden, explain it all would you? Justify the enormous cost of your very specialized soft-wear. `

`I was hoping you would explain, Sir.` the machine answered, deference in its tone `Would it be helpful to review the facts?`

`Oh yes please, Watson. That would be absolutely spiffing. Let's review them over and over again.`

`Spiffing` was another coded prompt, a secret between man and machine. Watson, as ever, took the hint. `John Savage appears to have expedited a most notable ruse, Sir, to wit, one daughter spirited, nay, one might almost say ghosted away into air that is most decidedly the frail side of thin. We have been waiting, with some impatience it might be added, for just such an escape. One cannot, heart on hand, claim to be even a crumb surprised. Irked in the extreme, yes, surprised, indefatigably not. The circumstances of the young lady's dematerialization have been the cause of a certain amount of consternation, Sir. The father appears to have provided some unwitting party with a mimic of your tag and then obliged said party to dispose of his daughter, aforementioned Beth Savage, poor gel, in the river Erewash, a small and most insalubrious tributary of the river Trent on the Notts-Derby border.`

`Damned cheek, what?` Sir David suggested, poking the Bertie Wooster *alter ego*.

`Unutterably so. The work of an absolute cad.`

Sir David released the machine from its Edwardian bondage by calling it by name. `Ask me some questions, Watson`

`Why the river Erewash, Sir?`

He liked it when Watson was stupid, it was a rare reminder that minds simpler than his own had devised the thing. `Keep asking.`

`Who was carrying your tag? Why did he throw his daughter in the river? Was it really his daughter who was thrown, or only her tag? Why were you the target of the falsification?`

`The last question, Watson. Give me three different answers.`

`Number one. Chance. Your name was chosen at random. The odds are seventy million three hundred and eighty four thousand nine hundred and sixty four to one. Number two. Design. A symbolic statement directed against those who administer and control the security systems of Airstrip One. Number three. A personal agenda beyond the remit of this investigation.`

Sir David smiled with satisfaction, picturing the programmers sweating away in unventilated rooms, trying to write out the past. John Savage had chosen him as a phantom carrier for very definite and very personal reasons and they would definitely be within the scope of the investigation but beyond the limits of poor prudish Watson. John Savage had chosen Sir David as a phantom carrier to signal his intent, to throw down the gauntlet one last time.

Sir David looked out across the floodwaters of the Thames basin. Across forty miles of mud, reeds and stilt villages he could make out the lights of the South Bank, strung along the Downs. The Harrow to Streatham shuttle cut through the water and scattered reflected light in its wake. He sighed, but not yet heavily. Much of the past was a burden to Sir David, but an invitation to play with his old adversary was not to be turned down. `He's playing a game with us, Watson. It's got his name written all over it. Clever man, very clever man, always was.`

`Most certainly, Sir.`

`We had thought he might be dead you know. But he'll never die,` Sir David mused, `just re-boot.`

`I recognize that as a joke.` Watson said.

How reassuring to have your jokes recognized, Sir David thought. No need for laughter, just recognition. When he was really bored he asked Watson to explain why something was funny. The explanations were always hilarious, far more so than any original joke could be. `The chicken's need to cross the road is understated in a form that exaggerates the trivial in order to...`

`John Savage chose me because he hates me. How about that one, Watson?` A nanosecond pause, whatever a nanosecond was. Sir David enjoyed those. It meant he was exploring close to the edge. The investigation could not be compromised by the need for tact yet the conflict made Watson hesitate very slightly.

`Is it possible that he hates you?` Watson asked, keeping it safe.

`Oh yes it is possible, Watson, it is possible, in so far as John Savage is capable of anything unvirtuous. Perhaps you would like to give me three reasons why he might hate me?` But he stopped Watson before he had really started. The formula would be the same, the third reason would be to do with a personal agenda beyond the remit of this investigation. He would have to be more subtle if he was going to lead the machine into the dark cul-de-sac of the forbidden past. First the leg work. That was Watson's speciality.

Sir David continued his musings for a while and than spun his chair to look out across the sea. The lights on the central London platform, where tourists were taken down to see the submerged sites, winked back at him as he plotted his next move. The prospect of success was making him nostalgic. `You see all that, Watson, the water, the marshes, the diving platforms, the lights of Croydon Docks? Fifty years ago you could have walked from here to those lights. A long walk, I'll grant you, but possible. Roads, streets, avenues, houses, shops, factories. Sixteen million people. All gone. All displaced. All re-housed.` Far more had gone in fifty years of course, youth, love and innocence with them, but of these he tried not to think. The four echoed demons paced the room as Sir David spoke, warming to to the changed intensity, pleased by the descent into hopeless gloom. `Can you imagine how it would have been without the System?` he continued, `Without complete control? Chaos. Like it was in half the civilized world. But not here. Thanks to our work every man, woman and child was re-housed, every business was relocated, every community given a second chance. Even the Germans came to us for advice. Can you imagine? The Germans! Asking *us* how to control people, how to keep things neat and tidy. We showed them. We did it for them. They were still groping around with silicon-based computers, for God's sake. Their entire tax records went in one day to a simple virus! John's machine could do it all and more on top. It was the same in the regions. Scotland and

Wales you could understand, but then Manchester, Liverpool, Tyne and Wear. They all wanted their own self-control, their own System, their own strict limits on resettlement. You know I grew up in Bradford, Watson?` The machine could have stated date, time, location, details of doctor, mid-wife, medication used, but refrained. `My ambition was to go shopping in Leeds. Can you imagine? It might as well have been on a different planet. Leeds was pre-paid plastic and on-line credit years ahead of Bradford. You could go there with real money but it wouldn't do you much good. Every shop knew you were loitering the moment you walked in the door. Commercial Tribalism they called it. I hated it, but it was a wonderful idea! The stuff dreams are made of. Leeds against Bradford, Lancashire against Yorkshire, North against South, street against street. We had to do it, Watson, we really did, we had no choice. There was no God or King or ideology to look up to. We gave them a satellite instead, John Savage and I!`

`John Savage, Sir?`

The demons stopped their pacing and became shadows playing on the wall. `We thought he was part of it. We thought he was one of us. He gave us the means. People gave me credit for some of it. Unfair that. I was never more than a crow following his plough. A metaphor, Watson. File it. Try and use it one day. He was the genius. He was the only one who understood it. Still is. Of course what we didn't know was his secret agenda.`

`His secret agenda, Sir?`

`John once told me a remarkable thing, Watson. Said he believed in Atlantis. Can you believe that? The country's top scientist, a Nobel prizewinner. Atlantis! Said that in Atlantis people had a choice. Some lived the good life, knowing it could only lead to death and destruction, but others wanted something more. They took to the mountains. Sheep and goats. Us and them. He wanted to ensure that those who wished it otherwise could take to the mountains. Live out the floods up there. The thing was, he didn't mean floods as you and I know them, he didn't mean water, he meant greed, selfishness, comfort.` Sir David shifted his focus away from the distant lights to his own reflection in the window. `What's the cure for schizophrenia, Watson?` he asked suddenly, changing tack.

`Do you wish me to answer that question in full, Sir?`

`You shoot one.` Sir David stated with emphasis. `None of this dialogue nonsense, talking the square into a circle. Therapy? Forget it! Take it from me, Watson, that kind of thing has had its day. You identify one half of the split, make a little ritual out of it and then have a mock execution. Works every time in my experience. You can't talk to yourself if the self you talk to has been shot at dawn, now can you?`

`Certainly not, Sir.`

`So now you understand the importance of our work?`

`The importance of our work, Sir?`

`How important it is to find Savage. To tidy things up. We live inside a mass schizophrenia, Watson. The whole nation has a split personality. Always has had, to be honest, us and them, Tory and Labour, home and away. We love a good clear split right down the middle. Means the enemy is always out there, always on the other side of a convenient line. Never in here. It's never us that needs to change. It's gone a bit far, that's all! Reached the point of madness, actually. Time to shoot one half.`

`Does that not contravene the official policy, Sir?`

`Ah! The official policy, Watson. What has the World Bank seeped into your electronic marrow? Ignore it, Watson, if they'll let you. Diversity? Those days are over. Who needs an unconscious? Can you answer that? Can you tell me what possible use it serves? It makes you impotent, Watson, if you'll excuse such a vibrant image, it makes you impotent just when the world's there to be screwed. That's what we're put on the planet for, to screw it, right? Diversity? Get rid of it. The Wildside, our great collective unconscious, time to move on, Watson, time to knock them into shape once and for all! John Savage is the Fidel Castro of the twenty-first century, the Wildside its Cuba. Time to have done with the relic.`

`I understand your last twelve questions to have been rhetorical, Sir. Are there any you wish me to answer?`

`Yes.` A change of mood. Demons fled for shelter at the prospect of clear thinking and the threat of action. `Start with this. On the day of the girl's disappearance, check all the names that didn't show on any scanner.`

It would not take Watson many seconds. They were known officially as the Invisibles. Everyone ill, at home and off work. About eight million usually, more if it was raining. Eight million people who had no need or desire to leave their homes. That might have made an interesting statistic at another time. Plans to extend the System's knowledge of the world into people's homes were well advanced, but in the meantime it was the only place to hide.

`Now add this. Lets assume that whoever dropped her tag off into that weir was either from Narnia or one of our own residents who then got cold feet and crossed over. Start from your eight million and check for all subsequent missing persons.`

`Seven million, four hundred and thirty three thousand and eighteen,` Watson corrected. `632 unaccounted for. They are probably still at home ill and not yet on doctor's records. `

`How many of those 632 have crossed over in the last year? Smugglers, dealers, authorized traders, that kind of thing.`

A moment or two as Watson delved into the bottomless pit of surveillance knowledge. `84.` he answered, the number bald on the screen in case of confusion, the names and addresses beneath. Whether because of drugs, adultery, or the urges of teenage excess, there were always a few. But Watson was still humming. `Two of those eighty-four have got red star status. Absconders. They are suspected of smuggling in the last twelve months but no action has been taken against them. There is no record for the day in question. Since missing. One took his fishing boat to Norway and has not returned. The other took off in a micro-light, a form of recreational aircraft. The suspected destination was Narnia.`

`The name, Watson?`

`Aeraxion Delta 3TS.`

`The pilot, Watson, not the machine.`

`Nathaniel Clegg, Sir, details as listed.`

Pages of it. Watson downloaded through the printer behind Sir David. He grazed through the dry data of Clegg`s life. School, family, army record, jobs, shoe-size. As ever there was no shortage of information. All that was needed was a touch of wisdom. And there it was, something Watson had not yet spotted, for all his billions of relays. Poor Watson, he really did have a lot to learn. Sir David uncapped his otherwise useless fountain pen and under-lined three words in the printout.

`Any tie-ins, Watson?`

Thousands of them. A Welbeck catering assistant's mother-in-law had attended a John Savage lecture twelve years previous. The building contractor who had replumbed the main toilets had also plumbed the house opposite Clegg's. Three of the hospital's eighty-four staff had attended the same university as John Savage and one had attended the same school as Clegg, although not at the same time. Kath Savage, the great man's sister, had once purchased a second-hand car from a retired nurse who had worked at Welbeck for six months, eight years ago, the same retired nurse who had attended to Danny, Clegg's brother, after a minor car accident. `Parameters, Sir?` Watson sensibly asked.

`Where was Clegg last employed, Watson?`

`Welbeck Secure Hospital, Sir.`

`And where is her brother...receiving treatment?`

`Welbeck Secure hospital, Sir.`

`Would you call that a connection, Watson?`

`A significant connection, Sir `

`Explain further.`

`Nathaniel Clegg was employed at Welbeck Secure hospital between August 2046 and September 2048. Beth Savage's brother is presently a patient in the hospital.`

But there was something else and they both knew it. If a computer could squirm and blush then Watson would surely have done so. Savage's wife, She-Who-Must-Not-Be-Mentioned, the only woman Sir David Armstrong had ever loved had lived out her final months in Welbeck Secure Hospital.

All the demons bar one had vanished. It remained as a shadow on the wall. It seemed to frown with weight and shifted in response to Sir David's gaze. `What else, Hal?` he whispered slowly, watching the shadow, defying the past. `What else? I want the whole of the family's past raked up, please. Everything.`

`I wouldn't do that if I were you, Dave.` came the soft and nightmare drawl.

`Oh wouldn't you indeed! I bet you wouldn't. Then lets try something else shall we, something a bit more ...spiffing?`

`Spiffing, Sir?`

`The Game, old boy. You remember the Game, with a capital `G`?`

`My recollection of said Game is most distinct, Sir.`

`It's time to play again.`

`A sentiment with which I can only comply.`

`It's time to play again.`

`And comply, I might add, with no little enthusiasm.

`It's time to play again, Watson.`

`Are you feeling unwell, Sir?`

PART TWO

Sometimes Thou may'st walk in Groves, which being full of Majestie will much advance the Soul...

Thomas Vaughan
Anima Magica Abscondita

SIXTEEN

Like a parched child sucking on a straw, draining it to the dregs, Arch drew it in, consumed it to the last drop: The Wildside. For every man a thousand trees. For every woman a thousand birds. For every child a thousand mysteries. Great oaks older than the nation's soul; sunken lanes dense and dripping with ferns and bracken; boulders hewn and worshiped by a dozen tribes across twice as many centuries. Blotched lichen on bleached stone, spotted orchids in dappled meadow, striped damselfly beneath spangled ash and willow. Herds of deer, skeins of geese, gangs of wild boar and the smell of woodsmoke, horse's flank and crushed bracken acrid in the thousand different types of warm damp. Slabs of rock and earth crumbled like mature cheese, wrapped in dense layers of green, as many greens as there are eyes to watch, as many nuances of light as there are minutes to the day and days to the year. Old forests and new, ancient hedgerow and juvenile, tree become copse, copse become wood, wood become chase. Hills, endless hills with secret folds, each with its own primeval name and untold history, each with long buried bones of nation-shapers and its half-forgotten myth and legend of boggart and fairy glamour. Man-made scars healed and opened a dozen times, each time the absolving green irrepressible, its appetite vast and all-consuming, no sin too great for its power of forgiveness. As many secrets as there are shrines, as many paths of initiation as there are blossoms on the hawthorn. And no lines. Perhaps there is the beauty of it. All the lines are rounded into curves, all the curves are humped into mounds and any shadows cast are rich and varied. All this and more for those with the eyes to see and a nose for the unknowable, which meant Arch, surrounded by unseen faces, alert to the silent voice of the subterranean truth.

He knew Clegg was in danger of enjoying himself. He remembered his own thrill and disbelief at the first discovery of outrageous freedoms. The tracks and roads to the west of Malvern were ideal for the scrambler and Clegg's state of mind. Why everybody wasn't out scrambling in the woods must have been a mystery to the new-born. It surely beat topping turnips or winding up radios or driving turkeys to market. Oh he must have enjoyed that! Though Arch had not seen it for himself it had been easy to piece together the evidence. Fifty of sixty of the things trotting stupidly ahead of two boys and their dogs, Clegg tearing a line through the middle, head down, birds exploding in all directions and the air dense with feathers. You couldn't do that at home, Mr.Clegg, now could you?

At one point Arch watched Clegg from less than a mile away as he ate some lunch and stared out across yet another wooded valley. Arch guessed that the trees would be making a big impression on the new man, just as they had done on him two years before. Every road was lined with them. Smaller roads were in the process of becoming tunnels of green as they had been at the turn of the previous century. Hedgerows were well kept and regularly studded with mature trees and those smaller ones, anything up to thirty years old which dated back to the birth of the Wildside and the first great programme of planting and regeneration. No doubt Clegg knew something about landscape as being the thing which had brought these people together and around which they had built their absurd constitution and retarded way of life, but Clegg could not know, as Arch certainly did, that what leapt skyward from every bank and road side, what filled the landscape with intense green was but an iceberg's tip compared to the dense underground chaos, ah, wonderful chaos!, where the roots met to conspire, to argue, to plan their manic campaign. The trees seemed to be in on a secret together, one they had not yet shared with their hosts but one which Arch had figured out straight away. They were taking over. For centuries they had been in retreat, forced to cower away in copses and small woods, tiny cells of resistance cherishing their plan from hedgerows and parks. Their time had come. They were fighting back. Now it was the people who were in retreat, struggling for room. Perhaps they needed waking up, before their world was choked with green and perhaps Clegg thought he was the man to do it. He would seek out their jugular, he would find their heart and rip it out if needs be. He would do to their Medieval pretensions and adolescent fantasies what he had done to the flock of turkeys, head down, feathers flying, Clegg the manic knight, tilting at their low-tec windmills. Just as Arch had thought and felt before the Earth Mother invited him in to her body, before he had learned to conspire on equal terms with myth and legend.

Clegg had worked hard for the scrambler. Arch was impressed. He had followed his nose, used the old instincts and training, observing quietly. He chose an area where the woods began to close even more eagerly onto the fields, somewhere between the market towns of Malvern and Ledbury. He picked up the trail in the mud even before he heard or saw the scrambling bike and set up camp in an old barn less than a mile from the farm. The theft was the easy part. Fuel would be the problem. But Clegg had obviously done his homework. He knew that each community had its own blacksmith. Those he had observed ran a forge for shoeing horses, of which there were thousands, and a petrol pump for fuelling vehicles, of which there were few. He watched a smith at work. Fascinated? Appalled? Arch could only guess. The beast-like hard work of it, the back bent double, the heat of the fire, the endless repetition of precise but heavy movements certainly seemed to captivate him.

Clegg struck on successive nights. Arch observed the one, sucked knowledge of the other through his nail. First was north of Ledbury, where Clegg jumped an old man delivering parcels, laid him out cleanly and took the well-worn document from the man's inside pocket.

The next evening at his target farm, thirty miles away, Clegg wheeled the scrambler away under cover of dark and attempted to bi-pass its ignition. He did so on the edge of a field that contained a very curious but very placid horse. The beast ambled up to Clegg and seemed to watch his every move with interest. At one point Clegg even felt the warmth of its breath on his neck but when he turned around the horse had politely stepped back. Clegg stood up and looked at it. He had never ridden one in his life, nor given it serious thought. His niece Bonny had. His niece Bonny had lived for horses as a child but they had grown inconvenient, too expensive, unfashionable. Here she would have had no choice. The state, such as it was, would have gifted her one on her eleventh birthday, obliged her, though it asked nothing else of its citizens, to care for it, to account for its well-being. For a few moments Clegg had toyed with the idea of abandoning the newly acquired scrambler and going native. The appeal was obvious. It would be a discreet way of travel and did not involve him in the daily quest for petrol. Then he thought of the pace it would condemn him to, and felt the loss of status and quiet superiority that would accompany such a choice. He dismissed the idea. Just the right side of dawn he got the machine started, sent the animal bolting for terror and let rip along the deserted tracks and back lanes. He bought petrol and a spare tank fifty miles further west, the three points of his three indiscretions neatly triangulated. He then dumped the stolen license to avoid the temptation of using it a second time. He would lift himself a new one once he broke into the reserve tank.

All according to the book, thought Arch, even if no one had yet written it. He tried fitting Clegg into various myths to see which one might explain him. The pictures came thick and fast from the Earth Mother's deep reservoir of green imagery but it was the Highwayman that stayed and fitted best, the archetypal nomad, the romantic out-law confined to the fringes of things, condemned to the wings from which he could interfere in spectacular but pre-doomed style.

Next Clegg allowed himself a little excitement. Roads and travel might be meager, but when everyone else was on horseback or humping through the mud then the illusion of power afforded by such a machine was immense. Only when he stopped at the edge of the clearing late in the afternoon of the third day and shut off his engine did Clegg pause for thought. The silence was appalling. You didn't need an army training to know that everything for miles around would be alerted to the intruder on his new scrambler.

What had happened to caution and stealth? Blame it on the air, though Clegg, lots of it, and the novelty of being untagged and unaccountable. Of course the memory of Jacobs' terrier spinning through the air was never far away but the youth didn't know he was being followed. The advantage was Clegg`s and he might as well enjoy it. Bare-footed. A stupid and dangerous conceit. He would make the freak pay for it yet. It was time to pick up the trail. He was dependent on success in Malvern but felt confident that for once in his life a lucky star was watching over him. He was trusting that Beth, having crossed over, would in some way be helped or in alliance with her pixie friend, he of the crossbow skills. Some how the girl's escape had been engineered from this side, not in the Comfort Zone, and whilst at home they might think Beth Savage had finished up in a river Clegg knew otherwise. They would be fumbling round, chasing their tails, arresting each other whilst he was already on his way to a prize the value of which was beyond imagination.

He lay awake beneath the night stars. Transfixed by their clarity he played a game remembered from childhood, extending lines from one to the other to create unheard of constellations, a mythical web known only to himself. Within this he slept fitfully, troubled by the unknown. Half a mile away Arch wiped wet soil from his nail, rolled up the copper wire, compacted the pen on itself and watched the same stars that Clegg watched, felt the same chill, heard the same night noises and heavy quiet and fell into a dreamless sleep, like a spider content with its own spinning.

SEVENTEEN

She decided to hate Finn. It would do him good, she thought, teach him humility. Not that he lacked it. Or much else. He was polite, apologetic, comfortable, just about the master of his shyness. He was talking about geese. Every year it was the same, he said, but every year it was repeated. Nothing, he insisted, nothing compared to the sight of tens of thousands of geese cruising the air, prospecting the drowned meadows, claiming their beat. Beth couldn't argue. There was nothing for her to relate to or make comparison with. He spoke of geese in the winter, on the ice. What did she know of winter or any season, of ice or any element? His name was Irish. She listened hard for a hint of accent but failed to find one. His eyes were less wild in the morning light, as though something had been resolved by sleep. Last night she had trusted herself to the advice of Moses and sought out this barge. It would take her across, he said, no questions asked, free of charge if she mentioned his name. Beth had felt instantly safe with Doctor Johnson, the white-haired owner, but anxious about his companion. Who would not have been? His feet were bare and callused. His crossbow showed menacing through his bedroll. His lean frame seemed awkward in the confines of the boat and Beth was uncertain as to who was most out of place, herself or Finn. He had apologized a lot. For the space he took up, for his crossbow, for the tap he turned the wrong way and the glass he nudged. Beside the awkwardness there was something unwashed about him, but less than dirt, something attractive, like the smell of wild garlic and woodsmoke on his hair. She had expected him to come for her in the night and cover her with his smell, like a fox marking its territory, but this was the Wildside, they did things differently, they took their time it seemed. He had sought her out that morning and now they were on the flat roof of the Boswell chugging quietly away from Stratford`s reach. He had asked directly, wrestling with his shyness: Why had she crossed over? Where was she headed? Did she need help? Beth's mistrust was competing with surprise at how direct and open he was. And polite. At first she was irritated by his manner but blamed herself, not him. When he had moved away to secure a trailing rope the smell had gone with him and Beth found herself missing it. She tried not to stare. He was a child of the Wildside, the real thing, bare feet and beautiful hands, veins like cord stood out on his tanned forearms. She felt like an observer at the zoo finding the bars and glass suddenly dissolved, the wild animal no closer than before but the certainty gone, in its place a terror and a thrill. Sam would be jealous, she thought, and then chastised herself. Sam would be delighted, teasing her with a glance.

Finn went from birds to history. It took her by surprise. Moses had said these people were living in the future, ahead of their time, not behind it, but here was a youth not much older than herself relating things back to centuries earlier. He explained without being asked. His eyes were on the distance as he spoke but Beth felt it was not with shyness, he seemed to speak from a vision perched somewhere this side of the wooded shore. `King Alfred ruled from Wessex and kept the Danes out.` he said, `I'm sorry if you know all this. Please stop me if you do.` She almost did. How dare he be so open and so friendly? She wanted to remind him she was from a different world, neither this one nor the other. But she kept silent. She suspected he might be expert in more than just history, that they might all be expert in everything and that soon enough she would be exposed not only as an intruder but as stupid. At the same time she felt a need to take it all in, as much as possible. It might be of use to her one day.

`The line then was not much different to the one we have now.` he continued, `They had a law, you see, slaves escaping from one side to the other would always be returned. Even though they were at war with each other they honoured that law. It was in the best interests of both sides.`

`Slaves?` asked Beth, unsure where this was leading.

`I'm not saying I agree`, he answered. `I'm just telling you how it was. Sorry.` He sensed her annoyance. `You've got red in your hair.` he said. `That's the Danes for you, the Vikings.` He seemed pleased with the discovery, as though it might be important.

`My hair is black.` she protested, `even darker than yours.`

It was also wildly untidy, falling different ways from the knot she had made at the back and being plucked at by the breeze. It was unusual for her to feel aware of her appearance but now she did and it made her uncomfortable.

`Of course it's black. I'm sorry. I'm not saying it's not black. I'm saying it's got some red in it, that's all. The black is the Celt. The red is the Dane. They won't send you back for that. Don't worry.`

She felt a sensation that she remembered from years before and one she associated with appearing stupid. It was the need to blush. She looked away, imagining that her hair, not her skin, had turned red. Half out of annoyance, half out of concern she asked him: how had he known? She had said nothing about herself.

He was a long time in answering, the need to apologize competing with a need to tell. `Erm...the clothes,` he muttered. `They are, well, they are quite different. You get a nose for these things. I'm sorry.`

Beth looked bleakly at what she had escaped in. She had spent the last weeks in the most unassuming and unfashionable clothes ready for the crossing. She had got it wrong it seemed. Of course Finn's clothes were all made of hemp. She imagined him stitching them himself, sewing by a fire with a needle he had made from bone and a thread he had spun from silk worms.

`Is it safe to trust the doctor?` she said, changing the subject.

`It looks like it. He would have turned you over in Stratford if he had wanted to. But you must be very careful. People don't just do it for the money.`

`But because they don't want us.` she added.

Finn looked at her apologetically, as though his world had paid her a grave insult for which he was personally responsible. `I'm sorry.` he said, nodding in agreement, `I suppose you're right. But we do make exceptions. Sometimes.` he smiled, glad to have found redemption. He looked at her softly, not a hint of malice or edge to his expression, any more than to his careful choice of words and quiet tone. He was not patronizing but seemed genuinely pleased with her innocence and her vulnerability. But also concerned. There was not a hint of red in his hair, Beth noticed, hoping they would have something in common. It was black, short and untroubled by the wind.

She had been up since dawn observing the barges come to life, the sky breaking up, the water birds arguing. Her ankle was sore but cleaned by the iodine. She had dreamed matter-of-factly, no significance hidden in absurdities, as though the escape had never happened. She wondered if the drugs she had used to sleep through the coffin trip had completely worn off. She had been tempted to explore the tow path and spy on Stratford before it woke but its reputation got the better of her as did the greater urge which was to preserve this delicate mood.

Finn had fried bacon for the three of them and stewed a huge pot of tea on the boat's tiny range. They had eaten together in silence, unspoken questions waiting for attention. The doctor seemed amused by the awkwardness of his two guests and had left them alone once they left the quay and were headed towards open water.

`Where do you live?` she asked him at last, hoping that the answer would be as complicated as some of hers had been.

It was. There were no disappointments here. Finn's past promised to be as unconventional as his dress sense. `I move around,` he said with a shrug. He told her about his parents, the floods, their lost farm. It was her turn to apologize but he stopped her and gestured to the water and reed around them. `And you can swim,` he said. `I swam from Stratford to Malvern in a day or you can canoe all the way up to Snowdonia or into the Kennet valley. My sister and I sailed across to Ireland one summer without telling our parents.` He stopped himself, awkward again. `I'm sorry,` he said. `You asked where I came from. It's not easy to say.`

Lucky bastard, Beth thought, lucky, lucky bastard. Sam and I used to hide in skips, build dens out of supermarket trolleys in the back of a burned-out garage. Sam and I used to keep our heads down. Lucky bastard.

`Have you seen movies?` he asked after a time.

`Of course.` she was on her guard now, uncertain of his direction. He took several moments before following up.

`I haven't. We can if we want, you know, it's not illegal. Its part of my training, you see. You have to learn to make your own pictures.` another pause. `Disaster movies?`

`Lots of disaster movies.` She was tempted to laugh at him, to get revenge for her clothes being unsuitable, and because he hadn't tried to sleep with her, but there was something touching about the way he asked.

`Which do you like best?`

`I don't. I hate them. I hate all of them.`

He seemed pleased with that and nodded as though to encourage more confessions. When none came he continued. `Melting ice-caps and rising sea-levels, they don't make for good disaster movies.` he said, suddenly the expert. `It's all too slow motion. The real thrills aren't on the coast behind sea-defenses. You don't really have refugees running away from huge waves. Have you seen films like that?`

She nodded.

`The real action is in insurance offices really. Or court rooms, government committee, places like that. It's not very visceral, I'm afraid.`

`Visceral?` Another of his fancy words.

`Blood and guts. Isn't that what people want? That's not how it is. Committees. That's where they make the decisions to abandon or relocate or new-build. My parents could tell you all about it. Insurance premiums and the prices of house and land, that's what does it. No government can play King Canute to market forces. Insurance premiums doubled on my parents every year for ten years. That's what makes people move. We took up fishing, not farming. It's that simple in the end. It's not a big disaster. You can't make movies out of it.`

`They can make movies out of anything,` said Beth, looking at him directly, no longer irritated or even uncomfortable, `absolutely anything. If they don't have a real disaster they'll make one up.`

`Oh yes, they're good at that. They could have stopped it, you know.` Finn said thoughtfully, nodding to the wet acres where his parents might once have grazed their cattle. `Sometimes I'm glad they didn't.`

Beth could see his point. The endless skyscapes, the variable moods, the non-stop concert of colours conducted by the wind, all owed this arena to political neglect and lack of will. And then there were the boats. Big ones for the big people to trade in, little ones for the little people to take their risks in, to cut their teeth, to explore beyond themselves. Beth could imagine Finn sailing in a small skiff to Ireland, the wind and the waves stretching him and his sister as taut as long bows, their parents trusting to their children's command of the elements in an elemental world. And school? Had this strange youth ever been to school? She was itching to ask him but didn't dare. Were they all like him over here or was he, like Beth, an odd one out? Would they all have bare feet and carry crossbows? Were they all shy but keen to talk and with wonderful stories to tell about sailing to distant lands?

`What could be better than boats?` Finn asked suddenly. It startled her. He seemed to have read her thoughts but was talking as much to himself as to her. She had an answer but kept it to herself. She had been thinking of it just seconds before. It involved a hot air balloon she had seen with her father and brother, it concerned a dream she had had ever since. But she did not wish to share it. Instead she imagined how it might be to float above this landscape silently, to cast only a minimal shadow and attract no attention that could reach you and so lovely was the idea that she felt guilty for not appreciating the boat and Finn's water. `I have a lot to learn about your world.` she said, perhaps meaning there was much to learn about herself and could he help her in this?

`It's not one world.` he said, more firmly than he had yet allowed himself. `Its not one world, don't make that mistake, Beth.` He was using her name for the first time, she noticed. `Its several, dozens. A hundred styles of anarchy. You'll see for yourself.`

Anarchy. Beth wasn't sure she wanted it on those terms. It was hard enough adapting to one new reality. Finn saw the distress on her face and for the first time touched her, lightly on the elbow, as though guiding her physically between obstacles. `But that's its beauty,` he said, eager once more, `That's what makes it the only place to be.`

Suddenly she believed him. Suddenly all the variety and unpredictable mess of it filled her with excitement. `Is it dangerous?` she asked, willing the answer.

`If you want it to be.`

`I do want it to be.` and she smiled, for the first time, straight at him, remembering the power and how to use it. She imagined her hair blushing red.

`I thought you would say that.` He looked away, embarrassed at how eager she had made him. `Look. I'll give you some examples.` He stood up and urged her to do the same. Uncertain of the boat and her own sea legs she clung to his arm but with feet widely placed they could stand securely and survey the estuary and the islands around them.

`You've seen Stratford and No-Man's-Land,` he said, dismissing all that lay behind them with a quick gesture. `That's the Wild West. Fire arms, shot guns, horse thieves, bounty hunters, you're well out of that. Way ahead is Malvern, you'll see that this evening. It's just a town. Shops, markets, craftsmen, guilds, honest business and a bit that's less honest. Beyond Malvern is Wales.` He shook his head theatrically as though peopling the place with dragons and demons. `A white-knuckle ride through a thousand years of history.` he said. `That's what they call it. It's not quite true. Sure, one minute you're in the 1950`s, the next it's the Dark Ages, one town lives by the Old Testament, in the neighbouring valley they think they're hobbits. Some think we owe it all to King Alfred. Others pay some kind of emotional tithe to King Arthur. Look at these.` he continued, pointing to two hills which drew towards them one on each side.

`Are they islands?`

He nodded. `Bredon on the right, Dumbleton on the left. You'll see them separate out soon. You heard of Dumbleton?` Of course not. Reality was often stranger than myth and didn't translate as well. `It's linked to the mainland by a causeway from the Cotswolds. Dutch settlers tried to reclaim the valley and the causeway's all that's left of it. Big Dutch community that way,` he pointed south, `And another up river. You can cross the causeway at low tide. There was a priest on the island at St Dunstans who used to give sanctuary to criminals during the civil war. He died about ten years ago but the tradition lives on. They say that if you commit a crime and get across with dry feet then you're free from arrest. You can cut a man's throat in Cheltenham before breakfast and take lunch with an easy mind on Dumbleton.` He might have been joking, but Beth was suddenly struck by the sensation that Finn, for all his mild manner, could cut a man's throat if necessary, that Finn could live in each of his country's styles of anarchy.

`You have to check the tides before you commit your crime.` It was the doctor who spoke, his head above the steering galley, peering past their legs towards the islands.

`So the place is full of criminals?` Beth asked.

`Used to be.` the doctor continued. `It's more like a self-run prison nowadays. Look closely as we go past. You'll see people with their little huts and vegetable plots. Perhaps they're criminals. Perhaps we all are at heart. Perhaps they just want a bit of peace and quiet. Shall we drop her off, Finn? Let her have a look?` They were joking but it reminded Beth that her progress for now at least was in the hands of strangers.

The island passed them slowly by and revealed very little of itself. By the waterline was a compact hut. A man was sifting through a woodpile next to the dwelling. Beth imagined him a brutal murderer even at this distance until he waved at them and she waved back guiltily. His neighbour's hut was even more bizarre. Old car doors and windscreens were welded together and brightly painted, all draped with Russian vine and with goats in its garden only yards from a bank of sand and rocks on which two grey seals were sunning themselves.

They weren't far across the estuary before the little barge began to tilt and struggle, the river current coming from one side and the wind from the other. Finn and Beth joined the doctor in the relative shelter and stability of the steering bay. Other boats, nothing much larger than this one, were making their way across or up or down the river. Some were under sail and might be headed for the mountains or down to Devon. One boat was accompanying a raft of logs, probably to the towns and villages of the Bristol Bay, others were fishing with lines or small nets. Only the wind and the surface of the water were in any hurry. Beth watched the shadows of clouds cut across the wake of the boats and the ripple of the water. Endless shadows, endless lines, each one its own story.

By late afternoon the Boswell was approaching Malvern. The steep little town looked pleased with its collection of boats and barges. For centuries the place had stood smug and distanced from the valley below, looking out across miles of farmland and motorway, dreaming of its coral reef past. Now it had drawn the sea back up to its doorstep and had a right to be aloof. It was the Wildside proper; it was what it had always wanted to be. Its people were promenading and admiring the clear spring air. It wasn't obvious which of Finn's several types of anarchy prevailed here.

It was understood that Beth would sleep one more night in the little surgery. She felt no inclination to explore the steep town and felt an awful weariness flood over her at the prospect of leaving the Boswell and exposing herself to decisions and choices. The prospect of danger was suddenly much less attractive. Perhaps a delayed shock from her escape, the drugs, her ankle, a combination of these was to blame for her sudden apathy. She had given Finn the look, sent him signals that no one could mistake. Tonight, of course, powerless, he would come for her, desperate to touch and be touched and she would arrive fully. Just as Timbo had been right for No-Man's-Land, no man as it turned out, then so Finn, bare-footed, wild-eyed Finn would be right for her Wildside initiation. She hoped there would still be enough light for her to see his forearms and the veins when he covered her and she was surprised to find herself excited at the thought, almost breathless. Amazingly Finn took his farewells. He seemed eager to be gone. She was suddenly very jealous of him and uncertain of herself. He was at home. He fitted into this place of strangeness, whilst she never would. Take me with you, she wanted to say, I am like you, I am one of you. We can travel together, you can make me smell of wild garlic, wear hemp, throw away my shoes. `Don't get cold feet,` she called after him as he disappeared into the evening, for which she felt stupid and fell asleep scripting what she should have said and how he might have replied in a perfect world.

EIGHTEEN

No demons yet, though the day was young. They came mostly in the night or late afternoon, sensitive to blood sugar levels and the possibility of long shadows. For now there was sharp light and the optimistic tang of coffee.

`A map please, Watson`

`Of what, Sir?`

Why was he always so polite to the machine? Was he so conditioned to correct behaviour that he could not bear to be direct? After two decades of great authority, he reminded himself, should he not have been free of deference? At least he could get revenge by pointing out its stupidity. `Central Britain of course. Rather slow this morning aren't we, Watson?`

`I am a crow following the plough, Sir. I was unsure which furrow we were turning.`

Sir David nodded in quiet defeat. The programmers had scored another point. He watched as Watson's screen became an outline map of what had once been the United Kingdom. The computer had already assumed to distinguish between Comfort Zone and Wildside. For political reasons the one was always tinted light pink and the other grey. Sir David smiled at the choice of pink, for what was left of a once world-smothering pastel. It was as though the loins of the old British Empire had withered to such an extent that they could no longer fill their own hose. Of course the map of these islands had changed countless times over the centuries but never more radically than in the last fifty years. No Dane, Roman or bastard Norman had achieved such total transformation. Rising sea levels were not even the most dramatic factor in those changes; symptoms, yes, cause, certainly not. A shame really. Treating symptoms was so much more lucrative than getting to the bottom of things. Sir David blamed the cult of the brand-leader, economic Darwinism's delight in crushing all opposition. But until the cult was exposed here as it had been on the Wildside scapegoats would be needed and in considerable quantity. Offer them up one by one, he thought, the public never tired of distraction politics. He studied the details. The main Comfort Zone conurbation extended north from Birmingham to engulf Derby, Chesterfield, Sheffield, Bradford and Leeds with Nottingham and Leicester on the eastern edge. Southeast from Birmingham through Coventy, Banbury, Oxford and Reading took the massive city to the Chilterns north of Reading where, together with the North Downs of Kent, London had been relocated. Kent was the only Comfort Zone county not to have been built solid but even it contrasted starkly with the wooded quiet of Sussex, the Wildside's most easterly arm. The Comfort Zone had a single tunnel connection beneath the Pennines to its Lancashire mass, a huge smoke-filled basin packed with people and their structures and hemmed in on three sides by high ground and on the fourth by marshes claimed by the Irish Sea. A land corridor from Leeds through York to the single city that had long-since engulfed Middlesbrough, Stockton, Durham, Sunderland and Newcastle completed the picture. The split was roughly east west, as it had always been, the myth of the north-south divide long since laid to rest. Scotland, as usual, had made its own peculiar arrangements but to all intents and purposes John Savage or Nathaniel Clegg or whoever else could travel by horse from Land's End in Cornwall, through the young forests of Dartmoor, across the reed and willow marshes of Somerset, the green patchwork quilt landscape of the Cotswolds, Shropshire, the Cheshire Plain, Wales, the Peak District, Pennines, Lake District, Cheviots and Southern Uplands without once alerting a sensor or crossing a motorized road, without once meeting a fast food outlet or tasting the bad breath of spent carbon. From the coast of Ayrshire a ferry would bypass the Glasgow-Edinburgh conglomerate and lead to the endless possibilities of the Scottish Highlands and Islands. As far as Sir David could understand there was no police-force in any of these places or any laws for them to enforce, beyond the magical constitution, and certainly no central government in the usual sense.

In terms of square miles it was by no means a large area, but in policing and control terms it was vast, as impenetrable as the Canadian or Australian out-back. Where to begin? Searching the Wildside, a wise man once said, was like searching your own childhood memories for the smells and tastes of half-formed impressions. No matter how you went about it you always ended up haunted and lost. There were of course `hot` areas in the various stretches of No-Man's-Land, places where illicit surveillance was carried out in secret conjunction with Wildside interests to control the activities of drug smugglers or absconders. Stratford on the Severn estuary, Blenheim Palace north of Oxford where official exchanges were made, York, where traffic through the land-corridor was controlled and to where the boat communities serving the Yorkshire and Lincolnshire Wolds turned for trade. Beth Savage had crossed over to join her father. Clegg, presumably an accomplice in the escape, had followed shortly afterwards. Where could Sir David begin his search?

`Show me the range of a micro-light aircraft, centred on the place from which Clegg took off.` he asked, pawn to king four, the obvious opening. The circle appeared almost instantly. It didn't take Clegg very far, nor did it take Sir David long to score one over Watson. `The circle assumes return flights. Double it please, we are looking at a one-way journey.` The range grew accordingly. Fifty miles. Across the estuary into Wales, down towards the Cotswolds, up as far as the White Peak.

`The escape routes we know of, sketch them in.`

A dozen spidery lines appeared on the map in a dozen different directions. They would reveal nothing. There were probably twice as many such routes that were currently unknown to the security forces but in this case and given John Savage's ability to manipulate the System he had almost certainly created one of his own.

`Show me Clegg`s previous crossings.`

The boat journeys to the badger island appeared on screen, Danny's expensively arranged blind spot easily exposed. They all started south of Birmingham, close to Clegg`s home and proceeded south west into the marshes and net-work of islands in No-Man`s-Land where he and Jacobs had plied their trade.

`Satellite pictures of possible crashed microlights.`

`There are none, Sir.`

`Which is odd, surely?`

`Which suggests he did not crash, Sir.`

`Or he downed in water.`

`A sensible possibility, Sir.`

Sir David turned slowly from the monitor to gaze at the wall. No shadows formed, no demons lurked in the corners of the room. Instead the cold and heavy wash of memory threatened to take his breath. The memory of friendship turned sour, of a beautiful woman caught between two admiring men, of late-night, dawn-early arguments about the brave new world and the shape of things to come. And somewhere, programmed out, a secret memory there was no one living left to share with. Which is a kind of demon. Let no one tell you otherwise, he thought. Let no one tell you otherwise. He turned back to the machine, ready to touch the edges of truth. `When the girl disappeared, Watson.`

`Yes, Sir?`

`I was apparently with her.`

`Apparently, Sir.`

`Who else was there?`

`Who else was where, Sir?`

`Follow the plough, Watson, don't pretend to be stupid. Who else was present when I threw young Beth into the river?`

A nanosecond. `It depends on what you mean by 'present', Sir.`

He could imagine them cringing inside the computer, pale-faced programmers caught in some indecent act. `Within one hundred meters.`

`The girl's aunt, Katherine Savage, walked with the girl almost until the weir and then went home.`

`Who else?`

`Nobody pertinent to the inquiry, Sir.`

Which left the possibility of those impertinent to the inquiry. `How did Clegg get to the weir?`

`We have no reason to believe he did, Sir.`

`We have every reason to believe he did. Clegg was John Savage's accomplice. It was almost certainly Clegg who was wearing my false tag. Let me put it another way, Watson. How did *I* get to the weir?`

`By car, Sir.`

`Thankyou. From?`

`The south of Birmingham`

`Close to Clegg`s home address?`

`Half a kilometer away.`

`Thankyou. Did I drive myself?`

`No, Sir.`

`Then I was driven.`

`Sir?`

`Elementary, my dear Watson. If I went by car and did not drive then I must have been...`

`Driven, Sir.`

`By?`

`A fictional accomplice, Sir.`

`How fictional?`

`Deceased. It is not a relevant line of inquiry, Sir.`

Deceased. What a massive word. It filled the room as no other could have done, it dispelled the light and hint of coffee in a second and conjured shadows where none had been thinkable. Uninvited but not unwelcome, four images of Emma Savage distilled from the past, one for each corner of the room. The first was tall, slim, classically elegant in a summer dress now twenty years out of fashion. The second was intense and argumentative, pointing at maps and diagrams, quoting politics and Greek philosphy, toting a pen and reading glasses. The third beckoned, questioned, gestured with arms and silent words but seemed in some way lost, as though denied an audience. The fourth he could not look at, not even its shadow. The fourth he ignored for now. `The name of the irrelevant deceased, please, Watson.` Of course he knew. He wanted to hear that name from somewhere other than his own memory. Emma Savage. She did exist because Watson says so. Emma, darling Emma, he thought, what have we done? What in God's name have we done?

`Emma Savage, Sir. John Savage's former wife. We have to assume abused data.`

Abused, thought Sir David, the smile frozen. `Much abused..,` he murmured, half to himself. `Much abused. Dead, buried and still so fondly missed.` He raised his voice suddenly, speaking to the corners of the room, to the view, to the expensive air, as though by rote, as though quoting catechism. `John makes a fool of me and I make a fool of Watson. In the fictional scheme of things I and the long dead Emma have thrown Beth into the river. In the real world John has used two drones to stage the disappearance and send us a rather complex message. Abused, certainly, dear Watson, but also very, very clever. And perhaps,` though the doubt in his voice was clear to sense and quite genuine, `Perhaps even a little... cruel.` Her dark eyes watched him, her frown deepened, black hair with its touch of bronze caught the light. All gone now and the dreams with her.

`Avalon.` Sir David said, coming up for air. `What have we got in Avalon?` Another of their secret codes. Another way of dressing ugly truths. He had chosen the name out of deference to the way he and John Savage had reinvented the new landscape decades earlier. New Bristol was Arcadia, Stratford was Camelot, Avalon was Malvern.

Watson listed the surveillance possibilities in and around the Malvern area. Their choices, though limited, were perfectly apt.

The solution, as so often happened, was not only right under Sir David's nose but was also the most absurdly playful he could have wished for. A long shot, risky, and therefore ideal.

`Inform John Savage that I accept his invitation.`

`Sir, we have no access to John Savage.`

`No access, dear Watson? No access? To a man who knows how much is in my bank account, who knows my blood pressure, my sugar count, my dental records? Put the message out there, Watson, anywhere, anyhow, any shape, any size. He'll get it. He always has done and he always will. Unless…`

`Unless, Sir?`

But no answer was forthcoming. Sir David was staring into the fourth corner. It was not Emma Savage who stared back but Sam, unblinking, half dead and utterly hypnotic.

NINETEEN

The pimps were out in force today, engine oil deep in every pore, a knowing nod or wink to regular clients, the discreet exchange of stained money licked from fat wads and stuffed deep into pockets. Clegg loved it. Clegg could not believe it. Clegg was in his element. His shades were in place, the swagger and boots were at last appropriate, only the cowboy hat was missing. Why not? He had seen them, nobody would sneer. Perhaps another time. When he had defeated them all. In the meantime he would cruise the red-light district, dip his appetite in rancid grease. All around him was something raw, magnetic, irresistible, all around him was a whispered appeal to the lower nature kept captive in the loins. Illegal, yes, but impossible to legislate against, even here. In the matter of engine emissions the Wildside was the world's devout nun, she had taken a lucrative vow of chastity, she had transformed desire into higher deeds. She had sold her rights to emit all known pollutants thirty years ago when such things were up for auction and the world was in a panic of self-doubt and climatic fevers. Of course licenses still allowed for exceptions of the medical and agricultural variety, but over-head satellites, like fussing chaperones, ensured that the vow was not broken. But chaste is one thing, and frigid another, and frigid the Wildside most certainly was not. Desire brooded in her virtuous loins, ached hot through the long nights of summer and found secret pleasures in the folded quiet of her night. Here, to prove it, was whore-mongering, pure and simple. Diesel engines dripped oil, motor bikes pouted curves, out-board motors flaunted their thrust, whilst winches, hydraulic gear, pumps, chain-saws, quad bikes, all seductively greased, all lovingly primed, all temptingly offered a variety of subversion. Whatever turned you on, thought Clegg. The pimps were no less protective than dealers in female flesh and had their own complex codes and jargon to protect themselves and their loved ones. They eyed Clegg suspiciously, ready to close ranks or winkle out his money, certain they could place his type. They prided themselves on being able to meet any fetish or machine-tooled deviance, to provide any service, no matter how filthy.

Whilst most of the gear around him was smuggled and shamelessly it was the stolen goods that interested Clegg. It was the only way he knew how to pick up the trail to the crossbow warrior. The stolen outboard. He might yet be glad of its theft. What else did he have? A few basics of equipment to put him a step or two ahead of the opposition: a compass, a small telescope, first aid, fire lighters, a knife. And maps, which like signposts, were illegal on the Wildside. Of course they circulated clandestinely and supplied a black market of their own but they were neither easily nor safely come by. The pouch of 2009 maps upgraded from satellite photographs that pressed between his skin and vest had cost hard currency. It was good to know they were there, to fool himself that this strange new world was as mapped and as measured as the one he had left behind.

The accents were Birmingham, as oil-stained as the machines and tools that were on sale yet spoken by men who had surely never been to the great city itself. The accent was in the objects they sold and the accent would live on in this part of the Wildside for as long as people wanted their boats and bikes and tractors to move them around. Even amongst emission paranoia there would always be carbon perverts like Clegg willing to pay the price and take the risk. His own scrambler was hidden deep in brambles some miles from town and he wondered how many of these honest citizens had similar smutty secrets hidden away in the unmapped interior.

The market was not all machines. Clegg watched carefully as an optician dipped through boxes of ground lenses to match the needs of a short-sighted knife grinder, as a barber removed hair with shears better suited to sheep whilst running a side-line in clockwork radios. His neighbour sold alternators and mini-turbines for use with domestic wind or water mills. All new this, beautifully made and expensive, in the hundreds compared to the pennies needed for a hair cut or to buy battered trout, pickled mushrooms, or a slice of the boar turning on its spit above glowing coals. Clegg fought off the revulsion. After an attempt at Wildside food he had spent hours squatted in bracken, his insides unused to such an assault of intestinal flora and bacteria. He craved white starch and pesticides but knew he would have to adapt. All the transactions he watched were cash. Pennies, pounds and florins, real coins, of real metal, much of it gold, not a card in sight and Clegg`s mouth watering at the opportunities this might bring.

His search, which he half expected to be hopeless, was successful beyond his dreams. Amongst the stalls catering for those who took their perverse and illegal pleasure on the water were a number of outboard motors and his own amongst them. Behind the stall, glaring at Clegg, stood a well-fed man of middle years, Caribbean-black skin exposing ivory teeth and eyes set above a ruptured mango of a nose. `Where did you get this from?` Clegg asked, pointing to the outboard. They were the first words he had spoken on this side of the Line. He half expected accent or language to betray him and for all eyes to turn in his direction. What a stupid question, he thought of himself, what a stupid way to begin his search. But what was the alternative? Here was his one and only lead. He took a fifty-pound note from his pocket and used it to point at the engine. He had got the money from Jacobs. Notes and coins enough to last a few days. The gold stitched in the lining of his jacket was from years ago. `Its like one I've got.` he said, `I might need a part for it.`

`Most people ask the price,` the man answered, looking past Clegg at people he thought more likely to buy.

`Most people don't have my problem,` Clegg replied, chewing hard on a piece of imaginary gum to deflect his concerns.

`Most people don't bring their problems to Machine Head,` the man said, `unless they're mechanical.` Machine Head. He spoke these words with a flourish, as though Clegg should understand this was no ordinary man he was speaking to but a man with a title as much as a name.

`Isn't everything.?`

`You a fuckin' philosopher or what?` the man growled, accusing Clegg with his mango. `If its philosophy you want you've come to the right man, but it costs does philosophy, like everything else on this stall. It all costs, see, in the end. Deals can be done, mind, I'm not saying deals can't be done. Know what I mean?`

`The mechanics of paying someone back,` said Clegg. `I owe someone. Whoever sold you this engine. That's who I owe.` It was true, he did.

The man shook his head, looked away, seemed to lose interest in Clegg but then pulled a surprise. `You got a strong left?` he asked.

Clegg told himself to keep steady, one step back, two forwards. `Might have. Who's asking?`

`The man with the spare parts. And the philosophy.`

`I've got cash.` Clegg reminded him.

`Of limited value, don't you find? Too much money chasing too little fun. You in a ring?` Machine Head could tell by Clegg's blank expression that he was not. `Alright, I'll give you a break. I run a book, right. Always looking for fresh blood.`

`Count me in,` said Clegg, not understanding but choosing to fly blind.

`Don't want punters,` he said, `Got plenty of punters. Fresh jockey is what I likes best. Man like you, passing through, unattached, looks fit, asks questions, might be just the ticket.`

`Ticket?`

The man laughed, Birmingham forgotten, West Indian rhythms let loose. `You help me, I help you. Ain't that how the world works? Don't worry, it's even legal, slightly. Arm wrestling, right? You've arm wrestled? Sure you have. Don't even have to win. I make my money on the book. Give it a bout and who knows what philosophy might be on offer.`

Arm wrestling sounded harmless enough, in the Queen's Head, two hours hence. `No holds barred.` Machine Head added slowly, almost as an after thought. `None-what-so-ever.`

There were times, and this was certainly one of them, when Clegg regretted his dislike of alcohol. The Queen's Arms by late afternoon was a fug of smoke and dazed consciousness in which no sober man could comfortably thrive. But he was not here to thrive, he told himself, he was to here to pick up a lead, to start out on his road to fame and fortune. The smoke and hollow laughter he would have to tolerate, likewise the sideways looks and muttered glances. It put him in mind of a saloon in a wild-west film. The floor was of bare boards, badly scuffed, with damp saw dust in the doorway to receive the street. A real piano played by a real person jangled away in one corner, the knock and clatter of skittles drifted in from a back yard and a horse stood in the doorway, restless for its owner as a dog might have been. Lengths of beer called pints shone like old leather through dull glass and somewhere the smell of chipped potatoes and curry hinted of left-over food. There was a conflicting mood, one of comfort and indecision but also something of expectation. It made Clegg alert but not uncomfortable. He was ready to enjoy something though he had no idea what.

Machine Head came at him from the shadows, teeth and eye-whites shocking in the gloom. The nose seemed polished for the occasion and flared in Clegg's direction. `You're on next.` he said, half smiling, `You're right handed? Then use your left, right? No other rules.`

`And the philosophy?`

`Sure, I'll give it now. I trust you, right? I'll give you the philosophy then you stay for your bout.` He placed a fleshy hand on Clegg's shoulder. The breath, when it came close, was tainted with ginger and cloves, not beer or grease. `How's that for business? Otherwise bad things creep out of the woodwork. You savvy? OK. A nice lad sold it to me, right? A very nice lad, as it happens.

Wouldn't want any `arm coming to `im, see, might hold a certain party responsible if there was `arm involved.`

`No harm. I promise. Regular supplier is he?`

`Regular? Nothing regular about this lad. Don't work for non-one, him, not a waster, mind, always busy.` A pause. `His name's Finn, salt of the earth, awkward bugger since you ask. And shy with it. Very shy. That lot usually are.`

He wasn't shy with the crossbow, thought Clegg, he wasn't shy with Jacobs' dogs. And what did the man mean by `that lot`? One was enough to worry about. The thought of an army of crossbow touting freaks was unnerving, even if they were shy. Clegg heard a roar come from a booth on the far side of the pub. The first bout had started. `Where does he live?`

`Won't find him round `ere, that is for sure. Don't approve of all this, immoral, you see. Mucky business. Bit beneath him, see. His choice. Live and let live, right? Of course right. Up a tree the last I `eard. Which tree? There's plenty to choose from. Look, I'll give you a break. This lad Finn moves around, OK. Can't pin `im down and that's a fact, way of the world, see, and good luck to `em, we've all been young. Always travellin` that lot, not a care in the world half of them. No one was more surprised than me when he turns up with this thing, I can tell you. Not his scene, see. Horses, that's more his style. Horses, not engines.` Machine Head turned to the youth behind the bar, `When's the next horse market, kid, Friday?` The barman confirmed with a nod. `Horse market, mister. Next Friday. Never misses. But don't you miss it, mind, when spring comes that sort buys a horse and just buggers off for the summer. Can't blame them really.` He paused, looked Clegg up and down, his expression somewhere between smile and frown. `Perhaps you should do the same?` he said, `You know, bugger off!`

Clegg was surprised that the man had parted so easily with the information and wondered if everything would be so child-like and easy in this new world. `We had a deal.` he mouthed, saying what was expected of him but not yet believing it. `You've kept your side, I'll keep mine.`

`I wouldn't like anyone to get hurt.` Machine Head's expression was suddenly soft, protective, making Clegg uneasy.

`Arm-wrestling?` he asked, amazed, but a roar from the booth distracted them both. The next moment the crowd parted as a man was dragged out, his face covered by a towel from which blood dripped. Machine Head looked at Clegg again, waiting for the penny to drop. No holds barred. This was the Wildside. It was not all daffodils and grazing cattle.

Clegg found himself seated at the gaming table, not certain how his feet had carried him there. A score or so of eager faces peered through the smoke at himself and at the man introduced as Mad John. Clegg was aware of money changing hands, of odds being chalked on a board. Arm wrestling. Why not? They did it in the army to kill time. Where was the catch? Fresh saw dust was spread at their feet and on the table. They gripped hands, left to left, the crowd cheered. There was no going back. He should have taken Machine Head's philosophy and advice, he should have buggared off long since. This one was for Jo, he thought. Don't tell your mum. No holds barred. Suspicion began to grow. Welcome to the Wildside, Clegg.

Their strength was well matched. Or else Mad John was holding back. Clegg certainly wasn't. He strained to keep his forearm upright but would not know how much he had in reserve until his opponent turned it on. The spectators hushed to a mutter, all eyes on the right hands of the two men, not on their clenched left. Mad John hit first. It was a sharp blow to the side of Clegg's face, easily beaten off. It was not a serious threat, it was aimed more at the audience response, but with the blow from the right came a slight increase from the left, a testing to which Clegg was equal. It was confirmation. No holds barred meant wrestle with your left, beat the shit out of each other with the right. Mad John leapt up, Clegg followed, one sat, then both. Their shared clench was a clear barrier between poised right fist and unprotected face. A kick on the shin. The table shook, the crowd approved, some pointed at the expression of pain on Clegg's face, another sharp blow followed, easily parried, a second kick, an increase in tempo. Clegg looked the man in the eye, sensed rather than saw a shift of position, parried a blow, put in one of his own, stung his knuckles uselessly against the man's ear, cursed. A ripple ran through the crowd. His name was muttered, shouted, `Take him John` rang out, horribly matter-of-fact, Clegg tasted blood from somewhere, licked it away quickly. His left began to drop. The money was on the left hand. At the end of the day whatever the right might do it was the left that earned the pay-out and attention was fixed as Clegg's left, inch by inch, was forced towards the surface. Lose and walk, he told himself, lose and walk, just like every other fucking time. Malvern market on Friday. That's why you're here, Cleggy, a boy and his horse, John Savage, the girl, a fortune. Lose and walk. Mad John gritted his few teeth, shifted his left shoulder up, sensed victory, milked the crowd and then looked dumb, startled, disbelieving as Clegg's right, economical as a hawk, shot against his jaw, once for Jenny, twice for Jo, the third time for Bonny, impacting the very centimeter that would crumple the cerebral lining and bring glorious oblivion. Slowly and precisely Clegg moved his opponent's slumped head to one side in order for his left to finish the formalities.

Be scared, he told Jenny, be very scared, because Clegg has come, and Clegg is invincible.

As ever, Nat,

This time I proved it, Jen. This time I took them apart, one by one. First the escape, then the scrambler, now the Queen's Arms, all-comers, no holds barred, six of them.

You must be very proud. What's next, Nat? Walk on water? Fishes and loaves?

Near dusk he celebrated. If Jenny showed no respect he could always turn the throttle. He found a green lane cut into the hillside, gravel and shale between dry stone walls. After a few miles of uncomfortable bouncing a downhill stretch of smooth road lured him on, his illegal roar wide across the dank valley. No horses. No tractors. No chains. Farms drew in on themselves as he passed, they flinched and trembled, hoping he would leave them untouched. Dumb cattle stampeded in the half-light, swarms of rabbits bolted into the earth. Clegg had the whole world to play with. To his delight the planet of Venus presented herself above hills to the west and directly in line with the road. He knew Venus when he saw her, just as he knew every constellation and planet. She would be his star. They had chosen each other. He roared down the track, shedding years of control and restraint and perhaps he let loose an elemental scream of delight or perhaps he was just about to as the rope pulled taut across the track, catching the front arch of the scrambling bike full on before sending Clegg, no holds barred, pirouetting through the air.

All over and done and the engine dead, one wheel still spinning but otherwise silent and not even a groan from Clegg the Invincible, as Venus winked, like a mother's eye, tearful above grim hills.

A man emerged from the side of the track. He went first to the scrambler, checking it for damage and next gathered up the rope, deftly fashioned a noose, hooked it over a branch which overhung the track and then and only then attended to the unconscious heap of Nathaniel Clegg.

TWENTY

Dear Sam,

His name is Finn. Like on a shark. Lean, cuts through the water and threatens a lot more. I don't know what to do about him. Like I didn't know what to do about Moses and Timbo. All three could see straight through me. And the doctor. They all know. It's like I've got no skin and they look straight into my insides and see how things work. You would know who to trust and how to hide from them, you would know straight away, but that's no use to me now. So how does he fit in? If at all. Am I going to meet people like him every day and are they all going to look at me as though I'm naked and stupid? Or is Finn special? I couldn't handle too many like him. Though he is nice, don't get me wrong, he is nice and he fits the world perfectly. He fits the world perfectly, Sam, can you imagine that? The bastard! I'm not supposed to trust anyone but I would swear, I would absolutely swear that he is in the picture somewhere, something to do with Dad and the letter. He's very shy in case you don't know, and awkward in one way, but very confident in another. He sometimes looks like a red Indian. His hair is short but very black, his eyes are a bit too big for his face and he has a hooked nose, like a pirate. His clothes grew on a tree. Really. Hemp and bark and natural things felted together. And he has a kind of smell, not dirty or unwashed, not animal. Halfway to somewhere else. Somewhere I've always wanted to go but didn't dare. He never seems distracted, always very concentrated and always too polite. And of course, you remember years ago when we saw those children across the motorway? The balloon? Of course you remember. Hold on to it Sam. Don't let go. He has bare feet. We tried it at home for a while but it was illegal, a health risk, an insurance problem or something. Well he has bare feet. Very fine feet with high arches and long toes and, I would imagine, because I haven't looked or asked, of course, incredibly tough souls. Well, they would have to be, wouldn't they? He could walk on glass with them, on fire. Infact *he has. Walked on fire. They do it at school, but when I asked about it he didn't seem to understand my question or why I should find it interesting. He was very beautiful in a way. I don't know if I would have written that if I knew you were definitely going to read this letter, and now I feel ashamed, as though I've let you down, because you are going to read it, every word of it, even me saying he was beautiful. Not like that, not in a film star way, he's too rough for that, but in a way that makes bare feet look beautiful. No, I didn't think you would understand. He needs a good sorting out is what Aunt Kath would say, which would make him presentable but he has probably never been `presented` anywhere or anyhow. Good luck to him, I say. So I asked the doctor about Finn, after he had gone. What did Finn do, that kind of thing. That was the first mistake. They don't `do` over here, they `are`. School is for finding your vocation, for finding whatever turns you on. They don't have jobs or careers, just a vocation or a calling. How do they find out, I asked? They try the lot, he said. No, it's not maths, or French or chemistry or whatever; its stone, wood, water, fire, words, lots of vague, bare-footed sort of things. Sweaty and feral, you've got the picture. I don't understand it but I know you probably would so there it is. More on this later. Perhaps. It turns out Finn is on a Quest. Part of school. He has a task to perform. Some kind of rite of passage. When I hear this I think of the shark's fin going about its business and wonder if he has teeth, if he's dangerous. Polite, shy and dangerous? They all do it apparently, a Quest, and you're not supposed to pry into the details but you are supposed to offer help, which the doctor did. It took me a time to realize that he assumed I was on a Quest, capital `Q` because it's kind of official, like exams. I told him I wasn't but he looked doubtful which made me doubtful. Because I am, on a Quest that is. That's exactly what it is. Funny thing is that the doctor realized it before I did.*

Next its horses, Sam. We knew it would be, but it has to be seen to be believed. Like an old cowboy film only better because have you noticed that in those films its only men who get to ride, never women and children? I swear I saw a girl of four riding to the market on a pony. Children, old people, everyone, on anything from little ponies to huge monsters. Thousands of the things, big, little, ugly, beautiful. Kids cruising, comparing, trading horse gossip. The doctor said they don't have social workers on the Wildside. Just horses. Sounds all right, don't you think? Yes, I know. It sounds like being on another planet. No, not everyone is barefooted. They wear shoes and boots, leather riding boots most of them, or cowboy boots. They argue and help and hinder just like at home. But I have to remind myself again and again, nobody is tagged. There are no sensors strapped to bollards, lamp-posts and traffic signs, there just isn't that same mood of everyone behaving because of invisible police men being strapped to their legs. There are no people talking into hand or head-sets, there are no TV screens with adverts on the street corners and in all the shop windows, but still there is a mood of anything and everything being possible. And people look you in the eye. Nobody is afraid of being seen. Just imagine that! Anyway, the doctor took me to the market. Sure enough, there was the treadmill, just like in the books, except that children weren't chained to it and no one was whipping the horses. It was a social thing, you got on it and pedaled if you wanted, you hooked your horse to it, again, only if you wanted. It was like a fairground ride but free and without the noise. It never stopped. That was a matter of local pride, I think. People got off when they found someone to take their place. I suppose the batteries were in the middle, certainly the wires ran from there to the different shops and stalls that needed power. We bought bags of grain and dried pulses from the back of an oxcart and curry powder from the little Indian whose elephant, yes, you heard it right, whose elephant was behind the stall chewing through a heap of cabbage leaves. We also got dried fruit, which the doctor later to gave me as a gift, a bottle of Welsh whiskey for medicinal purposes, and huge flat loaves of bread, still warm from the oven. We browsed through fabulous bolts of cloth which a Sudanese woman modeled beautifully on herself and her child, we sniffed and chewed at the dried cannabis leaf and the blocks of hashish resin and wads of qat. We got pickled herring from a Dutchman, there are lots of Dutch people on the market and running businesses. Nobody is stoned. Its not like they say. There aren't any hippies, not like in the books and the propaganda films. The doctor says life is too difficult for them, too much hard work. And at every stall there was lots of chat and gossip and the doctor told everyone that he would be holding surgery tomorrow, but mostly he was careful not to introduce me, even though people nodded and looked in my direction and wanted to know who I was. And last of all, the noise. Pigs, chickens, a donkey, a cage of jackdaws, lots of musicians playing the market's edge. And they all had wonderful instruments: violin, harp, drums and bagpipes, I'm sure it was all hand made and would probably be worth a fortune back home even though no one would know how to play them. But I shouldn't think like that, about the worth of things, the old man warned me. Oh yes, and I bought new clothes. But that's another story.

Your re-designed sister,

Beth.

In the midst of the market's bustle a girl touched Beth on the elbow. `Don't jump,` she said, belatedly. `I'm Anna. I'm a friend of the doctor's.` She pointed to Johnson who beamed a welcome and was immediately hugged for his troubles. The girl was Finn's sister. She was probably younger than Beth but had the confidence and front of a well-positioned adult. She was slight, almost transparent, with very pale skin and a habit of bending her head down and lifting her eyes up, as much to compensate for shortsightedness as to look cute. Like a fairy in *Midsummer Night's Dream*, was how Beth placed her. Her mouse-like hair was tied up in half a dozen little knots each with its own ribbon.

`What have you got for me?` she asked the doctor, eyeing Beth theatrically. `Finn warned me. Said there was work to be done. Don't worry.`

Beth wasn't sure she liked the idea of being worked on by Anna. The girl was as eager as her brother had been shy. Her self-confidence was dismaying, but Beth sensed she was not going to be given a choice in the matter. To make matters worse Doctor Johnson, having greeted Anna, now began to make his farewells of them both, leaving Beth with the uneasy feeling that he and Finn had arranged this earlier.

`Clothes.` Anna said, when the doctor had gone, gesturing Beth to a quieter corner of the market where racks of second-hand clothing blocked the street. `My brother said he hopes you didn't think he was being rude on the boat when he mentioned your clothes, he wanted me to send his apologies but I'm not sure I need to. Do I? ` She didn't wait for an answer. `He's always apologizing, you see. And he's always trying to help. Never thinks about himself, that's the trouble half the time. Did you like him? People say he's good looking. I wouldn't know, him being my brother. Never mind. Anyway, he asked me to look out for you. Said a girl would know better what to get.`

I will be friendly, Beth told herself, feeling dislike towards the girl, I have to. It was a means to an end. But her brother could have done the job just as well. Why had Finn not come if he was so concerned for Beth?

Anna's own clothes were typical for the time and place. She wore a bright red linen shirt to half way down her thighs. Beneath it were tights of wool, or hose as they were called, and above the lot a doublet of brightly coloured felt with dozens of pockets, each with a trinket or ornament. Totems, Anna called them, a mobile and hand-held diary of places, people and events you could add to at any time or exchange with whoever you met or give as gifts, suddenly and in response to the moment. Beth's clothes were too garish by local standards and nobody of her age wore jeans or had done for the last ten years. She might set a new fashion, Anna joked, by reviving the old. Anna then stood back and looked not at Beth's clothing but at her face and the shape of her ear.

`What's your tree?` she asked.

`My what?`

`Your tree type. It effects the clothes we choose.`

Tree type. Memories struggled to the surface along with the instinct to bluff. `Can't you guess?` Beth asked.

`I don't know you well enough, but Finn thought you were hawthorn.`

Then Finn can go to hell, Beth thought, because he doesn't know me either but still guesses right. Finn can go to hell and we don't like his sister. But then who do we like? Who can be allowed to help?

`Tough, attractive and a bit spiky` said Anna, laughing at Beth's pained expression. `Don't worry about it. What do you think he is?`

`Willow.` said Beth without a second's hesitation. `Lean and tender. Splits easily.` Two could play at this game she discovered. `Likes to be near water.`

Anna was impressed, but not as much as Beth was, wondering where her own words had come from. `I'm alder. Easily over-looked but difficult to get away from. Come on, hawthorn it is.`

They began to search the racks. The quality of tailoring was high and the range of colours breath-taking, almost African. It was not long before they had found several pairs of hose, two shirts, a beautiful doublet of green and purple patchwork and a leather saddlebag to carry the spares. Beth parted eagerly with what little money she had, in a way glad to be rid of it as it was suspect, stowed at home for years and for all she knew no longer valid, but the coins and crumpled notes attracted no undue attention. Beth's first experience of a cash transaction was completed. Anna advised her to destroy the old clothes. `Make a fire,` she told her, `make a ritual of it, you know the kind of thing.` No she didn't, she had not the slightest idea what Anna meant but couldn't say so. She covered herself with a newly acquired coat of waxed felt. And then the words she had been dreading. `So what now, Beth, where are you headed?`

Fuck off, she wanted to say, its got nothing to do with you, I don't need you or your brother. You're not in the plan. You're too confident. Its me, Sam, a letter and to hell with the rest of the world. But she also wanted Anna's comfort and help, desperately, or at least the connection to Finn. `I've got friends,` she lied, `outside of town. They're expecting me.` It came too quickly and too anxiously to have any chance of sounding genuine. She flushed and looked away, pretending to be distracted by a foal trotting proudly behind its mother.

Sensing how awkward she felt Anna was quick to offer relief. `Visit us if you have time,` she said, `At Knightwick Marshes. My school is there.` But she quickly gave her a second option. `Or Friday,` she said, `Finn will be here for the horse market. He knows his horses, does Finn. Might we see you then?`

Next Friday. Four days away. A lifetime. `You might.` Beth muttered, managing a smile. `I mean, I could be.`

Anna nodded, trying hard to read Beth's discomfort. `You'll need a horse.` she said, as though it was the most usual thing in the world. `We'll see you here on Friday. I have work to do at home.`

Home. Another coldly exclusive word if you were on the wrong side of the wrong line.

`Home's at school as well,` she explained, still looking to Beth for some more positive response, `Knightwick Marshes. Twenty miles north of here. It's not far.` With that she was gone, a Shakespearean cobweb vanished into the wings. Friday, like an island in a sea of uncertain currents, seemed very far away.

Make a ritual of it, she had said. But ritual is only possible when you are fed and warm. Beth had walked out of Malvern that afternoon as the market was drifting away. The track she followed varied from ridge to valley but had been deliberately landscaped to give shade, windbreak and views in alternation. Whilst the woods had something wild to them there was an extraordinary human touch which challenged her state of mind just as she was ready to warm to this strange new world. There was a grim and tragic mood to the place, dictated by the heart-rending statues, which lined the path on either side. Beth had heard of these, they were part of the artistic thing for which the Wildside was reluctantly praised back home. They were larger than life, black and glossy, each representing a road-death victim from the turn of the century. There were tens of thousands of them, made of an amber resin and all curled up in a foetal gesture of self-defense. Their faces, streaked with time and lichen, were contorted in mixtures of anger, pain and, most shocking of all, disbelief. They stretched for as far as the eye could see, half claimed by vegetation. Somewhere in their middle she came to a carved slab of marble. She read the words. This was the world's largest war memorial, it said, covering hundreds of acres, dedicated to the half million dead who had fallen in the century long war against the automobile.

After five miles the statement had been made and the statues stopped but their sorry mood stayed with Beth and an urge to curl up and be turned to agonized stone stayed with her until dusk when the sky lifted, the sun broke through and her nose for a quiet place took her from the path and led her to a perfect spot for her first night's camp, a river, slow and deep enough to offer pools for swimming.

How she would find her way between the theory of her father's instruction and the reality of endless woods and farmland was a question that hung with her as darkly as the statues. She had no training in these things beyond the games she had played with her brother in their tiny garden, gathering twigs and leaves to make a debris shelter, whittling at a stick to make kindling that would fire in even the dampest of weather, pouring over her father's old books on hedgerow skills and survival techniques. The reality was less comfortable but more thrilling, although for now she could rely on the pack of food she had put together with the doctor's help in Malvern. But soon it was time to light her first fire. She had practised many times at home to ensure the skill was there when needed. The string and knife she had brought with her but the rest of the bow drill she made from materials lying in the woods. Although she had matches she was determined to succeed without them and followed the rules to the letter, paring off slithers of wood for the initial kindling, crouching with her weight over the drill, bowing to a sustainable rhythm. The first whiffs of smoke lifted her spirits out of all proportion and when tiny flames licked at the tinder of wood and leaf she almost whooped for joy. Success gave her a sense of belonging that had been dangerously missing, and with it a renewed belief that she could survive in this world. To the loud and joyous singing of the late birds went the reassuring hiss of logs and with it a sharp air that promised summer weather.

Next she sought out the upright and diagonal struts that would make her shelter. These she installed on a flat piece of ground not too close to the water with its threat of insects and commenced to gather great arms-full of twigs and last year's leaves. It took her an hour before she was satisfied with the results by which time dusk was falling but a last touch of warmth was still reaching to the river and its shallow pools. With her work done it was time to make herself clean, and not just her body. It was time for ritual.

From her pack she took the strange clothes that Anna had helped her buy. She began to undress. Only her mother's watch would cross from the old to the new. The clear blue of the sky lit through the water to the stones and pebbles and fish that were still sunning themselves. Each item of clothing was a tiny sacrament. She placed them on the fire and watched them melt into flame. The jacket was for stealth and hiding in the alleyways of home, the jeans were for running in search of a world beyond her reach, the T-shirt was for school, smeared and smutty with lies and abuse, her pants were for those boys and youths who had stolen her childhood. Stripped bare to a last and cold layer of truth, still, in some strange way, virgin. In the smoke and flames a part of her was purged, tormented into the bright light of a pure evening. She had never loved this body, only the power it gave her. She had never enjoyed boys or men, only the humiliation she could inflict by tempting them. Her limbs and breasts had matured too early, gifted her a power she had never learned to control. Part of her had wanted to hold on to the unformed bones and neutral lines of the child but she had watched first with horror and then disbelief as a woman's future invaded her from within. But today would be different. Today she would step into her new body and let the creature she had been transform to smoke and ash.

Ritual? She would give them ritual. The memory came of a hawthorn tree burned by neighbours, of a pain too deep to describe. As the fire died she took the ashes of her old self on the end of a stick and smeared them across her face in jagged lines and made weird patterns on her breasts and midriff and thighs. She wanted a song or a chant. She came from a world without primal music and was a deaf-mute suddenly aware of the great orchestral conspiracy around her. She tossed the stick into the river and then waited. She felt the breeze touch every part of her, she felt it fresh beneath her arms as she ran her hands through her hair. She felt the ash dry and tingling. She breathed deeply and might have sung or let out a glorious scream had there been no one else on the planet. She took one last look at the trees that climbed away from either bank. She imagined him watching. She imagined him out there, bare-footed, speechless, large eyes grown larger, deference touched by lust, belonging to this strange world but longing to reach out to whatever she had to offer. This time he would come to her. She would let him touch the markings, add his own, perhaps a dolphin from the groin upwards, then she would take his Wildside madness into her body and drain him, vampire-like, until it was she who was tanned, feral, at home and he who was pale, uncertain and lost. She resented the feelings of jealousy he awoke in her but felt guilty for wanting any kind of revenge on his unassuming smugness. There was not an ounce of malice in the youth nor his sister, they belonged as naturally as the trout she was about to disturb or the birds now singing their last. Complete and total belonging. She plunged and for brief seconds flew, free of all weight. The water when it came was cold and final. Her few moments seemed like long minutes. She made no effort to wash off the markings or to dry herself. Within half an hour she was dressed as drably and as comfortably as every other Wildsider and was ready to sit by her very own fire until cold would drive her into the protective depths of her very own shelter.

TWENTYONE

Clegg on the wrong end of a hangman's rope. At times like these you see the imperfections. The usually handsome mouth is set in a strange downward twist, a throwback to childhood tantrums. His forehead is streaked with sweat although the sun has not yet risen and grime highlights the crow's feet that reach out from his eyes. For some reason beard growth has hesitated overnight, doubting whether it was worth the trouble and he looks unusually pale, a blue smudge beneath each eye, slate-grey eyes, yes, but blood shot. Above all he looks powerless, strange for those who know him because his wiry frame and sullen looks always give off a feeling of intent and capability. The rope might be woven from mindless dogma, the noose might be knotted with pointless hate but it can break his neck all the same and has the power to end his life agonizingly. His crime? A refusal to make promises, perhaps, to lend himself to the future? An excess of lies drawn from a bankrupt account? Cruelty whilst in His Majesty's Forces to those of a less perfect cast? Feigned affection to gain access to a woman's body? Not today. Today's offence, the one that might still kill him he would never have guessed. Polluting the air may have been his parents' birthright but it is not inherited. Emitting an endless stream of poison into the air we all breathe may have been the habit of millions over the last two centuries but nowadays the obvious joke is to say that the climate has changed. Clegg has obliged people miles away to take in his filth, to breathe it into their lungs, to lodge it in their delicate brains, to eat it in their seal-liver stew. Air, of course, is the community into which we are all born, but Clegg has been raised and reared outside all community, raised and reared as a dollar commodity with the single aim in life to consume. New rules, Clegg. New dangers. Air is our birthright and our responsibility. But of responsibility speak not to Clegg for he does not wish to know. He may once have heard that the Wildside sold its right to emit certain pollutants and invested the money in windmills and solar panels but he could not have guessed that this would lead to his life being hung, quite literally, in the balance.

This might have been explained to him by the passers by, of whom, to his initial relief but subsequent amazement, there had been several. The first, whilst Clegg was still naïve enough to trust in human compassion, had come just before dawn. Clegg hungrily anticipated the relief of being cut down, of rubbing his wounds, of drinking and pissing before looking for revenge. It was not to be. The rider slowed down, read the text which was daubed on a board just beyond Clegg`s field of vision, spat at him and continued on his way.

For minutes Clegg was too amazed to think straight. What kind of deranged person could ride past at the sight of a man hung by the neck? What kind of sick world had he stepped into? The passer-by must have been the hangman, that was the only explanation, he must have been returning to admire his handiwork of the previous night. But this theory lasted only until the next visitation. Textbook Wildsiders these, a cross between Amish farmers and Thomas Hardy peasants, cretinous parents with their two inbred children on a donkey cart. They passed, they read the text, they looked at Clegg with disgust and continued without comment. He hurled useless obscenities after them until his throat ached and the realization of thirst became an additional and very tangible pain. He had stopped hoping by the sixth passer-by; curiosity mixed with anger and a certain amount of fear and the advent, together with the midday sun, of a fever. It entered perhaps through the open wound and scalped skin of his left flank but advanced quickly to his head, there scrambling any last remnants of reason and clarity. By late afternoon its tactics were almost visible for Clegg, some mixture of boiling oil and bile livid in his throat, a mess of breached reason and frenzied defense somewhere between his glazed eyes and a blurred middle distance. His delirium ignored all the likely outlets. Instead of flying high above it all or racing through a mythical landscape on a voluptuous motorbike he found himself shoeing horses, and the faster he applied the hot shoes to the horn of the hoof the quicker they came at him. Soon he had shod every horse on the Wildside and those he had started with were returning and their owners ignored him completely, neither commenting on his skills nor bothering to pay for his services. Sick of horses and the smell they gave off he must have looked too long and too directly into the sun because the next moment he had imagined himself a total eclipse, the sun a black disk in a dark grey sky, the birds and animals all fallen silent and his eyes fixed to the line he imagined linking Venus to Mars to Jupiter and Saturn, each planet bright and distinct in the eclipsed daylight, as distinct as his mother. His mother? She had taught him this useless love of the night sky and it was his mother who was now directing his gaze, now admonishing him, who was now standing before him with a knife, like a butcher choosing a joint from a hung pig, like Mad John come for revenge, but instead of taking a part she demanded the whole, she cut the rope just above his head and he slumped in a heap on the floor. Jolted from his fever, skewered by the pain in his neck and side and suddenly aware of a woman slightly older than himself, bending down over his mess of a body, the knife still evident and wiping a cloth gently across his face and eyes. If not his mother it must have been Jenny, with little Jo close by, waiting for adventure.

You're very beautiful, Jenny, he tried, somewhere in the white noise of his skull, still in the habit of seeking her reassurance.

And you're baggage, the voice told him. Be quiet, you're badly hurt.

More beautiful than I remembered.

Why are men always full of crap? Roll over, let me look...

You smell of warm milk.

You smell of nothing I would care to mention. You are very lucky and probably very stupid. My name is not Jenny by the way.

I can hear your jewelry. What does the text say? What did they write?

It was chalked on the sign next to the road. Whether he saw it himself or whether the woman read it out to him he could never remember and it hardly mattered but it was biblical and swam in his head for hours, about filth and mire, about there being no rest for the wicked, which seemed both fair and appropriate, no rest for the untried blacksmith, exhausted and filthy in the smell and warmth of his own urine. Somehow the woman, no longer Jenny, briefly his mother, led him to a stream and made him wash. Somehow she settled him in the shade of a tree and made him drink, all the time watching him with slightly sad eyes set in a wonderfully mobile face, expressive without words, a great vitality hidden in each expression. Whether she administered medicine at that point he could not tell but the next thing he knew he was completely revived, unharmed, not a scratch to his body and the woman was Jenny transformed, long black hair falling gypsy-like over her shoulders as she mounted him, as she laughed at his discomfort and bared her breasts to the light of Venus, as she made love to him with planets and stars arrayed behind her and the jewelry at her neck moving in time to the beat of an imagined blacksmith's hammer. I am the anvil, he thought. I always wanted to be the hammer but now I understand. It is the anvil that transforms, not the hammer nor the swinging arm but the lowly anvil. In an instant of clarity he saw her for real once more, an unknown woman, clothed, intense, watching over his fever, fingering the bracelet at her wrist, keeping a vigil, their love-making an embarrassed fantasy.

Somewhere close to morning she spoke to him. She had made a fire and the stars had appeared for real, as had the pain. She had dressed his wounds expertly but now that the fever was receding he realized how badly he had been scraped and how well she had tended him. He sat up, groaned, looked at her clearly for the first time.

`You stink`, she said, of which he would remind her in happier circumstances. `Motorbike was it? You were asking for trouble. You're lucky they didn't kill you. They usually do.` Her eyes were as dark as her hair and Clegg found himself doubting her again.

`Who?` His first sensible noise through the numbness of pain. `Who did it?`

There was the glance of a smile as she answered, as though only a fool would ask, but might there also have been a certain sadness? For the extent of his ignorance, perhaps, or the strangeness of the world in general. `Arkites. Who do you think?`

What could he think? The Arkites were fundamentalists, a notorious cult born during the civil war, Old Testament ecologists who believed in a second coming to be prepared for in the most vigorous of ways, believers in the cleansing power of the Flood and in the need for a second Ark, this one of the Spirit and a second selecting out of those fit from those unfit to breed. Clegg`s worse nightmare, people with conviction.

`Will you be able to walk?`, the girl asked. Girl? Woman? She was close to thirty but seemed unfinished, still in the process of becoming. She probably knew men inside out and the world with them, but had never been a mother, that was it, she was of breeding age but had not yet bred. She had held something back for herself. She had not given all her youth away to babies and children, it still lived in the dance of her expression-rich features. She seemed genuinely concerned, one of nature's nurses, despite the slight smile. Clegg had not thought as far as walking. No amount of training can prepare for delayed shock, although whiskey can help, which the girl-woman now offered from a hip-flask. He took a mouthful, only to heave it out and break into contortions of coughing and to be treated again to the woman's slightly contemptuous grin. He took in her appearance. Capable. Comfortable in her body. Lots of dark hair piled up at the back of the head waiting to break loose and tumble down, like in the fantasy, when she had pinned him to the ground so wonderfully. A good figure, slight but strong. Her hands were beautiful with long elegant fingers, special hands, transforming hands, an extension of her lively and light-filled face. Lots of rings and bracelets. Gold. He thought of the wild fantasy that had taken him at the height of the fever, wondered if he had said anything, touched her, let her know what had been ranting away inside him.

`Thank you`, Clegg muttered, aware that he probably owed her a lot. He wanted to ask who she was, what her name was, why she was troubling with him, but none of those questions seemed safe. `Arkites?` he asked. `Who the hell do they think they are?`

`This is their patch`, she said patiently. Her words came slowly but he was content to wait, this was not a woman to be rushed. `Whoever you stole the bike from should have warned you. They don't allow machines here, you know. Nothing. Absolutely nothing. They ask forgiveness every time they use a knife to cut through bread or a plough to open the earth.`

`So that's why I had the road to myself,` Clegg mumbled, `and I didn't steal the bike.`

The girl shrugged, smiled, frowned. She could do all this and more in the tilt of one eyebrow but was suddenly distracted. They both heard horse approaching and in an instant the girl leant over him. `Now you're on your own`, she said quietly. The smell of milk again, the prospect of comfort confusing Clegg. `I've done what I can. These people are mad, remember that. Fanatics. You can never be quite sure of them. I'm sorry. Keep your mouth shut. Be humble for a day or two. They should let you go after that.`

Be humble? Clegg had not come here to be humble, Clegg had come here to piss on the lot of them, not on himself. She gave him one last look over: scabbed, filthy, bemused. `You look like shit!` she laughed silently, ruffled his hair like a parent leaving a child to the challenge of a school trip. `They wont want to hang on to you.` and then left him, walking towards the noise of two approaching horses.

He watched anxiously as she engaged two male riders in conversation. He wanted her back. She was safety. He wanted to watch her milk cows. The sky was turning pink behind them and he thought how pretty it all looked, two madmen on horse back silhouetted against the sun-rise, talking to a woman whose name he didn't know and who had probably saved his life. He could hear nothing but they gestured in his direction more than once before parting, the girl into the distance, the two men closing on Clegg with efficient menace, no holds barred, he reminded himself.

Grovel, she had told him. Be humble. A prisoner of war, he had been taught, should remain inconspicuous even at his own public trial. He should remain upright and square shouldered but avoid eye contact unless spoken to as an equal. He should do nothing to provoke anger or to show weakness that might draw out cruelty sooner than sympathy. He should observe carefully to identify the pecking order amongst the guards in order to befriend and possibly bribe...

A single blow to the head freed Clegg of both training and consciousness. The rope that had almost hung him was now used to strap him to a horse. Clegg would have to await his chance to grovel and apologize.

TWENTYTWO

Finn's school was all around Beth before she realized it. Kidding herself that she was taking an initiative and not just craving comfort she had negotiated the route from the Malvern Ridge down to the Knightwick Marshes. The wide blue and grey horizons of the estuary she had feasted on only two days ago felt very different for having a backdrop of uncharted Wildside rather than the glowering presence of the Comfort Zone. She was met and passed by a variety of ages on horseback who all greeted her casually but who all had a purpose which pointedly excluded her. For this reason she was delighted when Anna came riding towards her. It would have fitted the script well if the girl had dropped out of a tree, Puck-like, but she seemed genuinely surprised to see Beth.

`The clothes,` Anna said, `Are they right?`

`The clothes are fine.` Beth confirmed. `Thankyou.`

`No,` said Anna, suddenly serious, face down, eyes up reprovingly, `that's not why I asked, you know, not for you to say thankyou. Are they right, really?`

Beth resolved to try again. `The clothes are fine.` she said, sharply. The hose made her legs itch and it seemed strange to let the linen shirt trail so far down her thigh but she didn't say so. Nor did she say how much she loved the practical and spacious warmth of the doublet and how she could never imagine taking it off again or living without it.

`Can I show you around, Beth?` Anna asked, choosing to ignore the warning sounds. `Can I show you to our school?`

Beth almost told the girl where to stuff her school but realized that to do so would be habit, not common sense. She wanted to see and learn. She was less sure about being shown and taught. And she wanted to see Finn. She hated to admit it but she wanted to see if he was real, if the myth of such a person could endure for a second day. And she wanted to smell him. `Of course. I mean, please. I'd like that. Thankyou.`

For the last few miles the way was marked by wonderful sculptures, carved from the fallen and some standing trees: trolls, gnomes, giant snails, a sleeping bear. All were fashioned on a grand scale close enough to the path for viewing but far enough back for intrigue. Anna had dismounted to walk alongside Beth and pointed to one in the form of a lion. `Do you like these?` she asked.

`They're incredible,` said Beth, lamely, lacking the words to do them justice. `Who made them?`

But Anna answered with another question. `Have you ever been on a game show?` she asked.

`What?`

`A game show. You see, my brother told me where you were from. I mean, I hope you don't mind me asking. But I thought that everyone...`

`No I've never been on a game show.` Beth answered, confused. She knew plenty who had. Each channel broadcast several every night. She could understand why an outsider looking in might assume everyone in the Comfort Zone had enjoyed their moment of prize-winning glory.

The woodcarvings had now given way quite abruptly to the domain of a stone mason whose way-marking crosses and milestones tried to outdo the tree trunk spirits of the neighbour. After the standing stones came the wind-chime region where every large tree at an interval of about fifty paces had its own wind-chime, high up and active. Some were tiny and discreet like the twittering of goldcrest or tomtits. Others were the size and extent of large aviaries, complete with gongs and tubes which whistled like organ pipes to the right wind. Beth's favourite was the kingdom of plant pots, huge pots twenty feet high and wide, complete with a side opening to offer shelter to who or whatever. Others on their sides, cupping enough water to attract feeding birds.

`Have you been to Disney?` Anna asked after a while. The hopeful look in her eye almost made Beth laugh out loud.

`I'm sorry, Anna, I haven't been anywhere like that, my Dad didn't like that kind of thing.`

`A football match?`

`Sorry!`

`Have you driven a car?`

Beth smiled, shook her head, and then threw Anna a tit-bit. `I've used an implant phone.` she said, tapping behind her ear. `It was just here. It gave me a headache.`

Anna laughed. Before Beth could bristle the girl apologized and explained that she was laughing at herself, at her own stupidity. `It's just that I've never, you're the first... I should apologize again, but then I would sound like my brother. But it is interesting, don't you think so? Things are never like you expect them to be.`

Beth agreed but declined to say so.

`Like your sentences.`

`My what?`

`Your sentences. You speak in complete sentences. You know, beginning, end, verb, full stop. I thought...`

`You thought we didn't.`

`That's what I was told.`

`Who by?`

`I don't know. You just pick these things up.`

`What else have you picked up?`

Anna completely missed the hostile edge to Beth's voice and blundered on. `Well, boys for instance, and girls.`

`Boys for instance, and girls?`

`You know.` she shrugged, suddenly embarrassed.

`You mean we fuck like rabbits?` said Beth, `You mean boys buy and trade us like gum cards? Use us like cold wipes on a hot day? Is that what you mean?` Her anger was weary rather than hard-edged. She was amazed by the effect her words appeared to have on Anna. The girl became even slighter and even more transparent, gossamer-like. Her eyes had filled with tears.

`That won't happen here, Beth.` she said almost in a whisper. `That could never happen here.` Her hand reached out and touched Beth on the arm. This is Finn's sister's hand, Beth thought, her anger on hold. I have to allow it.

The two girls were quiet for some minutes, neither certain how to proceed. The next statue was the needed prompt. `I made that one.` Anna said, pointing into the woods. In the various territories they had passed were benches and bowers made of woven hazel or willow, freshly green and coming alive by the minute. It had not occurred to Beth that these, or the earlier statues and mobiles might be anything to do with a school, that people of her age and younger were actually allowed, encouraged even, to shape and shift the world they found themselves in, to be led to the conviction that it was theirs to transform and not just passively digest. Only when she saw the look of enthusiasm in Anna's face as she pointed to the willow bower did the awful suspicion confirm itself that all this excess of creative force was an expression of children and teenagers in the process of learning, and with this realization came an awful sinking sense of the distance, the alienation that would always exist between such privileged beings and the likes of her, starved and abused as she was in the soulless ways of Comfort Zone education. Just at that moment they came across a group of children being supervised by a teenager. Together they were struggling with a pole-lathe. It was powered by a long and lithe ash pole strapped to a tree, one end on the ground, the other in the air. From this highest point a rope was pulled down to a foot pedal via the simple but effective spindle of the apparatus. The two girls stood to watch.

`Did they make it themselves?` Beth asked, already knowing the answer.

Anna nodded and pointed to the roughly turned chair legs strewn on the floor. `They're making their own chairs and desks for school. They must be twelve, ready for sit-down work.`

Beth let that one sink in.

The youth in charge of the group recognized Anna and beckoned to them to come closer, but Anna showed more tact than Beth might have expected. `Would you like to have a go? He'll let you if I ask.`

Beth felt humiliated by her mixture of feelings. That she felt inadequate in the presence of these gifted people went without saying, that she would have given anything to try her hand with the chisel at turning a stool leg was beyond doubt but stronger was the wish to pass undetected and unnoticed, to observe Finn, Anna and their extraordinary world from the outside. She shook her head and Anna led them away from the clearing to where the noise of hammering and children's voices presented Beth with her next threat.

`Do you have a teacher?` Anna asked, `I mean, did you, at your school.`

Beth was surprised to see her guide blushing. The questions about game shows and Disney and school were part of an ignorance at least equal to her own. Beth had just assumed that she was the only one struggling to understand another world. In one way at least they were equals. `We have a coordinator.` Beth said. ` Mr. Jones. He's not a teacher, not really.`

`So who teaches you?`

Beth shrugged. She had never thought about it before. Anything worth knowing she had taught herself or got from her father. `We have a learning programme. Soft-wear. Its personalized every night and we work on it the next day.`

`You work on it?`

Something here was as alien to Anna as the pole-lathe had been to Beth. `Yes. We go to school. We all sit in a big room, about eighty of us. Mr. Jones has a control point. We download our personalized programme and do it.`

`Do it?`

`Yes, do it.` Beth was struggling to hide her irritation. Anna dropped the subject and looked at Beth, as though, fairy-like, she might dematerialize if rebuked again.

They had slipped from the path into the shelter of dark trees and were making their way closer to what seemed like the heart of the school, a clearing in the woods in which several large cone-shaped buildings were grouped around a central space. Each building was a construction of slabwood and ash-poles and had its own fire, some of which were lit to judge by the lazy plumes of smoke rising through the open peak of each cone. Some huts were quiet, either empty or home to more formal work, others rang to the sound of hammers on metal or the thrum of potters` wheels.

Beth had no doubt that the pupils, if that was the right word, had made the huts just as they had made the furniture and the sculptures and just as surely as they tended the animals and vegetable gardens which backed away from the clearing on one side. `You just do it?` repeated Anna, returning to the struggle. `What do you mean, you just do it?`

But Beth was too weary to explain. She was the guest and she felt the need to be rude. She ignored the girl's stupid questions and decided to ask some of her own. `What's that?` she demanded, pointing to a large clay and wicker built object, the size and shape if an upturned rowing boat. From its chimney rose a torrent of sparks and its mouth was being fed wood by pupils, not much younger than Beth, all of them hot and stained with soot and sweat.

`Its a kiln.` said Anna. `They made it last week. It's the first firing. They've been up all night keeping the temperature right. It should be ready quite soon.`

Beth had no idea what a kiln was and assumed the pupils to be involved in the preparing of food, especially as the area was littered with a variety of pots, some broken, some unfinished, but some quite wonderful in the extravagance of their design. She continued to watch but could find no point of reference from her own experience, nothing that would relate to anything she had ever done or even, more tellingly, ever dreamt of doing. If this was school then she was ready to begin anew, always assuming that it was not too late.

The two girls suddenly looked at each other as though they had shared the same thought at the same moment. `We're both as stupid as each other,` laughed Anna, putting it into words. `We should give each other lessons some time.` With that acknowledged Beth felt more at ease, more of an equal, less hostile.

`Would you like to see the boys?` Anna asked. `They should be making fools of themselves about now. Finn will be, anyway.`

`I think I should go.` said Beth, `I'm not sure...`

`They won't see us.` Anna added quickly. We're not supposed to watch but we can spy on them.`

That decided it. She wanted to see Finn but not be seen, she wanted to stay and be a part of things but peep in from the outside. Perfect. They heard Finn before seeing him. In the company of friends his voice was lighter, less cautious. He had shouted to others who had arrived in the clearing with horses, one of which he now mounted. Anna pulled Beth into the undergrowth and winked before leading her along a meager path that ran more or less parallel to the one Finn and the other youths were now riding down. They were trotting in the direction of the water, which was visible through trees on the far side of the school village. The girls carefully picked their way to the reed beds by the estuary, remaining hidden in the trees. Beth could see back across the estuary towards the east and knew enough to make out the distant summit of Bredon island but her attention was immediately taken by the gathering of horses and youngsters on a large sand bank left pristine by the falling tide. `It's a practice.` Anna whispered. `They play it for real next week.` The youths were half a mile away, about thirty of them, and there was no question of approaching any closer. Not only was there no more cover available but all the horses must have waded through a good yard of water to take their riders to where they were now mustering themselves for some kind of game or contest. The youths had all stripped, but Beth tried to take her cue from Anna, who seemed to find nothing remarkable in the nudity of the young men. A series of races was taking place, one-against one, in which the riders were not only intent on reaching the finish post first but in which they also tried to grapple each other to the ground whilst riding at full speed. Beth watched in amazement as reckless bout followed reckless bout, as screams and hoots of passion beat off the water, as fit young bodies crashed into firm sand or kinder shallows. Finn took and delivered his share of falls. One of the tricks was to bounce back up immediately, catch the bolting horse and remount before your opponent could lay claim to the trophy, a red or blue garland, which was hung around each horse's neck. Those garlands taken in mock battle were placed on one of two poles at either end of the sandbank. When all had been claimed a free-for-all broke out, a final ruck of horses and flailing limbs attempting to regain or to protect the `colours`, and all this as the tide played its part, silently and swiftly bringing water up to the hocks of the smaller ponies and making even more hilarious the falls which all continued to take.

Beth found herself wondering how many of these boys Anna had slept with because at home it would have been all of them, yet earlier the girl's reaction to Beth's anger had confused things. It would never happen here, Anna had said. Was she joking? The setting seemed designed for it and at home the sex would have been part of the game, probably its reward or stated purpose. Again Beth reminded herself that comparisons were pointless and realized in amazement that Anna was probably virgin, a thought that made her strangely envious but also filled her with contempt. How dare she be virgin? Beth asked herself, what right did she have? But there were no answers, only more questions.

Beth would have been content to slip away unnoticed. She was unsure how she should take her leave of Anna. She had felt painfully at odds with this new world even before the sights and sounds of the morning, even before their questions of each other had emphasized the gulf that lay between their two worlds. The already unlikely prospect of acquiring a horse on Malvern market was made even more improbable by seeing what use these people could put their animals to. The empty water and the dark grey of the far shore might have tempted her back if the last three days could be completely undone. There was no going back, but how could she ever truly arrive?

They took an awkward farewell of each other a couple of miles from the school compound. Beth felt exposed, certain that her pretence of friends and business locally had fooled Anna for not one moment, equally certain that she would relate to Finn every stupid question Beth had asked. Tomorrow on Malvern Market, Anna reminded her, she needed a horse, Finn would be there, Finn knew his horses, he would be happy to help. Of course Finn knew horses. Finn was perfect, she thought, reminding herself to hate him. It made Beth ache with loneliness to know that Finn would be there and she would not. Trust no one. Let no one follow. She would give Malvern a wide berth tomorrow. She would begin her trek to the northwest in pursuit of dreams and nightmares without their help. She left Anna for the cold comfort of a debris shelter alive with the imagined insects that had already cost her a night's sleep and the uncertain warmth of a meager fire on which she had absolutely nothing to cook.

TWENTYTHREE

`You should have known this, Mr.Clegg.` the eye seemed to say, `You should have been better prepared. Never neglect the details, Mr.Clegg. Didn't they teach you that? Didn't you learn the importance of preparation long ago? Didn't you pride yourself on being one step ahead of the oppo-fuckin'-sition? Two steps? Sorry, Mr.Clegg, if you say so, two steps it is. Then why, with all due respect, of course, no slight intended, as much due respect as you wish, naturally, why is it, if you're usually two steps ahead and sometimes more, why is it you are now chained by the ankle to a pillar set in concrete lying in your own shit? Difficult one that. No easy answers. None that don't include words like brainless or fucked. Why is it, to continue the theme, that you're lying, half-conscious, listening to a bloodshot eye as it speaks through a knot whole in the wood as if said eye was your only chance of salvation in a God-forsaken world, Mr.Clegg? Perhaps, deep down, you knew it very well, Mr.Clegg, perhaps for this reason you came to be hung yesterday, drawn today and quartered tomorrow, your safe assumptions spread to the four corners of this strange corner of a strange world. Assumptions, Mr.Clegg? Forget them, all of them, every single one. They will be your undoing. Not that you've got much more to be undone. With all due respect. Sorry, someone should have told you. Someone should have taken you quietly to one side and broken the news. They have a theory, see, Mr.Clegg, they have rules to live by, rules you have broken. Rules. They talk of things sacred to the human soul. They have appetites not of the body, quiet appetites for things *green* and *growing*, things caked in mud and crap. Incredible, Mr.Clegg. Illegal? It should be. Where you and I come from it is, Mr.Clegg, rest assured, where you and I come from such deviance was stamped out decades ago. If you can't get off on your own body, if you can't get happy by sticking things into yourself then don't waste our time, isn't that right, Mr.Clegg? Don't come whingeing to us about soul this and spirit that, don't go carping on about the *inner man*. Get busy with the outer man for God's sake. Buy a few add-ons, down-load a new trip. Otherwise fuck off. Cut your wrists. Eat rhubarb leaves. Jump under a train on a wet Sunday afternoon in November. Don't you agree, Mr.Clegg. Aren't I right?`

Clegg declined to answer. The eye had been tormenting him for what seemed like days even though it was beyond some kind of barrier, even though it blinked a lot and kept rubbing itself and disappearing for long minutes beneath pale white lids. He looked around again, for the dozenth time, still confused, almost out-of-body. Darkness had turned to dull light, details were being dredged to the surface one by one, cast up like rubbish on the beach. Clegg`s thoughts, still touched with the hangover of last night's fever, tried the Pig Trough as an option. Was he back there? Had Danny tricked him, pulled him back from the brink? Was the whole crossing, the micro-light, the scrambler, Malvern market, the milk and jewelry woman-girl, had it all been a dream? It was the Pig Trough. The police had raided, day light had been let in, the pigs were free and the punters had been dragged downstairs and chained, forced to lie in their own excess. The quiet hum of boredom and anxiety, of men fidgeting in their straw, one or two talking in hushed voices, the rub of listless limbs against stained boards, these were real. It was all real. But it was no night club. It was a huge hanger or barn, a great covered arena where agricultural shows had once been held, the kind of place that bulls were paraded, horses preened, tractors displayed, the kind of place farmers and their families came to reassure themselves they were not alone in their beef-rearing, or their pork-raising, their honey-gathering or their soil-tilling.

Clegg made the mistake of asking the eye again, not for the first time he realized too late, inspiring it to roll and glint manically through the knot in the wood. `They have appetites you would never dream of, Mr.Clegg. Soul-stuff. Quiet ones. They're the worse, Mr.Clegg, believe me, the quiet ones will keep you gagging for more the rest of your life. Want to get laid, Mr.Clegg? No problem. You know where, you know how, you know the price. A simple business transaction. Makes the world go round, that kind of thing, we both know it. Want to stuff your face, Mr.Clegg, eat till you vomit and then eat some more? Of course you do, we all do from time to time. You know the place, the price, perhaps even the chef. Easy! But you know where this is leading, Mr.Clegg, you know what's coming and its not pretty, its not nice, Mr.Clegg. You want to stuff your soul, Mr.Clegg, you want to get soul-laid, Mr.Clegg. You know the place? You know the price? Shit, you can spend forty years searching for that kind of fix, Mr.Clegg, you can spend whole lifetimes just trying to have a soul-fix, Mr.Clegg. We're talking seriously difficult merchandise, we're talking super-volatile shit, like you can't even hold it in your hand, Mr.Clegg, you can't even put a label on it for fuck's sake! Like a restaurant with no menu, no fuckin' door! I'll tell you. Mr.Clegg, since we're friends, because I wouldn't tell just anyone, right? I wouldn't give this away to any punk that might not appreciate it, Mr.Clegg, but I'm telling you straight up, from somewhere behind the horse's molars, Mr.Clegg, these guys, our hosts shall we say, lets call them our hosts, why not? Our hosts, they stuff their faces on nothing less than trees and green and the endless power of growth and re-growth, of birth and rebirth. Latter Day Church of the Inner Landscape, Mr.Clegg. "Landscape!" they cry. "Landscape! God was a tree." Lift the outer veil, Mr.Clegg. Lift it gently, behold the inner world of man. Landscape out there in the world is only a reflection of your own landscape, your own private wilderness. Ugly city landscapes are an expression of ugly city people, just like you and me, Mr.Clegg, no disrespect. Threaten the landscape and you threaten the sanctity of your very soul, Mr.Clegg, you had better believe it, because the soul, deep down, remembers its Garden of Eden. It remembers a place from before birth and longs to recreate that garden in the wilderness around and within.`

Clegg was no longer listening. Whether the eye was quoting its own creed or that of their `host` it was all gibberish. He checked his wounds. The woman had done well, presuming she had been more than a dream. He remembered the smell of milk, the sound of her jewelry, the fantasy of lovemaking. What was it she had said? It was difficult to separate the imagined from the real. Arkites, that was it. Extremists. Grovel. Keep your head down.

He took in the details. There were no light fittings. The building had been made `pure` of electrical and magnetic disturbances. The invisible background pollution Clegg had taken in with his mother's milk had been shown to nurture cancer in the body, and, according to Arkites at least, corruption in the soul. How did he know that? Had Danny told him, or the woman? Or had the eye been preaching at him all night, or longer? Was he the subject of some subliminal brain-washing technique? Large brass candlesticks stood around the walls. Pools of old wax had spilled onto the damp flag-stones, themselves a replacement for the once functional but politically unacceptable concrete. The walls were hung with biblical quotes, hand written on paper turned brown at the edges. The stall was of wooden boards on three sides and open at the front to a central passageway. The boards, where Clegg might have found the comfort of scratched messages, had been scrubbed and sanded fanatically bare. Across the aisle he could look into three more stalls each occupied, like his, with men chained and prostrate. One had clearly been in residence for some time. He had a small shelf with several books and had been allowed to decorate his walls with a magnificent mural of jungle plants and animals. The man took no notice of Clegg. He was reading. Clegg tried to stand. His fall from the scrambler had scalped one side of his left leg almost bare of skin and bruised, if not cracked, a number of ribs. He winced but managed to pull himself up. His shades were still in his pocket, broken into several pieces. One side of his leather jacket was marked as though by a lion's claw. He brushed straw from his clothing and looked around. The back wall was too high to peer over but to left and right, a yard or two either way he could look in on his neighbours. Both were sleeping. Clegg guessed from the light entering via the barred skylights that it was very early morning. He noticed for the first time that the back wall of each stall, his own included, had not only a biblical quote but a sign proclaiming the offence of its occupant, again like a zoo where species details and a map of distribution might have hung. `Air pollution.` his said. `Breach of emission legislation.` He looked again at his neighbours. `Chain-saw offences` to the left, `forged documents` to the right. The man opposite, the early-bird reader with book shelf and library, with the inner landscape of parrots and lianas was the real thing. `Murderer` stood out in bald letters, the subscript, too small for Clegg to read, seemed to give its Latin name.

The eye tried again. It was at knee height in the back wall and followed Clegg easily as he paced his enclosure. `They're all baddies.` the eye said, `Each stall's got a baddie. One for each sin. It's like Noah's Ark but with bad guys instead of animals. And no women. Not enough to go round. What they got you for?` the eye asked.

`Motorbike`, said Clegg, breathing out slowly, `Bad air.`

`You're a Highwayman, I knew it! French cocked hat on the forehead, bunch of lace wherever. ` the eye answered. `Bad shit. Man, you could be here for weeks, man, fuckin weeks. Motorbike plus Ark-heads equals One Long Time.`

`Where is this?` said Clegg, at last bending down to the peep hole, ready to confront the eye. `How long is weeks?`

There was a pause from the other side. `Stand back, man, stand as far away from the hole as you chain lets you. Go on, let me look.`

Clegg did as instructed. It was a perverse kind of surveillance, an eye through a hole measuring him up. He became aware of a noise coming from behind the eye's board, perhaps of grinding teeth. He returned to the peep-hole.

`For breakfast we get taken out,` the eye continued, `Party time, Mr.Clegg, exercise. Fresh air plus walkies equals three hundred happy boys. We can talk then. I'll be in the far corner of the yard, near the chapel. I'm called Arch by the way, not what I seem, far from it, but then who is, Mr.Clegg, honestly, who is? Oh, and by the way, I am definitely your man.`

He put Clegg in mind of an insect. His limbs were long and stick-like. His eyes were made compound by the large frames and thick lenses of his spectacles. His most distinctive features, however, were his Adam's apple, uncomfortably large for his gaunt neck, and the huge mop of dread-locked hair, bleached white. His complexion was light gray. It was as though his real blood had leached away into an ungrateful but thirsty world to be replaced by a transparent surrogate, a luke-warm extract more electric than organic. He sidled up to Clegg at the end of the exercise session. Cigarettes, as hard a currency here as in any other prison the world over seemed to be no problem for Arch. He handed Clegg a factory-made one that Clegg slid into his breast pocket. With the cigarettes went an ease of manner. Arch was every one's man, if Clegg was not mistaken, and perhaps even his own man at the same time.

`You're in deep, Mr. Motorbike. Post-Carbon Denial. It's a syndrome thing. They've got therapies for it. Most involve horse shit and long walks in the rain. Unless...` the briefest pause for thought, `You in some kind of game?` He sat next to Clegg on a bench and looked across the yard where some of the forty or so prisoners were playing volleyball. In Arch's hand two marbles rotated constantly, the cause of the grinding noise Clegg had heard earlier.

`I'm freelance.`

Arch laughed. `Aren't we all? At least we like to think so. But I'll tell you what you used to be, Mr.Clegg, before you became, er... freelance, you used to be a squaddie. Am I right or am I right? It takes one to know one.`

The steel tubular fencing around the exercise yard reflected back at Clegg twice, once in each spectacle lens, the light falling in such a way that nothing of Arch`s eyes could be seen. Clegg found it difficult to imagine this thin-faced figure in army uniform performing army tasks.

`I'll tell you what else, Mr.Clegg, when they ask why the motorbike, when they get past their spaced out ideas on air, then the shit hits full on, Mr.Clegg, at speed, because either you're here on a job, which means you're still army, which means they'll hang you, or you came over of your own messed up free will, in which case you can't get back. Or, like me, you're in the game.`

`Freelance.` Clegg repeated.

`Yeah! Like puppets on some pretty fucked-up strings. At home freelance helps you stand out. Over here they're all freelance, let me warn you, every last one of them.`

`So how long do you give me, Arch, assuming they don't ask any awkward questions. How long will they keep me?`

`Until the next one comes in. You could be lucky.`

`The next one?`

`You don't know shit, do you? Air-head to the power three divided by a load of crap. You really are freelance, unpre-fuckin'-pared! The army trains `em up better, Mr.Clegg. You're here until they find a replacement, until some other crap-head commits the same crime as you. You arrived yesterday, that was good news for the guy who had been in your stall. Six weeks he'd been waiting for you to turn up.`

`You mean...`

`Yeah, sure, I mean they have one of each, a token this, a token that. If you know a guy wants to commit murder you'd better do yours first because when he comes in second they let you out. Clever don't you think? It's all in the timing, Mr.Clegg. A good freelance should know that.`

`What's the point?`

`What's the point? What is the fuckin' point?! Answer that Mr.Clegg and you are one very rich man. Did you go to school, Mr.Clegg?` a nod. `Did that have a point?` a shake. `You were in the army, did that have a point?` another shake. `No? Then I've made mine, Mr.Motorbike man. Don't try and explain this world in the old way, you know what I mean? There is no point, maybe that's the point. Except for the shows of course, the guided tours.`

`What shows? What tours?`

`Highlight of the week, new friend, highlight of the week. School kids. They love showing us off to the next generation. Beats the zoo every time, Mr.Clegg. Freaks plus geeks times long hard chains divided by greed equals party time. They're even allowed to feed us, I joke not, they throw us peanuts. You think I'm windin' you? Man, Arch only jokes when things get serious. They feed us, Mr.Clegg, but don't get too excited. You and me are not the star attractions, you and me are not about to turn too many little heads. We're not the big cats or the elephants, don't you believe it, we're down there with the possums and the aardvarks, we barely get a glance. Kids these days! They head straight for the murderers and rapists, Billy over there, or Jack, they are star attractions. And I mean star. They've got waitin' lists of kids wantin' to see them, they've got waitin' lists of kids wantin' to adopt them, have their posters on the old bedroom wall. Those guys got peanuts to last a lifetime!` Arch dissolved into a nervous giggle, whether at the madness of it all or his own joke or Clegg's pained expression hardly mattered. He was a manic talker and here there was plenty to talk about.

The idea of criminals being on display was not new to Clegg. At home it was usual, it earned money for the prisons; a celebrity criminal, a serial killer or worse could draw in thousands, but the idea of one at a time, a constant rollover, one of each species, that was very new. `So why are you here?` he asked. `How do I know you're not the polar bear with cubs? What's your game, Arch?`

`How long have you got, Mr.Clegg? Man with a mission, that's me. Sounds weird? You better believe it. What's my game? Good question that. Been asking myself that one for a long time. Let's just say I hear voices. You know what I mean?` he tapped his head, `Of course you do, you're amongst friends, ex-army. I hear voices, you hear voices, so what's the score? What's my game? Rich shit, Mr.Clegg, 24-carat shit. Life is one big equation when it comes down to it. Doesn't add up, I'm not saying it does, don't get me wrong, doesn't add up one little bit. Unless you make up your own numbers.`

`That's why they put you in here? A numbers game?

`Good God no! I don't touch evangelists. Sorry, Mr.Clegg, you wouldn't understand the half of what I do. Not the half of it!` Arch began to laugh. He didn't understand it himself so why should anyone else, and he was certainly not about to explain everything to Clegg. Need to know. `It's all part of the Game, Mr.Clegg. The Game, OK. Big `G`, like very big. Might be wrong, though. Don't like to think about that.` He laughed at Clegg`s confused face. `A game, Mr.Clegg. You heard it right the first time. You in a game?`

`Not that I know of,` said Clegg, still missing the point.

`I wouldn't be too sure, Mr.Clegg. You in some one else's game without knowing it and you're going to get screwed up badly. Most people are inside a game or two. It's best to know it from the start. There might even be rules to play by.`

`Like in the army?`

`Yeah, like in the army. You've got the idea, Mr.Clegg. Biggest fucking game in the world, that one. Rules change every day, That's why we got out, right? Right. But I'll explain. You've played games, must have done, helmets and stuff, data gloves. You ever gone interactive? Tie-ins?`

Clegg was still shaking his head. He had the broad idea, but not the details. Some computer games combined the virtual with the real. For decades gamers had seen themselves as members of a secret club or society. They met in the cyberstreet, played a game, gave each other points, tasks, even money, gained some pathetic sense of self-worth. Some people got addicted to the whole thing, preferred it to real life, sacrificed work and marriage to an unreal alternative. It was second only to masturbation as the nation's most popular sport and equally as futile to Clegg`s way of thinking. Indeed with a data thong you could combine both activities. Yes, he knew all this and he knew people who indulged, but less common were the inter-active gamers, those who created real-life, real-world tie-ins for each other. The game could not be played only behind a screen or with a palm-top, its participants needed to photograph themselves digitally in front of well-known land marks or outside predesignated pubs, they needed to stalk each other in the flesh to win virtual `invisibility points.` Some even went further. A series of murders in London earlier in the century had been the first and most celebrated case. The victims and the perpetrators knew each other only from cyberspace, they met in the flesh only to attempt to kill each other. In a world so ordered and contained and safely organized the only real adventures and challenges were to be had in the shadow lands behind the monitor.

`I'm in a game, Mr.Clegg. Best game ever. A God game. You know the thing, except if you get to play in this one you have to accept that God is what you are definitely not. That's why I'm here. God sent me!` he burst out laughing at the idea. `Sure, makes me as mad as these goons, except I know that God does not exist. Not theirs anyway. Mine might. On good days. On bad days he couldn't give a shit. Me neither. And I'm doing well, thankyou. Not likely to win, but I'm not going to lose in a hurry, either. Arch plus God times infinite chaos equals zero.` The marbles gyrated as he spoke.

`How did you get in it?` Clegg asked, amused by the idea but also struck by the strange parallels with his own lot. Yes, he was in a game of sorts, but not one Arch and his geek friends would understand. The real world was still stranger than anything the Artificial Intelligentsia could dream up.

`Weirdest thing,` Arch explained. He had leaned forwards to speak into Clegg`s face. The light grey of his skin was tinged blue at the lips and temples. `I'm on a cyber trip, yeah? Lights and colours and stuff flying at me. Great programme. `Rainbow Geometry`, you should try it some time.` Clegg had done. It had made him sick. It was like being trapped inside a kaleidoscope with an out-of-tune orchestra, dolphins and synthesizers leaping at you from behind cascading waterfalls. It explained Arch. Junkies who tripped too often and too heavily had something in common with the lost souls of the 1960`s who had made similar trips with the help of LSD. Their grasp of reality was never, ever the same again. `Stuff's flying at me,` Arch bubbled, eyes rolling inside their fish bowls. `Colours, music, always different, never the same moment twice, and fast, like faster then your heart beat, faster then you can grasp them, when Pow! a voice. 'Welcome to the Game'. I nearly pull off the phones and lenses, this is seriously wrong, I'm like half way up the line to get my money back but I don't, I sit back and listen, calm, Arch, I say, its all a new experience, You've been in the army, you can handle this. Best thing I ever did, Mr.Clegg, listening. I even answer back. No voice card but you can't stop yourself right? Get the fuck out, I say, this is not moral. Moral, Mr.Clegg. Can you believe it. Me? No morality in cyberspace, that's the attraction, but I complain anyway, you don't crash another man's trip, okay? Welcome to the game, it says again, not just a voice, but a face, a Knight, medieval stuff, Simple instructions. A code number, three digits, can't forget that. Check your web account it says, You are one thousand down, refuse the challenge and you never see the money again. Take up the challenge and you get the money back twice over. One thousand times two equals two K, Mr.Clegg, a good equation that one. Got it? It adds up. You can't lose with that kind of equation. My web account is suddenly very red and this voice is offering to double my money if I play a game. I'm in. Of course I'm in. Phones and lenses off, check my web account Yep. Blown a whole in it. Key in the code number.

Welcome Arch, it says. welcome to an exclusive club, welcome to the Game. Capital `G` don't forget. Rules. A task. I'm in. Tie-ins from the start. Real people, real places, thirty or forty gamers, you never know for sure, and away we go. Money back and another grand on top. Then a month or two in, I'm hooked, man, I'm really hooked. Wouldn't you be? Sure you would, I can see it in your eyes. Stalked a woman through Birmingham, thousand pounds, get seen by some dude on a bus who is on the game, a thousand down, after three months I'm five grand up. Big money. Then the bomb shell. Stick a zero on the end, the game master says. Stick two zeroes on the end. Three zeroes on the end. He's serious. This is for real. One condition. The next tie-in is on the Wildside. You want to play this game you gotta cross the Line. You don't want to play this game, you want out, your accounts blown. They've got me, man. I'm over that Line. I'm in their fuckin` game, their fuckin` game is in me. Man I love this stuff.`

Arch stopped. Exhausted? It was hard to tell. The marbles might have given off smoke or been ground to dust by his manic enthusiasm. The place was unnaturally quiet, a handful of men throwing a ball to each other with no particular will to catch it. Magpies were picking up scraps from by the dustbins, ready to reclaim the exercise yard. Perhaps the reality of being confined, of being at someone else's mercy had impinged on Arch's dream, or perhaps he was too far-gone. `Funny thing is, Mr.Clegg. You kind of fit very neatly into my game. I think you'd enjoy it.`

`So how do you access it?` said Clegg, asking the obvious question. `If they don't allow motorbikes they certainly don't let that stuff in. All jammed. What's you way through?`

But Arch smiled and tapped the side of his nose. `Trade secret, Mr.Clegg, trade secret. Reckon I'm onto a winner, know what I mean? Can't give it all away first time, I have my pride to consider.`

`So what's the aim?` asked Clegg, `What are you trying to do?`

Arch chuckled, ran his hand down his neck, fondled the huge Adam's Apple. `I'm trying to find some one, Mr.Clegg. The Big One.`

`The Big One?`

`The Main Man. Who else? The one who holds the Wildside together.`

`And who might that be?` asked Clegg, for once avoiding Arch's eye, fearful of an answer that would touch on his own fragile reality. He need not have worried.

`His Holiness,` said Arch, letting Clegg down gently, placing himself firmly on the side of virtual sanity, `King Arthur!`

TWENTYFOUR

Beth woke before light to see cloud clearing from the west and to hear for the first time in her life the full-hearted rhapsody of a dawn chorus in which hundreds and thousands of birds took their part. At home, in the city, she had loved the solitary thrush and the mournful blackbird but nothing had prepared her for this. There were places at home where some residue of dawn chorus from parkland was a saleable commodity, expressing itself in the value of houses, and there were suburbs where caged birds were hung from trees to answer a nostalgia that had no clear memory of its reality. For almost an hour she sat listening, eyes closed, her face to the dawn and the wooded countryside which seemed to fall away in all directions, a great sponge of green saturated with song, an anxious hunger telling her it might be gone by tomorrow, that such bird song and such a dawn were aberrations, exceptions to a bleak rule.

She picked flowers. Great arm-fulls of campion, bluebell and wild garlic, their colour and smell bright with dawn, but then she threw them down, guiltily. What was she to do with them? Now they would wilt and die whilst those she had left untouched would continue to grace the woods for days to come. A memory came back, uninvited, one to which she had no right after all these years, one of her earliest, perhaps her first. Any details she recalled must have been added later, by her father, or even Sam, but the feelings were her own. They had visited their mother. Perhaps Welbeck was different in those days, a normal mental hospital with a secure wing. Or perhaps they had been made to visit as part of the official campaign against Savage and his family, because there was nothing much to see, only Emma Savage asleep, riddled with tubes and wires. But there were flowers next to her bed from the hospital grounds, pink and blue cornflowers. When they left Beth took one with her and when they walked to the car she dropped it or let it fall. They were in the car and about to drive away when a patient, his face flat and round, his tongue too large for his mouth, his neck as thick as his blunt head, lunged towards them with a great gush of friendly warmth. He came to the car window, he filled it with his face and grin and slobber and tried to hand the flower back to Beth. But Beth did not want the flower. She wanted her mother. Perhaps the unfortunate face filling the car window became the reason for all that was wrong. Beth flung the flower back at him and screamed as only two-year olds can. She was terrified, or inconsolable, or both. But why did the memory come now? The flowers lay on the floor, accusing her. They could not be unpicked.

Beth moved on, northwest to the hills where `the crowds gather`. The next stage of her route must now reveal itself. The fire's ash from two days before had started to rub away and in its place was a new layer of awareness and perception, heightened by the first naggings of hunger. For some reason she had gathered the remaining ash from the fire and crammed it into the waxed matchbox Finn had given her. The matches she burned. Their practical help was secondary now to the symbolism of the ash. Not knowing why she shoved the box in an inside pocket to keep it safe.

The track she followed had lost most of its tarmac to rain and was rutted deeply in places and fringed with flowers and bounded on both sides by new woodland, trees twenty to thirty years old which in a week or two would be dense with brambles but which now still let through light and small herds of wild cattle. She had heard of the cattle. They were harvested after a fashion but their main task was in the preservation and regeneration of the forests that had been so widely planted. Unlikely allies to the trees, they were the most surprising and one of the most comforting additions to the landscape. There were fields, sheltered by the woodlands and usually behind a house or cottage which would once have faced the road but which now all seemed to have turned around and to be offering back gardens to view, all well prepared for vegetables or stocked with chickens, goats, often a pig and sometimes an old tractor or two stripped of parts and nibbled by years of rust.

The people she saw nodded and exchanged polite greetings, whether from their gardens or the road on which they travelled variously by horse or tractor or their battery-assisted bikes and tricycles. The sanity of roads free of noise, smell and danger was overwhelming. It was a pleasure to be on such a highway and difficult to believe that not so far from here people had chosen for the awful opposite

Beth stopped in the afternoon and slept soundly. The debris shelter she had made for herself the night before would have graced any textbook on survival, kept off any amount of rain and even served in heavy frost, but for sleep it had been almost useless. Imagined hoards of insects and mice were still hidden in every rustle and their stirring had shod her imagination in red-hot shoes for all but the hour before dawn. She had spent most of the night thinking about Finn, imagining his dark eyes scanning the market, the look of disappointment settling when he was certain she would not be showing. She even fought the urge to decamp, to gather up her stuff and to seek him out in the marshes, to apologize and explain herself and her strange secrets. It was a relief to sleep by day with the prospect of another tortured night already very real. Now she slept effortlessly beneath apple trees in an overgrown orchard and woke to the unusual surprise of nothing having changed. The trees were still in bud, the sun was still warm, horses were still grazing in the next field and flicking off flies. She had left behind a world in which nothing remained the same, in which change had become a marketing ploy to feed the High Street and a disease to exhaust each customer, whilst here even the breathing of the trees and the movements of the clouds seemed reliable. Any change and disruption in this strange world would be caused by her, she thought, a little sadly, thinking of the flowers she had picked and abandoned. Even that would be nothing compared to the mess she had left behind, Aunt Kath being questioned, the house searched, lies in the newspapers again about her father and terrorism, administrators at school having to explain her away to their classes.

And all that whilst the birds sang, the horses grazed, and apple blossom littered the ground.

By late afternoon Beth was ready to start again on the construction of a shelter and the gathering of wood for a fire. Already she was weary of the process. There seemed little point when there was nothing to cook, no prospect of sleep and no fellowship to share at the fireside. She decided to confront her imagination. She chose a field corner not twenty yards from a derelict barn. She built the shelter, prepared a fire, nibbled on the last of the dried fruit she had saved by drinking far more than she was used to. Before dusk she left the camp intact, slipped into the woods and then embarked on a walk as circular as she could mange without breaking cover or straying too close to any of the farms in the area. She walked for almost two hours and approached her tiny camp from a new angle and in near darkness. She could make out a finger of smoke that had survived her inattention but the wedge-shaped shelter was lost in the dark. Carefully she picked her way to the barn and lay herself out on a nest of hay she had prepared earlier. She was exhausted and hungry. Whilst growing accustomed to the pleasant smear of dirt and dust on her skin and her clothing, her muscles ached for the old-fashioned relief of a warm bath. She might well have slept and made a nonsense of the experiment but for the insistence of the screech owl whose barn this was and whose frantically bobbing head and occasional scream seemed likely to occupy them both for the night. But when the owl left the barn and took up protest on the other side of the field Beth realized that she was only half its worries, that over there, beyond her fire and shelter, was someone or something else which had agitated the bird. She was right. She was being followed. The old world had not been shaken off, any more than the new one had accepted her arrival.

She sat up, rigid with fear, tiredness forgotten. She could sense rather than see a presence this side of an overgrown hedgerow. The owl had given her a clear marker but now she was certain that the shadows deepened and moved from one side to the other and sure enough the owl's agitation followed the dark suspicion. Whoever it was seemed intent on approaching Beth's camp from a point closest to cover. She knew it could have been anyone, any vagrant or traveller, even a local farmer or boy made suspicious by the fire. She desperately wanted it to be Finn, for the sake of her own safety, but dreaded such confirmation of his dubious motives. It was better to leave him innocently on Malvern market or riding naked in the marshes as a fond memory than have it confirmed that he was just one in a vast army of people who were to be feared and mistrusted and who would gladly come between herself, her father and the preservation of the Wildside. A twig snapped to confirm her worst fears yet strangely the owl gave up its vigil and disappeared towards the farm a mile or two away to attend to its business leaving Beth alone with the intruder. Then her first real sighting, a movement at ground level by the entrance to her shelter. Whoever it was was carefully checking to see if she was at home and asleep, might even now be reaching into the false comfort of her twigs and leaf litter to haul her into the open. The moon, which had been hidden, chose now to cut through the low cloud and send a pathway of light sleekly through the field and right into the recesses where Beth had imagined herself to be lying. The intruder minded not at all. He lifted his head casually towards the woods, his features exaggerated by the moon and its squadron of shadows. It was a fox, drawn by Beth's smells and the prospect of food, a fox which had so alerted the owl and so alarmed Beth that she was now in a bleak sweat of anguish and relief. She almost laughed. The beauty of the animal was overwhelming and the sharp innocence of its features melted her. She felt duped but glad of it, suddenly flattered that such a perfect creature had deigned to visit her imperfect camp and impressed with her own woodcraft and her ability to trick it. She would leave it to explore, there was nothing for it to take and she was content with her shelter in the barn. But then the fox looked to Beth's left and bolted. Its casual elegance was turned into a guilty lope and in seconds it had vanished, taking the moon with it.

Something had frightened it, and it had not been Beth. If this was terror she felt then no words were left to describe the sensation that followed when the hand reached out and took her firmly by the shoulder. Her inexplicable failure to scream saved the moment.

`I'm sorry. It's me.` Finn sounded as anxious as she did, as though he too was haunted by the movements of the night. `I'm sorry, Beth, relax. It' all right. It's Finn.`

Of course it was Finn. Who else could it have been? She had expected him all along. Finn had come to rescue her. Finn, in consultation with the good doctor, had brought her food and comfort, the smell of wood and garlic, he was here to ease her on her way. They would have sex, make a plan, share food. Or Finn had come to betray her, to follow her to her father, to act out a huge conspiracy. She slapped him. There was not enough light to show the livid mark on his cheek and she wanted to do it again but the sound of it was too hollow, too silly. Instead she glared as he took it in silence, accepting his deserts and seeking no explanation. Of course she should slap him, that was what people did when you scared them senseless. But knowing what to do next was harder. She wanted to burst out crying, to bury her head in his shoulder and be comforted, so badly did she want this and the warmth he seemed to exude even in the cold dark that she tore into him. `Bastard!` she said. `How dare you? You scared me to death. What the hell are you doing here anyway? Bastard!`

Finn knew better than to answer her straight away. `Let's go to the fire,` he said, rising up from the shadows, picking his way carefully through the barn. At the fireside he began to blow, teasing the embers to life, adding a few small twigs. Beth imagined the red mark on his cheek where she had hit him. She even imagined a look just short of tears in his eyes. She wanted to say sorry for the way she had reacted but to her annoyance Finn anticipated her. `Don't apologize,` he said, `You did well!` he rubbed his cheek by way of a compliment. `You were looking after yourself. That's good.`

`Not well enough. I didn't see you or hear you.` Perhaps that was why she was angry. He had out-crafted her. Invaded her illusion of control. `I had set a trap for you and was on the look out...`

`You were expecting me?`

She cursed herself for admitting as much but then decided to come clean. If he could creep up on her unawares and frighten her half to death then she would do the same to him, in her way, on her terms. `Yes, I was expecting you. I'm not stupid.` Confused, she could have admitted, frightened, but she had seized the initiative. `Who are you, Finn? What do you want?`

If her heart had not already gone out to him then now it certainly did. Sitting back from the fire that had now caught well he stared into its flames and looked as dejected and as down cast as Beth had previously felt. `I'm a failure,` he said, `that's who I am. I'm a complete failure, I don't deserve any better than a slap. I have been given a job to do and I've failed.`

`What job?` she asked, already guessing.

`To follow you.`

`Why?`

`To make sure you're not being followed.`

`And am I?`

`No you're not.`

`Wrong, Finn, I'm being followed by you. That's more than enough. And why? What do you want?`

He swallowed his wretchedness and looked apologetically at her. He lowered his voice even further, as though fearful of the fox or the owl. `I know who you are, Beth. I know who your father is.`

`So? What's that got to do with you?`

`I'm supposed to help you`

For a second she thought she may have missed the clues. Finn was her fondest dream, being stalked her worse nightmare. Finn belonged in her father's coded message. But it did not work like that, it was not so simple, no matter how badly she wanted it to be. `Why should I let you?` she asked, ` Why should I trust you? You creep up on me in the middle of the night, you poke your nose into my business, you even kit me out in your clothes. Why? Go on, why should I trust you?` She was desperate for him to win the argument and deserve forgiveness.

`I'm sorry.` he said quietly.

`For what?`

`I don't know. What do you want me to be sorry for?`

`I could give you a list, a long one.`

`I'm to ask you for some proof.` he said a little sheepishly.

`Of what?`

`Good faith.`

`No proof. No good faith. How is that?`

Finn tried to ignore the anger in her voice. `I was told you would probably bring a watch. Your mother's watch.`

`Who told you?`

`A friend of your father's.`

`You're a liar.`

`Alright, your father told me. He said you were sure to bring the watch. It's a kind of proof. `

`No watch. No proof. Now will you leave?`

Sensibly he ignored her, more out of confusion than policy. After a few moments she reached into her jacket and took out the watch. She passed it to him. He turned it and held it to the light in order to read the inscription.

`Mum's watch.` she said. `She was a nurse. It's the kind they pin on their aprons. It's the kind you wind up. Satisfied?`

Finn read the inscription on the back. `"If thou shouldst never see my face again, Pray for my soul. More things are wrought by prayer Than this world dreams of."` he read. `It's very beautiful.`

`It's sentimental crap.` she said. `Tennyson. He was good at it.`

`And do you?`

`Do I what?`

`Pray for her soul? Your mother's soul?`

`It's nothing to do with you,` she said, taking back the watch. `So you know about the watch, so what? Why should I trust you?

He surprised her. `You can't.` he said, `You mustn't. You mustn't trust any one. I only know you have to find your father. That's who I work for. That's who lots of us work for in different ways. But we have to keep him safe, we don't want him taken back. I'm just a foot soldier, a pawn. I don't need to know where he is, it wouldn't be safe. But I do have another job. It's one I don't quite understand.`

`Which is?`

`I have to make sure you *are* being followed, by the right person. By a man.`

`Followed! What man?!` Beth was horrified. Finn she could cope with, but the idea of another unknown shadow out there in the dark was too much. `What are you talking about?`

`I don't know. I mean, I know who the man is, I've seen him, but I don't know why, I don't know why your father wants him to follow you.`

`You don't know what you're talking about.` she snapped, `It's all bull shit. What do you mean, followed? The whole point is that I'm *not* followed!`

Finn could only shrug, he no more understood the plot than she did. Her outrage was perfectly reasonable.

Beth fell silent. She could not even begin to guess why her father had arranged such a thing, if indeed he had. The letter was explicit: trust no one, and Finn had said as much about himself; he was not to be trusted. But why would he make up such an unlikely detail?

`You said you wanted danger, Beth.` Finn reminded her. The light of the fire had touched his darkness with red and Beth thought of her hair and its betrayal of mixed history .

`Did I?`

`On the boat, you asked me if it was dangerous.`

`If I wanted it to be, you said. I don't want it yet. Not until I've slept. Not until I've got you and your stupid sister out of my hair.`

Finn ignored her.` I was also told to fix you up with a horse. I was even given money to...`

`Who by? You might be making all this up. You might have wanted me on Malvern market to hand me over to the sheriff or to make sure I could be followed easily.`

Finn nodded. There was little else for him to say. Beth was reacting exactly as he had hoped, cautious and defensive in the face of possible exposure. `I was told to give you this,` he said, reaching to an inside pocket. `It's a sign of good faith. They said you would understand it.`

`They`. Always `they`. She hated them. Why not use names like normal people? But `they` had prepared well. It was a jay's wing feather. Seeing it made her want to slap Finn a second time. He had won. He was on her side. She had been wrong in her suspicions. He was closer to her father than she was. He knew at least some of the rules and the extent of the game, far more than she did. Instead of slapping him she took the feather and closed her eyes. She imagined herself as a quite different person, neither better nor worse, just different, an alternative Beth-who-might-have-been, and the different Beth was able to reach out to Finn, and kiss him gently on the cheek she had hit. She opened her eyes and dismissed the fantasy, alarmed that he may have been reading her thoughts. Without another word she slipped into the dark interior of the debris shelter and fell into the deep life-saving sleep of the exhausted.

TWENTY FIVE

`Army intelligence.` Arch tapped the side of his nose wisely and attempted a wink. He was answering Clegg's questions. Somebody had smuggled dope into the arena and Arch was unusually mellow, the marbles caressing each other gently, the Adam's apple sliding smoothly about its business. `I worked in army intelligence. Never left my desk. Computer whiz-kid.` he exhaled slowly, a long and succulent plume into the bright morning air.

But Clegg was far from mellow and only half listening. Beth would be meeting with Finn on Malvern market about now. The trail was dead before he had even picked it up. His lucky lead via Machine Head would count for nothing now. The size and emptiness of the Wildside was beginning to suggest itself to him. This was Clegg`s second meeting with Arch in the exercise yard, his second morning in captivity. He was still too bruised to have thought about getting out, still too busy piecing together the impressions of scattered turkeys, smashed scramblers and a woman who smelled of milk. And now this. `So then the Game?` he asked, distracted.

`I'd been out of the army for three years before the Game found me.` Arch continued through smoke rings, `Yeah, sure, I thought of that one. I reckon they knew who they were getting hooked. You make a lot of weird friends in that business. When they get pensioned off they get bored. One game rolls into the next, that's all. It's kind of funny ending up here, though. These people blame it all on the likes of us. The computer stuff, its all our fault.`

`That's new to me.`

`Keep it that way. It sucks, but I'll tell you anyway. They say...`

`They?`

`They, them, the Wildside, the Green Men, the unwashed and mellow, the ones who dreamed it up, not this lot, this is just the lunatic fringe, Welsh Amish and English Ammonites, something like that. No, I mean the serious puppeteers. They like the landscape, yeah? Shared communal experience and all that crap, Shamanic masturbation and its role in the sustainable eco-orgasm, the lost heritage, natural work of art, heart and soul of the nation, blah, blah, blah. They say the destruction began in the 1960's when the good old binary age flipped its egg. People became fixed in this new habit of thinking, right, in straight lines, A and B, zero and one, that was their *inner landscape.*` He made the last two words sound mystical, as though reading from a crystal ball or a tarot deck. `The outer landscape got fucked up. The electric fence replaced the hedge, the drainage pipe replaced the ditch, the fly-over replaced the winding road. Kind of `game-over` for olde England, all that crap. People bought computers and went on-line and the trees came crashing down. Wheee!` Arch mimed the fall of a tree with his forearm and hand. `Did you know, Mr.Clegg, species became extinct in direct proportion to the sales of the big software companies? It's a fact! We sucked on the lush and bountiful Microsoft nipple while all those little bugs and beasties gave up the ghost. So you can do anything with statistics, right? World-wide-web meant a worldwide grid of plastic landscape. Sick, don't you think? Give me an electric fence and a flyover any time, Nat, easier to maintain. Less hassle, much less hassle. But they called it an illness, profoundly sick, terminal, the works. Symptoms? You want symptoms, Mr. Nathaniel Clegg? Climate, sea levels, floods, asthma epidemics, that kind of thing? You've got them, thick and fast. But, listen carefully, Mr. Nat, listen very carefully. That was just the outside, Nat, just on the outside. Wait for the sting in the tail. Wait for the big one. Wait for the New Age Big Bang! They invented another world, Nat, this one was not enough, they sent a colony off into space, into the depths of an inside world, inside your soul! The soul, for fuck's sake! What's a soul, Nat? Can you tell me? Can anyone tell me? Some kind of virus? Some kind of glitch built into the programme so you have to keep upgrading? God stuff, yeah? In my book God is the number one purveyor of bugged soft-wear in the fuckin' universe; not a monopoly, I'll grant you, but still number one. Still a major player. So floods bring a cure, okay? Sure? Wash away a few cities, float bits of Antarctica up north like battleships to beat the crap out of the suburbs, fill the sea with bloated bodies. Like all good illness, Nat, a great fever of floods and panic, sweeping away all those grubby little cities. But the inner illness, Nat, the soul-stuff, like the soul-illness, that was a different matter, the inner illness took on millions of names, man, shit, you must remember them, tabloid headlines for a day, but all the symptom of the same disease. Did you know, Mr. Nathaniel Clegg, that at the start of our proud century one in four children was receiving treatment for some form of mental illness? So fuckin what? I say, what are pills for anyway? But they didn't buy that, not these guys. Suicide was the main cause of adolescent death, they said. Big deal! They want to top themselves let them get on with it, Nat, so long as its not all over my carpet. Politicians told them they had never had it so good. But did they listen?`

Arch could have been talking about Bonny, about any one of tens of thousands who lived the Comfort Zone dream. Clegg was beginning to feel cold in his company but found the narrative gripping. There was no knowing how much of this history was real, how much of it was just Arch's cynical version of things. Yes he had heard most of this before, but Arch's spin on things was horribly compelling.

`Heal landscape and you heal yourself, Mr.Clegg. Heal yourself and the Garden of Eden re-seeds itself around you. The Civil War was part of the healing, yeah? Like a fever, an illness like none before it, each individual at war with themselves. If lifestyle makes you ill either change it or shut up. Those who wanted change, those who had a belly full of media, of denatured food, synthetic childhood, virtual relationships, they went west, right? They came here. They spawned the Wildside, used the new surveillance technologies to break away, then covered themselves in shit. The rest went east, reached for the handset and the crisps, worshipped the great cultural anesthetics, waited for the electro-magnetically-induced cancer to herald the final episode of the ultimate soap opera. This is not new, Mr.Clegg. Tell me you're not hearing this for the first time?`

`You give it your own slant, Arch.`

`You're a diplomat, Mr.Clegg, we could work well together. Court cases, Mr.Clegg, they were next, after the floods, after the ice-caps got the squits, court cases, about mobile phone wave lengths and the labeling of food and the building of roads and imported margarine. Court cases raised the financial stakes more than a little bit. The President of the U.S.A. spreads shit on his breakfast toast then so must you, Mr.Clegg, then so-must-you. Sheep and goats ended up using different currencies.`

`So where does that leave you and I, Arch? What does that mean for our hosts as you call them.`

`Difficult to judge, Mr.Clegg. Extremists have clouded the issue. Always do, in my experience. Landscape Bolsheviks, the Ayatollahs of Conservation, the Millennial Luddites, the National Trust's Militant Wing, all wankers, Mr.Clegg, serial wankers, ten-times a day, that bad. And the Arkites? Not many of them, Mr.Clegg, thankfully few, but their inner landscape is not one you can ride motorbikes through, Mr.Clegg, certainly not. Strange world. At the end of the day you're either Green-man or Machine-Man, right?` he mused almost to himself.

`Green-Man or Machine Man?

`Machine Man,` Arch held out one hand as though affecting an introduction, `Wants to rule the world with machines, control everything with machines. Amoebae becomes ape, ape becomes man, man becomes machine, OK? Earth equals Planet Machine, the Death Star, right? No room for humans in the end, Nat, not efficient, see?`

`Or?`

`Green-Man,` he held out the other hand, `Or Bird-Man, Plant-Man, Tree-Man, whatever. It's either or, Nat, a war to the death, they can't live together. When men listen to birds or paint pictures of trees or grow roses they get turned off machines, they stop buying, they stop devoting themselves to Planet Machine. Bad news. Or if men get off on machines, Nat, the other choice, if men get off on machines they've got no time and patience for living things, because living things only show up how pathetic, crap and feeble the machines really are. Can't have that, Nat, bad publicity, bad for sales. No. Sorry. It's a war to the death.`

`So whose side are you on, Arch?`

The marbles stopped. The last smoke ring drifted away. Arch was shaking his head with no intention of answering such a straight forward question. `They couldn't have done it without us.`

`Done what?`

`Created this place.`

`If you say so.`

`I do say so, Nat, and you'd do well to listen. How did it all happen?`

`Tell me. I'm listening.`

`The whole constitution was a web thing. The first constitution in history created for the people, by the people, on the net. And then the game.`

`Another game, Arch?`

`Sure. Don't take the piss, another game. A God game. Like SimCity. You've played it, every one has. These guys put one out for free. Brilliant graphics. Except it was different from the real one. The real one you had to keep taxes low, encourage business, that kind of thing, very American parameters, that's what we call them, Nat, parameters. You screw people and let people screw each other and your SimCity takes off. These guys changed the parameters, Down loaded a game on the world where things only got better if you got rid of cars and planted fuckin trees. Very popular, big time. They dreamed up this constitution and bred it into the game, game changed as the constitution changed. The Wildside was born in cyberspace, Nat, make no mistake. The

Wildside is one of ours, one that got away, that's all. They don't know who they owe it all to, that's the only problem. Best virtual game ever.`

`You're fond of `they`, Arch, `they` this and `they` the other. Who is `they` in the end? Who wrote the programme?`

`Don't know,` said Arch, sounding genuinely sad. `Don't know. Wish I did. I'd kiss his arse to know the rules he plays by.`

Arch removed his glasses to clean them and exposed a face suddenly ten years younger, half boy, half embryo, unformed and unfocused eyes awash in pale watery flesh. He got his instructions from the Black Knight, he said, and was trying to find King Arthur. As far as he knew it was the only game with tie-ins on this side of the Line, which was why he had been so anxious to place Clegg, to explain him on his own terms. He had been playing for nearly two years and was not even close to either winning or losing. Clegg was a disappointment to him, his questions showing again and again that he did not understand the unreal world of the full-time gamer. Arch was in another league and Clegg was not sure he wanted to keep up.

`So is King Arthur real?` Clegg asked at one point.

`He might be, he might not, it doesn't really matter.` Arch sighed, hardly believing that anyone could be so stupid. `Only the other players are *real* real And some of those are made up. There's two of me, for a start.`

Of course, thought, Clegg, as many as you like.

`I'm Arch and I'm also Keith. Other gamers don't know. Keith's up near Appleby, horse-trading. Keeps people off my scent. But I don't know if they know. Some of them might. Or they might think Keith's for real and I'm not. Suits me. It does get confusing.` Clegg was relieved to hear it, glad to know he was not the only one made dizzy by the convolutions of Arch's world. `Take this witch in Cardiff, for example.` Arch seemed to do just that, gripping the evil nonentity between first finger and thumb, piercing into her with his vast lenses. ` She's brilliant, got to hand it to her. The tart laid a whole load of past stuff into my biography, virtual, okay, one day I'm well adjusted, the next day I'm the victim of childhood abuse. Can you imagine how that feels? I can't undo it. The bitch has recreated me overnight. Suddenly I'm unhinged because of what my dad did to me twenty years ago. It would make the old man turn in his grave.`

`Virtual or real?`

`Virtual, man! Come on, keep track, Mr.Clegg. We're talking virtual here, I created my virtual dad and he's a great guy, no way he'd do what she made up. No, my real dad was a shit. That's another story. The Cardiff bitch is owed one. You agree?`

`I agree, Arch.` It was easier that way.

`I've put an AIDS contract on her. I've bought in a guy in the Cardiff area. Expensive. Virtual AIDS, real cash, but it might pay off. This witch sleeps around. Frigid as shit in the real world but we mixed up her genes, goes like a rabbit now.`

`So how does she get AIDS?`

But Arch only laughed, full of sympathy for Clegg's struggle. `Lets just say its a virus within a virus. One real, the other virtual.`

`But the money is real?` asked Clegg, returning to a point that had troubled him from the start. How could the game down or off load money from Arch's account without the System knowing and raising the alarm?

`My first question, Nat, my very first question. I told you, right from the start they doubled my account. I drew it down, moved it around, made sure it was real. No doubt about it. But when the stakes got higher these boys got clever. Now you're talking gold, man, real gold.`

Now you're talking bullshit, Clegg wanted to say, now your fantasy doesn't fool me. `If it makes you happy, Arch.` Clegg conceded, not bothering to hide his contempt.

But Arch only laughed. `I don't expect you to believe it, Nat. And I don't care. So now we're both happy. But I'm telling you, if I find King Arthur ahead of the other shits then I'm one million, count my fingers, Nat, read my lips, one million in gold bullion up on the non-believers.`

Chasing imaginary shadows for imaginary reward. Clegg looked at Arch's bright but watery eyes and zealot's grin with a sudden feeling of dislocation. At least the poor bastard admitted it was all a game and at least he had some rules to play by. Clegg wondered whether it was him or Arch who was mad, which of them both would sound most convincing if called on to plead sanity. `And have you got a lead, Arch?` Clegg asked, sympathy mixed with genuine curiosity.

`What if I have, man? You going to rip me off? Don't trust anyone, Arch's first rule. Arch's only rule!` but then he laughed, the intensity in his eyes turned to amusement, the Adam's apple thrust taut against his throat like an alien trying to escape its host. `Yeah, I've got a lead, Nat. You're my friend, right? Once a squaddie always a fuckin' loser, right? We have to stick together, Nat, or they'll grind us down. I've got a lead. These freaks meet once a year in a special place, place changes, freaks stay the same. Like, I'm talking serious druids, man, like weird stuff they'd lock you away for at home, like praying and chants and stuff. Macbeth`s witches on speed. You got the picture? They call it the Valley of Healing. Can you believe it? They heal a valley, for fuck's sake! Freaks, poets, vestal virgins, all these guys with bare feet. Arch thinks if King Arthur's not with those dudes to dance on Midsummer's Day then he's nowhere, you know what I mean?` But Arch could see from Clegg's frown that he was not sure of anything anymore. `It's okay, Nat, you stick with Arch,` he said holding out his hand and the two glass balls. `Arch plus Nat equals one hell of a ride. And at least you know I've got my marbles.`

TWENTYSIX

By late afternoon Beth had tired of asking Finn questions he could or would not answer. She had moved on to her next challenge. The pony was a Connemara called Whisper, a beautiful pale brown mare with hidden layers of white, which seemed to lift it up and give its trot an extra lightness. Although she had never ridden before the pony's forgiving nature and Finn's patience, matched by her determination not to look a fool in front of her trainer all combined splendidly. They had found a large patch of fallow ground punctuated by clumps of gorse and hazel but very level under foot and here spent most of the day as Beth was introduced to the basics of riding. Before dusk, with Beth struggling to hide how sore and stiff she had become, Finn, to her surprise, took his farewells. He had brought her sausage and fresh bread and fairly deluged her with final tips and last pieces of advice, anything to delay the moment when he must leave her alone. They neither of them found it easy, which made them curt and matter-of-fact with each other.

Although Finn had assured her he would not be following her and nor, sadly, was anyone else, another uneasy night lay ahead for Beth. Again sleep only came close to dawn when the breathing of the horse and the soft hiss of the logs were joined by the first songbird. At least Beth slept late, waking to the sun full on her face and the horse a hundred yards away happily foraging. She was appalled at how stiff her back and legs had become over night and the thought of riding almost made her sick, but once she had hauled herself up on to Whisper's back and taken the reigns in her hand she felt once more the thrill of her Quest, if such it was, and felt suddenly an enormous wave of gratitude to Finn for having sought her out, despite herself. Even if he was only doing a job, being a pawn in a complex game, he was doing it with care. She remembered how hard she had slapped him and she remembered the imagined kiss and she found herself smiling at the memory of both.

`Go where the crowds gather` her father's strange letter had said, an alarmingly vague piece of advice and a subject on which she had only been able to question Finn indirectly. She had asked after markets and Finn's sketched map gave her the clear option of Leominster one day followed by Ludlow the next. Both lay more or less to the north west and seemed as likely starting points as any.

In Ludlow a pleasant looking man in his early thirties approached her as she sat on a doorstep watching the market. He was selling pies and gave her one for free. You are not the man following me, she told herself, you are not important, and for that alone she felt inclined to talk and glad of his company. He was a dead-end, quite neutral and therefore a welcome relief. He seemed surprised when she accepted his invitation to drink coffee in a quiet café and even more surprised when she asked to see his bakery and how he made his pies. At every step his innocence and lack of involvement in any plot increased his attraction to Beth and she was happy to cast him the look, to feel him snag on the bait of her body. She flirted with him on the way to his home and of course he started to fumble over her hemp clothing in the dusty quiet of the bakery. She could have ended it there, she knew his type, he would have accepted her terms, but her need for reassurance was strong and she enjoyed the feeling of power as it returned. Finn's indifference had made her doubt it's universal appeal. At home it had been her only strength, her only means of manipulating the world. It was good to know that it was still potent. But outside of the plot, she reminded herself, only where it didn't seem to matter. Beth suspected from the man's haste that there was a wife or girl-friend somewhere in his life but what of it? They were using each other for comfort and the man, if nothing else, was gentle, though not hesitant as he undressed her and touched her, following the remnant lines of her ash ritual. She thought of Finn and the veins on his forearms. `Fuck you.` she muttered under her breath, which the baker took as encouragement but which she directed at the middle distance beyond the man's hunched back where Finn might have stood, watching in torment. She sensed him there in the shadows, sullen with lust, cursing his missed opportunity and to punish him she encouraged the baker with the kind of sounds and movements men seemed to like. But suddenly the illusion was shattered. Beyond the imagined Finn was a real poster on a real wall. It was advertising a touring attraction, the text embraced by the shape of a hot-air balloon. She strained to read the date and details and as they formed the baker lost all innocence and all appeal. He was no longer removed from the scheme of things, no longer a neutral space in which to pause. The pie, the coffee, the sex, all were suddenly implicated, all had led to this, the next piece of the riddle. The baker took the scratching of her nails as a sign of approval and her sudden change of mood as typical of a woman satisfied. She pushed him off, grabbed her clothes, ran to the poster, which she ripped from the wall and dressed hastily. `Thanks for the pie`, she said, mindless of any irony. Outside in the street she found a quiet place to read. It was advertising a touring attraction which was to be seen at several locations in the area, `depending on suitable winds` it claimed theatrically, the text printed within the outline of a balloon, a hot-air balloon, the basket of which contained several figures in silhouette, each acting out Beth's dream. It had not been Finn watching her from the shadows of the room, she realized, it had not been poor wild-eyed Finn burning there with envy, angry with desire. It had been Sam quietly pointing the way.

She found them two days later. By now she and Whisper had found a pace to suit them both and Beth had calculated rightly that the performance at Walcot Park to the south of the Long Mynd would be comfortably within her reach. She camped on a hilltop overlooking the valley and the next morning watched, thrilled and anxious, as people began to approach from all directions. Horses, traction buses, walkers, cyclists by the score, everyone in party mood, or at least she imagined, observing from a distance. At last Beth approached the park with its flag-waving mansion and sentinel trees. Three or four hundred people were stood or sat around a large circle. Yellow and black tents were behind the crowd and a roped-off path linked the tents to the arena. Beth held back for a time, made nervous by the crowd, but soon their cheering and good humour drew her a little closer. Some children had climbed the huge chestnut trees on the edge of the arena in order to see over the crowd and Beth pulled herself up to share their view.

There was no sign of a hot air balloon. A single rider was crossing the circle enclosed by the crowd. It was a woman, not young but very handsome and strongly built. She was wearing a strange hat on which was fixed some kind of upright tuft. On her raised wrist was a beautiful hawk, possibly a peregrine, lost in worlds of its own. On reaching the centre of the circle the rider stopped and in one movement flicked the hawk from her wrist and fixed something to the tuft on her hat. The hawk bobbed lightly away, two or three wing beats lifting it effortlessly beyond the edge of the field and directly above Beth. In the flick of a wing it changed from nonchalant to lethal. With a stoop that brought a gasp from the crowd and a flurry of the air the hawk darted towards the circle where the rider was now cantering in tight circles. It was the first of several fly-pasts, each one bringing vast appreciation from the stunned audience until finally the bird grabbed the bait from the rider's hat a second before she reined in the horse and reared back dramatically. The snort of the horse and the shouted commands of the woman were drowned by the clapping and cheering of the crowd. The hawk had returned silently to a perch on the circle's edge where it was now tearing its reward vigorously.

The lady on the horse was wearing an outfit of black and yellow squares, as were half a dozen others on the edge of the circle. It was two of these who now stepped forwards, each holding a magnificent eagle, a sea eagle if Beth knew her birds.

The creatures seemed to ignore each other and the crowd but cast repeated looks up at the sky as though weighing up the odds of an escape or looking to settle some bet concerning the weather. Then the crowd, Beth included, saw what the birds had been seeking and a great gasp went up followed by applause. Beth's eyes almost filled with tears. Her father was alive and well, her father's reach was assured and comforting, even in separation, for there was the proof of his wisdom and his sense of fun and, most touchingly, of his knowledge of her. A hot air balloon appeared from beyond a ridge of trees. The crowds were gathered to witness a part of her dream and it was here somewhere, somehow, beyond her worst nightmare that the contact would be made, or at very least the clues would become concrete and her path would be clearly marked. The balloon was more than a stunt or the pride of a family circus; it was a talisman, like the orange balloon that had drifted across the motorway so long ago, proof of something far more important.

It was low enough for the three figures in its basket to be seen waving to the crowd. Above the basket the balloon itself was livid with the red and orange of a huge eagle's face, its massive eyes and beak seeming to threaten the crowd silently. As the beast floated closer the black and yellow livery of its crew could be distinguished, as could the fact that the smallest of the three, a child, surely, was sat on the basket's edge, dangling his or her feet sickeningly into the air. Almost unnoticed by the crowd the two eagles had been loosed and were now circling their lazy way higher and higher into the blue, seeming to ignore the balloon and each other.

A sharp jet of flame followed by its deep roar gave the final adjustment to the balloon's height. Next came a long and eerie throat-call half red Indian and half throttled from one of the crew in the basket.

The crowd watched in disbelief as the eagles, each in their own good time, began their descent. First one and then the second approached the balloon effortlessly, its orange eyes seeming to forbid their disobedience. They landed each in turn on the basket's rim and their weight was made apparent by the slight swing and tilt of the whole apparatus. The balloon was now two hundred feet above the crowd but sufficiently back from its edge for all to see clearly what happened next. Even those who had seen the spectacle before gasped as the child leapt from the basket and the two eagles rolled casually into the air. For a second they adjusted their flight as the harness, only now apparent, lost its slack and the twin straps the eagles were clutching pulled tight on either side of the child. The balloon had belched once more and was pulling away, the yellow and black clad infant was waving and smiling, the two eagles were dropping steadily to the circle's centre and the crowd was cheering and clapping in a great and astonished body of sound as they delivered their cargo, not simply to the centre of the circle but to the arms of a second lady rider, the child's mother perhaps, as she trotted bare back around the circle.

Beth wanted to share it. She wanted to see Sam's face as the eagle girl descended, as the hawk swooped across the circle, she did not want to keep it as her own private memory. She wanted to be the little girl, not for the sake of applause or bright colours but for the chance to trust her life to those birds, to show them with one simple step into empty air how magnificent and powerful but above all how trusted they were. She wanted to reach past the butcher and so many like him to the dream of weightlessness. She wanted to look down on circles of people, to see the patterns they made in the grass and to look down into their marveling faces and then, in the flick of a wing, to be free of them, to belong to the air.

She climbed from the tree, elation turning quickly to doubt. On the ground she sat heavily on the grass and took her mother's watch from her pocket and watched as the audience started to drift away. Now what? Her dream was there clearly to be seen. But the nightmare? And to whom should she drop hints and clues about her lost flute, who amongst all these people was watching and waiting, perhaps as anxiously as she, for the code to be broken? And where was Finn when she needed him? Nursing his cheek she hoped. She read the inscription on the back of the watch. I have never prayed, she might say to him, I have never prayed and never will, but if you want to pray for me, if you really have to, then do it now. But never let me know.

TWENTYSEVEN

Arch was in poetic mode. He only knew the one, he said, and its hour had come. `They'll look for you by moonlight, though hell should bar the way!` he chuckled as Arkite guards shunted them from one room to another. Clegg was his highwayman, hunted by the red-coats, some black-eyed Bess was out there, waiting, longingly. That they came at noon made no difference to Arch, he seemed to know what they could expect, seemed happy with the confusion and quite fearless. Only the threat of rehab worried him which apparently meant rehab from image addiction and which would involve weeks without TV and film. `They make you draw and paint,` he said, in horrified tones, `they make you *observe, talk, listen* and *commune.* `They make you stare at the fuckin soil until it stares back,` he said, `they make you stroke trees until you get a hard on. It's brain washing,` he conceded, `But I want mine filthy, just the way it is.`

Clegg and Arch were amongst the lucky ones. They and a handful of others were led as a chain gang from the arena down to the Market Square of the adjoining town. There was a small crowd gathered for the show, of which Clegg was apparently a feature. He looked beyond them to the turf-roofed houses and the inter-active shops, he watched the horses and the electric buses, he heard music from a solitary instrument and the unlikely sounds of laughter. Tea-break at a film-set, he thought. Somewhere around the corner was a cowboy film in the making, or a documentary about 1950's England, or a science-fiction film or a feature on African migrants trading drums and jewelry. But no one was filming. No one had costumes to remove or real homes to go to. Behind the town hills closed in, the slow invasion of trees waiting to claim every last public space.

A man was speaking, some kind of clerk or court official, enjoying the highlight of his year. He seemed ignorant of the trees that menaced behind him, blind even to the bit-part actors who pretended to listen. His sermon was long and tedious and made much of the virtues of living in the Dark Ages, often by reference to the bible, most of which seemed to mention animals far more than people, Clegg noticed, and people only when considered as 'tribes'.

With the bleak sermon over the prisoner's crimes were read out, each in turn, whilst the crowd muttered, moaned or cheered in accord with the punishments on offer. Clegg half expected a director to leap up from somewhere, to shout `cut` and to regale the crowd to do it all again, from the top, this time with feeling. But nobody obliged. The extras were for real, or as real as anything else Clegg could see, including the punishments. One man, a shoplifter, was to be confined to the stocks for a day and a night. Two others, whose crime was brawling in a public place were fixed up with arm-hobbles, metal calipers which prevented them from bending their elbows. For the next week, it was decreed, and in public view, they could starve or feed each other. Clegg felt a glimmer of respect for the Arkites as he tried to imagine the two men spooning soup into the other's mouth. Toilet arrangements would also need a high level of co-operation.

Arch and Clegg were last. Clegg had been surprised to see his manic marble-fondler in deep conversation with one of their guards earlier in the morning and even for laughter to have been traded between them. It was not difficult to imagine Arch negotiating some deal with their captors, ingratiating himself like a tapeworm into the judicial bowel movements of the Arkites to score virtual points which he could eventually exchange for a shield of invincibility. But not yet. Perhaps he had traded points to be with Clegg, because the leg hobbles were uncomfortably real. Clegg had seen them used in the army on prisoners. It was only necessary to restrict one leg in order to have the prisoner at the mercy of the key-holder. One band fitted around the upper thigh, one each just above and below the knee and one at the ankle. The same key locked his and Arch's calipers, a key that vanished into the deep pocket of the clerk.

With no further explanation Clegg and Arch were led from the square, swinging their new legs awkwardly and to the amusement of those who remained to watch. They were helped onto the back of a cart that was loaded high with rounds of cheese and bolts of muslin. The cart's driver turned and nodded. He was an ageless man, anywhere between the mid forties and late sixties. His skin was like finely scrubbed leather and his eyes were strangely impassive, either all-seeing or else windows to a dulled intelligence. His smile was friendly but he had no need of conversation, preferring the fellowship of a tobacco pipe. He drew the horse and cart out of the town, Clegg anxious to memorize the details of the clerk's appearance and the lay out of the streets in which the key to his hobble would somewhere reside, Arch waving to the bored crowd, no doubt imagining himself some kind of celebrity.

By early afternoon drizzle had set and Clegg's self-doubt was palpable. The deeper he got into this wretched place the less it seemed likely that he would find his target, let alone bring him out alive. The appeal of Bonny's world was suddenly strong. Slumped on a couch, heavy air reassuring with the smells of alcohol and rendered fat, blood-stream bathed in a cocktail of valium, serotonin and retilin, the senses numbed with bright images and senseless noise, the mind set on zero, everything warm, dry and apathetic. What would Clegg have done if offered an exchange? He dismissed the thought, moved on to his task. Would they pay for John Savage dead? He doubted it. Danny had said it was the man's knowledge they wanted, there would be no warm welcome at the border for Clegg with a corpse. But how did you get someone out against their will? You couldn't bundle him into the back of a van over here or just pay the local heavies to do the job. Nothing Clegg had learned on the street or in the army would be of much use in these wilds. The gold from the lining of his coat was gone. His maps, like pornography, had been confiscated to judgmental sighs and frowning. Only his telescope had survived the scrambler accident and Arkite regulations. He would have to invent his own rules of engagement. He would have to escape overland which meant horse and cart for discretion or something illegal for speed. Best of all, as they had taught him in the army, was when your victim wanted to come with you, but not even Clegg had that amount of charm. But why worry, he reminded himself. By now Beth would have made her rendezvous with Finn, she would have acquired her horse and disappeared into the wilds. There would be no finding John Savage that way.

A few hours later and with the drizzle turned to steady rain Clegg saw a monastery sign-posted ahead. Arch had been strangely quiet all afternoon, hunched miserably under an inadequate poncho but as they entered the monastery grounds he peered out and showed some interest. The order was housed in an old manor and in another time and another place it might have passed itself off as an old-people's home or a hospice or even a commune, where now it was all three and more besides. There were plenty of old people sitting around in the conservatory playing cards, chess or piano, plenty of elderly men and women working in the large walled garden, despite the rain, and several more in the huge green house which had been turned into a weavery and where beautiful rugs and hangings were slowly taking shape. But there were also young people around and children, not visiting but part of the whole. Further away from the buildings and partly hidden by trees was a strange shanty town of tepees, benders, tree houses and yurts in and around which Clegg could see only teenagers.

`That's the place to be.` grinned Arch, speaking for the first time in hours. `A DIY initiation centre. Rites of passage. You want to get laid, Nat, that's the place for you. You want to find God, there he is. Or one of him.`

`One of him, Arch?`

`Two Gods, Nathaniel Clegg. I've always been a faithful worshipper. One for each religion.`

`Two religions?`

`My dick and my stomach. You can't quite worship them both at the same time. I recommend about five minutes in between.`

`With this on?` Clegg asked, tapping the caliper.

Arch shrugged and sank back into his poncho, theology over.

The tree houses were linked with ropewalks and several large totem poles decorated the site. Music was coming from a small group around an open fire playing flute and drums.

They were passing by when a lean and wide-eyed girl of about eighteen waved to the driver of the wagon and came over to talk. She wore the tight hose that seemed in fashion, all her curves exposed, together with a leather waistcoat and cuffs of lace frill, like something from *Robin Hood*, thought Clegg. She nodded to the two in the back, unconcerned by their obvious status. She was telling the man that most of the `village` were sleeping in the mountains tonight, preparing a sweat lodge and ritual for two of their number who had decided to marry. Did he want his two `guests` to sleep in the lodge, the large central teepee, there was soup and bread, she said, if they wanted it. Not now, the man said, Agnes would be waiting.

The girl smiled at Clegg and Arch. `We'll be neighbours,` she said, `If Ralph here hits you too often, you're welcome to escape to us. If there is anything you want.`

`To suck your tits,` Arch muttered, scarcely under his breath. Clegg kicked him and nodded to the girl. Yes there was something Clegg wanted right now. He wanted to run bare-foot with the pack on the mountains or explore their maze of tree-houses and swing from tree to tree, or else blank out to Bonny's world. But this he kept to himself, taking it all in, the lay-out of the estate, the suggested layers of social nuance. There were no families in boxes by the look of things, no easy allocation of labels to foreheads. He wanted to try their world out for size, without Arch gabbling away.

Within a mile of the encampment and still within the rich estate of the monastery they arrived at a farmyard full of poultry and free-range pigs and with white doves perched dream-like on eaves. The driver climbed down stiffly, walked round to the two men and introduced himself. Ralph Bailey, he said, cheese-maker. He hoped they weren't too wet. Good to start as they probably had to continue, he added. He eyed his new acquisitions with a mixture of curiosity and sympathy. He was clearly a man of few words but one who felt nothing awkward in his own silences.

Looking at the house, the trees behind it, the deep hills beyond, Clegg had the feeling of sinking deeply, of peeling back more and more layers of the Wildside's mystery. No maps, no sign-posts, no reference points, the place was growing bigger by the minute, huge in his imagination, limitless as only the sky had been in his previous life. The feeling hardened when from the farmhouse a woman emerged and Clegg had the sudden conviction that he had misled Arch and himself all along. Of course he was in a game, why hide the fact? Of course there were rules, it was just that no one had bothered to explain them to him, or perhaps he dreamed them up for himself in the night. He had certainly dreamt this woman, just as he had smelled warm milk when she was close to him, just as he remembered her jewelry. It was the girl-woman who had cut him down from the noose, the one who had tended his wounds so well and advised him to grovel. Ralph Bailey's daughter or a much younger wife? It was not clear, nor did it matter. What mattered most and what put Clegg on his guard was that she showed no surprise at seeing him, only the usually agile range of friendly expression around the dancing eyes and the insolent, suggestive smile. She was introduced as Agnes. She wiped her hands on her old dungarees and shook hands first with Arch and then with Clegg, before apologizing, gesturing to the calipers. `It's not our idea of justice,` she said. `The Arkites are odd but they keep their word.` But she could tell from the expression of her two new charges that very few words had been exchanged back there in the town, certainly not enough to be either kept or broken. `You are to work for us,` she explained. `Didn't they tell you? After a couple of weeks, if we have no complaints that is, they'll unlock you and you can be off. If you want.` She added this last whilst fixing Clegg with a sideways look that left him eager for his smashed shades. She laughed at his discomfort, bright, like water on a dry day, but also matter of fact, just as she had been when she had found him dangling from a tree. `I'm glad to see they didn't fix that thing to your bad leg.` she added as an aside to Clegg, an acknowledgement of whatever they had shared those few mornings ago.

The two men followed Agnes awkwardly towards the house, Ralph behind them. He smelled of cheese, Clegg noticed, not mature cheese but of some halfway stage, warm and sweet, not unpleasant. They stopped in a cobbled courtyard and took in their surroundings. This was the kind of house for which the Wildside was famous and which would have been inconceivable at home. Beams and tree trunks came to an apex above a high triangle of windows ahead of them. From the apex the roof spiraled down in two or three linked terraces of turf to the walls of bright pink cob. There were guinea pigs grazing the roof and a large fire-pit in the courtyard with a spit across it and tree stump benches around in a circle. As the south-facing front was all glass it afforded a view of both floors, much of the space full of vats and churns and hanging linen. Clegg imagined he saw Agnes' room, perfectly bare but for the rib cage and vertebrae of some huge marine mammal, possibly a whale, hanging down from the angled wooden ceiling. In the main room into which they were led a table and a handful of chairs battled unsuccessfully for space amongst the rubble of Ralph Bailey's industry. The place was ripe with the smells of milk, pig dung, wood smoke and last year's apples. Each chair was unique, handcrafted, bright with polished wood and wax and each with its own resident cat. The table was a massive hand-carved slab of oak and was cluttered with cheese samples and half-empty bottles of port. Agnes attended a tile-lined stove, rings and bracelets caught by its sudden glow and Clegg recalled her fingers and saw again how beautiful they were and how completely at home she seemed to be in her compact body.

`Do you like the house?` she asked.

`I like the house.` said Clegg, careful not to say he had seen nothing like it before in his life.

`I designed it.` she assured him.

`You're an architect?`

She laughed. `What a strange idea.` she said. `No, I designed it when I was at school.`

Clegg knew he was about to be challenged again in an unspoken way. He decided to ignore the house and its beautiful, hand-made furniture, its brightly glazed crockery, its rich wall hangings and water colour paintings. Wildsiders bought nothing in boxes, it was said, Wildsiders had everything made, by hand, uniquely for, or by, themselves. All this he would ignore, but in looking around the room he came across a different snare. Above the hearth was an embroidered quote. He read it, keen to place these two people in a context he could understand. It was a mistake. Agnes was watching him, feeding off his discomfort.

`*Welcome to the Land of the Grail. Where each man is a Wilderness unto himself. Where each man may seek the Grail castle. Where each man may attain to the Grail. Where each man may bring life to the Wasteland of his own Soul.*`

Shit, he thought, more zealots, but she looked at him as though challenging him to comment. Her eyes were laughing but her mouth gave nothing away. Each capital letter in the text was like a thump on the table, a call to change before it was too late, but here were no other signs of fanaticism or religious excess. On the contrary. The table had its whiskey bottle, the cupboard had its DVR, his hosts, apparently, had a sense of humour because Ralph Bailey had poured them all a glass of port and was proposing a toast to the Second Flood, which was the Arkite's main article of faith, but he did so with a wink in their direction.

Clegg was suddenly alarmed by the suspicion that he might feel at home here, in so far as that was possible with a cage of iron strapped to his leg and in the company of a man who thought he was tracking King Arthur. Even the pigs coming in at the front door or the stove backfiring smoke into the kitchen had a certain charm after the grim little world of the Arkites.

`They don't mean any harm.` Agnes added in defense of the extremists.

Are you his daughter or his wife? Clegg wanted to ask. Do you sleep with him or do you sleep alone? There was no placing her just by the way she spoke. She would be independent even as a wife, it surely did not matter who she belonged to by law. Of course they had no laws, Clegg reminded himself, only the landscape thing.

`Short of taking my head off, no harm at all` he suggested.

`Short of taking his head off.` Arch repeated in a show of solidarity. `No harm at all, Miss Agnes, no harm at all. Do you sleep by yourself?` he suddenly asked, to Clegg's embarrassment but the amusement of Ralph and Agnes Bailey.

`I sleep with whoever I want.` she answered with a laugh. `Which is probably more than you can say.`

`Put me on the list.` said Arch, unfazed.

`You're straight in there at number ninety seven.` she said, raising her glass as though in a fresh toast. `But the Arkites,` she repeated, apparently serious again, `they only mean you to work off your debt.`

`What debt?` Clegg asked.

`We'll all be in their debt,` she answered, amused by how quickly Clegg had bristled, `If they save us from the flood.`

`Alleluia!` wailed Arch, making them all jump, waving his hands gospel style, `Alle-fuckin-luia!`

Agnes rolled the port in her glass and took a piece of cheese from one of the many rounds on the table. She knew that Clegg was in danger of taking her seriously even if Arch had no intention of doing so and decided to play him a while longer. `Doesn't matter that sea levels are steady,` she added. `It's the tide of moral filth that matters. Moral filth,` she repeated, goading Arch with a sharp glare. `Technology and the abuse of nature set it all in motion, you know. Machines. Like your bike, Mr.Clegg.` She raised her glass as though in a toast. `Now it's time to honour God through nature and build Arks.`

`Build Arks?` Arch exclaimed, calling her bluff, perhaps sensing a rival game. `What might you mean, Miss, *build arks*? And will there be room for me?` He had stopped gyrating the marbles, as if they too were intent on the answer and a stay of execution. `We could share a stable. Repopulate the earth.`

`Not real ones.` Ralph Bailey assured him, speaking slowly, his voice heavy with pipe smoke but with a boyish glimmer of mischief. `Communities of pure and simple souls. Islands of moral rectitude in a sea of corruption. Oases of culture in a desert of degradation.` He spelled it out methodically, as though reading from a shopping list. It wasn't clear if he was quoting or poking fun. `There's an Ark above the Beacon,` he continued, `Inside the old Iron Age hill fort. Twenty families, fifty or so people. Fine people. Pure, simple, free from corruption.`

`And all as miserable as shit!` Agnes added, stealing his punch line, downing the port as her father dissolved into laughter.

Clegg conceded defeat. He and Arch had been nicely confused by their new hosts. He noticed the lines which ran out from Agnes's eyes when she smiled and how they made her look more, not less attractive. She was very pretty in a well-worn sort of way and her untidy hair and mobile eyes made her look comfortable, the sum far greater than any single part. She might even have been plain as a teenager but would be stunning by forty. Her clothes were simple and dull which made it all the more strange that she wore an exquisite necklace and matching ankle ring of gold chain, real gold if Clegg knew a good thing when he saw it. He did a quick calculation of its market value. He was impressed. She slept with whosoever she wanted, he reminded himself.

`No more jokes.` Ralph suggested, mildly, as though this one would serve them for a day or two. `I've got work to do.` this to himself, the quiet fire of his private discipline addressed.

Agnes played the housewife. She gave them soup and bread and followed it with tea, biscuits and the ubiquitous cheese. She then set them to work, unloading the cart, moving cheeses and boxes around endlessly. Next she showed them to a room in the old stable block in which beds had been made. And there, next to his bed, Clegg saw the strangest of things, the final madness of a world with stocks and calipers: a glass jar, half filled with water, and in the water wild flowers, real flowers, picked and placed there, he was sure, by her, like subversive totems.

TWENTYEIGHT

`She doesn't have a home to go to.` the woman was saying. `Any fool can see that!'

It was difficult to argue with her. Beth was dirty, cod-eyed and running a cold. She had slept so heavily that these people and daylight had caught her unawares, asleep beneath their wagon. She had dreamed neither of balloons nor flight but felt as though she had been riding all night and was suitably stiff.

The man who had been poking her with a stick and urging her to shift gave off at the woman's insistence. `She'll need feeding,' he said in a Welsh accent. `They always do.' He looked at her with a mixture of sympathy and disgust.

Beth sat up, alarmed, embarrassed, clutching her bedroll and cracking her head against the wagon's axle. She had not intended to blunder so obviously into their midst but here they were rising to an outdoor breakfast, three horse-drawn caravans, seven adults, a clutter of children, three horses, two eagles and a hawk. The sight of their camp late the night before had been too much for Beth. Like a moth to their flame she had been drawn in the face of all risks.

They backed off as she stirred. They looked more concerned than suspicious and the Welshman with the stick and accent spoke to someone behind him. `Get her some food. And you little ones leave her be a while, she might bite you.'

Which seemed an appropriate warning. Beth felt like a cornered cat. Part of her wanted to snarl or squirt some kind of verbal lighter fluid on them and set them alight.

Only the youngest ignored the man, a girl of perhaps three, fearless of being bitten, the girl who flew with eagles. She stood and watched wide-eyed as Beth rubbed herself awake and wormed her way from beneath the wagon. `You're funny.' the girl said. She was holding a stick in the form of a miniature shepherd's crook and her long dress dragged in the mud as she skipped away to a life of few obvious cares.

Beth wondered how they had trained the little girl, how they had convinced her and the mother to trust to the eagles and how it had felt the first time. Beth thought how it would be when the child would be too large and too heavy and would have to abandon the trick and confine the experience of flight to an ever more distant memory. The thought saddened her, and seeing the balloon collapsed in a heap had a similar effect on her mood. Flight was an illusion, flight of any kind. Gravity was the only constant, the one thing to be relied upon. But wasn't that another of her father's heresies? No gravity. It was a myth, he said. Levity was the future of science. But Beth could not imagine levity raising the balloon or lifting the girl from the ground once her bones grew as heavy as her own now felt. As if to punish her for doubting and with perfect timing John Savage reached out to Beth, there on the floor, next to the wagon. She gasped. There was no escape from her father's insight and planning, no hiding place from the shadows moved by Sam. Beyond the baker's arching back the shadows had spoken and now, from the deflated heap of the balloon her worst nightmare approached.

The man was offering her a bowl. Her reaction to him was that of a small girl having a spider placed down her neck. Or of a bereft child having a cornflower thrust into her face through a car window. She cringed impulsively and found all her reflexes drawing at her extremities. It was not simply fear or disgust. It was an ancient memory she could share with no one and barely with herself. The man seemed to have no neck. His thick tongue protruded like an enormous slug from his moist lips and his spectacle lenses were heavy with grime. She had seen pictures of people with these deformities, knew them as Down's Syndrome, although `Mongol` was still the school-yard term, and knew rationally that her disgust was inexcusable, but her horror of deformities of any kind had been common knowledge in the family since she had been old enough to point whilst screaming. She had certainly never spoken to such a person, not least because they were a very rare sight in her perfectly designed world. Given the choice between talking to the man or leaping from a balloon strung to an eagle she would have chosen the second without hesitation. And yet her feelings were mixed with those of thrill and hope. The coded message had reached her again. This was confirmation, beyond even the balloon, that she was close to her father, for he better than anyone had known her worst nightmare.

`Porridge,` he said, offering a wooden bowl and a big smile. `Eat it up. You must be cold.` He waited for her to nod, but Beth was suddenly the more handicapped of the two, incapable of a normal response. `Don't worry,' he went on. I was cold. It'll go away. There's been a dew. Did you see the dew?' Again she could only nod stupidly. `Where's your Mum and Dad?' he asked suddenly, getting straight to the point. This strange man, free of normal codes, had instant access to the important things. Perhaps that was why Beth had always feared such an encounter.

`A long way away.' she finally managed.

He nodded, satisfied. `What's your name?'

She had thought about this a great deal. She could hide her surname, but to pass herself off as anything other than Beth would be beyond her. It was not an uncommon name. `Beth.` she said. `I'm Beth.` She said it reluctantly, as though it would give him some power over her. And then, with a huge effort: `What's your name?`

`I'm Andrew. That's Owen who told us to get you some food. I hope he didn't hurt you with the stick. Owen's in charge of things really. Owen's my brother. And that's Betty, his wife. And over there you can see Dai and Megan. They're all my brothers, really, and the twins, Jamie and David.

`Where's my horse?` Beth asked, suddenly very anxious and very alarmed.

`With the others,` Andrew said, nodding to a field into which someone, on Beth's behalf, had turned Whisper loose.

Beth sighed, feeling the need to apologize, but instead asked after the little girl. She was struggling to hide her feelings, ashamed and angry but still under their sway. She was pleased to have managed the question.

`Little Mo? That's Megan's girl. I'm her uncle. She can fly. Have you seen her fly? Have you seen the eagles? People usually want to see them. Come and look. They don't like the dew but its okay.`

Andrew and his enthusiasm could not be denied. He touched Beth lightly on the arm, just as Finn had touched her but this time she stiffened visibly before following at a safe distance to the far side of the next caravan. The eagles sat sullenly on blocks of wood. Even in the shadows their dark feathers hinted at bronze and umber whilst their white necks seemed shockingly bright. The hawk was elsewhere, never comfortable with the bigger birds. Andrew offered them proudly for viewing. `Sea-eagles,` he said, `They live by the sea.` but then he grew quiet in their presence and didn't go too close. He noticed that Beth had not touched her porridge. `You want a spoon! Come to the fire and get a spoon. Come on, don't be shy.`

Betty Morgan took over where Andrew left off, Beth's relief almost visible. Andrew had given Beth a spoon and then left in the direction of the horses. Betty offered tea and prodded one of the children to make room for the new guest. `Have you come far?` was all she asked, not wishing to pry but sensing Beth's need for a bit of sympathy as well as privacy. She was a handsome woman in her early forties, with very steady eyes and a knowing but not a weary look. She had been the rider in the show, from whose head the hawk had taken food. Beth noticed the woman's hands, rich with rings and pads of flesh, large enough to control horses and eagles but adorned with the most perfectly groomed nails, filed to an unnatural roundness, her one small concession to femininity.

`From your last show`, Beth said, `I watched you yesterday. I didn't mean to follow, well, I suppose...`

Betty laughed. Her teeth were as perfect as her nails. `No need to explain,` she said. `People do. Follow I mean.` The reaction of the children to Beth had already suggested they were used to people joining them for a meal or a day or a month. `And when did you last eat?` she asked, watching how Beth wolfed down the food.

`More recently than me.` Owen Morgan joked, joining them at the fire and claiming a bowl. He was a round-faced and round-bodied man with a large beard turning grey at the edges, a Welsh Father Christmas in the making. `Where are you from, then?' he asked, `You must be from somewhere.`

`I'm not sure anymore,` Beth answered, not trying to be clever or to hide anything but telling a kind of truth. And then something jolted Beth to her senses, shook off the heaviness of sleep and the shock of her reaction to Andrew. This was the moment. She must not let it pass. They might travel on without her very soon, there would be no reason or excuse for her to tag along with them. Except that her father had provided one. `I need to earn some money.` she said, as casually as she could manage, but feeling herself blush, the words suddenly huge in her mouth. This was like raising the coffin lid again, rising from the dead in the marshes. `I play the flute. It was stolen and I have to buy a new one.` There it was. She had launched her balloon, she had reached out across the divide, she had thrown herself at their mercy. Somewhere a buzzard called. Empty spaces were filling with life. But not this one.

`You won't earn much with us,` said Owen, apologetically, ignoring the prompt. `What can you do? Can you cook?`

`She doesn't need to cook.` Betty said, `She needs to eat. Leave the girl alone.`

`Well I might at that.` said Owen, quick to concede to his wife's authority. `I was only thinking how we could help the girl. Imagine if someone stole your drum. You'd end up beating me if you didn't have that thing to hit.` It seemed that banter was the usual way between the two of them.

`Its not a drum its a Bodhran and I get more sense out of it than I do out of you. Where can she find work?`

`Clun on May Day.` Owen answered. `That's where we're headed. It's a big holiday, always work to be picked up.` He made work sound delightful, synonymous with good food and rich living.

`That's my birthday.` Beth said and then wished she hadn't. Why would these people want to know about her birthday? She was a minor event on their never-ending travels. They must have had more than enough birthdays amongst them to wrap the year around in their own family intimacy. But their reaction was polite.

`We can have a party!` Andrew exclaimed, he had rejoined the circle without Beth noticing and was watching her through milky eyes. `We like parties.`

`Clun is a nice place for a party,` Owen agreed, as though he had known Beth all his life and accommodating her birthday was an annual event. `Nice place, and the best time of the year. You a virgin?' he asked, taking her off guard just as she was beginning to feel slightly comfortable.

`Owen Morgan!` Betty exclaimed, eyes wide. `What kind of manners are these? Shut up and let the girl get some food inside her. Virgin indeed. She's young enough to be your granddaughter.` She had cuffed her husband for his troubles.

`I was only asking out of interest,` he added, feigning hurt, `nothin' personal you understand, its just that Clun on May Day, can get lively as you well know,` he winked at his wife, calling on some old but intimate memory. `They puts on a show of Maidens, see, fertility rites, all good fun, no harm in it, but a barrel of cider for everyone on the main cart. You can sell it on afterwards.`

`You earn every drop by the time the Green Man's finished gropin` you.` Betty added. `You do what you like on your birthday, Beth, and don't let him talk you into nothin.`

`I'm sorry, lass, didn't mean to embarrass you. I was just thinking practical, like. Have to take your chances when you travel.`

`I can wash pots.` Beth said, sorry for his embarrassment more than her own.

An ironic cheer went up from a young lad whose turn it must have been and who had been eyeing the porridge pot sulkily.

`You'll do no such thing,` Betty said, `not on your first day anyway. If you want to pay for the porridge, lass, you can't, but if you want to go and fetch water for the horses and swill out their mash buckets you're most welcome. When you've eaten, mind.` Betty's hands, surely made for swill and mash and porridge, touched Beth lightly on the knee.

Beth needed no more prompting and was glad of the chance to step aside and watch them from a distance but glad also to have been drawn very slightly into their orbit.

Owen saved further awkwardness by inviting Beth to join them when they struck camp and lumbered their carts and caravans onto the road. She had little choice but to travel with them, hoping that her coded message would now have registered with whoever was supposed to help her on her way. Surely one of them would approach her discreetly when the chance arose and reassure her that she was on the right path and direct her to her father. Perhaps Clun was the key and Owen Morgan was discreetly playing his part in the conspiracy.

They travelled north through gentle farm land in a broad valley and stopped in the middle of the day to eat beneath a huge oak tree, massive in girth, enormous in height and without a single flaw or break in its complex crown. It had all the vigour and vitality of a young tree and had stood there, at least Owen believed, since the time of the Armada, when it had probably been planted to celebrate victory. So powerful was its presence that they all felt a reluctance to leave it in mid-afternoon and Andrew hugged the trunk for as long as he could before his brothers urged him on.

When Owen fell in next to Beth she was sure that the moment of revelation had come: I am to lead you to your father, Beth, your worries are over. But Owen had something else to declare. He seemed very different with his wife out of earshot, more confident and more concerned, less the performer. `Its Andy,` he began, `don't get him wrong. I've been watchin`, and he likes you. You're not used to him that's all. He's like mortar between the bricks with us. He can't ride a horse or tame a hawk or juggle a single ball but without him we would all fall apart. I make the jokes, see, though I'm not soft. I tame the acts and make the decisions and get all the blame, but he's the sun of this little solar system, I'm only the moon. Don't be scared of him. Please. If you hurt his feelings he can go off in a sulk for days.`

`I wouldn't dream of...` Beth started to say but Owen shushed her.

`No of course not, of course you wouldn't my dear. Just watch him, is all. You won't find a better friend.` He left Beth to dwell on that. His words had been gentle but she was stinging with shame for the feeling of disgust she felt in Andrew's presence and at her inability to hide them. But she was beginning to translate Andrew's secret into her own language. He too had crossed a line, one even further removed from normal life. He had crossed it before his birth and like Beth was only a visitor here from another world, with strange secrets and insights into the so-called normal.

That evening brought Beth's first real meal since the Boswell and in this company sleep took her easily. When she woke in the night it was to find that someone had moved her from the fireside and laid her out next to the caravan and covered her with a blanket. At first she was alarmed to think that she had slept through being lifted and moved but the dog which had curled up in the small of her back seemed to reassure her. The stars, like the bird song of the previous morning, were an amazement to her. Like a dawn chorus frozen, ready to thaw with first light and soak into the landscape. But then a tingle of fear, a feeling that she was always awake to. She was being watched. Again. The memory of Finn and the fox rushed back. All around was the sound of sleep but eyes were on her, cold and intense. She turned slowly towards the balloon basket that was carried on its low cart. Her watcher was silhouetted black against a small orchestra of stars, its outline perfectly still. It was an eagle. Whether it blinked or simply closed its eyes she could not know but it released her from its spell and then paid her its highest compliment. Or was it an insult? It tucked its head deeply into its shoulders and returned to sleep.

TWENTY NINE

Why had he come? But then again, why had he kept away? And whose choice was it anyway? It seemed to him that the sheets were held in place by starch more than anything beneath them. The face, obscured by tubes and electrodes, bore no resemblance to the one that haunted his sleep. So often at night when he lay awake he had seen the wasted form of Sam Savage hovering in a hospital bed, bars of light playing across perfect sheets. Now he looked at the reality and acknowledged that the silent youth had won. He had played Sir David like a Pied Piper luring the king rat to its doom. He had been silently writing the script all along, pulling strings, casting shadows, providing prompts to which Sir David, and others like him, had unfailingly responded. Here no blackbirds sang, no sirens screeched, no uniformed officers jumped to the great man's command. Here only the insistent pulse of the monitor, the background drone of polishing machines, the efficient click of nurses' heels broke the peace. The chastising silence of dust unsettled Sir David more than anything. It was all so non-judgmental, so politely neutral, so morally bland, all so empty but for the certain presence of Sam Savage and the rather less certain presence of Doctor Khalil. Oh dear. Poor Khalil. At least somebody else in this room was horribly uncomfortable and genuinely afraid. Yet Khalil hid the feeling of panic well, preferring to speculate on the impossible. He knew that Sir David's seeing Sam in the flesh was going to add nothing to written reports, and seeing Khalil in person would only waste the time of all concerned. Khalil consoled himself with the ridiculous thought that perhaps his senior officer had a conscience after all. Perhaps he needed to see for himself the torture chamber they had condemned the boy to, to smell at first hand the modern day equivalent of burning coals and wracked flesh. Or perhaps, forgetting conscience for a moment, and this was a thought Khalil tried hard to put aside, perhaps Sir David was the type to gain pleasure from such things. Perhaps he was the type to gain a cold and clinical reassurance from the warm glow of life-function monitors and the smell of disinfectant.

D.I.Alice Jones was wondering the same. She was accompanying Sir David as his recently appointed assistant, although both of them knew that she was here on the advice of dear Watson, whose concern at a number of Sir David's recent questions and responses had been alerted to security. The prospect of hospitals unnerved Alice Jones at the best of times. Suffering was for others and had little if anything to do with her nicely sterilized world. She had led nearly a score of murder investigations in her short but successful career and not once had she exposed herself to the victim's corpse other than through photographs. Murder was a bore. The System knew the moment it happened and who the offender was. Surprisingly few people had the imagination to shuffle tags around or stick them to well-trained collie dogs, with the Darwinian consequence, at least this was the theory Sir David had tried on her that morning, that police detectives had reversed evolution. They had become increasingly like apes, dull and uncreative, capable of mimicry and repetition but no creativity. Their foreheads were getting lower, their opposable thumbs expert only in holding beer glasses. She had not known whether to take his idea seriously or to laugh at it and had resorted to grooming her nails in silence. It was also part of D.I.Jones' unwritten and unspoken brief to keep Sir David out of the firing line. The old boy's love of hands-on action was legendary even though he had reached an age when not only should he be delegating all practical work, he should even be having the delegation done on his behalf. It had crossed her mind more than once, and most insistently as she walked down the final corridor and entered the private room, that Sir David was toying with her, rubbing her pert little nose into something foul smelling and unavoidable. She was worried for him, the whole department was worried for him. He had been distracted of late. She had learned to respect his clear thinking and incisive manner, but these had been very little in evidence since Beth Savage had managed to abscond.

Sir David introduced D.I.Jones to Dr.Khalil and made a joke about them all having titles, a knight, a detective, a doctor, he said, and where was the candlestick maker? which none of them understood, so he asked for the whole story, pretending that Jones was ignorant of the background. Khalil knew this was a charade, he knew that his orders came directly from Sir David and that no one would be allowed into the bowels of this particular hospital without being very much in-the-know. He took it to be another example of his host-nation's love of theatre.

`He was hit by a vehicle, Inspector Jones, we believe a lorry, just over a year ago, whilst crossing the motorway. There were head and neck injuries only, so he was probably clipped by a wing-mirror, nothing more than that, but at one hundred kilometers an hour...` The doctor left the rest to Jones' imagination `Although the neck was broken we have fused the second and third vertebrae. The surgeon was confident that the spine was not damaged and that sensation and control would return. But we have no way of knowing until...`

`Until he's conscious.` Sir David added.

`Precisely.`

`Which he hardly was to start with.` Puzzled looks turned in his direction.

`Is he a vegetable?` D.I.Jones asked. Sir David noticed how pale his new assistant had become. How simply awful it would be if the girl keeled over, feinted dramatically onto a medicine trolley perhaps, sending all the glass-wear flying, cutting herself as she fell, earning a bandage to which they could all knowingly nod in the corridors and canteens of power. Sir David smiled at her, willing her to pass out. If she suffered it might absolve him by just the smallest amount.

`Oh no, absolutely not.` Khalil answered. `There are many degrees of coma and his is by no means the most severe. There are eye-movements that indicate dreams, he has talked in his sleep, incoherent, but speech, certainly. Also, on several occasions...` the doctor paused, embarrassed, `he appears to have cried.`

`Cried?` Jones looked as though she had been slapped across the face. Sir David stared blankly at the back of his hand.

`Yes, Inspector Jones.`

`You mean his tear gland is active. You're not suggesting *emotional* activity.` Jones turned to Sir David for support and for confirmation. Vegetables she could understand, emotion was another matter entirely. She had not been trained to respond to only a limited range of feelings.

`I am just saying he appears to have cried.`

Sir David leant across Sam's body and placed a hand on the good doctor's knee. `Miss Jones wasn't asking a question, Doctor Khalil. A very subtle thing the English language. She was making a statement. Is that not so, Alice? We just want you to confirm for us doctor, or at least for Inspector Jones, you are not suggesting emotional activity.`

Five years earlier Khalil and his entire family had fled the flooded ruins of northeast India where his Bangladesh nation had lived in mounting misery. Four years ago he had been interred with tens of thousands of refugees in a Turkish transit camps. Three years ago he had left his family to work as a volunteer intern in a filthy disease-ridden Birmingham hospital, helping to contain the latest out-break of malaria. Only a year ago had his family been allowed to follow.

`There is tear-gland activity,` he stated, avoiding Sir David's eye, deferring to the woman's discomfort. `I don't think it is worth mentioning in any reports.`

For a moment Sir David was almost embarrassed by the extent of his own power, delighted with Khalil`s answer and strangely thrilled by D.I.Jones' discomfort. Seeing her reaction put him very slightly in touch with his own, deeply hidden, response.

`Can you imagine how it must be inside there?` he asked, staring at the ghost-white face static on the pillow, addressing Khalil and Jones or neither. `In your own private no-man's-land? I wonder what he thinks.`

There was a single window to the room, high, affording no view. For a few minutes of every day, weather permitting, the sun broke through, sufficient to light up a thin shaft of dust motes floating aimlessly around. By a trick of timing or chance not only had the sun arrived but both Khalil and Sir David found themselves transfixed for a few silent seconds by the pointless dance of illumined dust.

`One assumes he doesn't think at all.` offered D.I.Jones, breaking the spell. The two men looked at each other. The shadow of the window's central bar reached across the bed and onto the floor, dividing them from her.

`Oh does one?` Sir David said, like a theatre aside, whispered dramatically, `Does one indeed? How convenient for us all. An irritated tear-duct and an endless, dreamless night. I wonder what the good doctor thinks of that? Fed, watered, ministered to by the best specialists, free to think absolutely... nothing.` a pause. `Or free to think exactly what he wants? How many of us can do that, Alice, how many of us are free to think our own thoughts?`

`I'm not sure...` she started to say but before she could finish he had cut across her, addressing Khalil.

`Do you know what this place was?` he asked, `All these under-ground tunnels, the huge ballroom we passed through, the electric train set that links each office? People dismiss it as a folly, you know, the work of the eccentric earl, the mole earl, who had it all dug, what, two centuries ago? Do you know what it was when it started life?` Nobody answered. `It's what we all want to do deep down, that's what it is. We all want our own hidden and secret world. He wasn't mad, the earl, he was just rich enough to have it done. Have you never wanted that, Alice, your own private world?` No response. `A doll's house? A hide-away in the garden?`

Incomprehension. `This youth is in his own secret world. The earl of Welbeck tried by digging tunnels but failed. This boy has succeeded. His father succeeded. Don't we all feel just a tiny bit jealous?`

D.I.Jones was wondering if this was the kind of rambling nonsense she should be alert to and if she might have to report it at some stage. Watson was inactive, in Sir David's breast pocket. She would have to be cautious.

`What's the prognosis?` Sir David asked, suddenly bright and breezy, nodding toward the bed.

`Normally we would have expected the patient to emerge from such a coma.` Dr. Khalil spoke.

`Normally.`

`In this case we have been advised to use a regime of drugs I am not familiar with. To stabilize the patient.`

`Stabilize!` gasped Sir David, stroking his long fingers over his endless forehead. `What a wonderful word.`

He let them both dwell on it. Each made of it what they would. For D.I.Jones it was suitably sterile, suitably clinical and detached. Sir David, a connoisseur of such things, delighting in its subtlety. For Doctor Khalil it meant keep the patient slightly this side of dead, whilst stabilizing the political ambitions of Sir David and his corrupt world. Khalil knew he was no more than a puppet on Sir David's strings. Each line he spoke had a hidden sub-text. He could only marvel at how the first lie had grown into this absurd shadow play. Armstrong's `stability` meant that the patient's chances of recovering from the neck surgery grew less by the day. But Khalil did not need to know the reason why. He had his opinions on what thoughts a coma patient was capable of thinking, opinions he was sensible enough to keep to himself.

`If you stopped administering the drug...` Sir David began tentatively, addressing the doctor but looking at D.I.Jones as he spoke, making sure nothing was lost on her. `How long before...`

`He might be sitting up and taking solids within two weeks.` the doctor was cautious, alert to another game of Sir David's.

`Two or three weeks. That is one possibility. And if you continued the medication but stopped the feeding?`

Khalil looked shocked. Did he really need to answer such a question? `He would die. Of course.`

`Of course.` Sir David said, apologetically, he had no wish to humiliate the doctor, `I mean how long would it take?`

`In this state it's hard to tell. He is very weak, but then the metabolism has adapted to a slow tempo. Probably no more than ten days.`

Sir David dismissed the speculation with a wave of the hand. `Ten days. A second possibility. I am pleased with your work, doctor, very pleased. Oh, has the family settled?` He knew they had settled. He rarely asked a question to which he did not know the answer. Pennine Newtown wasn't it? A grim high rise, but an improvement on the camps.

`Yes, Sir. They have settled very well.` Khalil was careful not to mistake the question for genuine concern.

`And the camps,` Sir David continued, `Do you have any contact with the camps?`

`Letters, Sir, from friends, infrequently.`

`I hear they have got worse.`

`I hear the same.`

`Your family, Doctor, it might be time to make their status more permanent, more secure. Such things are possible.` It was also possible to have them expelled that afternoon, to return them to the floating cholera-infested rat-heap they thought they had escaped from. `I will look into it for you,` he said, `In the meantime keep up the good work. Oh, one last thing, the patient's visitors?`

`Only the aunt and sister are authorized, Sir. That has not changed. The sister has not been for some time.`

Sir David and D.I.Jones both let their thoughts drift briefly across the border to wherever Beth might have been.

`What do you remember of the sister?` D.I.Jones asked, some instinctive notion of police work nudging her to pursue inquiries.

But Khalil had no revelations. `Very little.` he answered. `A young lady. Very forthright. She always spoke to me.`

Sir David wondered if Jones would ever get closer to Beth than now. He doubted it.

`What about?` Jones asked.

`Bangladesh.` he answered, for some reason half swallowing the word and looking away as he said it.

`And the searches?`

`Always the searches, Sir.` Khalil answered. `Always very thorough, ending with a shower.`

`A shower?` It was D.I.Jones who queried this detail.

`Doctor Khalil and his staff were instructed to make sure that the two visitors never took anything away with them.` Sir David explained.

`A shower, of course.` Jones smiled, pleased with the efficiency of the arrangements.

`Much of your culture is unusual to me,` Khalil said, speaking for the first time without being asked to do so. `I have learned to accept a great deal that is both new and strange. Religion is different all across the world and I respect that.`

Now it was the word religion that left Jones confused. She looked to Sir David for an explanation, but he was smiling, amused by Khalil's angle on things. He watched the dust dance in the sunlight, charmed by its carefree purpose. He could end the visit right now, but why miss the opportunity to play? `Would you like to explain that, Khalil.` he asked, `don't worry about offending us. We know ourselves to be odd.`

Khalil looked anxiously from the knight to the detective, unsure of his ground. He was not in the business of causing offence.

He wished he had never mentioned religion bur realized there was no possibility of retreat. `These practices vary from nation to nation, from people to people.` he repeated, `It is not my place to criticize or judge what other ...`

`Tell us, doctor, please. You are amongst friends.` Sir David patted him on the elbow, impressed by his own sincerity.

`In the Christian religion you drink the blood and eat the flesh of your God. Every week. Forgive me if I find it slightly offensive.`

`Did they do that? Did they take communion here?` D.I.Jones asked, as though stumbling across some strange cult ritual that must be eradicated.

`I use it only as an example,` Khalil answered, `Blood is very sacred. To all religions. To mine, to the Christians. Also to yours.`

`Our religion?` D.I.Jones could hardly believe her ears. She had been accused of many things in her time but never religion. `I'm afraid I don't understand.`

`He means the DNA.` Sir David told her gently, as though breaking news of a terminal illness. `The visitors were DNA stripped to make sure they took nothing away from the patient: hair, skin, blood. Is that not correct doctor?`

Khalil nodded.

Sir David looked wistfully at D.I.Jones. `How are you on religion?` he asked, smiling slyly.

`Sir?`

`You heard me, Miss Jones. Religion.`

`I understand that Christians take communion, my grandmother used to...`

`No, no, no,` he waved her to a halt. `You. Us. What is our religion? Doctor Khalil is not stupid.`

`I'm not sure I have one, Sir. It hardly seems appropriate in this day and age, I mean, our choices, our genes...`

`Thankyou, Miss Jones. Thankyou. What to you seems as natural as fresh air seems as strange to Doctor Khalil as drinking blood. It's all in the genes, isn't that what they say? When I was your age the world was so anxious for a new faith, Miss Jones, so very anxious, desperate I might even say, quite desperate. Ideally one which demanded nothing of the individual but gave lots in return.` Sir David stood up and walked to the monitors and fixed his eye on the persistent lines. He was still surprised that the room was empty of demons, this room of all rooms, though he suspected it was somehow too full of Sam to allow anything else. `You know the kind of thing, Miss Jones, one which had no wish to rant and rave about morality and obligation but allowed us all to feel good.` He suddenly dropped his voice to a whisper, as though sharing a secret. `We found it, Alice! Didn't anyone tell you? We found it. We invented the religion to fit the national mood.`

`You're talking about Genetic Absolutism, Sir. I'm sorry, when Doctor Khalil said religion I assumed he meant...`

`Something stupid? Something wrong-headed? Something superstitious? Of course. But try looking at it from a different angle, Miss Jones. Genetic Absolutism. A science? Well it certainly fitted the bill wonderfully. Its only imperative was sex. What could be better, Alice, really, what could be better? A new creed for a new world, all based on sex. Just think of the marketing possibilities! Endless! No soul or spirit, Alice, God forbid. Just the body. Sex! Darwin! The old religions, the ones you assumed Doctor Khalil to mean, they've long since been confined to the theme parks. You should visit one. Excellent for a rainy day with the children. Virtual churches, that's all we're left with, where you can buy communion wine and candles on the way home, where you can bottle the goodness to freshen your bathroom, absolve your sins with a donation to guide dogs, that kind of thing. By the time I was a student, Miss Jones, at the start of the century, there were no crusades any more, only sales campaigns, there were no theological debates, only media witch-hunts, no parables, only sound bites. The new God was DNA. Brilliant! The only wonder was that people had managed so long without it.`

He fell silent, sat next to the bed and ran both hands slowly over the dome, once, twice, three times. `I must thankyou, Doctor Khalil. I would never have thought of all these clever words unless you had talked religion. You know this youth is here because of his father? We should never forget that, not for one moment, his father condemned him to this as surely as any articulated lorry. But that's not genes. That's politics. And bloody awful bad luck.`

With that Sir David rose, nodded a thanks to Khalil, gestured to his assistant and was gone from the room seconds behind his own shadow.

THIRTY

`So what does it mean for you?` Clegg asked. `What's your Grail?` He had surprised her. The noise of the pigs had masked the scrape of his caliper against the floor and table. She was standing at the sink and holding something small and apparently delicate up to the light. She jumped and for the first time in his experience seemed vulnerable. He had not been so close to her before and he wondered how someone so slight of frame could seem durable and tough. She smelled of metal now, which surprised him.

`Why do you ask?`

Clegg nodded to the quote above the door. `I'm curious.` he said. `There's a lot to learn around here.`

`There's always a lot to learn, Mr.Clegg, it doesn't matter where you are.` There was the slightest hint of impatience in her tone. `Where's your friend?`

Just what Clegg had been thinking. Arch had started to behave in even more bizarre ways. One minute he was confiding all in Clegg, as though they had been working together in never-never land for years past, the next he was sullen and suspicious, accusing Clegg of trying to muscle in on the imminent and not-to-be-doubted rewards. Today he was as taciturn as Ralph, with whom he was now busy in the dairy.

`He's not my friend. We were thrown together. Chance, that kind of thing. Did you arrange with those people for me to come here?`

`Those people?`

`The Arkites.`

`Why would I do that?`

`That was my next question.`

`You ask a lot of them.`

`How many am I allowed?`

She smiled. `A maximum of ten. You've used more than half. Lets just say I don't believe in chance. You looked worth a bit of effort. Of course I might have been wrong.`

He took it as a compliment and nodded his thanks. `Do you believe all this.` he asked, `The Grail stuff. Did you put it there?`

`It's been there since the house was built, and yes, I do believe it.` She said it matter-of-fact. This was no fanatic or zealot fixing Clegg with her gaze, this was a woman worth a great deal of effort, to use her terms. He remembered the fantasy and imagined trying to make love with a calipered leg. For a second he had the distinct impression that she was reading his thoughts. She was certainly smiling. `You don't laugh much, Mr.Clegg. Infact I don't think I've seen you smile since you got here.`

`I don't have much to smile about.` he said, tapping the caliper.

She shrugged, unimpressed. She had finished at the sink and turned to him. Again the smile. Clegg had never fallen for a smile before, Jenny had rarely smiled, but he thought this one might be worth cultivating. Either that or he was growing old. `You asked me what my Grail is.` she said, `Come on, I'll show you.`

She took a key from a rack above the sink and led the way outside. Instinctively they both glanced towards the dairy to make sure Arch was not about to blunder across. Clegg was taken by a second fantasy, one in which she took him to an outhouse, unlocked him and then slipped out of her long dress, smiling so much that he was unable to perform. Back in the real world, on the opposite side of the yard, she unlocked the door to an old stable or outhouse. Entering brought a surprise because the slates on the far side of the roof had been removed and glass put in their place. The room was flooded with unexpected light that fell directly onto a workbench. It was immaculately tidy. Miniature tools were hung on a rack, each in its allotted place and the tiny vice on the bench's leading edge seemed almost to shine.

Clegg watched as Agnes sat herself on the swivel stool and gestured proudly at her little kingdom. She reached for a cigar box, one of several stacked neatly to one side. She opened it carefully, as though something inside might be sleeping or on the point of flying away and offered it to Clegg.

The box was lined with silk on which rested an imitation cobweb, or at least an exquisitely delicate necklace. It looked as though breath would undo it and yet the details of tiny stars, suns and crescent moons suspended in its gossamer heaven were clear enough to marvel at. Clegg reached out to touch them but thought better of it, leaving it to the delicate fingers of Agnes to perform deft gymnastics with clasp and links. She undid the top button of her blouse to better show him her handiwork. The blouse was silk, he noticed, and her skin beneath it surprisingly brown. She was already wearing a diamond pendant and to this she now added the necklace. It rested below her throat and showed clearly the eight highlighted stars in the form of Virgo, with the lowest resting discreetly between her breasts.

He was suddenly unsure which he found the more desirable, the jewelry or her. Nor did he know which unnerved him the most, the prospect of her body or the threat of her smile. Even now it seemed she had an unexpected control over him. She had him in a noose of her own making and it made him cautious.

`Beautiful` was all he could manage, but when she said nothing nor changed her gesture he stumbled on. `What's it made of?`

`What would you like it to be made of?`

`Gold?`

`Then gold it is. Do you want to touch?`

He could not believe she was ignorant of the ambiguity, the unspoken offer of her breasts, especially when she invited him once more to feel. She seemed now to be smiling at his torment but defused the moment by reaching behind her neck and unfastening the chain. She placed it in Clegg's out-stretched palms. It was surprisingly heavy.

`Pure gold?`

`What else?`

He examined it closely, weighed it from one hand to the next. Without realizing he raised it to his nose, eager for the smell of warm milk and Agnes' body. He glanced up. She was watching his face minutely for a reaction. He handed it back cautiously. `It must be worth a fortune,` he suggested.

The spell was broken. Breasts, milk, fantasy, all gone in a second. She put the necklace away briskly, returned the box neatly to its pile and did up her buttons.

`I wouldn't know.` she said sharply, not looking at him.

`Why not?`

`Why should I?`

`I presume you sell them.`

`Don't presume too much, Mr.Clegg. If you must know, I give them away.`

`You what?`

`I said, I give them away. I make them for fun. Ever heard of that? Fun? There's no profit in this business. The Grail is the human heart, Mr.Clegg, not a bank account.`

`Just for fun!`

`You heard. Think about it. It might do you good.` But then she softened slightly. `Well, not only for fun. If I'm honest I have to admit to another motive. I make them to corrupt people as well.`

Clegg was out of his depth. He shook his head but could think of nothing to say.

`Not everyone in the Comfort Zone is happy to be fattened for the snare.` she said. `Nothing stirs things up more than beauty for its own sake.`

`You really do give them away?`

`Why not?` she sounded almost angry. `How else can I reach people who are half-dead and three-quarters buried? They've got nothing over there I want so I give these away. Let's say it's my quiet alternative to being an Arkite. My way of undermining everything they stand for over there.`

Clegg felt like protesting that he at least stood for nothing whatsoever but suspected he was being led to that very conclusion. `But the gold?` he asked, trying to keep things practical. `What about the gold?`

She smiled again, this time sympathetically as she climbed down from her chair. She led him through a second door that gave onto the inside of a large greenhouse. Various plants were growing in small patches but the prominent crop, in raised boxes, appeared to be cabbages.

`I grow it,` she said, as though it were the most normal thing in the world. `I feed them a chemical or two. It's called Phytomining, I believe.`

`I've heard of it. I never knew it worked.`

`Only if you talk nicely to your cabbages,` she said. `Over here we do.`

Over here. Another subtle way of placing Clegg, of confirming that she knew.

`You talk to them?` It hardly mattered what she did to the cabbages because Clegg had seen the result poised on her breast. `You grow your own gold, you turn it into jewelry, beautiful jewelry,` he conceded. `And then you give it away, so as to corrupt people?`

`Perfect, don't you think?` she laughed, the girl within the woman suddenly free. `I would prefer mineral gold, mind you, it's easier to work than the homegrown. It's impossible to get. Criminals on the other side need it all to play their games, there's nothing left for the honest jeweler.` She had led them back to the workshop and had taken a wristband from a box. It was made of two dragons inter-twined and without asking she slipped it over

Clegg's wrist. When he made to protest she placed a finger to his lips. He was stunned by this tiny intimacy, more flattered than if she had bared her breasts or thrust his hand down her blouse. But he knew there would be a price to pay, there always was.

`I've told you my secrets,` she said. `And shown you my Grail, if that's what you want to call it. Now you. What makes you tick? What gets you full of fire? You don't belong here. You probably don't belong anywhere. What's your story, Mr.Clegg? ` She was leading him from the shed, locking the door behind them and walking back to the kitchen.

`My name's Nathaniel,` he said, just as he found himself holding open the kitchen door for her to enter ahead of him, `Nat. Mr.Clegg makes me sound official. I'm not used to being official.` Nor was he used to holding doors open or being spoken to like this. The big sister had become a bully but he didn't know how to resist. He had a passion, it was true, in the clouds, flying. Or was that his escape, his way of avoiding the emptiness that arises when nothing fills you with fire? By telling the truth he would hide something deeper for a while longer.

`I'm searching for a girl,` he said .

`Ah! Jenny I suppose?`

`Jenny?`

`Perhaps I imagined it when I was dressing your wound. You seemed to think a lot of her at the time.`

`Not Jenny. And I don't mean that. I'm looking for a girl. Following her. It's her father I want to meet.`

To meet. It sounded very different to capture, abduct or sell, it sounded perfectly respectable and worthy.

Agnes looked at him long and hard before daring the next question.

`Are you a bounty hunter?` At last a label. A name. Even the worst symptoms seem lessened by the diagnosis of a name. Yes, Clegg was a bounty hunter, not a pointless, feckless, amoral loser.

A bounty hunter. `You've crossed over haven't you? You're from over the Line.`

`What if I am?`

`Then you need to be very careful. The Arkites would kill you for a start. Burn you in fact. I should turn you in. Claim the money.`

She was half taunting but half serious, weighing up her options.

`I'll be gone soon,` he reminded her.

With an ironic grin, she tapped against the caliper. `Not far, you won't, not with that. So why do you want them? What have they done wrong?`

Another impossible question. Clegg had never assumed his prey to have done anything wrong. Or right for that matter.

`He's crossed over. Two years ago. I need to take them both back.`

She nodded. `For money. You're doing it for money.`

`What else?`

She laughed, but looked at him with sympathy.

`Because it'll go wrong! If you do it for money it will go badly wrong. It always does. It will be you who ends up corrupted. Try and find a better reason.`

There wasn't one, at least not one he was about to share.

Agnes reached down to the hearth and picked up a small piece of coal and then removed the diamond pendant from her neck and placed the two items on the table. `You see these, two, coal and diamond? They're the same thing at heart, Mr.Clegg. Carbon. They're both carbon. But why does some carbon turn into the one rather than the other?` Clegg shrugged as he was supposed to. `The man of coal gets thrown in the fire and comes out as clinker and ash. The man of diamond gets to rest here.` She tapped the cusp between her breasts, close to her heart and looked into Clegg as though defying him to think the wrong thoughts. `The choice is yours.` she said as she replaced the pendant.

`So I'm a man of clinker and ash, is that it?`

`If you are a man of coal then you're not the only one in this world,` she said wearily, `but you've got the right idea. Go into this for money and you will come out clinker and ash. Sure. Go ahead.`

`What's the alternative.`

`Transformation.`

`You'll turn me into a diamond?`

`You need an alchemist for that, Nathaniel, a miracle worker.`

`Isn't that what you are, an alchemist? Turning cabbages into jewelry, turning me into a gem?` He felt enlivened now, at last ready to challenge her domination.

`I've got skilled hands, but that's asking a lot. Unless you want it, really want it, more than anything else?` It was half-question half challenge and to confuse it further Clegg's desire offered a cheap way out of the probing questions, an alternative to the threat of transformation.

`Then I get to rest here.` he said, placing his hand between her breasts and next to her heart.

`You get to screw yourself in your own private wasteland,` she said, brushing his hand away, quoting from the sign above the kitchen door. `Where are they, this girl and her father?`

`I don't know. I've lost the trail.`

`So what will you do?`

`Play a hunch. It's my only choice.`

`What hunch?`

`Arch gave me an idea. There is a place, Cwm something or other, where they heal a valley. I'll ask around.`

Her expression was now a strange mixture of pity and contempt. `You could be killed for this.` she said softly. `For what you are and where you've come from. If it was up to me…` She seemed to hesitate but then regained her outrage. `Nobody would miss you there, would they? Nobody would notice. Tell me I'm wrong.`

`You're not wrong.` this said with no hint of bitterness, `No one would miss me. Perhaps that's why I'm here. But listen, I want to take somebody back, that's all, a criminal. The police want him.`

`He won't want to go,` she said, stating the obvious.

`Of course not. He'll go to prison.`

`No. I don't mean that. I mean he won't want to leave whatever he's found here. They never do.`

`Other people's choices aren't my worry,` he started to say, but she cut him short.

`You're a fool, Mr. Nathaniel Clegg. A complete fool. I saw it there on the road where I cut you down. And you're a fool to drag Arch around as a friend.`

`He isn't. I don't. Chance threw us together, just like you and I.`

`Don't bet on it. I told you, I don't believe in chance. The clerk said Arch was free to go. He bribed them to get sent here. How do you explain that?`

He couldn't, it made no sense at all, but before he could ask her more she had moved on.

`He's the least of your worries. Unless you're careful you won't want to go back either. You'll be paying out bribes to do strange things, just like Arch.`

`Now its you who shouldn't bet.` Clegg answered.

`Oh, I wouldn't put money on you either way, but you've been warned, Mr. Clinker and Ash. Stay too long and you might just wake up, you might just realize that there's nothing to go back for.`

`What about comfort to start with?`

She gestured around her to indicate the food and drink and shelter. `Go on,` she said. `Tell me. What is there to go back to?`

Go on Clegg, tell her. Tell her about the 42 varieties of washing powder, the 284 TV channels, the 187 teenage suicides daily, the prescription rates for Prozac and Retilin, the army of Bonnys spewing up the crap they have force fed themselves. And tell her about the best of it, the great sleep of the soul, the great warm bosom of apathy and indifference, Bonny's couch.

`Flying,` he said, `Since you ask. I love to fly, that's what I'll go back for.`

`And why do you fly?` she asked, sensing victory.

Tell her, Clegg, tell her why you fly. You fly to escape. You fly to be rid of the disease. The only thing to go back for is a means of escape. `I'm awake,` he answered, avoiding the question, `It's this whole place that's asleep.`

To his surprise she was nodding. `Yes, in a way. This whole place is asleep. It's the country's subconscious, the part of yourself you and yours have been destroying for centuries.`

You and yours. The Wildwood, without and within. The lost primitive. Clegg had heard the theories, read their limp and listless poets at school. He had suddenly had enough of being bullied and took the initiative, largely out of self-defense, and also to conclude because Ralph and Arch had just crossed the courtyard from the dairy.

`I have my Holy Grail,` he said, before the others entered the kitchen. `And I know there's no money in it. I'll show you one of these nights when the weather's clear. And I'll show you not to judge a man by the things he doesn't say.`

THIRTYONE

She slept with Owen's younger nephew, Jamie, out of pity. He had a squint half hidden by thick lenses but was the softer of the two, less territorial than David. She had felt guilty about taking the group's hospitality whilst giving nothing in return and knew that this would be expected even if she paid her way or washed porridge pans every day. But like the baker in Ludlow Jamie seemed surprised by her compliance. Even his `thankyou` was odd. It put her on her guard. Perhaps her alien status made it special to him, like sleeping with a black girl might have been? Why else would he have been so nervous, his voice and hands shaking as he explored her body? Indeed why else should the baker in Ludlow have looked on in awe as she undressed herself? Perhaps she was something exotic, something to boast about. But the baker in Ludlow had not suspected her origins, surely? And what about David, the other twin? Why had he not pushed for equal access? This was the Wildside, she reminded herself, they did things differently. They had no Blockers, no pills to curb the sexual urge, but there seemed to be something else at work here, something of which she had no experience. Incredible though it seemed might she have been the first girl he had ever had sex with? At fifteen it seemed very unlikely. Again she wondered why Finn had not used her body. Without its power she would have no point of entry into their closed world. Jamie's obvious thrill and his complete surrender were a great reassurance to Beth, something good to place alongside the usual emptiness.

The following day the two brothers woke her before dawn. She had been dreaming of hospitals and boats, some mixture of Dr.Johnson's barge and an operating theatre. She wanted to dream of balloon flights but was still waiting. Gravity won. But at last the shaking got through to her.

`Do you want to come?`

At first she assumed they wanted to share her, but there was something missing in their faces, the hunger was replaced by a child-like vigour. `Where?`

`Sssh! Don't wake anyone. You coming or not?`

This is it, she thought. They had heard the message, they knew her next step. They were part of the plan. Don't ask questions, she told herself, not this time. Trust.

She leapt from her sleeping bag, forced on her boots and still had to hurry to keep up with them as they ducked behind the caravan, avoiding the horses, and dived into the woods on the far side of the lane, swift and fluid in their movements like animals of prey.

`We're after a bit of breakfast.` David hissed. That was all. The only other clue was the bundle under Jamie's arm and the pointed sticks they were carrying. The bundle was a net of course green nylon, an old fishing net most likely. `We need help. We tried it yesterday but we need a fourth person.`

Beth was thrilled.

`You might be less useless than you look.` he said, shifting the mood.

Useless or not, she belonged, at least for a time, in whatever the two were planning. She had been starting to fear that once in Clun she would have no choice but to leave the Owen family despite being not an inch closer to finding her father, but now something was afoot, something was shifting in her favour.

The boys picked up a trail through the woods and dropped into a loping stride which Beth did her best to imitate. After half a mile they stopped and listened. A whistle came from the undergrowth, followed by a figure. It was Andrew, surprisingly light-footed and with a broad grin on his face. Beth struggled to feel neutral.

`Any luck, Andy?` one of the twins whispered.

Andrew nodded but said nothing, gesturing to them to follow. They raced through the woods. Birds ignored them, rabbits bolted, dew clawed at them and shook itself from low growing plants, Beth making more noise than the other three combined. After what seemed like an age they stopped. Beth was heaving for breath and could not hide it. But the boys and Andrew were just warming to the task. They ignored her discomfort. To their right a patch of earth had been turned over. The clean white of nibbled roots and the dark black of dung told them enough. Jamie felt the droppings to be certain and nodded back to the others with the beginnings of a grin.

`You just do what we say.` David whispered. `There's no danger. At least not likely. We need you to run her out, see.`

Beth tried to straighten up but was still sucking for wind. Run who out? She felt too stupid to ask. It was time to watch, time to trust in these unlikely looking huntsmen. Beth stared in horror as the twins took the dung and smeared it over their arms and faces along with some of the surrounding leaf-mould. Was this belonging? A memory. She had acted out some primitive form of this by the river with her ashes, not knowing why, not aware that perhaps it was the most primal way possible of belonging, of being part of the real world. Andrew grinned at Beth to share her disgust. She would be up wind, they said, no need for this. But they had to swing in behind, she would see.

She soon did. Coming to a ridge in the woods they combined crouching with crawling. At the top of the ridge they stopped and pointed. Beth swallowed hard and struggled to keep her breathing under control. The boys had already exhausted her, it was barely light and now the real work was to be done. They were pointing at a wild boar, a large female. Around her five or six chestnut coloured piglets rooted silently in the soft earth. They were no more than fifty yards away and the two boys and Andrew had done their work expertly. Beth had never seen anything so exquisite, so perfect, not even the fox by moonlight or the eagles carrying Megan.

`Show me your watch.` one of them asked. She upinned her mother's watch and handed it to Jamie. He looked at it carefully, front and back before nodding. `Four minutes, no more. After four minutes exactly, just stand up and walk towards them. She won't see you at first. Its good that you smell, she'll smell you before anything else, perhaps hear you. Keep straight towards them. Andrew will stay here with you. Keep time, Andy.` he handed Beth's watch to her worst nightmare. He nodded eagerly.

They were gone. Before she could question them on details or ask to back out they had vanished, one to the left, one to the right as silently as shadows, leaving herself and Andrew in the middle of an adventure which had not even been explained. She could not have refused. She was trapped in their world now, for better or for worse. She watched the wild boar go about their business. She feared for them, glad that they were innocent of the boys creeping up on them and whatever fate was about to disturb their harmless grubbing. Mothers of any species could be frantic in defense of their young. She looked at the nearby trees to see which ones would take her if the sow refused to obey the boys as easily as she had. The time crawled. Four minutes had never passed so slowly. She compared herself to the boar. Unsuspecting, ignorant of horrible things lurking around every corner. Andrew nudged her and pointed to the watch. Her mother's watch. The watch her mother had held and set. Now Andrew's plump fingers gripped it clumsily. Four minutes had passed. They both took deep breaths as though preparing to dive under water. They stood up and started walking. There was no response from the group for several seconds. Then the sow grunted in alarm. She had heard something and swung her snout vaguely in their direction. A second grunt followed by an explosive burst of speed, mud, trotters and vegetation as the entire group leaped almost as one away from Beth and Andrew towards the densest patch of vegetation behind them. Beth could not believe how fast the beast was travelling within seconds of standing still. It's speed took her through brambles and fallen branches with the piglets trailing very slightly behind and moments later it was as though they had never been there, the whole thing an extension of her dreams. Only the fresh evidence of rooting suggested it had been real, that and the new and brief silence of the songbirds, startled into caution.

Andrew gestured her to sit. `We just wait now.` he said.

`How many will they kill?` she asked, less comfortable with silence than with small talk.

`Only one. The mother can count to four.`

`And will we eat it?`

`Of course not!` Andrew laughed, amazed that any one could be so stupid about fresh meat. `We hang it for a couple of weeks. But there is a man up the valley we can give this one to and he'll give us one we caught last time.`

Of course. Simple economics, the type you learned at school on the Wildside.

Suddenly Andrew turned to her and fumbled for the handkerchief he used for cleaning his glasses. `You lost your flute?` he asked, making conversation Beth assumed. She nodded. `Owen told me,` Andrew continued. `Said you had it stolen.` Beth was listening for the twins, anxious for them to return to save her from small talk, something she felt incapable of doing with Andrew. `So you have to earn money to buy a new one?` he asked.

Where were they? Poor Andrew, he did not deserve Beth's indifference and she knew it. The twins were marvelous with him, they talked and behaved as equals, they had no inhibitions about their uncle's missing or extra chromosome or his strange appearance. If only she could be as easy with Andrew as they were. She had still not looked at him properly, she had still not listened to his questions, even as she answered them. She was still stupidly ignorant of what should have been so obvious.

`Then you must be John Savage's daughter.` Andrew said, returning his glasses to their rightful place. `I know how you can find him. I am supposed to help you. I have a letter from your father.`

Before Beth could react with even a gasp the twins emerged from bushes fifty yards away. Andrew had already leapt up to join them, leaving Beth winded by the revelation. The net was slung between the boys and in it lay the freshly slaughtered piglet. Beth had been spared the butchering. The piglet's squeals had been cut off before the mother could consider it lost. She would already be feeding, they said, settling down to a fresh patch, a mile covered in five minutes, certainly, but already she would have forgotten the whole business. Andrew reminded her that the sow should be left with four. She could count to four, it was cruel to leave her less. Beth realized that he had explained the same fact only a few minutes earlier, but this time she listened, this time she took him seriously, this time she looked at him as though he were more than a human being, only minutes ago she had unknowingly dismissed him to the level of some kind of subspecies. He was the one. Andrew was the one. Not Owen, not Betty or Megan or Dai or the twins, but Andrew, her worst nightmare, it was Andrew to whom her father had trusted his whereabouts. She should have known from the very start. The world was never quite as it seemed with John Savage in charge. He had devoted his life to shifting lines, angles, expectations, to unsettling the settled, to undoing the predictable. He was one of life's clowns, a court jester. Of course he had chosen Andrew, the one least likely to attract attention, to arouse suspicion. If anyone had followed her this far waiting for her to receive a message then Andrew would have been the perfect foil, the ideal hiding place for whatever clue had been left waiting. Andrew was the triumph of levity over gravity.

The four of them walked back steadily through the woods. With the job done and the piglet to carry it seemed much further and no one was inclined to talk until they were back. Beth was desperate to be alone with Andrew. Suddenly he remembered his jacket. He had left it in the woods and went back to find it. Beth made to go with him but he waved her on. `I'll see you soon` he said, `I won't be a second.` With that the twins and Beth continued, but not before the boys had exchanged glances and a few words to each other in what Beth assumed to be Welsh.

Back at the camp there was to be a further surprise. As Beth prepared to strut and boast, to walk differently, to announce her arrival in tiny ways the twins stated their intention of delivering the piglet now, five miles up the valley. They were insistent that she should accompany them, take her share and credit in the kill. Of course she would go. She belonged. She was one among equals. She could help them pick out some choice cuts, make sure the butcher didn't short change them. Andrew would probably meet them there. That decided it. She collected Whisper and fell in behind them, wondering what the meat of a young wild boar would taste like fried on an open wood fire. The camp was stirring as they left. Betty was watching sideways on, not quick to interfere with the comings and goings of the youngsters but curious. Her large hands held slabs of bacon.

`I'll have breakfast ready when you come back.` she called.

Beth nodded her thanks but the two boys said nothing. They followed the road for about three miles until a track led them down to a large farmhouse, limed white and neatly kept with a great meadow of wild flowers where a garden might once have been. Several shire horses were grazing in the paddock behind the farm, gigantic beasts each the weight of a dozen ponies and with strength enough to work machinery on the heavy soil here in the valley bottom. A man was leaning on the paddock fence, watching the horses graze. Anything less like the local butcher was hard to imagine. He turned at their approach and smiled. He was well in his sixties but a shock of white hair and a military baring suggested he might still have decades left in him. He seemed to look straight past the boys and their catch, alert to the presence of Beth. After a few moments he seemed to snap out of some fixed thought and addressed the twins in a friendly but surprisingly soft voice for a man of his build.

`Jamie, David! Good to see you boys again. I heard you would soon be in out part of the world. You headed for Clun? The whole world is it seems. What have you got for me?`

`Caught it this morning,` said Jamie, `Can't get any fresher than that.`

`I won't argue with that, lad. What do you want for it?`

`The usual.` said David.

`Have you got proof?` the man asked. `You know we always need proof.`

Betty's fried breakfast was suddenly very far away, so too was Andrew's vital but untapped knowledge. `We've got proof,` one of the boys said. `She's got an ankle scar. But it's the watch that really gives her away.`

THIRTYTWO

`We make the stuff in our own image.` Ralph Bailey was explaining, `Though nobody thanks you for pointing it out.` He was chopping curds with a large butcher's knife. He kept it in a bucket of pig's urine over-night because the pigs were fed on whey and their urine, so he insisted, was a perfect antiseptic.

Clegg was feeding the curds through a peg mill and adding salt, breaking the mats of cheese into thousands of little lumps that would coagulate afresh when pressed into linen-lined tins. He expected Ralph to continue, to explain his theory, but the cheese-maker was fond of silence. At times he was as dark as Agnes was light, sullen to the point of hostility. Perhaps he saw in Clegg an unwanted rival or something contagious. Arch was ill with a cold and had been given the morning off, a relief to them all. Both Clegg and Ralph were happy to work quietly, without Arch's constant sparrow-like chatter.

Clegg's knife was blunt and he asked for a stone. Ralph stopped work, wiped his hands methodically and then walked over to a shelf on the far side of the dairy. He lifted down one of the two stones, walked slowly back and handed it to Clegg without comment.

`This is a dry stone.` Clegg said. `I need a wet stone.`

Still without speaking and repeating exactly the same meticulous and unhurried movements Ralph took the stone from Clegg, placed it on the shelf, took down the one next to it, handed it to Clegg and returned to his work. But with a difference. He was watching from the corner of his eye, or watching the blade as it smoothed itself a warm slick of saliva and grit. Clegg satisfied the knife by removing a few hairs from the back of his hand. He wiped both the blade and the stone on the outside of his free leg and returned the stone to its shelf but before he could address the curds Ralph Bailey grunted something through the side of his mouth. He gestured to Clegg to join him at the bench that ran half the length of the dairy. He had in front of him a small round of cheese. He gestured for Clegg's knife, tested it himself for sharpness and then cut several small chunks. He handed one to Clegg, who duly ate it.

`I want your honest opinion,` Ralph said, nodding to the cheese. `take your time.`

Clegg was confused. Talking to Bailey was more a process than a dialogue. Hours of silence could be broken by a five-minute lecture, questions left over from the previous day might suddenly be answered without preamble. Clegg saw through the trick straight away. The cheese was differently wrapped and finished. Agnes had made it. He smiled at the description he could have come up with. Mature. Subtle. Deceptively full-bodied. Best taken neat, after desert. He might try a few on her, she was not lacking in humour.

`I prefer meat,` said Clegg. `Sorry. Never been a cheese man.`

Ralph Bailey dismissed the apology. `I have a lot of theories, Mr.Clegg. Agnes says I have too many but you must be the judge of that. As many theories as types of cheese. You must stop me when you don't want to hear them.` But Clegg had no intention of stopping the man. Whenever there was something to learn Clegg could listen long and patiently. `I believe there are two kinds of men on this earth, Mr.Clegg,` he looked at the cheese as he spoke, chewing slowly. `Some people like it more complicated than that but I'm happy to keep it simple.`

`Two kinds, Mr.Bailey?` Clegg asked, certain of something more substantial than Arch's two gods.

`Two kinds, Mr.Clegg. Those who know how to use a sharpening stone and those who don't.`

It was all so simple. Clegg envied Ralph Bailey the uncomplicated universe he inhabited. It would take a braver man than Clegg to challenge its theories.

`Never trust a man who does not know how to use a sharpening stone.` he concluded, `Never.`

Clegg was suddenly unsure as to which side of Ralph Bailey's great divide he stood. He had learned to use a stone in the army. He was certain he had done it correctly, indeed the blade was proof of that.

`And why do you tell me this, Mr.Bailey?`

But there was to be no answer for now. Ralph Bailey had returned silently to work and expected Clegg to do the same. Together the two men checked that morning's milk that was heating slowly over two gas rings. Ralph wouldn't let Clegg anywhere near the rennet or the starter, his secret ingredients. The starter had been cultivated in a pan in the kitchen and owed as much to flies, wood smoke and bacon fat as to science. Comparing people to cheeses was a complex game when you saw what went into the process. Left to himself, what kind of cheese would Clegg come up with, he wondered. It was too easy. Tough on the outside and sour in the middle. It was obvious. Words like `nutty`, `mature`, `mellow` and `smoked` were too subtle for Clegg's bland cheddar. He couldn't help but smile when he looked at the cheese Agnes had made.

Although an hour had past since Ralph had expounded the Theory of the Sharpening Stone and presented Clegg with Agnes's cheese it was understood that the same themes still hung in the air and could be called upon at a moment's notice without any preamble. For this reason Clegg was not surprised when Ralph again laid down his tools, wiped his hands thoroughly on a cloth and gestured Clegg to follow him outside. There was a simple bench that gave a view over an untidy garden that fell away to woods in the middle distance and gorse covered hills beyond. The two men sat, each awkward in his own way.

`I know what you are, Mr.Clegg.` he began, `I'm not stupid. It might have been better if they had let you hang back there on the road.` His voice was stained with the black bile of nicotine but his manner was changing, he was ready to show something of himself to Clegg.

`I thought you weren't one of them,` said Clegg.

`One of them. What does that mean? Not an Arkite? Not a lunatic with a convenient label. Shall I give you some advice, Mr.Clegg?`

`I'm always grateful for advice, Mr.Bailey.`

`I believe you are, Mr.Clegg. I do believe you are. Your friend Arch, he doesn't know how to use a sharpening stone.` To make things perfectly clear he added. `Don't trust, him Mr.Clegg. I fear you must not trust him.`

It had never occurred to Clegg to trust Arch but he was still amazed to be receiving this advice from Ralph Bailey. But there was more to come. Much more.

`You see all that,` Bailey continued, `The Garden of Eden. It has its faults, but we've done our best to make a garden of it.`

Here we go again, thought Clegg, the Landscape God. But he was mistaken.

`Do you know your history, Mr.Clegg?`

It was a genuine question and Clegg answered it honestly. `As a matter of fact I do, Mr. Bailey. I had a liking for it once.`

Bailey nodded, approving of the answer. `Do you know how the Civil War started, Mr.Clegg?`

`There are lots of theories. As many as there are cheeses. I know the usual view. Devolution, health scares, new towns, the bomb at the World Bank, the immigrants from Africa and the east, that kind of thing.`

`And the one about the trees?`

`I know something about the trees.`

`I'm sure you do, Mr.Clegg, I'm sure you do.` He sighed. His eyes swept the trees that topped each hill and filled each hollow. `When everyone finally believed in nothing or had their own private religion the time was ready for the trees. A great healer, trees. A great healer. And then there was the merchant banker in Devon who quietly started planting them. He thought it was for pheasants but he was wrong. A thousand acres, I think it was. No one noticed at first, but after about five years, when the oaks were waist high and the alder and beech up to here,` he gestured to his own eye-level, `people began to notice, you bet they did. They began to stop their cars, walk their dogs, spread their picnic rugs. Some of them didn't even know what drew them, but it happened, like magic, it happened. Then adjoining villages donated fields, named them community woodlands, a legacy here, a gift there, some small, some, like the old R.A.F. airfield or the valley owned by the Church Commissioners were huge. After ten years, by which times the oaks were head-height and unbendable people started selling up and moving to be closer to it, politicians began to argue about it, for and against. Teenagers ran away from home to build themselves a bender somewhere in its middle, opponents tried to burn it down or plough it up. Within fifteen years of the first acorn being heeled in you could walk from the South Devon coast, up the Dart valley, round the bottom edge of Dartmoor, north of Exeter, up through Somerset all the way to the edge of Bristol without ever breaking cover. And if you could do it so could the deer and the birds and all the rest.`

`So that's how it started?`

`Too vague, Mr.Clegg, too vague. They could have lived with the forest, made it their own, put a price on it, turned it into an asset, sold its soul. But we got them where it really hurt.`

Clegg waited.

`What really got them worried, Mr.Clegg, what really pushed them over the edge were the take-over bids.` A coarse cough cleared a path through the current layer of old tar.

`Tell me more.` said Clegg, accepting his role.

`I was part of an organization, Mr.Clegg, very well funded, good public image, whose reason for existence was to buy up and then close down hostile industries.`

`Hostile?`

`Yes, Mr.Clegg, hostile. Hostile to the Landscape constitution which was then being drawn up, hostile to the future and freedom of this country. Mobile phones, soft wear management, chemicals, nuclear power, food processing. I was in a consortium that targeted the genetics and cloning industries. We launched a hostile bid for the biggest. People sold us their shares even though they knew we would dissolve the company, sit on their patents, destroy their lives' work. Did that stop them? It most certainly did not. They took the money and they ran. Can you imagine living like that, Mr.Clegg? Your only ideal is to make money. Your only reason for going to work is to make money. People made a choice back then, Mr.Clegg. What we did forced people to make those choices. That is what started the Civil War.`

`Why are you telling me this?` asked Clegg, suddenly suspicious.

`Because as a young man I was placed inside the target company. They employed me as a financial adviser. I was a traitor. I was there to destroy them.`

Yes, Clegg could imagine living only for money, having no ideals. He could also imagine a young Ralph Bailey quietly working his way into the target company, a patient and conscientious mole, bent on destruction. `And?` Clegg prompted.

`Mary Magdalene,` he said, apparently changing tack. `What does the name Mary Magdalene mean to you?`

Another theory was burrowing its way to the surface, uprooting orthodoxy on its way. `Wasn't she a whore?` asked Clegg, `One of Christ's followers.`

`She was first at the tomb on Easter Sunday, Mr.Clegg. The first to see the risen Christ. She mistook him for the gardener. The gardener. Have you ever thought about that? Don't apologize if you haven't, you are not alone in that. The woman who knew him better than anyone alive mistook him for the gardener. It is the single most important line in the bible, Mr.Clegg, some might say the only important line. The thing is, she wasn't mistaken. Christ is the gardener. And this is the garden.` He gestured outwards. It could have been comic if the tangle of bramble and plants in the foreground had caught the eye but Ralph Bailey's conviction went far into the distance, to include the fields and hills beyond. The earth was Bailey's garden. Tending it was his religion. `If our two worlds had flags, Mr.Clegg, flags that meant anything, Magdalene would be on ours. Next to the tomb. Holding the Grail.`

`And the other one?` asked Clegg, obediently, `The Comfort Zone flag?`

`Judas.`

`Iscariot?`

`Hung from a tree. Thirty pieces of silver spread on the floor. The whore and the traitor, Mr.Clegg. Not much of a choice you might think. Give me the whore any time. Over there, in your city-world they have chosen for Judas, wall-to-wall Judas. They hang from a noose of their own making, they grovel in a thousand shades of shit to dredge out their lost silver.`

`Not much of a choice, Mr.Bailey, not when you put it like that.`

`Don't let me get you down, Mr.Clegg. Things are never as bad as they appear. In Dorchester there is a church window, I've never seen it but I've often thought to take a walk that way.`

`A church window?`

`Judas, hanging from the tree. Funny thing is, the thirty pieces of silver falling from his hand have taken root. They've turned into flowers.`

`Flowers?`

`For the whore to tend, no doubt. You see, the fruit of betrayal is not always as bitter as you might think. Of course you, Mr.Clegg, you are a child of Judas.`

`An accident of birth, Mr.Bailey.`

`Don't despair, Mr.Clegg.` His expression changed. It was as though something had struck him for the first time. `Perhaps Judas was the good guy.` With that the sermon was almost over. `You will need a key, Mr.Clegg, to the caliper. I will arrange it in the next few days. You will need it if you are to put distance between yourself and Arch. And you will certainly need it if you wish to test any of my theories. `

THIRTYTHREE

`I've killed people for less.` the sheriff was saying, `A long time ago it might have been, we danced to a different tune in those days, right? But the melody lingers on. I've killed people before and I would do it again. Ask Owen.` But there was no need. Owen had briefed Beth well, preparing her for the worst of Robert Melrose. A veteran, Owen had called him, a legend in his own and very eventful lifetime. A man who had graduated to authority via anarchy and periodic prison sentences. Robert Melrose was born under ground, they said, Robert Melrose first breathed God's air thirty feet below the roots of threatened trees, Robert Melrose had learned to walk amongst the fumes of disabled diggers and to the background music of police sirens and his parents' protest chants. He had been at Twyford Down, the M11, the early Geneva riots. He had been one of the first to blow up mobile phone masts, to picket the oil refineries, to crash the bar-code systems, to rip up trial crops. But of course his speciality, his calling card was the midnight garden. Driving the bulldozer into the car park late at night, his comrades-in-arms waiting with skips to remove the tarmac and trucks to bring in the top-soil, Melrose the Midnight Gardener would be gone before dawn, streets reclaimed, trees planted, the press tipped off in advance, prime-time exposure pre-arranged. The Street Tribe. Composers of the Urban Song Lines. Revolution by Compost. He had done the lot. For years the media had struggled to describe Robert Melrose and his comrades, just as the authorities had failed to double-guess them, ascribe them to a box or recognize any formal structure of command and leadership. For years Melrose and hundreds like him had drifted from protest to protest, frustrated idealism burning its way through the world's apathy. Until the Wildside had given them a focus, until the Wildside had offered an alternative to the all-consuming world order. War on the Inevitable, they called it, because nothing is. The steady take-over of people's lives by cars, by wires, by pills, by networks, none of it was inevitable. There was as much choice as you chose to exercise. The myth of consumer inevitability was a marketing trick, Melrose claimed, it was conjured up by the corporate magicians to hypnotize the global audience. Like rabbits caught in the headlights, two generations of Europe and North America's finest had been willingly flattened by the juggernaut of Inevitability. Work, spend, work, spend, work, die. Inevitable? Death, yes, but the rest was negotiable, the rest was a matter of glorious choice.

But right now Robert Melrose was short of choices and was being less than honest. He had never killed. He had never come near it. The facts had corrupted into myth over the last thirty years, the history of the revolution rewritten a score of times. He had nearly been killed. In London, when the oil companies had sent in agitators to discredit a demonstration, an iron bar had removed a piece of Robert Melrose's incaution. Since then he had found comfort in more gentle forms of revolution. He had planted ten thousand trees in the Wildside's first five years, at the same time separating out and spreading close to a million wild daffodil bulbs. From there he had advanced to wellington boot administration, walking thousands of miles to monitor the acre-mile-tree rule, the rule that required one hundred trees to every mile of hedgerow and one mile of hedgerow to every five acres of land. Now fate had cast him in a role his former adversaries would never have believed. Sheriff and Magistrate of the area, guardian of the new-world order, poacher turned lord of the manor, master of Beth's immediate fate. As sheriff and magistrate it was his duty to pay out the bounty to the twins, which he had done, and deliver Beth to Shrewsbury, which he was arranging. There was no reason for him to explain his actions, but something about Beth seemed to demand it. He ran long fingers through his mane of white hair before rearranging the papers on his desk. He examined the water colours above the fireplace as though in search of inevitability.

`I've told her the legal position.` Owen said. `I've told her its your job to send her back.` he paused. `But I've also told her it might not be that straight forward.` Owen Morgan recognizing spontaneous bureaucracy when he saw it. He was in trouble for having sheltered Beth, however unknowingly, and now had nothing to lose in trying to prevent her deportation. But there was another complication. Since the twins and Beth had parted from Andrew in the woods early that morning Andrew had not been seen. Coincidence? Owen was not certain and had no wish to see Beth lost to officialdom if Andrew was off in a sulk. `She says she would rather die than go back.` Owen repeated.

Both men looked at Beth. She sat like a caged animal, her dark eyes fierce, her knees drawn up to her chin, her expression a cross between contempt and outrage. She was not restrained in any way. She was a prisoner in name only. She was in Robert Melrose's large office, the front room of the farmhouse. He had forms to attend to, procedures to follow but so far had written nothing.

Melrose was wary of her, sensing her anger, attracted by its quiet threat. `You have to understand,` he said, as though addressing a drill-hall of new recruits, `every year they send people to destabilize things, to spy, to spread rumours. They're jealous, you see, angry. We have to assume the worst. It's our job. Paid paranoia. Isn't that right, Owen?` he didn't wait for an answer. He had the old and stale paranoia of the retired dope-head, but with it the desperate need to forgive. `We pay out a bounty, return the prisoner, make an official complaint and wait for the next one. I'm sorry, Owen, I've heard it all before.` Which was not quite true. He had never heard of one so young, nor one who claimed to have the future safety and well being of the Wildside in her hands. But for as long as she would give no further details his options were limited. The girl was dangerous. She reminded him of himself at that age.

Beth had given up looking for any logic. Events had moved too swiftly for that. Andrew's disappearance so soon after declaring his hand confused things horribly. Perhaps he had known what the twins intended, or had found it out too late and had gone off in a huff. Such was Owen's theory, and no one knew Andrew better, indeed Owen confirmed that Andrew had been fascinated with Beth since her arrival. `The lad is always falling in love.` he pointed out. `And falling hard.`

Melrose nodded and reverted to old habits. `Who can blame him,? he said. `She is a pretty girl.` He looked at Beth for a second too long. `But you can't be suggesting we break the law for the sake of your brother's crush, Owen?`

That was exactly what Owen was suggesting. `I would do anything for my brother,` he said, `You know that, Robbie. We break this particular law until we find him, how would that be? We'll take responsibility for Beth. Until Andrew turns up. Do you hear that, Beth?`

No. She had not heard. She was staring at the two men blankly. Owen would do anything for his brother, he said, and Melrose had called her a pretty girl, which meant that in return for sex he would co-operate. But it didn't mean that, she realized, not here, not like at home. It reminded her of Finn's rejection and her own lack of power. And then something snapped in her. She was back in the land of unfinished sentences, back as a child into the habit of doing things to make the boys happy, unspeakable things. And why had she done it? Why the first, from which the scores of others followed? Why had she let them wipe their lust all over her? To save Sam, that was why. Because if she refused to do what they asked they used to beat Sam to a pulp, they used to torture him to make her do their wishes. Because she was a pretty girl. And because she would do anything for her brother. And nothing had changed. Here she was, for Sam's sake, because of Sam, and here were the same old signals, though somehow confused. `I'm a pretty girl am I?` she said, taking a deep breath, straightening herself in the chair, leaning forwards. `A pretty girl. Is that what you see? Is that really what you see? What a simple little world we all live in. And what am I supposed to see? An ugly old man? Some old has-been hero? I suppose you'll let me stay if I smile nicely, or is that not quite enough? Will you let me stay if I flutter my eyelids? Or do you want more? Because they usually do. A lot more.`

`Beth!` Owen tried to stop her, knowing her anger would lead them no nearer to a solution, but once started there would be no stopping her.

`Because its never enough, is it?` she continued, `Are you just the same as the rest of them? Give me a list. The things I have to do. Or shall I write it, because I know what will be on it, from the first to the last, every filthy fucking bit of it. `

`Beth.` Owen tried again, reaching out to touch her on the shoulder. `It's not like that. It's different here. Robbie is trying to help.`

`Prove it.` she snapped, her eyes on the sheriff. `Prove it's not all words and theory.`

Melrose took his time. He was equal to her anger and met it with complete inner calm and not a hint of judgement. Perhaps there had been daughters of his own once.

`Why do you think there is a border, Beth?` he asked, denying the instinct to address her as `young lady`. `Why do you think the two halves of this country should be kept from each other?`

Beth looked from one man to the other and sighed. There was more at her disposal than anger but for now an awful weariness threatened to deny her an answer. She knew that only by playing to their rules could she get what she needed. She would have to tell them what they wanted to hear. Which was the truth. `Because over there its awful. There is nothing to live for and hasn't been for half a century. Over there the world is full of zombies. People who are more like machines. They don't believe in themselves any more, they don't believe in anything, only shopping and entertainment. They measure everything in money. Everything. If it makes a profit, it's good. Oh, and they watch you, all the time they watch you. Everything you do, everything you buy, everyone you visit or talk to, they know everything. Drive in a box. Live in a box. Fit in a box.

Pop the pills, watch the movie. It can make you angry, ` she said, the closest she would come to apologizing, her voice strangely level, her eyes fixed on Melrose, `It can make you very angry.`

Her words created a silence in the room, both men unsure of their right to speak. It was Melrose who finally found the courage. `Which is why the Line should come down,` he said, wrong footing Beth and Owen. `Think about it. You've just explained why it might be time to put an end to the way things are.`

Beth shook her head, not understanding. The room, the desk and the man all spoke of the new order and the revolutionary *status quo* but he now seemed to be rewriting his own rules. Here was a man, like her father, who had helped draw the Line. For the sake of preserving it he was going to send her back. But now he was talking of the Line coming down.

`You must excuse us, Beth. Owen and I go back a long way and have chewed over these things lots of times. We're close to Offa's Dyke here. Offa's Dyke. You've heard of it? Hundreds of years ago people lived and died for that thing, keeping the English out. Wasn't that it, Owen? Or the other way round? It makes no difference now. And it makes no sense either. Sure, it's a useful footpath, but that's all. It's a relic of a dead way of thinking, not a border. One day the line through this country will be just the same. People won't believe what a fuss we made about it. All those people in the Comfort Zone, you want to abandon them? You want them to live on in the misery you claim to be running from?`

`Yes.` She said, without a second's hesitation. `If it means I can stay. How is that for selfish? Or do you want me to lie? I will if you want. And I know what you're going to say next. I've heard it before. The line is inside each one of us, isn't that it? We've to get rid of the line inside ourselves to make sense of the world. Isn't that what you're going to say? Go back home and work on the Line from inside? That's what my Dad used to say. I understand all that, but it's too late. People should have done that fifty years ago when they still had the chance. It doesn't change things here and now. I've done that, I'm an expert at it but I would rather die than go back. And if you send me back you'll regret it.`

The threat again. And mention of her father, the key to all this but a subject on which she would reveal nothing more.

`Let me tell you something,` Melrose leaned forwards as he spoke, abandoning the comfort of pen and paper. `Let me tell you why the Line will have to come down one day. You can judge people in all sorts of ways, Beth, that's what the twins did, they judged you by your watch, by your ankle scar. There are other ways, what people wear, the company they keep, what their trade is, how much they earn. But I'll tell you, Beth, that's all unimportant at the end of the day. The only thing that really matters, the only thing on which we have the right to judge another person is whether they believe.`

`Some people don't believe in anything.` Beth offered.

`I didn't say *what*, I said *whether*. Some people have made a religion out of not believing, Beth. Tragic, don't you think? That's why this strange little country dares to exist, dares to poke its presumptions into the face of the world. We believe in something. We're not always sure what, and you can make fun of that all you like. Life is a school. There are things to learn, and the first lesson is out there, in the soil, the land, the landscape. It's our Grail. We live the Arthurian myth. Fifty years from now it won't make sense, they'll laugh at us, just as they would have done fifty years ago, but that doesn't matter. Fifty years from now there'll be a new crusade, a new mythology. So what?`

`But what has this got to do with me and sending me back?` she asked, quietly impressed.

`I'll tell you, Beth. Everyone who crosses the Line brings something with them, a little part of a big illness. Even with the best will in the world we can't soak it all up, no more than we can feed the whole of Africa or house the refugees. You have brought something from your past, just like the rest. You probably don't know what it is: a wish, a want, a lie, anything. To us it can be like the common cold was to the Incas or alcohol to the Indians. It could destroy us. We send it back. I'm sorry. We have a job to do.`

`A job?`

`You see the stones in that field?` he said, `Every year we pile them up. Every year more come burrowing to the surface. You can't pretend they're not there, not if you keep blunting your plough against them. But that's what people do, at least in your world, Beth. Sorry, in the Comfort Zone. They pretend there's no history or myth or legend, no past. They don't even bother to plough anymore. You could say they skim the surface at best, they let it all go to weeds if you like. No ideals, no beliefs. But you see, Beth, there is one secret bedded so deep and so wide in that soil that no amount of ignorance can hide it. It's a myth I happen to believe in, very literally as it happens, for which some people consider me a fool. If you know your history, Beth, you'll know that a score of times in the last two thousand years the freedom of Europe has been destroyed and that here, in these islands, some vague glimmer of hope has always been kept alive, has always hung on like a candle in a dark night to offer a way out, back to freedom. That's what the Wildside is, Beth. Illogical, imperfect, implausible. But a candle in a very dark night.`

It's King Arthur crap again, she wanted to say, its myths and legends instead of real people. Occult fascism. This was how they killed Mum, arguing over theory and ideas. Dogma fodder. We're all King Arthur now, she thought. Don't they know that? We're all the whole myth rolled into one. The sleeper awakes, it's not some knight in a cave, it's inside us all. `So you send me back into the darkness in order to save your little flame?` she snapped.

Owen flinched. He knew how far Robert Melrose had come in softening towards the girl. He could hear the anger in Beth's voice rising again and knew how little it would help her to antagonize the old warrior. Owen scrolled the tips of his beard through anxious fingers, willing Beth to behave. She had a surprise for them both.

`I saw a helicopter yesterday.` she said, `Are they allowed to cross the Line? And if they are, why not me?`

It was true, sufficient for Melrose and Owen to exchange glances. They had all seen the helicopter. It had roared in low, late in the morning, about the time that Owen had arrived to explain why Beth had been travelling with them.

`Why do you ask that, Beth?` Melrose was cautious.

`It was from the Comfort Zone, wasn't it? It was one of theirs. But what do you do to stop it? If things like that can still happen then why not let one person pass quietly through?` She was gripping the edge of the table and her knuckles were white, her eyes fierce.

`We'll complain about the helicopter.' Melrose answered, `On Midsummer's Day there will be some reply from us.`

`But what will you do to stop it?` she demanded, emphasizing every word.

`What are you getting at, Beth?` It was Owen who intervened, also impressed by how pertinent her question had been.

`I mean you can't stop them, can you? Isn't it true that they are less worried now than they used to be about you messing with the System?` She didn't wait for an answer. `That helicopter,` she said, sensing a way out, sighing away the anger but far from surrendering, `they were looking for me. They are trying to take me back. Doesn't that show something?`

For a second it seemed she had done her case no good at all because Melrose was shaking his head and Owen looked away. It was left to the Welshman to explain.

`It happens every few months, Beth. It's illegal but difficult to control. Somebody over there pays a big bribe and over they come.`

`Why?`

`Hunting. Deer, boar, bustards, birds of prey.`

It had been a long shot claiming the helicopter as part of her own drama and she regretted it. But there was worse to come.

`It might also explain Andrew.` Melrose said, avoiding Owen's eye, but needing to explain to Beth. `You see, its not always animals they hunt.`

The awful implications of this hung in the air and Robert Melrose, to his credit, allowed some time to pass silently. But the Owen family were performers, born and bred, the Owen family could fly and defy gravity and had a sense of theatre. Into the silence burst Betty Owen, not bothering to knock or to concede to the sheriff's authority. More important things were afoot. Her large hands and perfect nails came down with intent on Owen's shoulders before he could even turn around. `It's Andrew,` she said `They've found him. Come quickly, both of you.`

It was unclear who was included and who excluded by this command, but all three sprang from their chairs and followed Betty to the courtyard where horses were tethered, Whisper amongst them. Betty was already leading the way and would answer no more questions, Beth made to follow but Melrose pulled in front of her, waiting to make sure Owen could not hear.

`Go.`he said, his tone awkwardly between military precision and real warmth. `This is not your war. Don't let me see which way you take, just go.`

So easy. But to go away without Andrew's little store of knowledge would be no better than returning home. The trail stopped here. Suddenly all her anger was spent. She looked at Melrose with pity, not contempt and surprised them both with her tone, though not the words. `Thankyou.` she said. `I'm grateful, I really am , but you're wrong. It is my war. I'm sorry.` with that, and to no ones surprise, she fell in behind the two men and proceeded to follow Betty's lead.

Andrew was covered from head to toe in mud. One lens of his spectacles was cracked and blood from a head wound had caked dry into his hair and against his forehead. Snot ran from his nose and his skin was blue with cold and exhaustion. They had found him staggering down from the hillside. It had been in thick mist most of the day and the first assumption was that he had got lost, nothing more sinister. But there was more. He had heard the helicopter, he said, though not seen it. Then there had been men running through the woods, one of them firing shots, the others shouting. Andrew had run into the mist, up the hill, fallen into a stream, rolled, twisted his ankle. He had heard the men arguing but the mist had confused them. He thought they must be playing a game but they didn't seem to be enjoying it. He had hidden in the stream, literally in the water, for most of the day. He had heard the helicopter some time in the afternoon and after that followed the stream down, out of the mist and into the back yard of a pub, in the bar of which he was now sat, telling his story between heaving shakes which wracked his body every two or three minutes and great slurps of sweet tea the landlady was plying him with.

Owen was livid, trying to hide his anger for Andrew's sake but making a poor job of it. `There's no reason for it!` He was saying, `Why pick on Andy? Why pick on anyone? There is no reason for it!`

Beth watched from a distance. After several minutes of fussing with tea and ointment she moved closer to Andrew. There was a reason for it. It would not shape itself into words but something compelled her to search through his pockets and draw out the watch. Her mother's watch. The ferryman, the sheriff, they had both talked in different kinds of riddle about leaving things behind, of letting go of the past, but neither could have guessed how exact and literal their warnings had been. She turned the watch over. There was a tiny rubber seal trapped between the back and the face to keep water out. But somehow the seal was wrongly inserted, it was pinched between front and back and stuck out a few millimeters at one point. Beth looked up. Owen was watching her face. Without a word he produced a pocketknife and handed it to her. With concentrated effort she flicked the back off and let it fall, its despised quotation face down at their feet. She looked at the blank discs and slabs of plastic, not certain what she was looking for. Owen pointed. A tiny object had been inserted between the mechanism and the casing. It was no bigger than a grain of rice, but was clearly of a different age and technology to the rest of the watch. Trust no one, her father had urged. Trust no one. Here was the awful link between herself and Andrew's ordeal, a link between her own desperate attempt to justify her status amongst these people and the truth of her task. Her mother's watch. What else? It was the perfect point of betrayal, the place where sentiment overcame common sense. During the hunt for the boar it was Andrew who had become the timekeeper, Andrew who had taken the watch to count off the four minutes. The watch that crossed over with her. She did not understand how and certainly not why, but this watch, or its tiny bug, had led the helicopter's crew to within a few minutes and yards of who they thought to be Beth. Her instinct was to throw it to the floor and grind it with her boot but she caught Robert Melrose's eye. It only took a second before the sheriff felt able to speak for them both. `Its alright, Owen,` he said, `Its alright, Andrew. Don't worry. You see, Beth and I have a plan.`

THIRTYFOUR

`I'm surprised you're still here.`

`So am I.` he said, also lying. `It might be something to do with this.` he tapped the caliper. `Your father told you about our talk?`

`Yes he told me. He thinks Arch is bad for you. I'm surprised he even cares.`

Agnes had approached Clegg as he sat outside the farmhouse, stitching his jacket. He had patched the holes left over from his scrambling-bike 'accident'. It was the kind of maintenance work that helped him stay whilst preparing to go. Ralph had promised the key sooner rather than later but Clegg found himself strangely indifferent on the matter. With the caliper on things could remain as they were, in a pleasant state of indecision, Clegg kidding himself that he was preparing a master plan. The reality was very different. Something in Arch's ramblings had struck a cord with Clegg. This talk of King Arthur and the forthcoming assembly of people in the so-called Valley of Healing revealed Arch's madness but also made clear something very awkward to accept. They were both similarly engaged. The mystery of Arch's bribe only made it more likely. Had Arch purchased Clegg's company for a reason, or was it the kind of random act the game-player appeared to thrive on? He had not tackled him on the subject and had no intention of doing so, yet.

And then there was Agnes. Clegg felt that she had something for him, that there might still be a reason why she had found him on the track and claimed him from the Arkites. More than the bracelet of gold and the prospect of sex and the quiet drug of her smile was the suspicion that he could somehow use her in his plan to extract John Savage from the Wildside. Quite how was still completely beyond him.

Some minutes passed in silence. Without knowing it they were watching the sun go down and listening to the bird song. Lots of birds, lots of song. A bit like reading the Bible, Clegg thought, suddenly the expert, a bit like visiting someone else's life, you could take from it exactly what you wanted. This was not the first time he and Agnes had taken the air together. She was fond of showing him things in the landscape important to her, pointing out trees she and her father had planted, a pond they had made, nesting boxes. Clegg had tried to see some sense in her talk, how landscape could live and thrive in the same way as any plant or animal and how people could only find happiness in a place if they first attended to the landscape. He kept his doubts to himself, but at least felt no need to scoff. Agnes was genuine, which both attracted him and made him uncomfortable. Because Agnes came close to touching his secret. Agnes was not the first woman in Clegg's life with convictions.

They started to climb the hill together, Clegg now skilled in swinging his hobbled leg in the right rhythm to keep up. They were met with a wonderful view; endless hills rolling away from purple in the foreground to black in the distance, the valleys puddling with dark even as they watched.

`I'd like my son to see this.` said Clegg. Jo was only a stepson, at most, but Agnes need never know. Clegg suddenly wanted to claim the boy as his own. He could not have explained why. Perhaps it gave him a stake in Agnes' world.

`So how old is your son?` she asked.

The truth forced its way in. `Step-son.` he corrected, unable or unwilling to sustain that particular lie. `Ex. Like a lot of things. He's four, nearly five. I'd still like him to see it, though, even if he isn't mine.`

Agnes looked at him strangely, as though he had said something ridiculous or offensive. `You might have to be quick.` she said.

`Which means?`

`Which means you might have to be quick. There are those who would like to destroy it. All this green, all these growing things, all this free beauty. It corrupts the soul.` She let him chew on that one before continuing. `Once upon a time,` she said, `about a hundred years ago this country still had the most perfect landscape ever created by man and nature together. Did you know that? An old partnership. Centuries old. Planting, culling, husbandry, sensing what was needed. Trees, hedgerows, drainage, common land, pasture, roads, it was the most perfect eco-system for its latitude anywhere on earth.`

So what? would have been the old response and something still itched in Clegg to burst this particular bubble and to hurt Agnes for her passion, or for the fact that she was right, too right, Jo would never see this or anything remotely like it. Worse still, Jo would never know it was here to be missed. Yes, Clegg knew about landscape theory, about nostalgia for a past that never was, how the machine age changed the way people thought and then screwed up the landscape. He was, after all, almost a child of his time. Almost. Almost a child of the linear, binary, digital desert of the computer screen, where everything was black and white despite the colours, where everything was wonderfully unreal, dead and predictable. Almost. His friends had gone all the way. Their heroes, like Arch's, were in cyberspace, their first erotic fantasies had involved virtual thighs and breasts. For those who had done little more at puberty than up-grade from a computer joy-stick to nature's equivalent it was not easy to get off on the subtleties of a Saxon hedgerow or a Celtic field pattern.

But Clegg had survived. Above, in the night sky, at his mother's beckoning had appeared a landscape immune to all systems, a universe with more stars than the computer had pixels, with more mysteries and options than the most sophisticated of games. The night sky was the ultimate computer bug. It made all systems crash. Take a long look at the Milky Way. Game over. It had corrupted Clegg, saved him from complete absorption into the binary conspiracy. It had opened his ears to Agnes in a way he could only resent. For this reason he said nothing. For this reason he left Agnes to her ideals a while longer.

They sat on the hilltop, by a gate in the hedge. There was no moon and the night was mild. Perfect for what Clegg intended. He had never sat for so long in silence with a woman. At first it unnerved him, he was sure he was doing something wrong, that she was waiting for him to make a move, but after half an hour he was comfortable with it, it seemed the most natural of things to do. He was even surprised when she finally spoke.

`Your Holy Grail?` she asked, `Prove me wrong. Please.`

The `please` was genuine, a plea from the heart. He looked at her. He would never have bothered to find her beautiful in his past life, he would have looked straight past her, but there was something about her correctness, her belonging, her complete and total absorption into this strange world that made her shine, made her eerily attractive. He turned away and nodded towards the sky. `Its all there.` he told her. `As delicate as your jewelry. It costs nothing, and it corrupts the soul.'

`How?`

He asked her to lie next to him so they could study the same piece of sky. `Even the most powerful of warlords can only look at all this and feel tiny, puny. Alexander, Napoleon, Hitler. They've all done it.`

`It doesn't seem to have stopped them.'

`Perhaps it drove them on.` he suggested, `Perhaps it made them so inadequate that they just had to go out and kill.`

`Do you know their names?`

`Yes, I know their names. There's Mars. And Jupiter.`

`I know that one.` she said, pointing to the pinprick of light to the north of Arcturus. She didn't need to say anything else. Everybody knew that one. It was God's Eye, watching every breath and heartbeat of the Comfort Zone, the System's relay satellite.

`And there's your star-sign, Virgo.`

`How do you know all this?`

`My mother taught me.`

Clegg regretted the words before they were even out. Big boys don't discuss their mothers with women they want. But it was too late. Clegg's appointment was with his dead mother as much as with Agnes. `It's what kept her going.` he said, seeing no other way out.

`It was just you and her?`

`And Danny, my kid brother. Danny's dad was around for a few years, but most of the time there were just the three of us.`

`Was she a scientist?` Agnes asked.

Clegg laughed at that one. `Sure, the same way you're an architect. No she wasn't a scientist. She was a watcher. She saw something bigger than herself and loved it. If that makes her a scientist then OK. She was just a mother, really.` The biggest put-down and compliment. Clegg might have added that as a child, if he woke in the night and needed her, she would be in the back garden, huddling in blankets against the cold, watching with the old binoculars and taking mysterious notes which Clegg never understood or tried to. As a youngster he had spent many a freezing winter's night on the hill behind their house, waiting for the street and house lights to fade away and for some obscure comet or planet or moon to come into view. Clegg's first real act of violence had been carried out gleefully on a schoolmate who had called his mother mad. She had not been mad. Abused, yes. Hard-done by, certainly. But no more mad than the world she was captive to. Through all his youth, through the army, right to the present day, Clegg could not look at the night sky without being reminded of his mother's excitement at the arrival of a planet or her anger at the interference caused by reflective satellites with their death-like glow. Agnes, picking over the fine tracery of her golden chains, had reminded him of his mother pointing out a constellation or nebula. Agnes explaining how trees and fields must balance the contours and allow colour to move in and out of the valley, reminded him of his mother explaining the great rhythm of stars and galaxies. Both loved a different kind of landscape, both were genuine, both left him feeling distinctly odd.

Agnes was observing. `I've never taken much notice of them,` she said. `Strange really. Nobody ever took the time. I had my interests down here. How do you know it's my star-sign?` she asked suddenly.

`A guess. The jewelry you showed me. Although it wasn't accurate.`

`It wasn't meant to be accurate, it was meant to be beautiful.`

`The night sky is both. Look,` he pointed to the southeast, placing a hand on her shoulder and directing her gaze from behind. For a moment his cheek pressed into her hair and he could smell a mixture of soap and warm milk. `That's Mars, the red one. Now come this way to the bright star in Virgo. That's Spica, then the next bright one. That's Regulus, in Leo.`

`What about them?`

`If you imagine a curve going through them all and carrying on to over there in the north, that's the ecliptic, the line on which the planets can be seen. That's how you know where to find them. Back to Spica. It means ear of wheat, by the way, then up to the head of Virgo. Do you see those smudges? Look slightly to one side of them. They're galaxies, dozens of galaxies. Here.` He handed her his pocket telescope and redirected her towards the Virgo Galaxy clusters.

`Beautiful!` she gasped, `Yes, I've got them.`

For a moment he was distracted by the beat of her pulse in the vein of her neck and felt a strong urge to touch it lightly, to feel her life-blood going about its work. `The middle one, if you can find it, M87, its got a black hole in the centre. You see, even your beautiful Virgo has a black heart.`

`Don't spoil it!` she protested. `Numbers and black hearts. Is that your kind of accuracy? Tell me something nice about her.` She handed back the telescope to take in the bigger picture.

`The Greeks called her Demeter. The goddess of fertility.` Now there was a thought. `And justice.`

`Justice, that reminds me.` She sat up and reached for the key around her neck. She unlocked the four rings and drew the caliper off as Clegg cautiously bent his knee for the first time in a fortnight and sighed with relief. He could have pulled her towards him, there was nothing to stop him now. In the fantasy of his fever she had made all the moves, she had lowered herself on to him, she had taken him for herself and extracted part of his deception, leaving him spent and exhausted. The reality might be different. She turned and laughed, once again giving him the impression that she had read his thoughts. Without speaking she removed the gold necklace from her breast and fixed it around Clegg's head like a crown.

`You want to be king?` she said `Isn't that what they all want, all men, their own little kingdom? It suits you. Perhaps you're cut out for the job.`

`And you'll be the Queen?`

`I think the modern word is whore!` she laughed, `I know my place, and I know how men work. But not yet,` she said, suddenly serious, suddenly acknowledging that they were both thinking the same. `Find your girl, Nat Clegg, perhaps even her father. Who knows? It might make you rich. It might make you feel clever. Then bring your stepson to see all this. Then we'll negotiate terms.` With that she stood up, removing Clegg's crown as she did so. `Leave the caliper with us. Its time for you to go. Arch's already one step ahead.`

THIRTY FIVE

At least one. More likely dozens. Scores. Or was it just seven? Arch was not sure any more, Arch was finding it hard to keep the chaos moving. The tendency of the mess to distill into an awful order was getting almost too much, even for him. He might have to admit the pattern, acknowledge the truth, concede to the Black Knight. The Black Knight? But that was only half of it. Or less. The Black Knight, clever though he no doubt was, all-pervasive as he often seemed, knew, Arch was sure, only part of all this. There was stuff bubbling up from the earth that pre- and postdated the Black Knight by aeons, stuff that would have the Black Knight quivering with fear, certainly rage. Stuff about the feather, its black against blue, the sharp barbs and their shadows falling into place, stuff about the World Truth echoing in a great silent cave, shaping light in a way that had made Arch quiver and moan, stuff about the mission of the Britons, saving world freedom. All this was far beyond the Black Knight. And the Arthur stuff. Arch had assumed that was part of the illusion, the Black Knight's marketing spin, but he was beginning to doubt it. He was beginning to suspect that just as he was caught up in the Black Knight's game then so the Black Knight was caught up in someone else's game. Or some thing else's. Some *thing*. Like the Earth Mother, but bigger, something more... Arch struggled for a word other than fundamental but could not find it, fundamental, like in foundations. The Black Knight was no less a pawn than Arch, the difference being that Arch half knew it and was beginning to see through it.

He dared hardly pierce the turf. He held the nail in his hands for longer than usual, stroked its length, breathed deeply to steady himself. He half knew what would come and what would happen; he half guessed the faces and their voices even before they came. So had he invented them? Had he dreamed them into being before he penetrated the ground, or were they always there, always waiting, screaming in silence into the void, waiting for those with ears and courage and no sense of fear? And did it matter? Whatever, thought Arch. Well, for once it just might, for once it might just be worth a sleepless night or two, if only to clear his head of that damned jay's feather and the sound of that light rippling like water over the ceiling of a distant cave.

They took mercy on him. They came slowly, one by one. Different Camelots. Why not? Different Arthurs. It was not a man, it was a title, a rank, like priest or general. The first was the best. Arch liked the first one's style. Breast plate and iron, sword, shield, pony-tail, bad breath, all the traditional stuff, nothing he couldn't have dreamed up. He was a real king, though, Arch could tell that. The nail seemed respectful, its iron mellow with blood. It was a real king who had fought against the Danes, his Merlin was a real wizard, too. Or at least clairvoyant. Perhaps, like Arch, this Merlin guy had a nail, a secret means of penetration. But the next ones he could not have invented. The next ones were real but so unlikely that Arch knew this was the purest data, that perhaps he was the first to have sucked it from the earth since it had seeped there centuries earlier. Caratacus, another King, but less than the first, fighting against Romans, then a woman, Elisabeth. Her Merlin was not one man but several, spies, plotters, a man called Walsingham was in there somewhere, another even had a code number, 007. It was too incredible not to be true, but already Arch could see the pattern, he thought, but then came Joan of Arc, French. That blew his theory. Or did it? Her Merlin was an angel or two, dubious characters in grottoes muttering revelations. Where had Joan hidden the nail? Arch wondered. But she wasn't even English. A voice told him it didn't matter. She fought against the English to help them, to keep them to their rightful job, something to do with freedom, saving the world. Then Churchill. Arch had heard of Churchill but didn't know anything about him, not enough to make up a story, anyway. In the war with Germany. His iron nail was radar. No, don't laugh, he told himself, just listen, all these guys, whoever, wherever, all these mystic Arthurs, they all had one thing in common, they all had a voice whispering in the ear, they all had some unseen, unknown lead on the opposition. Arch had his nail, Joan had her angel, this Churchill guy had radar. Whatever, don't knock it. Who was Arch to doubt any of this? Just keep it coming, he thought, this is leading somewhere, this is a groovy script and miles more fun than the Black Knight crap. Radar, sure, a kind of nail stuck in the air. German pilots thought the British had the edge over them because of carrots for God's sake! Radar was the last centuries answer to Merlin. Kept these islands free. Enjoy!

But then is stopped. Arch almost jolted forwards it was so sudden. It stopped and the empty silence was frightening. Worse than that. Lonely. There was a great dark loneliness down there and Arch did not like it one little bit. All the swirling Arthurs, all the whispering spies, the drone of spitfires in the sky and sea-ships firing cannon, all gone. And in their place, slowly, steadily, resolving out of the dark, tubes and wires linked to flasks and monitors, flesh floating like an afterthought beneath sheets more solid than the body they hid, the whole thing, body, sheet, tubes, floating up and out, through the window, to be burned up by the sun.

THIRTYSIX

This was no worse to walking through four lanes of speeding traffic. At least then the object had been clear, bright and orange on the ground. Now the object was vague beyond words. It was something to do with revenge on the one hand, belonging on the other. Winning acceptance, certainly. Using the anger, Robert Melrose had said, far too wise, but right. The sheriff had not rushed to explain his plan but allowed the fuss around Andrew to run its course before taking her aside to ask more about the watch and how she might have been parted from it briefly, at the hands of the silent boy and his grandfather perhaps? Outsourcing, Robert Melrose called it. There was no all-reaching maw of security forces, he explained, and more was the pity. The enemy, if there was one, worked through dismembered bodies, each ignorant of their part in the greater scheme of things. Somebody, somewhere, had paid for the right to hunt on the Wildside. Someone else had connected them to the carrier of this particular watch. It made no difference to them whether Andrew or Beth presented themselves as sport on the bare hilltops or the dense valleys, they had paid a fee and they expected to take their pleasure accordingly. There were people in No-Man's-Land who were paid by Comfort Zone interests to place the bugs. If you crossed over you were fair game. If you could be tracked you were of value, whether for hunting, smuggling, or security force surveillance was of no interest to those who placed the bugs. Moses and Timbo were the only suspects. Whilst Beth slept they must have removed and doctored the watch. The consequence was this feeling of being raw and exposed, the feeling the body experiences when lowered into a hot bath in a very cold room, the feeling she always had when her power had been spent. Beth would not have recognized it as loneliness, but it certainly was. She was surprised to feel no anger towards Moses and Timbo. Their paymasters, yes, and the goons who would blunder about in the wilds in an approximation of hunting, certainly, but for some reason she felt the old man and his grandson innocent of anything more than opportunism.

`So they didn't come for me?` Beth asked, not sure what answer she wanted.

`They came for the watch, not you.` Melrose explained. `And they will come for it again.`

`So I'm to help you.`

`Only if you want.`

`And if I don't want, then you send me back?`

`I would no more blackmail you, Beth, than I would dare patronize you a second time for being pretty. If you don't want to help then you should take your chance with Owen and his family. I won't stand in your way.`

He could not have been fairer. She felt a slight regret for the anger she had directed at him earlier but suspected it had done her prospects no harm at all. `I'll do it.` she said. `You knew I would.`

`I saw your face when you understood what had happened to Andrew.` And with that he explained the plan. She would not get to fly with the eagles as the little girl did, but it would come close.

An osprey was patrolling the small lake with little passion or purpose. Almost certainly one of last year's fledglings it had no mate or nest to occupy its instincts and it drifted from lake to lake over a large area constantly being chased away by the settled pairs, trapped awkwardly in its adolescence. Here it was left alone to sulk, but there were few fish to interest it.

The bird's white was vivid against the sky's perfect blue. April was giving way to May, warmth would soon supplant the showers. The green of the hill was at its most virile, lifting it extra feet upward.

The bird had seen Beth but it was too far away to be a worry. She had another five hundred feet to climb. Already the soft hedgerows had surrendered to sparse rowan and ash and limestone boulders, soon even these would concede to heather, bilberry and constant breeze from the West.

The Long Mynd is a strange intrusion into the pastures of what once had been England. Its shoulders are all primrose, Maythorn and quiet pubs, its head is grouse, bog and wretched sheep. It is a boundary between two worlds and as such has its own elemental laws.

Beth was thinking of Andrew as she climbed. He had fascinated her from the start. She had seen pictures of such people but never dreamt that they still existed much beyond conception or that they could live 'normal', lives amongst 'normal' people. She certainly did not connect him with her visit fourteen years ago to her mother in hospital. Despite her revulsion she had sensed from the start that what the world might call his handicap was really his gift and that here it was treated as such. Andrew had no boundary between himself and other people. Their concerns were his concerns. Their joys were his joys. Even after the horror of being hunted he was full of love and warmth for the huge family of everyone he met. Of course there was no place for the likes of Andrew in the Comfort Zone, where mothers designed their babies before conception. Such beings were out of fashion, a genetic 'disaster' that could be easily avoided. Flushed down the toilet, as Andrew put it, the fact's of genetic screening and simple home-induced abortions having once been explained to him by Owen or Betty. It was ironic that the Comfort Zone hunters had stumbled across Andrew by mistake, because hadn't they finally got him? Hunting, making sport, taking pot shots in the dark, wasn't that what they did anyway with their so-called genetics? If they could cull and persecute and impose 'final solutions' on their own bodies and destinies, if they saw themselves only as animal hunting grounds how easy it must have been to take the next small step and to hunt a real, live freak with real, live guns.

But then why stop at the likes of Andrew?

It was impossible to retrace exactly where Andrew had been directed because his descriptions were vague, but the most commonly held theory was that he had been scared upwards on to the Mynd. They must have had a sighting of him, but the weather and their indecision had saved him, of that they were all certain. Less certain was whether they would try again.

The osprey dispelled any doubts Beth may have felt. It swung silently away from the lake and flew towards her, disturbed by somebody or something on the summit. She may have seen a figure move high up in the heather but she could not be certain. She continued climbing.

The top was inconclusive. It rolled away in all directions, each part of equal height and bulk but she could make out two important features. One was a stand of pine trees to the east, leaning and spindly. The second was a helicopter, its grey-green belly comfortable in the heather, broody, like a hen.

`Let it start.` she muttered to itself. There had been enough waiting, she had been the spectator too long. Even if it went wrong, even if they caught her or killed her surely it would move things on, shake the world, her father, Finn, make them cherish her at last. She would show them. Let it start. Cut down the tree, smear on the ash, torch the neighbour's washing. Suddenly, as though to order, bursting from a point directly ahead a scrambling bike spat up mud and smoke and a vulgar noise as it tore towards her. She froze. There was barely a script to play from, only improvisation and a huge wind-blown stage. She wanted the chance to spit in the face of whoever had devised this whole thing, to show contempt for what they had done to Andrew and now intended for her. Melrose had called it the future of Social Darwinism, whatever that meant, the rich hunting the poor for fun. People had been doing it to her all her life.

The man was bundled up in scarves and helmet. `Can't read?` he shouted above the noise of his own engine. `No trespassers!` He suddenly killed the engine and shocked them both with silence. `Don't worry,` he sneered. `Suppose they didn't tell you. Better be off. No, not that way, across. Cut across. Down the other side. If anyone sees, just run. Friends of mine, see. They don't mean any harm. Mad, that's all they are, stark raving mad.` Incomplete sentences, like Anna had said, something Beth had never been conscious of before. It meant she had arrived, she could recognize the Comfort Zone in someone's way of speaking, in the vague muddle of their half-formed thoughts. `Now move!` he suddenly shouted, at which she felt herself grow, she felt a cold strength rise up inside her frightening in its intensity. She willed the man to shout again, to swear, to rant, to implore, knowing that she would feed off him endlessly and become huge in her power, untouchable. But the man was finished, already sucked dry by the way she fixed his eye and stared him out. He gunned the engine and sprayed her with dirt as he belted down the valley, presumably to block her retreat. She looked ahead. At first nothing, but then to left and right and about a mile away, others had appeared, two on each side, watching. More. She wanted more men, an army of them, scores to be humiliated, to make her great in their failure. They were so stupid, so unbelievably stupid. Their plan was obvious. Child-like, just as Melrose had told her. Once over the flat of the top she would descend into a valley like the one she had just climbed. They would cut across the moor, one pair to each side of the valley where cover might give her the illusion of a chance and the men the fun of tracking her. She imagined first luring them into the woods and then turning on them, hooking each with the power of her body, making them twitch like beached fish.

She ran straight into the startling blue. There would be no mist today to spirit her away as it had done Andrew, nor sleep of drugs and coffin lids as there had when she crossed the Line. It was her legs against theirs for the moment. Was she mad to be enjoying this? She had never been more terrified in her life and yet the wonderful thrill of being hunted was carrying her along almost above the heather. Was this how the fox felt, or the stag? In various stretches of No-Man's Land, around Stratford, Leeds and Liverpool, where the crazies lived and hunted each other, was this what drew to-comfort-born teenagers, this thrill of flirting with death? But not Andrew. He would have felt no thrill as he blundered through the undergrowth, blood and snot streaming down his face, terrified of being flushed down the toilet. He had almost certainly gone straight ahead and into the valley where the wind would have tunneled the saving mists to gather him up.

Beth was doing the same. The path was crazed to miss pools of mud and a straight line would have had her bogged down in seconds.

Suddenly her eye was drawn beyond the nearest two men to the helicopter a mile behind them. Its side door was open and to her keen eyes it looked as though a small group of people stood there with binoculars raised. Spectators? When you have lived all your life in an electronic fish-tank, spectators are unmistakable, you have the instinct of the watched. But spectators need spectacle, something spectacular. Beth had been watched all her life, frowned over like a sparrow in an aviary of hawks. She would give them spectacle. They were what she had been running from all her life, their hollow souls craving a fix of entertainment, their dried out hearts aching for the heat of borrowed blood.

At the last possible moment she veered back and to the left, closer to two of the men but in a direct line for the sorry clump of fir trees. Come and get me, she muttered. Come and get me, you're fucked, every one of you, and always have been. The men changed course, whooping like apes and loosing off shots in the air. Amongst the pines she would be trapped. They were broadly spaced and offered no ground cover. Only an old sheep-shearers' shack made any kind of focus or feature. They would be thinking of rape, she knew it, they would not be able to help themselves, the fantasy tripping them even as they sprinted towards her. Let them think it. Let them grow fat and stupid on the idea. Judging her dash to the second Beth entered the wood and belted for the hut just as the two pairs became a foursome and split again to approach her from all sides.

At the helicopter the spectators were growing restless. The pine trees obscured their view of the action, and the vehicle, which should have taken them down into the pre-determined valley, could not cut across bog land to reach the trees. They had paid well for this, even as prospective clients for a subsequent hunt of their own. They could excuse last week's weather, but this was poor form. Perhaps the trees would have to be felled. The sharp sound of gunshot offered them a conclusion of sorts but now came a very long and frustrating silence, then the muffled shouts that barely carried. Then nothing.

The eagle, when it rose, was of course silent. Like a balloon. From a different world. It carried a small bag or pouch and seemed at first reluctant to obey. The tiny radio receiver strapped to its ankle literally buzzed with a few simple commands: climb, away, release, return. None of the spectators had ever seen such a bird. A sea-eagle common around the Scottish coast, had no place so far south or inland. It flew high and lazily towards them. It circled thoughtfully. It dropped the bag. It flicked its way nonchalantly back to the fir trees.

The small bundle landed no more than fifty yards from the helicopter with a dull thud. The spectators had been joined by the beater on his scrambling bike and he it was who collected and opened the bag, spilling its contents in a jerk of revulsion. The severed first fingers, the trigger fingers fresh from four mutilated hands seemed variously to beckon, goad and point. As though to a script the eagle let out a strangely unmajestic screech and wheeled back towards the woods.

THIRTYSEVEN

Agnes was right, Arch had gone. He must have had his own key, stranger still, he must have had his own reasons for coming to the farm, for living amongst them and for disappearing without a word of explanation or farewell. Addiction could do strange things to people, especially to one as dangerously bright as Arch, but addiction to a game, to a fantasy world, if such it was, that was a new one on Clegg.

Agnes offered a symbolic farewell. They travelled to Clun for the May day festival. He owed her a proper goodbye, Agnes had insisted, and he owed himself some real music. She could not believe that he had never heard real, live music.

Clun was a small town dominated by its ruined castle. Tents and marquees covered most available space with stalls and sideshows to cater for the wants and wishes of a widespread community. There were festive events on every street corner and attractions all stunning in their triviality. Tug-o'-war, dog races, parrots, bonsai, sheep-shearing, snakes, Morris dancing, lace-making, ditch-crawling, best pickled beetroot. There seemed to be no limit to the way these people entertained themselves. Clegg viewed it all as a window-shopper might who had no money to spend. If he enjoyed anything it was through Agnes who seemed to know half the people on offer and who could be as enthusiastic about a child's miniature garden as she could about sheep dog's haring up the hillside in perfect response to the faintest of whistles.

At noon the Green Man paraded through the streets, surrounded by fawns and fairies in costumes almost as spectacular as his. He was decked from head to toe in a tangle of leaves and ivy stalks that made movement difficult. He wielded a short stick of obviously phallic importance which the women were advised to keep well clear of unless they wanted a sharp prod in the crutch or buttocks accompanied by the hoots and howls of a suitably lewd audience. At the castle gates he was raised on to a cart which was garlanded with fresh green and flowers and from a throne of foliage he held court for those couples brave enough to take the jokes and banter. A call went up for Maidens to accompany him on his farewell journey, at which a gaggle of girls, too young to understand the significance of it all and beautiful in their innocence were lifted onto the cart as it was pulled away by horses to the accompaniment of pipe music and drums.

They ate by the river at a restaurant set up for the day and which roasted its boar in the Arab way in clay ovens which had been built by local children in the run-up to the event. The same ovens were also firing pots, made by the same children, and by early evening the freshly made pots were in service for the scores of diners who made the most of the long evening and the good weather.

Agnes shopped around for the best music but it was soon obvious that the Church House Inn close to the castle would attract the likeliest. It was a large pub with a wooden floor and high ceilings that would give the music an extra kick. The clatter of glasses and the murmur of talk were on equal terms all evening to the solo whistle and violin players, but now the talk was getting less and more deference was being shown to the string of musicians who offered a jig or a reel. Clegg had to admit it was different. Not only had he scarcely heard live music before, he had never heard music made by instruments rather than machines. His ear may have been corrupted over the years but it didn't stop him from tapping his feet and feeling great envy for these people as they reveled like children in wave after wave of their own making. He even envied them their alcohol, they're swimming in and out of consciousness, the great social heart they were all forming together. Stone cold sober had its advantages, however. He watched their faces and feet, he watched the musicians tuning up and discussing technique, he admired the raw energy not only of the youngsters but those even a decade or two older than himself who had the gusto and energy to drink and sing and dance the night away. He watched the teenagers flirting, the old boys muttering, their wives gossiping, he watched

Agnes move easily amongst them all, like a priestess amongst her congregation, laughing and joking with ease. He felt a twinge of jealousy when one youth, a teenager surely, cupped his hand to Agnes' buttock and was glad to see her clip him, although perhaps too playfully. She was a handsome woman. She had almost been his. She was willing to talk terms. They could carve that on his gravestone if nothing else.

A woman had started singing. It was low, soft and mournful and the pub had fallen silent. It may have been Welsh or Gaelic or some cobbled-together folk-English but the text did not matter because the mood was both subtle and electric. After a couple of verses unaccompanied she upped her pitch as a violin picked up the melody. Next came a side flute throwing tragic thoughts high above the voice and strings. Then the drums. They too were soft and insistent to begin with, Irish side drums, three, all played by unlikely looking women, one at least in her eighties. The voice did not let up but became more intense, more searching, a whistle toyed with the flute, a second violin urged on the pace and then bagpipes, Breton-pipes, not that Clegg would have known, laying a drone that threatened to move his bowels and by now a tempo carried by the drums but also spoons and tapping feet which had even Clegg in its thrall, clapping and swaying and just when it could get no better up stood two women who placed what looked like tea-trays on the floor and on these they started their flat-foot dancing to a rhythm and at a speed which had Clegg struggling to hide his disbelief. His whole body was now caught up in the rhythm. The entire pub was, everyone hobbled by the beat. Almost spontaneously the floor had cleared and Agnes, God-bless her, was centre stage, tapping and swirling, her skirts wide with the movement and her face flushed with the heat, her breasts taut against her blouse, hair flung back and plastered to the sweat of her temples and then a great whoop of delight as she was joined on the floor by some kind of freak, his great slug of a tongue glistening in the lights, his hand shooting back and forwards to return his slipping specs to the bridge of his nose, his grin inane and animal-like. At least to Clegg's reckoning, but weren't they all made animal by the music and the drink? For a second he had to grip his chair to stop from leaping up and tearing the freak away from Agnes, but the noise and the rhythm would have drowned him and the floor was filling with others caught by the music. The singer had conceded gracefully but the instruments raced on until by a wonderful feat of timing all stopped at the same moment except for the drums which raced into their deep heart-beat solo, ending all to the accompaniment of cheers and clapping from the entire pub.

Angry. He didn't even ask himself why. Five years ago he would have thrown over the tables and smashed glasses, he would picked a fight with whoever dared meet his eye and would have ended it all in the gutter or an army cell. Now he sulked into his elder berry juice. Why should these people strut and leap and squeal like pigs and enjoy themselves whilst he could only sit and glower, whilst Bonny and thousands like her slit their wrists or puked up the day's intake of junk? What right did they have to be so happy and self-righteous, brothers and sisters in some great carnal sin? They were meant to be grim. They were meant to top turnips, to live in a damp depression, to envy Clegg and his kind, to lust after slick machines and Japanese wizardry. Who did they think they were conspiring together, witches around a cauldron, initiates in a profane rite to which Clegg had not been invited?

His rage turned suddenly ice cold and found a focus as his ears picked up a hint of something momentous. The group in the corner, the freak, an old man, some Welsh louts, a pretty girl, they had turned themselves into a birthday party, they were toasting the girl, singing her name. Only on the third time did it hit him and jolt him from his frenzy of disgust. Happy birthday, dear Beth. There it was again. Happy Birthday, Beth. A common name? He had no need to weigh up odds, to dismiss the chances, to count the risks. He knew. He knew as surely as he hated this place and its wonderful music that this was Beth Savage. This was the girl who would lead him to the pot of gold. This was the girl who had somehow snarled up his life. She had been there all night, right under his nose. She was next to the freak, she was laughing and drinking. She belonged. She was one of them. An insider. Something Clegg would never be.

`Nat?` It was Agnes. `Nat? What's wrong? You look like death.`

You have never seen death, he thought. One day I'll show you, then you'll know that this is worse, far worse. This whole place is worse than death. It has no points of reference, no logic, it makes no sense. `I'm all right,` he lied. `Do you know all these people?` he gestured wildly into the crowded room.

`Of course not. How could I?`

`You seem to know most of them.` he muttered, trying hard not to make it an accusation. He tested her on a few, leading her off the scent, gaining control of his anger as he did so. She must not know, she must not see through him in this as she had done in everything else. He asked her about the barman, the old girl on the drum, the fiddle player. `And that one?` he asked, pointing to Andrew, aiming as close to his real target as he dared.

Agnes obliged. She knew most by name or reputation. Andrew belonged to the Owen troop, she told him, circus people, just passing through. His thoughts raced ahead. He was stitching together clues, building a map of possibilities, wrestling with the unreal odds. His anger had turned to something vibrant, something closer to a thrill, the excitement of the chase and the likelihood of failure. But this also passed, and in its place, to his great surprise, like exhaustion after the fight, a feeling of resignation, a feeling that it might not matter in the slightest if he never found John Savage.

The girl had stood up and was leaving her group in the corner, heading for the door. Clegg waited until Agnes had gone to the bar for fresh drinks before slipping quietly from his place and following the birthday girl into the night.

THIRTTYEIGHT

Beth's birthday came a day early in the form of a letter. It was handed to her with great ceremony by Andrew, who was now much restored since his ordeal on the Mynd. The fact that they had both been through a similar experience pleased him greatly and he was no longer reluctant to talk about it. Giving Beth the letter cemented their relationship as far as he was concerned, they were in this together, he lisped, come what may. So was Owen. Andrew had been given two letters three months earlier by `a young man with bare feet`, one for Beth and one for Owen, neither of them to be delivered or referred to until the girl arrived in search of money to buy a flute. Keeping the secret from his brother had been Andrew's biggest problem, but now the waiting was over and the secret was out. Owen had known John Savage well and was amazed to find himself in the thick of a plot to which Andrew was party but about which he had been kept in the dark. He had been John Savage's bodyguard at a time when he was touring the world, giving lectures about his alternative science and improbable politics. Owen's old loyalties were immediately activated by the letter of explanation from his old friend and employer, a letter which also apologised for using Andrew as a reliable but thoroughly unlikely courier, an extra measure of security that had certainly worked.

Beth ripped her letter open eagerly but then hesitated to read it in company. A sudden dread came over her as she tried to guess its contents. She took herself away to a quiet corner of the woods before daring to move closer to her father.

My Dearest Beth,

You are truly, truly amazing! You have done so well to reach Andrew and now I can begin to hope that we will all soon be together. Even Sam, God willing.

I am sorry I had to lead this far by riddles but I am sure you understand the need to keep people off your trail. I have asked

Owen to accompany you to a place called Llanidloes. He will know the way and make a good companion. You can trust him. He will tell you endless stories about the times he and I spent together. Don't believe everything he tells you! What he does not know is that our time is running out. My body is not well, Beth, you need to be aware of that. I am happy, as always, and long to see my children, but my body, poor thing, is really not well. Owen does not need to know, but I thought it best to warn you. In Llanidloes you will be given exact information as to my whereabouts. The church doorway will carry a message for you when you arrive. Don't worry, we will know you are there! I cannot wait to see you again and to hear of your adventures and to hear what you think of this strange world of ours. Be quick, for all our sakes!

Your loving father.

What he left unsaid she could only guess. All these precautions to make sure she was not followed made a nonsense of what Finn had told her, yet it was not Finn she found herself doubting. There was something she was not being told and the feeling of being only partly trusted was not a comfortable one. Furthermore the thought of her father's illness inclined her to both hurry and delay. There was something in the prospect of it that repelled her; she was not aware of ever having seen him weak or vulnerable. Although she felt sympathy and concern and hurt for him she also felt slightly let down. Surely now, when she needed him most, he should be strong and able? She found herself sighing, as much at her own situation as his. But she would hurry, if only for Sam's sake. If her father was weak then at least Sam was strong.

A birthday party in the company of strangers was not what she would have chosen for herself, but Owen, Betty, Andrew and the rest insisted on the need for celebration. They found a pub with lots of music and dancing and Andrew succeeded in making her laugh. Then came a present from Betty, her old Bodhran. The twins said they would teach her how to play it, the least they could do, Jamie said, which was their way of apologizing for having turned her in to Melrose. Beth appeared gracious but hid her true feelings. Nobody would teach her to play the thing, she thought to herself, because very soon she would be gone and forgotten. Owen's obligation was to John Savage and the past, not to her own future.

During the music and dancing Beth slipped backwards and forwards between two extreme moods. One minute she was elated, thrilled by the company and her own achievements, the next she was morose and silent, brooding on what was still to come. The episode on the Mynd stood out as the high point of her journey. Although the idea had come from Melrose and the back-up was thorough Beth knew that up there she had been alone, and most importantly beyond the planning of her father. He had orchestrated everything in his own wonderful way, but up there she had been beyond the reach of his letters or contacts or hidden agendas. He would certainly have been angry with her for taking such a huge risk when so much was at stake, but what if he was? The thought of it only made Beth more certain of herself.

But her journey also had a low point. It was a constant nag she had not expected. Whether it came from the anxiety bred into her or the instruction to trust no one or Finn's revelation hardly mattered, the fact was that the feeling of being watched and followed, a feeling she had expected to leave behind in the Comfort Zone, was more or less constant. It struck her now in the noise and good humour of the pub and made her sullen once more. Even here, she felt, even in the confused crowd and half-light there was a presence out there, something that weighed on her and would not let her free. She peered into the corners of the pub to convince herself that she was wrong but failed. At times it seemed as though dozens of eyes were watching her through glass bottoms or mirror reflections. The fact that no one was looking her way only confirmed the fear. She watched the shadows of hands and faces huge and distorted against the walls, moving as though they had a life of their own, as though their human counter-parts were the illusion. Suddenly she wanted to be out of their reach, not of the people but their shadows, the half-truths cast by everyone in the crowded room, by everyone she had ever met. During a lull in the music she slipped out of the pub, apparently for fresh air. Jamie made as though to follow her, an expectant look on his face that Beth dismissed with a shake of the head and a glare. Whatever comfort she sought could not be provided by him. It was a mild evening and the town was lively enough for her not to stand out or feel unsafe, although it was not long before some instinct took her towards the castle and the river, away from the noise and lights. No doubt there were people down there to spy on her. Or one person. A man. That was all Finn had known or would tell her. Make sure she was followed, he had said. But by whom? And why? With the letter delivered and her destination known it seemed even more vital to understand the plot, but how could she when her father did not trust her? Why was he doing this to her? It was her father's doing, somewhere, somehow, though Beth could not even begin to guess how or why. She heard a noise. A cat or dog? It was heavier than a cat, more stealthy than a dog. She had imagined it. There it was again. And a movement. Jamie? Surely not, he had read the signs and was meek enough to obey them. It was in the shadows by the river side, under the trees. Her first instinct was to run, her second was to lunge at the shadows, to call the bluff of whoever was out there. She had not felt like this on the Mynd. She had been certain then of back-up, Dai, Owen and Melrose's men and there, in the light, the threat had been obvious and somehow blunt, as though she had been up against children playing a game. And it had been her own choice. This was different. She listened to the breeze in the undergrowth and the chatter of the river, both of which could have hidden the noise of a stalker or even the sounds of a struggle if somebody jumped her. She turned suddenly. A figure moved in the bushes. `Jamie?` she called, without conviction. `Stop playing.` Nothing, only silence, the menace of her own imagination, her voice small and flat. A shape again. A man? She sensed rather than saw it. Or an illusion, a demon of her own fear? There it was again, a parting of branches, a silence in the dark where there should have been the play of breeze on leaves. The next second a scream snatched in her throat as a hand came down on her shoulder. She turned and drew away at the same time but the hand gripped her tightly and its owner stepped into the lesser dark, caught the hand she had raised to strike with, and pulled her forwards. It was a man, she could smell it, she brought her knee into his groin but he was too fast and caught her under the thigh. The next moment they were kissing, anger still coiled in the nails she dug into his back, but relief intense as he eased her away, brushed the hair from her eyes, started to apologize, stammer and grin all at the same time.

`You had better slap me again,` Finn said, softly, waiting for her judgement. But instead she started to laugh; relief and pleasure confused. She laughed like a young girl, as she had not done for a long time. She tried to kiss him again but after a few seconds the laughter returned and it was her turn to apologize.

`If I'd had a knife,` she started to say.

`But you don't.`

`How do you know?`

She knew the answer before he provided it. Because he had been watching her. She also knew something else. Finn could not lie. He was incapable of it. He had never learned how. She knew that if she framed her questions right he would squirm and apologize endlessly but he would never lie. She suddenly felt sorry for him. It was as though she had discovered a secret that would give her limitless power over him, a power she was quite free to abuse.

`Why did you kiss me?` she asked.

`It was a birthday present. I'm sorry, I shouldn't...`

`Why did you kiss me?`

`Because you're beautiful.` he confessed.

`And?

`And I've been following you.`

`And?`

`I've been watching you.`

`And what have you seen?`

Before answering he looked around. He had left his bedroll and crossbow by the river but he led her towards a bench some distance away barely in the light of a street lamp. Once seated he reached into her jacket pocket and took out the matchbox. A million years ago Beth had burned her own clothes by the river, she had decorated herself with the ash and stared into the woods, thinking of Finn. It was the matchbox she had filled with ash by the fire and had carried safely, apparently for this moment. `It's just an idea.` Finn said, opening the box, taking wet ash onto his finger tip. 'You don't have to. But you must have saved it for a reason. It won't change anything if you say no, I mean we still have a job to do. I won't let it get in the way.`

If Finn had been following and watching her he would have seen her ritual painting with this same ash, he would have seen her with Jamie, with the baker, perhaps even with Timbo. She wondered what secrets she still had from him. Was it worth the pretence or the effort? Why not show him her father's letter, or did he already know about that? For now he had obviously come to claim a piece of her for himself, as she had expected him to on Doctor Johnson's boat. She had felt confused by his lack of interest then. Now she felt irritated that he had sprung it on her in this way.

`Let what get in the way?` she asked, already knowing the answer.

`I was wondering,` he said, `If you wanted, I mean it's only symbolic, but...` She feigned patience. `If we could become a Tribe of Two.`

`A what?`

`I'll understand if you don't want to, I mean...` his voice trailed off bleakly.

Beth sighed. She was bored by the coded deference. If this was Wildside euphemism she could live without it. Suddenly the disappointment was like an ache. She had thought that Finn was different, in some way above all that, but she had been wrong. He was the same as all the others who had assumed she was there to answer their needs. Bitter experience told her it was better to get this kind of thing out of the way as soon as possible.

`OK.` she answered, the contempt clear in her voice. `Here?`

`Why not?`

Why not? Why not in the pub itself or the main street? At home men took what they wanted wherever it suited them. `It's just the light` she said, `perhaps you'd prefer...`

`No the light is good, we need the light to see if we're doing it right. I've never done it before.`

She was too confused to laugh at him. She started to unbutton her blouse but Finn stopped her. `Just the face,` he said, `That's all we need.`

Before she could respond his finger, dipped in the ash, had reached out to her face and was softly drawing a line on her skin. Confused, her mouth hung open, her breathing changed, the disappointment she had felt began to shift. She felt a slight thrill.

`Now you do the same.` he urged.

She took the ash and imitated on his face what she had felt on her own: a strong black line, waving slightly across the forehead. He made marks on her cheeks which she copied. He finished with a dot in the centre of her brow. She did the same and then gasped. Tears were rolling down her cheeks. She wiped them without thinking, realized she had smudged the markings and looked at Finn for guidance. He took her hand and made her smudge his own. They started to laugh. A Tribe of Two. Finn *was* different. He kissed her again, but so softly it felt like another kind of apology. How can I tell Sam? She thought, stupidly, Sam would never believe this. But then she realized that Sam already knew and had known for a long time and that Sam would thoroughly approve.

`What now?` she whispered. She found herself wanting him in the usual way, something she had never dreamed would be possible, but she was afraid of losing the mood, of slipping back into the shadows they seemed to have left.

`It's like being blood brothers.` he said. `We look out for each other.`

`What else?`

He started to kiss her again, this time without apology, but after a second he leapt up and Beth stiffened. There was a noise in the bushes by the river, a presence too close for comfort, followed by a splash. Finn ran to the water, waded out a yard or two and fished out a bundle. His bed roll.

`Who...?` Beth started to ask but stopped when she saw the direction of his gaze. Above their heads and hanging just out of reach was Finn's crossbow.

THIRTYNINE

Judas was the good guy, Jenny.

Whatever you say, Nat.

Whatever Ralph Bailey says, Jen. Ralph Bailey knows a lot. Theory number ninety four.

And the other ninety-three?

This one seems to have stuck. This one won't go away.

A fresh trial, Nat, is that what's needed?

For Judas?

For both of you?

It's all down to motive, Jen.

So what's yours, Nat?

If it was money, if he did it for money then let him swing.

Yours I said.

Let the crows take out his eyes.

Not Judas, Nat, you. What's your motive?

But if it was something else, Jen.

Something else, Nat?

If he did it to turn the world upside down, on its head, inside out. After all, the fruit of betrayal is not always bitter.

Whatever, Nat.

No Judas, no Grail.

Why are you telling me this?

You trusted me once.

More than you trusted yourself, Nat.

I can't tell Agnes.

Why not?

She'd laugh.

That might not matter.

Might not?

Sure. It all depends, Nat.

On what?

Motive.

Clegg took instructions from Agnes. A walk, a train, a further walk, hills and forests strung together in her description much like stars in an unmapped heaven. The Valley of Healing and perhaps, just perhaps, priority number eighteen, beat Arch at his own Game. Capital `G`.

He had half expected a steam train with a face painted on its front and filthy carriages full of farmers and their livestock. At home rail travel had almost been killed off by making it free to the unemployed, a move aimed at boosting car sales.

The reality was impressively different. The train was battery operated and the central carriage of three housed a large friction wheel that used the centre of the track and the sleepers to resist the train's down-hill movement and to recharge its batteries at the same time. It gave off a reassuring hum throughout the journey and enabled track to take steep gradients, most of it having been laid on old roads. The energy equation was balanced at each of the frequent stations where a five-minute recharge was standard.

The passengers were varied, comfortable and nearly all seemed to be transporting more than just personal luggage, a trend aided by the large sliding doors and the in-built storage space. Bicycles, bolts of cloth, a bundle of willow lathes, a wheeled crate of pottery, a windmill kit, a cello or double bass, bags of seed corn and any number of children's push-chairs made their entrances and exits as Clegg watched as discreetly as he could.

At one point the train was delayed. It stood for more than ten minutes at the head of a valley, side on to a broad view. Out of boredom Clegg tried looking at it as Agnes might have done, rather than thinking how much all that timber would sell for back home. He remembered a neighbour from his childhood, a sad old recluse who everyone avoided but who had turned his large back garden into a ridiculous model. He had made of it a toy landscape with tiny fields each the size of face flannels, hedged in with moss and even minute walls of gravel cemented together. He had planted heathers and low shrubs to look like woodland, made a concrete river bed and put in tracks and paths for the model tractors and cows. In a better world he might have won a prize for it, but in this world he was lucky not to have been put away. Clegg and his mates had done him a favour. Bored one summer's day they had knocked on the old man's door and asked, as sweet as pie, if they could see the famous garden. The poor fool had almost wet himself with excitement, showing them the tiny trivia of a foxes' earth and a salmon leap which he had recently added, pointing out where his pretend house would have been had it all been real, plying them with biscuits and invitations to return.

They had returned all right. They had parked their ankle tags on a warm-blooded accomplice who had remained outside, within range of the street-corner sensor whilst they had climbed the garden fence and smashed the whole pathetic sham, ripping up the plants, torching the model houses, pissing in the toy lake.

The man had died a year later, which led to two surprises. The first was that Clegg's mum had gone to the funeral, the second was the discovery that an almost secret society of model-makers existed, similarly deranged men and women whose way of revolution was to create in miniature what their hearts ached for on a real scale. Several had been at the funeral, unashamedly.

Wasn't this the same? The fields and hedgerows and walls and woodlands, wasn't it all a similar model, a pointless waste of time, an escape from the real grind of life? Wouldn't Clegg be doing them all a favour by smashing it all up, grubbing out their ridiculous fantasy, pissing in the lake of their collective folly? You got nowhere by going backwards, and standing still had never been an option. These people needed to move ahead. As though reading his thoughts the train lurched slightly and resumed its way, leaving the valley via a tunnel that offered Clegg his own reflection, staring back from the window. For a second he was shocked by the look in his eye. He hadn't seen a mirror since crossing over. His hair was cropped short and never a problem and he had let his stubble do its worse, but his eyes, just for a second, were not his own. His eyes were his mothers, looking into a landscape of infinite wonder. Suddenly the tunnel was gone and with it the reflection, but Clegg found himself fingering the bracelet. Two dragons entwined with their heads joined by fire. He had worn it to please her of course, but he was tempted to keep it boxed and perfect, to sell for more when he got home. Dragons. Mythological crap. He had read once that myths belonged to mankind's childhood. Mankind's puberty came with the scientific age, with illusions of power and sensuous plenty. Mid-life crisis came with the millennium. Doubt and angst and no direction. Over here they had coped with mid-life crisis very easily. They had just returned to childhood, like the man with his model. Perhaps it was time to wake them up to the Comfort Zone version of death by boredom.

Clegg tried to feel smug and slightly powerful. Agnes was on his side, it seemed. She had answered all his questions about routes to the Valley of Healing and had fixed him up with food and advice. She had looked a little wistful at his parting and had kissed him firmly on the cheek. Clegg could still smell the milk and imagined gold. If she had known of his true intention then she would surely have turned him over to the Arkites knowing it would be the death of him. She trusted him. Now he was free to betray her, to undo the world she believed in. And yet Agnes was no fool. There was a nagging doubt at the back of Clegg's mind that perhaps she knew more than she let on and that perhaps he was the one most likely to be screwed. Judas as the hero? Either they were trying to tell him something or this place was making him paranoid. He allowed himself to think the unthinkable. Agnes knew. She knew everything, or at least more than Clegg knew, which was not difficult. She had saved him at the road-side, she had arranged with the Arkites to have him deposited with her, she had taken the time to weigh him up, to check him out, she had warned him against Arch, and finally she had even taken him to Clun in order to pick up the trail. It was all too awful to be true. It would mean that the

System, perhaps via Danny, or at least via a mistake made by Danny, had followed him, had picked up his trail. The System knew what he was about, they wanted him to succeed. He was being used, now as always, to serve the ends of others. It was easier to allow for coincidence, to keep Agnes in a neutral space, tomorrow's whore, not today's Judas.

Clegg left the train as Agnes had advised and found himself in a broad bleak valley with domed hills humped on either side. From here he would have a day's walk to the so-called Valley of Healing, to the great jamboree of madmen. He liked to think he was prepared for everything. He liked to think that even if his route via Agnes had been manipulated that he still had the power to double guess the lot of them. After all, how could they know what he was doing when he had very little idea himself?

By early evening the rain had stopped and the sky had cleared. He followed the road cautiously, listening all the time. Perhaps half an hour before final dark his suspicion was rewarded. The noise was unmistakable. As pleasant to his ears as it was offensive to the song birds it silenced, as sweet as a woman purring under his touch, the insistent noise that proved to Clegg, if proof were needed, just how clever he really was, just how irresistible was his thrust for those thirty or more pieces of silver.

He buried himself in the hedgerow as the scrambler went past. His scrambler. Agnes had been right. Arch's Game might have rules of its own but they could still be guessed by anyone with a suspicious bent. The bike was obviously undamaged, something its new driver might not be before the night was done.

FORTY

Clun had a hangover. There was litter in the streets and the shops were reluctant to open. Beth, Owen and Andrew set out early to avoid the congestion of stall-holders who would soon be decamping. None of them felt the need to talk. Beth, in her silence, was beginning to understand Finn's rejection and was angry, not at him but with herself. She wondered if by abstaining, which seemed possible here, even normal, would she become virgin again, clean enough even for Finn? She knew the obvious answer but ignored it. Perhaps she was virgin, beyond her body at least, because she had only given herself for the feeling of power that went with it. She was beginning to realize that abstinence brought a far greater power, something inestimable in its ability to move people on in their lives. A Tribe of Two. It made her uncomfortable. She had given too much away, because where was Finn when she needed him? Last night, after the confusion of being watched or made fun of, they assumed by children, Finn had vanished without a word of farewell. And where did all this leave Sam? Sam had felt close to her all this time but now seemed absent just when their father might be within reach. Or was Sam angry? She carried the mood like a cloud, confused, resentful towards Finn, thinking of him all the time but annoyed by it, cool towards Owen and Andrew. She tried talking to the horse but it ignored her. For the first time on the Wildside the trees were silent, the birds muted. She felt guilty for not feeling light-hearted. And she felt scared but could not admit it, not even to herself.

Owen found the solution. Having followed the Kerry ridgeway from England into Wales and made good progress in the perfect spring weather he proposed a detour. They dropped from the ridgeway and cut across heath land and young woods to the edge of a lake where they tethered their horses before creeping forwards to this hiding place. After a wait of nearly two hours they were rewarded. Two adult beavers feeding and preening, although no sign of young. At such a time and in such a place the shadows are pure, cleaner than light. It is impossible to resent them.

That night they found an inn. Beth and Andrew chose to sleep with the horses but they persuaded Owen to treat his older bones to a bed. They met in the lounge, dark but for a log fire and listened to Owen. `Its European beavers, see,` he told them `Don't make no big claims on anyone or anything. Not like those Canadian yobs. Very polite beavers all in all. Doesn't need great dams and lakes, gentle with the world, on the whole.`

`I could have watched them all day.` Beth answered, aware that her mood was lifting. Owen explained the theory that every restored species returned something to the soul of the land. Beaver, bustard, eagles, storks, boar, kites, polecat, marten, corncrake and a dozen types of hawk and harrier had reclaimed their part in the landscape. Each returned species was a small miracle of healing, he said, nodding sagely at Beth.

Her need was to share them. With the balloon and eagles she had wanted to share them with Sam, to see his face as the little girl trusted herself to the air. But now Beth was in a tribe of two. She imagined returning here, not with Owen and Andrew, not with Sam, but with Finn, showing him something of his own world, seeing his eyes grow even wider and his breathing even stiller. She found herself telling Owen and Andrew about Moses the salvage man and his talk of them all being in a story, of everyone needing a story to live by.

Owen was impressed. The warmth and light of the log fire seemed to encourage confessions. `The old man was talking sense,` he said, `even if he did lumber you with a bugged watch. We do all need a story, more now than ever before. Years ago, before I met your father, I traveled the world a bit, watched it fall apart. I went to Brazil. Just at the end of the last century it must have been. The future was there to be seen, really, in places like Brazil they were living our future years before we woke up to it.`

Beth asked him to explain.

`I mean the street children, the have-nots, the waste product. Tens of thousands of them. Tens of thousands. Even then you could be put in prison at the age of four. Prisons full of little children, can you imagine? No, don't even try. Food and TV, that's all they were given, all day long, TV, nothing else. If you walked in there they didn't even look up. If you could teach them a trick, how to pick a lock, that kind of thing, then they would, then they would watch and listen, but otherwise, nothing. It was like being in the land of the dead.` He stopped, moved by the memory of it. He checked to make sure Andrew was not too upset by the tale. `I went there with a friend,` he continued, `A lady friend. A teacher. They told her the children would tear her to pieces if they didn't ignore her. I went with her and watched. After half an hour of being in there every single child, from four to fourteen was staring at her, open-mouthed, fascinated, transfixed they were.`

`What was she doing?` Beth asked.

`Telling a story. A fairy story. That's all it was. Telling a fairy story. Every child was lapping it up. She went back every day after that, became a feature, she did. A wonderful thing. A very wonderful thing. Your man was right, we all need a story to live by.`

Nobody spoke for several minutes although by the time Beth came out with her question Owen had arrived at the same point in his thoughts and probably by a very similar route. `You knew my father.` she asked, suddenly nervous. `Does that mean you knew my mother?`

`I met her, Beth. I didn't know her well. She was as busy as your father in those days. Don't forget I was with your father on his lecture tours. Your mother stayed behind. They often had to live separate lives.` So far so good. Nothing awkward or edged.

`So what was special about Dad? What was his story?`

Owen was taken by surprise. He had braced himself for more questions about Emma Savage, knowing full well that Beth had known the one but not the other. `He is a very gifted man. And he always seemed big to me, Beth, a big man, though he never was.

But most of all he's warm. A big heart. Always interested in other people and concerned for them...`

`I don't mean that.` Beth said, `I know all that. I mean the other stuff. There was a book wasn't there? There were things in the papers, civil war stuff. Some strange ideas? There was a story. Something to make everyone listen.`

It was safe ground but Owen had no way of knowing how much she knew and how much her father had chosen to keep quiet. The book she referred to was written when Beth was in nappies. It was certainly old, but as Robert Melrose had said, some stories never quite die.

`Oh there was a book, Beth, certainly there was, and a theory. Plenty of theories around then, you see. Two a penny they were. Mind, it was quite popular, I can't deny. There was a newspaper that took up the idea. It caught the public's imagination. You know how these things happen.`

No, not really. If anyone had made a habit of avoiding the media and the popular mind it was Beth. `Tell me about it.` she said, making it sound like an instruction, not a request. Hearing her own tone she softened a little. `If you don't mind,` she added.

`Well it was to do with history,` Owen began. `But so was everything else. A lot of interest in history back then, there was. The whole country was busy reinventing itself if you ask me. It was a time of crisis, even before the Civil War. Scotland had broken away. Sunderland and Newcastle were virtually at war. London wanted independence. Its difficult to imagine now just how things were. Everything was negotiable, that's how they used to describe it, everything was negotiable in a way it hadn't been for hundreds of years.`

`The theory was about King Arthur wasn't it?`

`It was, Beth. It was. A mess of clap-trap and second rate journalism if you ask me.`

`So you didn't believe it?`

`No, I didn't say that. You should never believe everything you read, that's all. It was about King Arthur waking up. And like your friend said, every one should have a story to live by, just a bit odd, mind, in an age when myths and things had all been dumped. It was always said Arthur would wake up when the country needed him, when freedom was threatened, that kind of thing. A lot of talk about freedom then. That's something else that comes and goes.`

`And King Arthur would save the country?`

`Something like that.`

`Someone has to.` she said. `But first you have to let go of all that stuff. We're all King Arthur nowadays. And Merlin. And Galahad. We're all responsible for the good and the bad. We can't blame it on heroes anymore. Why not you and me, Owen? Save the country shall we? You ready for it?`

Dear God, he thought, she is like her mother. Bright, direct, beautiful. No wonder they all loved her. No wonder John couldn't hold on to her. And this one, she would break hearts as well, far too many than would be good for her. They were disturbed by the sound of Andrew snoring, his head slumped against the wooden settle. It made them both smile and without saying anything they knew the subject was closed and it was time to sleep.

The valley of Llanidloes is centred on the town with its old bridge, physically at the centre of old Wales. Both the Wye and the Severn rise hereabouts in the mountains of Plynlimon to the west, but for all its natural beauty there is a certain gloom about it, even in the sun. Perhaps the hills are too close to one another or the rivers too restless or the town in some way ill conceived. Whatever the reason those whose job it is to decide such things have agreed that Llanidloes needs healing in the hope that the surrounding countryside as well as the present town and valley will prosper and be healthier. Scores of people have gathered to watch and to participate in the festival of music and dance and ritual which will return the valley to a state of health. Some have been here for weeks, sensitives who will offer their opinions and observations to the appointed priest, people who live for such gatherings and who spend their lives travelling from venue to venue. Others have arrived only at the last minute, self-confessed hangers-on to whom the rituals mean very little but who see the chance to sell a horse, find a wife or pick a pocket.

The priestess is housed in a large white tent pitched next to the river. She has not been seen for a week now and rumours are going the rounds that she will want the bridge pulled down or all the sycamores felled or an acupuncture stone set in the town square where the stocks now stand. But the rumours come from gossip and fire-side speculation, not from the priestess's tent. Tomorrow such rumours may indeed become fact but tonight Beth's own act and ritual of healing was about to start and it is for the church she was anxious to head, perhaps too anxious. Blame the letter, blame the waiting, blame Owen's local knowledge. Or Merlin whispering in the ear. It was Owen who told Beth the legend of St.Idloes church, although he could not remember how he had learned of such a thing. If you walked around it twelve times, he told her, on a certain night of the year. Which one? He shook his head, shrugged his shoulders, unsure of the details or their significance. If, if, a hundred times if, then you could peep through the key-hole of the door and read the list of next year's dead. Next year's dead. Who would read such a list for fear of familiar names? How far could such a list cast its lines and shadows into the world of here and now? Beth would read it and Owen, annoyed at himself for putting the thought there as well as anxious to watch over her success would accompany her. But Beth lied. Forget it, she said, its not important, lets sleep. Once Owen had retired to his room and Andrew was installed in the hay she left the dark silence of the inn for the shadows of the future.

It was a lively night and at first the town seemed welcoming and festive, but away from the square and approaching the church a more sober mood hung around the doorways. The church itself was dimly lit and seemed a little too grand for its setting. Perhaps guilty, its beautiful arched bays having been filched from the plundered abbey of Cwmhir half a millennium ago.

`Which way, Sam?` Beth asked the night. `Widdershins,' she answered, not waiting for an answer. Anti-clockwise. You always had to go widdershins in the fairy stories, she thought, and you always had to go against the flow to get anything in life. Behind her the dark bulk of the building looked as though it might reach out and make its deadly claim. Finn was far away, Owen and Andrew were sleeping. Almost alone, except for Sam, except for his voice in her ear. How else could it have been in the end?

There had been a change. A weak light, previously unlit now cast dull yellow on the dark wood. An envelope was pinned to the door. Beth's name was on the envelope, as she had always known it would be. She knew what it would say. It would lead her to the great John Savage. It would list next year's dead. But she didn't care where it led. She understood now.

FORTY ONE

Arch on the end of a hangman's noose. At times like this you see the imperfections: the meager store of fat turning generously to sweat, the eyes sunk half into his skull and the rope snagged against the Adam's apple. What an excellent start to the day, thought Clegg, looking at his catch, what a perfect beginning to an ideal end.

`Can we be straight with each other?` Clegg asked. A generous offer. He was sat in the shade of the trees, paring the rind from a cheese, laying slices on fat wads of Agnes's rye bread. Arch by contrast had to stretch his toes and torture his calves just to prevent the rope from throttling him.

Arch tried to shake his head. He had an inconsistent honesty that might yet be his undoing. `Can't promise,` he croaked, `Not in my nature, Nat. You know that, come on, man, give us a break. Who kept you in advice back there in the land of the dinosaurs? Who taught you the rules? The sound of one tree clapping? You're my highwayman, Nat, I'm your red-coat.`

`Who pulled me off my bike?` Clegg asked, very composed. `Who nearly broke my only neck and handed me over to the primitives in the first place?`

`Some clown who should have known better.` said Arch, `Some one who got it wrong. I've finished with him, Nat, he's off the staff, I promise, he's out of here. I'm straight now. Get me down and we can talk. You know as much as I do, but I can tell it better. Please.`

Clegg ignored him. `Twenty questions. I'll ask you twenty questions, Arch. You're into games, right? It's one I learnt from Agnes. Try it by my rules. You answer them right and I'll be nice to you. I might even let you go. But you get even one wrong, you hesitate, repeat or deviate and this knife starts on your rind.`

`Number one, Nat. Go on, I'm good at this. Try me.`

`You're ready?`

`Yes! I'm ready.` he screamed. `Nineteen left.` He was half laughing half crying, caught between the need to toy with words and get himself out of the mess.

`What's the aim of your game, Arch?`

`To win.`

`To win, sure, but how do you win?`

`You have to reach the goal.`

`What's the goal?`

`To win. No!` Clegg had stood up, a show of impatience and the knife at the ready. `To find King Arthur. The aim of the game is to find King Arthur.`

`And who is King Arthur?`

`King of the Britons. Scourge of the foe, champion of the down-trodden. She used to wear lace around her neck, smoke cigars. No, I'm serious.`

`His real name?`

`Don't spoil it, Nat, you lose points if you spoil it.`

`Do I have to repeat the question?`

`His real name? This time round, this time round, right, I'll explain another time, I promise, for now its John Savage. John Savage is King Arthur. Or his son. Or the girl. It gets a bit confusing.`

`Who do you work for?`

`The Black Knight.`

`And who is the Black knight?`

`Some bastard on the other side who set this whole thing up, who set me up and any number of others and who probably wants us both dead.` This came in a rush, Arch's best effort yet at genuine honesty.

`Is Agnes in on the game?`

`No. Not that I know of.`

`Is Agnes straight?`

`Man give me a break. Is any one straight around here? Ralph suck-my-Cheddar Bailey might be the chief of police, his daughter might be minister of finances. How the fuck do I know? She's not in the game. I'd put money on that, Nat. Eleven down. Nine left. Please, Nat, this thing is killing me. I'm no use to you dead.`

`You're not much use to anyone alive, Arch, remember that will you? Question twelve. Is there a girl in the frame?`

Arch seemed to think about that one and Clegg suspected he was not bluffing. Behind them the sun had started to set, sucking long sharp shadows towards a flame-red vanishing point. `There wasn't. Listen, Nat, I'm impressed. You know more than I thought. There wasn't, but there is now. The rules have changed since we were buddies.`

`In what way?`

`Find the girl, that's the word rising up. Find King Arthur's daughter. Meant nothing to me, Nat, but you've got it, you're on to something. We could make a good team, we could crack this case.`

`Can you send them a message, Arch?`

`Who?`

`The game-master. The Black Knight. Can you send him a message. From me.`

`You don't want to do that, Nat, he's a mean one. Slip away, out of sight, that's my advice. Don't let him know you're here. Black Knight plus Clegg equals very bad shit.`

`He already knows.`

`I am thinking not, Nat, I am thinking not. I am thinking he suspects, I am thinking he's worried, but I don't think he knows for sure. I'm his eyes and ears, Nat. I don't tell him everything. I need secrets like the next man.`

Clegg had heard enough. He cut the noose above the knot and untied Arch's hands. `Take a message.` he said.

Arch looked doubtfully at Clegg, shook his head and then squinted into the sky. The sun had almost gone. He shrugged and set to work. He unsnagged the pen and nail from his tangle of dread-locks. Within a few seconds the sun had activated the cells on the back of pen's monitor. At last he nodded and then shook his head. `I can do it, Nat, as you well know. I can do many strange and wonderful things, but this one is the opposite of wise. This one is the suicidal side of healthy. Don't say I didn't warn you.`

`Tell him Clegg says `hi`. Tell him to split the money between the two of us. Tell him I want mine in gold bars.`

`I can't tell him any of this, Nat. He'll think it's a joke. He'll tell me to jerk off. This guy hasn't got time for jokers. Give me something hard.`

`Tell him I'll hand John Savage over to him on Midsummer's Day. In Stratford. Tell him I want an amnesty, a fresh start. And tell him I want an explanation. Then tell him it's not a joke. I've got references. Tell him a man called Armstrong recommended me, David to his friends. If he's got any.`

Arch did as he was told. It only took a few seconds, but there was no time for a reply. Clegg took Arch's pen and the wraps and pocketed them. He directed Arch towards the scrambling bike `It's yours,` he said, `if you can fix it. Mind it doesn't get you into trouble.`

`You're winding me up, Nat. You're killing me with kindness, is that it? I never wanted the fuckin' thing in the first place. The noise, Nat. It's not good for a sensitive soul like Archibald.`

Clegg looked at him, fighting off sympathy. The game was for real and Arch had not realized it. Someone, somehow, had set him up to penetrate the Wildside, to hunt for John Savage, alias King Arthur, and latterly to tie-in with both Clegg and Beth. Would Arch have lost interest if he had known how real the people and the dangers were? Would he have left the reality in preference for an alternative game? Clegg was impressed by the minders of the System. They must have known what he was trying to do. Their tentacles reached far indeed if they could manipulate a crazy like Arch into playing a game on their behalf. Brilliant, he had to admit. You put in an agent undercover, you gave him instructions and tasks, but best of all you kept his identity secret even from himself. A game within a game within a game. Clegg was reminded of the railway carriage riddle that had absorbed him as a child. At night, in a train, your own reflection, and beyond your reflection was the reflection of your reflection, and beyond your reflected reflection was...It ended when the eye was no longer capable of following the logic into infinity. But here the eye had access through a satellite to a colossal database and had no limits, and where the eye could not reach there were moles like Arch who stuck a nail into the resonant earth and played the same game but by different rules. Here the eye and its servants could wrap Arch and Clegg and however many more it wished to add into an infinite loop. Sure, Arch was in a game, but it beat the shit out of the game he thought he was in.

`Go on then,` Clegg said. `There's the bike. Now go and play.`

But Arch was shaking his head, looking at Clegg sadly. `I can't.`

`What do you mean you can't?`

`The world wants me unhappy, Nat. The world wants everyone unhappy. Unhappy people spend more money, unhappy people need cosmetics, add-ons, placebos, drugs of solace, stuff to fill the void. They need serotonin, Nat, and I need a fix.`

`Then stick the nail in your head. You might get some kind of message.`

`Nat, irony, don't, it's not your strongest thing OK? I don't mean that kind of fix. Really, I don't. I'm allergic to artificial serotonin, right? The stuff they put in the ice-creams.` Arch had finished a half-hearted inspection of the bike and now slumped to the floor. He removed his glasses and gave Clegg a weak smile.

`So what makes you happy, Arch?

`Well since you ask, Nat, and we're learning to trust, since we're really connecting here, opening up on new levels, heart to heart, that kind of shit, I would rather like to beat the shit out of the Black Knight.`

Clegg said nothing. He knew this decision was important. He also hated the idea of Arch behind him. `So this serotonin,` he asked. `If you're allergic and it's got to be the natural stuff, is beating the shit out of someone the only way to get high?`

`Practically,` said Arch, smiling at last, sensing that Clegg was going to include him. `Realistically. And we're talking real time and real space, right? There is another way of getting the stuff, so I'm told, another way of getting happy. But let's stay real.`

`Another way, Arch?`

`Sure, for saints. Some crap about doing the good.`

FORTYTWO

Dear Sam,

Seeing him so ill made me angry. But who was there to be angry with? It wasn't his fault. I was angry with myself for being angry. I even tried being angry with you, Sam, for sending me into this, for making me do what you should have done, but it didn't work for long. Would you believe it? I can't remember his first words or mine but I remember the flowers in the vase by the window. Who put them there? And the picture above the fireplace, not his taste, I thought, but then why should it be, and why should I even notice it?

Was it like losing him for a second time? That would be too simple. He looked so ill and so wasted that I thought breathing too heavily might peel off his skin and turn him to dust. He almost wasn't Dad; he was almost an imposter, a fraud. Perhaps that was why I felt angry. You will see him, I'm sure, but in one way I hope you don't. In one way we should let him go just before the end. He is horribly ill. He can prop himself up with drugs and function for an hour or two a day but his time is running out, Sam, even quicker than ours. Function. Do you remember how he hated that word? It was in a school report: `Beth functions adequately in the science lesson` or something. He went mad, he went wild, he wrote letters and complained to the school manager. Humans don't function, machines function, he said. Perhaps illness is like a machine, or it turns the body into one. Two years ago the cancer was already there, it must have been. Dad must have known. People on this side must have known. Perhaps knowing that time was limited forced his hand and theirs. Or perhaps he just wanted to save you and I the pain of watching him die in slow motion.

I know what you're thinking. You're thinking that meeting him could never have satisfied me, it could never have lived up to my expectations, because in the end it wasn't him I wanted, it wasn't him I wanted brought back to life, at all. It was Mum. Even Dad healthy and giving all the right answers and bringing you out safely would have left me empty. Think what you like, Sam. I was angry with him but managed to hide it.

But it wasn't all grim. Okay, there were no violins or trumpets but we did laugh. Dad was propped up in bed by the window. It was a comfortable upstairs room in the town square pub and he had seen Owen and I from the window before we even found the note. He had been watching out for us. The nurse said how difficult it had been to make him rest for the last two or three days. She was just one of several people who seemed to hover in the corridor and the doorway and the next room to look after him. Along with the nurse there were two Finn look-alikes, bare-footed, and an older man who prepared the food and medicine. I remember Dad shrugging at one point when the room seemed to fill up with all these people and me thinking that even in death he would be public property.

The letter on the church door had invited me to bring Owen and Andrew. Dad wanted to thank them but I think he was uncertain about being alone with me. I was glad they were there to start with. He winked at Owen and made a joke about something from their past. Andrew hung back, very shy I suppose. It was beautiful to watch, but Dad wanted to include and thank them all for whatever they might have done to help.

We told him about the beavers and he said something about wolves and bears and got very excited for a time, but I wasn't listening too closely. I was noticing how the one of him, even sick and withered, seemed to fill half the room while the three of us and the nurse only half filled the rest of the space.

The wolves were in Snowdonia, he said; shy and timid. Owen got down on one knee next to the bed and it reminded me of one of those old religious paintings and I felt like telling Owen to stand up and not be so stupid but they went all nostalgic on each other and I left them to it. Dad said something about this being his death bed. Owen said it was a sick bed but Dad only laughed. He told Owen he didn't need a bodyguard anymore because there wasn't enough to fuss over.

Then it was my turn. Owen must have backed off, I can't remember how or even if he and Andrew stayed in the room, but soon it was me next to the bed. He started talking about how happy people were on the Wildside, had I seen it for myself? They made mistakes, he said, they grew old and died, but it made sense, life had a purpose. I couldn't disagree because I had seen it for myself but then I mentioned you. `Sam would love it.` I said and the mood changed.

He stared into the open fire. I'm sure by then we were alone in the room. A log fell and sent up lots of sparks and I felt you were there with us, Sam, living in the shadows. `You haven't even asked how he is.` I said. I don't think I sounded angry. It was just a fact.

He sighed and looked at me. You remember how he used to sigh? Deep and slow, very sad, but not for himself. I had never been aware of his eyes before, how blue they were and how certain, but seeing them look very weak and very tired reminded me of what he had lost. `There could be lots of reasons why I haven't asked.` he said. His voice was almost a whisper. `You think I'm obsessed with my own little scheme of things. Wolves in the mountains? I am. I always have been. But perhaps it hurts me too much to think about him lying there.`

I put the knife in. `Like Mum.` I said.

He didn't speak for an age, just looked at me, as though trying to read my thoughts or to understand what was going on for me. `Like Mum.` he eventually said, `He's in the same place, isn't he? Probably the same room, even the same bed. Kath's letters have found me, they made sure of that, they made sure I knew what state they held him in.`

`And they offered you a deal?` I was surprised at myself for asking it straight out. I had sat on it all my life but it seemed the only thing worth talking about and that nothing would get in our way.

`They have asked nothing of me, Beth, they have not made a single ransom proposal.`

`I don't mean, Sam.` I said. I mean Mum.` I felt strange saying it, as though I had no right, as though it should have been you. He stared into the fire as though he might see some kind of escape and it gave me time to realize a few important details. Things I have never told anyone, not even you. Like the fact that I don't remember her. You and Dad told me about her and I had the photographs. I hated the photographs. They didn't tell me what she smelled like or how her voice sounded. You could just as well have saved her skeleton for me and hung it up on the wall. And then I told Dad something I didn't even know myself. I didn't know it was true or important until it came out. `I miss her hands.` I said. `I think I remember her hands. And I miss them.`

I hated him for crying. It was me who should have been crying not him. It was me who should have let it all out and been comforted by an arm or a hand, but it wasn't, it was him. He cried like a baby and I have never felt worse in my life, helpless, useless to him and useless to myself. And then I hated myself for hating him and thanked god there was a fire to mess with. I put logs on and poked it, but I didn't run away from it. I stayed with it, even though he had to cry my tears for me. `Sam told me about her.` I said. `Everything I know about her is from him. I feel Sam's loss as much as my own.`

He had closed his eyes. For a moment I thought he might drift into sleep and I wondered if that was the only escape allowed to him, that and death, but his fingers suddenly tightened on the bed sheets. `Did he say I could have saved her?` he asked. `Did Sam tell you I let her die for the sake of all this?`

I nodded. Even though his eyes were still closed he knew what the answer was.

`Poor, Sam.` he said. `Poor bloody Sam.`

I waited for him to open his eyes. If Owen or Andrew or the nurse had come in then it wouldn't have mattered. They would have seen us and gone, they would not have dared intrude. I told him I wasn't angry. I told him I just needed to know. If he had let Mum die for the sake of all this was he going to let you go the same way. And me?

He surprised me by sitting up straight. The crying had been good for him and so had my questions. I recognized that business-like look he used to have when things needed doing. `We're like an old carpet over here,` he said. `They just want to roll us up and chuck it all away.`

`The Comfort Zone,` I said. `They want to debug the System. Get rid of all this. Build thirty million houses. Isn't that what they've always wanted?` I nearly added that was why I couldn't remember Mum's hands but there was no point.

He said that in the end it wasn't about houses or building or trees. It was about being human, about honouring an agreement with God. He said that two years ago they, the Comfort Zone, had made a break-through, a discovery. Although it was probably by chance there had been enough of them on the job long enough for it to be inevitable; not if, but when. They got close to the Big Secret. It was a security measure that Dad built into the System right from the start. They had tried code words and random numbers by the billion but the System's control levels still remained beyond their reach, they were still working with a programme Dad had devised to keep them out of the Wildside. But they had discovered their way in, or at least taken the first steps to that discovery. I can tell you, Sam, but I think you already know, I think you've been half way there for a long time. It's our blood, Sam, our DNA. It's our blood that keeps this whole world the way it is and always has been. Blood. Kind of appropriate, don't you think? It put a lot of things in their place. That's why we were always searched and showered after visiting you, they wanted to be sure we were taking nothing away like hair or skin or blood. So what about me? I asked him.

`They will have taken what they wanted. Hair from a brush, some blood courtesy of the dentist. They've got your secrets.`

`So now all they need is you?` I said, beginning to see the picture. `It's kind of Genesis in reverse. They get hold of God, draw off his blood and reverse creation.` I didn't mean it the way it sounded. I wanted to say sorry even before I saw him flinch but I didn't know how. I suppose he took it for my sake.

He shook his head. `I'm not important by myself, Beth. And I never wanted to play God. Yes, the System was built around my DNA, because blood is sacred and unique and I wanted the sacred to be hidden in the heart of this right from the start. But it didn't have to be mine. As my children were born I used theirs to make access even more difficult and even more secure.`

`I understand that.` I said. `Two down and one to go. If they follow me and get their hands on you, or they get hold of a hair or a piece of skin then it's all finished.`

`Not quite.` he said, eyes closed again, voice sinking to a whisper. `Your maths is not right, Beth. It's two down two to go. It's time I told you about Nathaniel Clegg.`

FORTYTHREE

She was not much older than Bonny, Clegg thought, she might even have been to the same school, made some of the same choices. He watched her carefully as she sat talking to the bull-necked, thick-tongued youth. She was showing him a trick with thread and fingers, cat's cradle, patiently hooking and unhooking strings over his clumsy fingers. It was difficult not to compare her to Danny's daughter when Clegg's experience of young girls was limited to these two extremes. But Bonny had never sat comfortably on a street corner watching the world go by. Bonny had never been given respite from the demands of shopping for God.

`Look the other way.` he whispered to Arch. `We don't want her to see us together. The plan wont work if she does.`

`You look the other way, man, the other way is a brick wall. She's dangerously desirable. She's got that fold of fresh fat just above the knee that says she's arrived, the sex is on-line, hormones down-loaded. Too young for you. Move over, Nat, know when you're finished. This one is for Arch. This one is ripe. Two young thighs divided by Arch equals bliss. Brief, but pure.` But there was more that Arch did not say. Like how well he knew the girl already, like how his imagination had already licked the ash markings from every inch of her neat mermaid's body, how seeing her here had sent a bolt of recognition through him that had raised far more than sweat.

Three days had passed since Clegg had cut Arch down to size, three days in which certainties had started to shift but were yet to reform. Clegg had been tempted to end their working relationship, but something told him that Arch could still be of use, that Arch was happy to play along with any game so long as its rules were complex and its aim obscure. He guessed rightly that Arch was addicted to being messed around, an addiction that might stand him in good stead.

`Take a good look.` said Clegg, `That's all. For now. Business only. Pop a Blocker if she gets to you. We don't want your dick-god in the way of this. Then try and act normal. Try very, very hard, Arch, you might get half way.`

`You mean normal, Nat, or you mean like the rest of these people?`

It was a good question. They were in the market square. The priestess was going to announce her findings. The healing of the valley was upon them. Her discussions had come to an end the evening before and she had spent the night revisiting certain sites in and around the town. She was a handsome woman with untidy hair and an intense but good-humoured face. Her nose was midway between regal and aquiline but the intensity of her eyes detracted from its size. She wore her femininity in great swirls of skirts and scarves and bracelets and her voice was deep and sensuous. Her status was as tangible as the cloud of perfume and incense she seemed to inhabit.

`Look at her.` Arch hissed, happy to be distracted from Beth, `Look at her groupies. They have sex with dolphins, these people, they listen to the didgeridoo of their own free will, Nat, and still believe in God and you ask *me* to be normal.`

We're fifty miles from Birmingham, thought Clegg, trying not to shake his head in disbelief. Bare-footed children picked their way through horse-shit, vendors sold their qat, their hash and their hams of wild boar meat, Beth's quiet beauty cut a path through the crowds. We're fifty miles from Birmingham, they're back in the Dark Ages, they're happy, and just like the rest of them, she's mine to destroy. What a strange world we inhabit, he decided.

`The girl's with two men,` he said. `The one she's sitting with and the older one, over there, grey-beard. Watch them closely.`

`Who is the young one?` said Arch, nodding towards Andrew.

Clegg shrugged. `Evolution. That's the way they're all headed over here.`

`No seriously.` said Arch, surprising Clegg with a change of tone. `He's a chosen one.`

`Whatever. Watch him. They can be strong.`

`Strong? Nat, you don't know a thing. Strong? You had better believe it.` He went quiet for a moment. `I used to have one.` he said, almost in a whisper. `I used to have one. I used to play with it. They took it away.`

`Took what away, Arch?`

`My brother. I had a brother like that. Downs Syndrome. I loved that brother, Nat. He was the sweetest brother a boy ever had.` Silence again. `They took him away.`

Clegg ignored him. The priestess had started to speak.

`At first we were drawn to the air` she was saying. She was standing on the steps of the town hall and needed no lessons in projecting the voice. The pronoun `we` was all-inclusive, not royal. Others had offered their advice and opinions who would be included in the `we`, but privately the priestess would also acknowledge the help of spirit-beings who had concerned themselves with the town's well-being for centuries and with whom she, in prayer and often fraught meditation, had consulted. `The air is fresher both north and south of the town and seems to get trapped around the bridges and the High Street.`

`Evolution?` whispered Arch, ignoring the priestess and picking up on something Clegg had said. `You believe in that crap?`

`What else?` asked Clegg. `Its proved.`

`Fortunately the air isn't the problem,` the priestess went on, `because air is always difficult to work with.` No, she assured them all, the problem was the river as everybody suddenly seemed to know, to judge by their nods.

`What's proved?`

`Evolution, we're evolved from apes. If you don't believe it, look in the mirror. Now shut up and listen.`

`There used to be a series of stepped weirs just below the bridge, you'll find remnants of them if you look. About 800 years ago the monks at the Abbey had them dismantled to let the salmon through. But the village had grown up around those stepped weirs because of the trout, because of easy crossing and because of the light.`

`You might be, Nat. You might me evolved from a fucking ape. That I could believe, that I could very well believe. But leave me out of that crap, leave me well out of that crap, and leave him out of it to.` he gestured towards Andrew.

`The pools, I think about six of them, were like big mirrors. They made the air and the light healthier. And they slowed it down. Since the weirs went the river has rushed too much, agitated the air and sucked energy out of the town.`

Arch made a sucking sound, like water escaping from the bath. `Sounds as convincing as your Darwin crap.` he hissed. Clegg poked him in the ribs.

`We have also given some thought to another old tradition.` the priestess said.

`Burning witches?` Arch muttered just loud enough for Clegg to hear.

`We have been told that a local woman, a Lady Jeffreys, has been associated with the bridge since the 18th century. When she died she became a water spirit and was `prayed down` into a bottle which was placed under the Short Bridge.` People were nodding, obviously familiar with the local legends and with this strange terminology. `The New Bridge, the long one, was built in 1848.`

`Back in the time of Darwin,` Arch whispered, picking up the theme again, shaking his head once more in Clegg's direction. `I thought the world had moved on since then.` he almost spat.

`The story says that a boy found the bottle with an angry fly in it and put it back. Lady Jeffreys was probably a diviner,` the priest continued. `She would know that the confluence here of the Severn and the Clywedog would need reconciling. The bottle almost certainly contained correctly charged water. If the boy found it with a fly in then it had obviously emptied itself. It will need recharging.`

`How?` rose the obvious question.

`60,000 volts to the genitals.` Arch hissed. `Nat, tell me its not true. She's been unfaithful to me.`

`Who has?`

The Earth Mother, he wanted to say, someone else had been screwing her for her secrets, tapping the dark places with a nail or a cigar, this priestess for one. But he was not ready to share all this with Clegg and for now kept up the act. `Tell me we've been abducted by aliens. Her science is as screwed up as yours.`

`Silica eggs.` the priestess replied. `They will pacify the two rivers.`

`Get me out of here, man.` Arch hissed. `Fuckin water spirits, man. You heard it. Did you hear it? Tell me I'm wrong. Tell me this is a game. No, don't. Don't say that. Games make sense. Leave me my games, Nat, don't let them fuck with my games. Where did they evolve from, Nat? Where did she evolve from? A dolphin?` But Arch knew the answer even as he asked it. She had evolved from Merlin, the same as Arch, she was just the latest in a long line.

Clegg was not in the mood to argue. Two hundred people were stood around giving credence to a woman who talked of water spirits but they showed no sign of lynching her. They showed no sign of hooting abuse and shouting her down. They showed no sign of drifting off, embarrassed on her behalf. In the army they would have known how to deal with her. They would have wiped the innane smile from her face, taught her the true meaning of women serving the military. Here they listened. Here they nodded. Here they humoured her with questions and deference. Clegg looked sideways to the girl. Beth was now standing in order to see the priestess. She seemed to be taking it all in. She was one of them. Clegg was the alien, the only sane one in the place.

`Darwin was an ass-hole, Nat. He admitted it himself. Got it all wrong. Like this woman. Look at her. What the hell has she got to do with apes?`

`Leave it. I want to listen to her.`

`Proof! You are the exception. Only the son of a chimp's louse would want to listen to that instead of to Arch.` He was jealous. The woman was good. There were things here not even he could have pieced together with the help of his nail and the contorted underground voices. He found himself wanting to keep it from Clegg.

`And now we come to the dam,` the priestess continued.

Ah, the dam, the crowd muttered, a culture away from Clegg's discomfort and Arch's feigned outrage. There was a raised level of murmuring because the dam was a favorite subject hereabouts. The 237 foot high concrete beast was now well embedded in the landscape, or at least the reservoir behind it was. Water levels were kept constant and it was a place of great beauty, although entirely man-made. But that was not the issue. The issue was that the reservoir, along with those of Elan, Claerwen and Vyrnwy, provided water for the thirsty Comfort Zone. Only these four had survived the terrorists' bombs earlier in the century when the country was still making its choices. There were plenty on the Wildside who saw no reason why bad habits in the east should be supplied by water from the west. But the priest was not interested in the politics, only in the health of the landscape. The tension caused by the dam was carried by rock strata right into the town, she explained. Acupuncture stones, carved with runes to her prescription should be placed at agreed points on either side of the valley. She likened the dam to a pair of spectacles pressing lightly behind the ears and causing chronic headaches. Placing acupuncture stones would be like spreading the weight of the spectacles so they would sit more easily. `So you can all continue enjoying that beautiful lake.` she added as a passing nod in favour of the status quo.

`Dynamite.` Arch mumbled. `Why not dynamite? Blow the thing up! Tell her, Nat, tell her, its the only choice at the end of the day.`

`Perhaps they know something we don't.` Clegg snapped, suddenly irritated with Arch's interruptions.

How true, thought Arch, suck my nail, Nat. Tremble in the face of your ignorance. `If only.` he said. `Perhaps they're all fuckin crazy, Nat. Like you. Don't let them get to you. Don't let them in. They're invading you, Nat, they've got you!'

Almost. They had a secret. They had a world and a language and a purpose, something worth while. When were they going to let Clegg in on it?

Now the priest was talking about lead pollution from the ancient mines above Van, closed down in 1921 but still tainting the water minutely. Lead was the metal of Jupiter and beech trees were under Jupiter. Beech planted in the area would flourish famously by taking up the homeopathic excess in the soil. Oh no, she corrected herself. Plant juniper. That would keep grazing animals off allowing beech to establish itself.

`Its de-volution, Nat, since you ask. Devolution. We are de-volved, not e-volved. Think about it.`

`From what, Arch?`

`From what, Nat?

`What are we de-volved from?`

`Ask the high priestess.`

`The Green Man.` she said, as though scripted by Arch, `The Green Man was the original name of the pub now called the Queen's Arms. We believe it should revert to its original name because nothing annoys the elemental forces more than to be denied or to have their old symbols and images repressed.`

Arch shrugged, dissolved into laughter. `You're evolved from an ape, Nat. I'm devolved from a fucking pub. Suits me!`

There he was again, thought Clegg, ignoring Arch. The Green Man, as in Clun. Clun made him think of Agnes. She was the kind of priestess that never preached. She could devolve gold from cabbages and in her quiet way she might to do for Clegg what this witch was doing for a valley.

There should be some reconciliation between the pubs, the priestess concluded by saying, because they represented the two primal forces. The Abbey Inn stood for order, ritual, routine, hard work. The Green Man as it should now be called stood for chaos, fun, spontaneity.

Arch was on the floor, his head buried in his hands, rocking from side to side, mumbling to himself. He had heard enough.

The Abbey Inn had gained the upper hand. The priestess proposed a wrought iron arch linking the pubs and spanning the High Street, proclaiming both names. Annual tug 'o war between clients of the respective pubs would raise the sub-earthly struggle to a human level which all could acknowledge and enjoy.

Clegg caught Beth's eye. She was watching him. Did she smile? Had she recognized something in his expression? He realized to his horror that he had blushed. The glance of a sixteen year old girl across a crowded market square had made him blush. How long was it since he had experienced such a sensation and what had the Wildside exposed of him that it should come to this? He felt an irrational fear that she had recognized more than his skepticism, that she had seen his great deceit and treachery writ large like a stained aura. Bright girl. And Arch was right. That fold of fat just above the knee, bare thighs turned brown by Wildside sun, she was ready, on-line as Arch would say. He looked away, concentrating on the witch woman with all his might. Soon, very soon, he would make his move. She was within reach. Three cheers for the Abbey Inn, thought Clegg, they could draw him a pint anytime. Three cheers for the company of bright girls like her, girls to flatter him at the moment of his greatest confusion. Perhaps he should pull on the Abbey Inn end of the rope against Beth and the others. Or had Agnes and this weird place corrupted him so much that he was now one of the Green Men, from which all was devolved, his soul lost to chaos and fun? As the crowd thinned and the two pubs beckoned he thanked the God he had never believed in that he had no faith to lose, no point to make, no sickness to heal.

FORTYFOUR

`Of course we might be cursed, Alice. Have you thought of that? John Savage might simply have put a jinx on us? No I thought not. A clever man, I've told you that. A very clever man.`

`Certainly, Sir. But a jinx?`

Sir David was in conference. It was necessary to revue the case formally every two weeks even though the resulting summary would be for his eyes only. Heavy eyes. D.I. Alice Jones wondered how her boss was sleeping these days. He seemed to spend longer in the office than the rest of his staff combined and the time he did spend here was largely passed staring at the view across the estuary or toying with a single note pad on which he had taken to making extensive and rather worrying doodles. There was also the question of his mumbled monologues, his habit of talking into empty corners even when others were present. No one dared challenge him on the matter. Today each corner was occupied. Emma Savage hovered reluctantly in one, Sam stared blankly from a second. The remaining two had something electric and unreal squirming between them, subhuman but conscious.

`I'm not sure it is something we could quantify.` she added, as much to reassure herself as the computer. Training manuals referred to luck and its absence, but a jinx was altogether different, a jinx implied something controlled, conscious, something beyond the reach of police procedure. `I think we have had reasonable success.` she added, not sure whether it was her place to defend their shared failures or to criticize her boss for an uncertain record.

`Wonderful success!` Sir David beamed. `Quite wonderful. We allowed Beth Savage across the Line, we found her, we lost her. We allowed Nathaniel Clegg across the Line, we found him, we lost him. Would you care to define success?`

`The irregulars have been effective.` she pointed out. `One of them has located Clegg.`

`I beg to differ, Alice, Clegg has found us. None of those goons had the slightest interest in real names and real people and then suddenly my name appears in bright lights on top of the Christmas tree. It must be obvious that John has penetrated even the Game. He has used dear old Arch to alert us to the fact.`

Arch. The third and fourth corners suddenly made sense, Sir David's memory of him stared back through a mist of static and bright edges.

`But at least we know where the message came from.`

`We know only that such messages can no longer be trusted. I'm sorry, Alice, if you have been instructed to cheer me up, to console me a little, then you will have to find another way.`

`The satellite pictures are inconclusive.`

Sir David sighed. He failed to see how anyone could put such faith in the ability of satellite photographs to chart the whereabouts and progress of three million people on the Wildside. He knew that an army of men and women huddled in basements somewhere analyzing such pictures and he knew they had come up with a dozen or more Beth Savages picking their erratic way across hill and dale. The very nature of the Wildside made it a thankless task. People came and went, people shimmied and shifted, people moved willy-nilly or in response to whim and fancy. How could they analyze that? If the game-player's contact with Clegg coincided with satellite collateral then the chances were it was down to coincidence, not police ability.

`I'm sorry, Alice. No one is more fond of the Game players than I am. Cheap and unreliable. They are half crazy to start with, half lost to the real world which is probably why I feel comfortable running them. Watson is fond of them too, aren't you Watson?`

`Fond of them, Sir?`

`What can we expect when we start shifting reality around them? Arch was too clever by far. They all are. I sometimes wonder who is manipulating who.`

`Whom.` D.I. Jones corrected.

`Whatever. The point is we still do not know what Savage will do next. `

`We must persevere, Sir. The rewards will be immense.`

`What do you mean by that? Please, Alice, amuse me with tales of reward and success.`

`It's just as you say, Sir, We don't know what Savage intends to do next. If we can find him and confront him with his son's situation then we can oblige him to debug the System, we can extend surveillance to the Wildside. It will mean an end to crime, Sir, an end to anything and everything illegal.`

Her passion impressed him slightly. It was encouraging to see the poor girl enthusiastic about something, but Sir David shook his head sadly. How things had changed in twenty years. It was true that crime was almost impossible. Crimes of passion, of feeling, jealousy, anger and the rest, they would linger on, but honest-to-goodness bread and jam crime revolved around money and if there was one thing controlled more tightly than individual people and their day-to-day movements then it was money. Every single financial transaction was conducted by plastic and was therefore subject to control and monitoring. Cash was illegal, it was quite simply the currency of crime. The black economy had been eradicated by the tax-man's grip on all exchanges of services, goods and money.

`You do remember money, don't you Alice?` Sir David asked, abandoning the review for a nostalgic siesta. `No. Of course not. You're too young. When we were children there was still a kind of money for the under-twelves. You could be given pocket money and buy sweets in the old way but only at certain shops. Most traders couldn't be bothered with the stuff. Even the small amount in circulation gave rise to crime. Wonderful, really. Children can be so innovative, you know. At least they used to be. We could beg, borrow and steal, unlike our parents, unlike anyone above the age of twelve in fact, because at twelve you went on-line and that was it, you were stitched up. Your financial status signalled itself at every shop you entered.`

`I was born on-line.` she reminded him, she had only just turned thirty. She was of the generation fed into the System by the midwife, before the first feed or wipe down or nappy change. She had known nothing of cash transactions, of choices, of moral responsibility.

`It's rather a wonder we have a job,` Sir David pointed out. `Fortunately for us there is no limit to criminal ingenuity and no end to history's sense of humour.`

`Sir?`

`Gold.` he reminded her, `Don't forget gold, Alice. Oh yes, and barter. When we all went on-line and credit got more and more sophisticated, that's when our behaviour regressed to the good-old days of gold and barter. You know the value of gold has risen in direct proportion to the legislation and legal disincentives directed against its use? I find that quite reassuring but I shouldn't. It all made our work very simple, Alice. Even random acts of violence or drunken brawls are easy to tidy up now. What does electronic tagging give you? An exact and retrospective picture of who has done what to who. Sorry, whom. Wonderful. That's why we sit around in offices all day. That's why we grow fat and pasty faced, present company excluded, of course. Which is why policing is so low-key. Oh you have no idea! You know what percentage of police officers never moves from behind their monitors, what percentage sits day after day, year after year, matching data with data, crunching movements of people with the appearance and disappearance of virtual cash, or keeping tabs on each other to check for System fraud and hacking? Ninety eight percent, Alice. Ninety eight percent. Which means, lets be clear, even pedantic, that only one police man or woman out of every fifty ever ventures onto the streets. John Savage has made us almost redundant, Alice, by giving us the System. Perhaps it's out of sympathy that he keeps us busy. Bringing John to account will be this country's last police act, he will be this country's last ever criminal. Just think about it, Alice, at last, a debugged System, blanket surveillance, an end to the Wildside, an end to Midsummer's Day, no more crime. We can all go home. We can all go fishing.`

`I think it is to be desired`, she said, weighing her career prospects against Sir David's uncertain Utopia. `We have a duty to protect each other from the criminal element.`

But Sir David was not listening. Arch had vanished to be replaced by an imagined Beth, naked on horse back, broken light from the tree canopy hiding her modesty. He leaned forwards as though to examine her closely. `Can you imagine it over there, Alice? Can you imagine being free to rob, murder, rape, anything you wish, being able to travel, to escape, to disappear at will, to reappear whenever and wherever you want?`

If she heard the wistful longing in his tone she certainly did not react to it. `It is difficult to imagine.` she agreed. `It does seem a strange thing to choose.`

Sir David laughed. On his note pad a virile tree had taken shape from which an ever increasing and elaborate network of branches reached out to the edges of the paper, choking out the white. `Soon my generation will be gone, Alice, soon no-one will remain who was born into the other way. Already you people outnumber the old timers. You know what Khalil told me? That religion is a sense organ. What do you think of that? He said you can develop it in different ways but the best way is by doing good deeds. Can you imagine? Hardly practical. Said most people have the sense organ blunted, said we're all like deaf people trying to make sense of an orchestra. Something like that. Cooked frogs, Alice, that's what I told him. Cooked frogs.`

`Sir?`

`Watson, tell D.I.Jones our cooked frog theory. I have taught it to him, you see. He understands it and applies it to certain analyses he is asked to run.`

`The cooked frog theory, Sir, states that if you put a frog in boiling water it will immediately jump out.`

`I'm sorry, Sir, I don't get it.`

`Hush, listen to Watson. Make a spiffing story of it, old boy.`

`However if you put said frog in warm water of the luke variety and then apply heat incrementally our dear amphibian will remain in the water until, if you'll excuse me, your lady, boiled alive.`

`It stays where it is.` Sir David added `It cooks to death. It doesn't even think of jumping out. Interesting observation. A twentieth century philosopher, I believe.`

`I don't quite see the point, Sir...`

`Don't you?` he suddenly snapped, irritated with her stupidity, with their age difference, with the whole business of growing old, of passing on a world he had helped create but no longer believed in. `Don't you, Alice,? I rather think you do. I rather think you know exactly what I mean, and millions along with you. You're born into luke-warm water, Miss Jones, and by my age you've been boiled dry, nothing left, just a shrivelled up skin of pretence, Miss Jones, just as if you had been thrown into boiling water right from the start. Some knew it and acted. There were plenty who jumped very quickly and very violently, Miss Jones, I can tell you that for nothing. Put a lid on the saucepan and those frogs will smash their brains out in trying to lift it off. Take the lid off, Miss Jones, and there is the Wildside, a place to jump to.`

`But still we have crime.` she said, outraged by the implications of her boss's diatribe, shaken by her own uncertainty. `If we could extend tagging across the whole country, if we could close down No-Man's land, cut off the smugglers, impound all the gold, put an end to Midsummer's Day, there would be no crime, ever, no crime. No fear of being robbed or raped or mugged.`

`Wonderful.` Sir David agreed, wrapping D.I. Jones in a very thoughtful, very protective smile, `Wonderful. No crime, no fear. Tags and monitors watching and listening. Who, where, how, even whom, all of it known, all of it recorded. Except for one thing, Alice, one thing beyond the reach even of the most sophisticated and the most comprehensive of surveillance techniques.`

`Sir?`

`The one thing, Alice that your System will never monitor and never detect, the most important thing of all.`

`Which is?`

`Let me show you. You have a lot of respect for these things, I'm sure?` he nodded to Watson's monitor.

`They are an essential tool in our work, Sir.`

`Just watch how good he is. Watson, how old is Nathaniel Clegg, to the hour?`

`Twenty eight years, four months three weeks, two days and four hours, Sir.`

`How many fillings does he have?`

`Six, and one extraction.`

`What size shoe does he take?`

`Size nine, Sir.`

`His last recorded weight?`

`86 kilos.`

`His last known liaison.`

`Jennifer Riley of Birmingham, Sir. No legal framework.`

`What do we know of his movements over the last six weeks?`

`Absconded on April 28th by micro-light recreational aircraft, suspected destination was Malvern. Lost until May 14th. Reported to be temporarily resident in a detention centre at grid reference SO313632. Moved from there on the 28th, travelled over land to Montgomery in Wales. Suspected of illegal transmission via police networks on the 8th of June.`

`Why did he cross over, Watson?`

`Supposition, Sir. To evade arrest.`

`So why did he send me a message via the police network?`

'Supposition, Sir. None viable.'
'Rephrase for D.I.Jones, please, Watson.'
'Motive, Sir. Quite unknown.'

FORTYFIVE

Arch had a vehicle. Infact Arch had a whole network of strange machines and dubious contacts he had built up over two years of skulking around the Wildside. He led Clegg to a small quarry, overgrown with brambles and hung over with manic little oaks lurching into nothingness and showed it off with pride. It was an extraordinary hybrid, a charcoal burner, but also a means of bending emission laws. It looked as though somebody had dropped a caravan from a great height onto the chassis of a good-sized truck, one that had started life as a Mercedes Unimog if the lettering was to be believed. The green-painted caravan was fixed to the chassis and the rear wheels loomed large against the caravan windows on either side. As if this weren't strange enough the Unimog's steering column had been extended through the caravan and on to its roof, where a small gantry had been added around a tractor seat so that the thing could be driven by someone perched on its roof. The sides of the caravan were lined with fuel cans, chains, ropes, fishing rods, a winch, barrels, boxes and baskets and only the fresh mud tracks leading into the quarry denied the suspicion that perhaps the thing had stood here for decades. Welded to the rear of the caravan was a large metal box from which sprouted a profusion of chimneys and herein lay its disguise, because a mobile charcoal burner was a legal form of locomotion, exempt from most restrictions. Arch kept the scrambler hidden in the back.

`How fast does it go?` Clegg asked.

`Fifteen. Twenty down hill.`

`So we put him in the back of this and take six weeks driving to the border?`

`Its the best I can do, man. You're the practical one. You want him on the scrambler? They say he's past his best. Bits might drop off. Then what?` He pretended to sulk and muttered something to the marbles cupped in his hand.

But Clegg could see no other way, unless John Savage was ready to come voluntarily, unless they could somehow tempt him nearer the border. `Has your Black Knight got any ideas?` Clegg asked.

`The Black Knight doesn't do details, Nat, he leaves the details to the infantry. The Black Knight deals in the Big Picture. Anyway, you've made him a promise, he expects you to deliver.`

`Not in this, Arch. You couldn't deliver the post in this.`

`Don't knock it, Nat. Look on it as an option. A fuckin useless one, maybe, but surely its better than no options at all.`

`Do you trust me, Arch?`

`Dumb as a dog I listens, Nat. But do I look stupid?`

`Yes. Most of the time you do. Trust me. I've got an idea. I promise you'll enjoy the first part.`

`And the second part?`

`I don't want you losing sleep over the second part, Arch. Believe me, you would if you knew it.`

`If it works I'll forgive you, Nat.`

`Don't bet on either, Arch, don't bet on either.`

It was risky but Clegg could think of nothing better. When he explained it to Arch it sounded even more fragile but it gained a grudging acceptance. There was more to Arch than met the eye. There would need to be.

That night the two men avoided the town and found a pub in the next valley. It was flying the white flag to show that the home-brew was available. Arch was in one of his quiet moods, more unnerving than his sermons. Clegg made the mistake of drawing him out. He asked Arch about the army. Why had he joined? What had his work been? Why had he left? For several minutes Arch was evasive, shaking his head, giving one-word answers. Then he reached to the back of his head and pulled out a small metal tube from somewhere close to his scalp. He opened it, unrolled the square of paper it contained and handed it to Clegg. It was a photo, much traveled and much creased. It was of a beautiful black woman and her even more beautiful child.

`Are these yours?` Clegg asked, incredulous. `Family?`

In saying nothing Arch gave Clegg time for envy. He had no photo of Jenny or little Jo, no right to one, he had nothing to conceal in any metal tube. He tried to dismiss the feeling, tried to wish Arch all the good things in life.

Arch took back the photo, rolled it up, returned it to its tube, concealed it in his hair. `I was in Tolouse.` he said at last. `Arab France. Front line Pyrennes. You must have heard the stories. Half of black Africa clawing their way over the mountains. Half the Arab world hiding smack up the blackies' arses. We looked at satellite pictures, waded through data, sent conclusions down the line. All very nice and comfortable. We still couldn't stop them. Millions of them. What do you do? The Moroccans had their death camps, the Algerians had their hit squads, we had satellites. Okay, so it's a team game. Then we find this guy with a glass eye. He's from Senegal we think, or Nigeria, whatever, black as bad news, big teeth, the works, but a glass eye. At first we don't notice, he's just one of hundreds to be sent back to a slow death, but someone sees the eye and has and idea, someone talks to us and the idea lifts off. The guy is clear of AIDS, unusual and good news. So we talk him through it, right. I talk him through it. Arch the spy-man. I've picked up some Edo by now. Quick at languages is Arch, Arch plus lingo equals sonnets by the end of the month, I exaggerate only slightly. Goldeneye we call him. He's going back to try again, they all try again, they just get turned round and back they come, but this time we've got him tabbed, this time we put a bug on him. That's a break through, right? They have their networks, see, they have a whole industry trying to help them through and at every stage these guys get searched for bugs. No one takes any risks, right? Not the whites running the escape routes, not the Arabs pushing drugs through, everyone is swept clean twice a day. You got fillings in your teeth, don't even bother, don't even think about it, because none of the brothers are goin' to help, right? Too risky. But this guy is clean, except he's got a hiding place no one would usually check. Behind the eye, right? So it's a deal. We send him back. And he starts the journey again. And we track him every inch of the way. And we nail every contact he makes, every official he bribes, every network he touches. We roll half of black Africa up behind him, like a carpet. He walks through Niger. He goes to ground in Tamarasset, that's Algeria. He crosses the desert *de bidon*, that's what they call it, its French, it means he has a water can, nothing else. He's six months in Algeria, working in a prison camp, a kind of semi-official slavery. They do their work without complaints and then they're allowed to move on, to Morocco, someone else's problem. Then he goes underground. We know he's at greatest risk now. Calamocarro is not far away, and Calamocarro means the end of everything, glass eye included. But there are systems, there are people, plenty of people, all making a packet, all fiddling each other, all bending things this way and that. Another eight months and he's in the hold of a fishing boat on its way to Portugal. He's been buggared more times than the Foreign Secretary, this his fourth attempt and he's still a million miles from any kind of permit or passport.`

`And you're watching him?`

`And we're watching him. And he's motivated. He knows if he gets through to Toulouse we will give him his fucking wings and harp, we will welcome him like Saint Peter at the pearly gates and give him a permit to shovel our shit for the rest of his life. That is one lucky black out there on the screen, that is one Golden Boy. He gets through and he wins the Lottery, three meals a day for the rest of his life, two and a half more than he's likely to see at home in the jungle. So he walks. You would walk. You would walk until your feet were stumps, you would walk till you drop, and then some more. We watch him walk. The satellite follows him. We watch him walk, sleep, shit, everything. The technology we put on him, man, street value, even second-hand you could feed his nation for a year. Anyway, he leads us to caves full of dealers, to dock-yards full of rackets, to government departments full of graft, he's a walking, sleeping, crapping gold-mine.

`At last he's within reach. We meet him in the mountains, on the Basque side. I'm not sure why I'm there. We had to do thirty days a year in the field, right, get some fresh air, that kind of thing, why not? It means I can see the Main Man, I can thank him on behalf of whoever. So we make camp. A group goes out to jump the dealer he's with, nail the others and bring Goldeneye back to base. Two miles from camp. Two miles from Arch and a whole bunch of other geeks, of hard-wear illiterati. Shit, was I scared! A gun goes off. You know what we did? Me and the other guys in the camp, you know what we did? A gun goes off and we giggle, like school girls at a funeral. We giggle till we nearly wet our pants. I don't know what we're high on but it beats the shit out of fear every time. We giggle until somebody shouts. The moon goes in. The squaddies come running into the camp full of crap, higher than we are. They're giggling too. They've done it, they've nailed the dealer, six blacks have escaped, but what the shit, we can hunt them down tomorrow, and here is Goldeneye, here is the golden boy, the goose carrying the golden egg that's led us neatly across half the scam's on the Africa trail. Except its not. It's a guy I've never seen before. They all look alike, right? Like shit, do they. This one was smaller, younger, this one was Goldeneye minus about twenty years, but my hand-held says he's our man, he's carrying the bug so out comers the eye. Yeah, you've guessed the rest. Why do I bother?` Arch faltered, looked away, removed his glasses, wiped them, returned them again. In their few seconds of nakedness Clegg saw his eyes like albino mice, pink and vulnerable, shivering against the cold. Don't cry on me, Arch, Clegg thought, it's your story, not mine. Both men looked around the pub, anxious to go unnoticed. Clegg did a strange thing. He reached in his pocket for the shades that had long since been discarded. With no where to hide he decided to touch Arch. He chose the elbow. `Yeah, I've guessed.` he said, `You don't have to go on.`

But Arch needed to. `Both eyes, Nat, both of them. Can you believe it? This guy had been crawling through shit for nearly two years and we take out his eyes.` His voice had dropped to a whisper. The usual bravado had vanished. He was close to whimpering. `Its Goldeneye's brother, right? The two have done a deal. Goldeneye is back on Bongowongoland, his kid brother has been given the golden ticket, passport to the eternal Burger bar. I'm out of this, you have to understand that. I'm not a front line man, I'm a geek, a gatherer, so I'm standing back, watching, throwing up, whatever, except we're all high and nobody is going to remember in the morning who did what and there is a thing called guilt by association, right? Doesn't mean shit until you see a guy writhing on the floor, both his eyes in the dirt, then it means something, believe me, it means more than you ever thought possible.`

`There must have been a commanding officer,` suggested Clegg, `There must have been the guy with the knife.`

`Chains of command get a bit confused when everyone's high, Nat. It wasn't me, that is for sure, but I was six feet away. This guy's blood is on my boots, right? And it is not a game, Nat. It is very definitely not a game. So where is the bug? As if it matters. As if we believed any of it by then. But these guys get steamed up in combat, Nat, these guys do strange things. And if you've taken a man's eyes out, what's left? What's holding you back?`

`So where was it? And what's with the photo?`

`The bug was in his stomach. He swallowed and shat it out two or three times a day. His money was in the large intestine. This,` he tapped the place in his dreadlocks where the tube was hidden, `this was in his colon. On its way out. His wife and daughter.`

The two men sat in silence for the next five minutes. The baby mice were screwed up in tight little balls, their owner rocking slightly backwards and forwards. Clegg took in the warm comfort of the pub, the quiet chatter, the open fire. He had never felt complacent in his life but now it seemed an option, like an item on a shelf. Reach out and take it, warm in Bonny's bath. Leave Goldeneye's brother in the dirt, have another drink. `So you left the army?` he asked, still needing the moral of the story to be spelled out.

`I left the army, Nat. I left the fuckin' planet. I've not been back since. Been in orbit, see.` Another long pause. `If you want to protect what's yours, Nat, if you want to keep the next man out of your back yard then in the end that's what you do, that's what we all do. You take his eyes out, one by one, you gut him, you lift his secrets and treasures from his insides, you even search his turds for useful scraps. Africa, the Arabs, the Slavs, whoever.`

`So what's the answer, Arch?`

`Watch for me by moonlight,` he answered, holding up the marbles to the light, examining them as though they were amputated eyes, `Wait for me by moonlight. Come for me by moonlight, though hell should bar the way!`

`Which means what?`

But Arch had finished. Eyes closed, he lapsed into silence.

Heaven is a pub, thought Clegg; warm dry, complacent. Hell is the view from the window.

Arch took Andrew from behind with a blow to the head and then felled Owen at the knees. The brothers had been watering the horses by a small river. Beth was a hundred paces away making tea over a stove, close enough to hear the grunts, too far away to take in the details, but before Arch had tied up the two men she was already on her feet, a scream trapped somewhere in her throat and a knife in her hand. The knife was not in the script, but Arch had either not seen it or was too blinded by the action. He came charging towards Beth with his eyes manic behind their lenses and the Adam's apple straining at its neck. He was deceptively strong, his limbs long and his grip tight. His weight brought her to the ground with a sharp thud which sent the horses bolting as the kettle spilled onto the ground with the knife. The confusion was a blessing, there was no time to think thoughts of rape or worse, just an all-consuming stupefaction as though she had been stunned by a horrible light and explosion. She might have emerged from the bright darkness with the question `why?` but Arch was already trying to apply a gag which bit into her gums and compressed her tongue painfully into her throat.

What happened next was never clear to Beth. Her eyes were fixed on Arch's in the hope that some spark of reason would compete with the passion or madness that had surely overcome him. Instead she heard a thud and probably stiffened, ready for some fresh horror. She saw Arch turn his head and then fly upwards, half lifted, half leaping, as a second man appeared from nowhere and hurled himself at them both. The struggle was uneven and quickly over, the newcomer stood thoughtfully over Arch for a second before doubling him up with a kick to the ribs. Not a shot had been fired, barely a sound uttered, hardly seconds had passed but the second man had done his work. He looked briefly at Beth before gathering up the rope that Arch had been about to apply to her hands and feet. Within seconds it was Arch who was bundled up. The second man took great care in removing her gag, showing a strange delicacy for one who had seconds before over-powered his adversary with brute force.

`Its all right,` he said, speaking for the first time. `Its all right, you're safe.`

But it was not all right. She had been attacked. She had been violated, Owen and Andrew were still prostrate. It was far from being all right.

`Tea.` the man said, gesturing to the spilled kettle. `A good idea.`

`Who are you?` asked Beth, clawing her way back to the real world, ` And why did you help us?`

I am your nemesis, Clegg could have said, slate-grey eyes tight in a tanned face. I am your undoing. I have come to destroy all you love and wish for, I have come to spit deep into the throat of your stupid, misplaced innocence, to take your eyes out one by one. I have come to destroy the Wildside.

He looked at Beth long and hard before answering with a slight smile. `My name is Nathaniel,` he said, `Nathaniel Clegg. Let's just say I'm the helpful type.'

PART THREE

He who is destined for the Grail brings with him his brother.

Trevor Ravenscroft
The Cup of Destiny

FORTYSIX

Dear Sam,

He say's he's a jeweler. He says his sister taught him and he works with gold. Can you believe it? He says he grows it on cabbages and it's secret. Can you believe that someone finds it so easy to lie? To invent yourself like a clay model, to make it all up, all rubbish, confident that people believe you and can never find out the truth? He invents it well, but he's not perfect. He can't hold your eye when he says it, he keeps looking at the ground or away into the trees, as though there's something out there that might catch him out. Perhaps there is. I held his eye. I said I was a falconer, that I trained them and had done since I was a child. He nodded, not sure what to say, probably impressed by how well I could match him. I was tempted to go further, to make up ridiculous things, to make a fool of him, knowing that he would just nod and smile, thinking himself very clever. I almost felt sorry for him.

I know her, Agnes, I've met her, I'm sure. I've past her in the street or in a shop, looked at her, and not just in the park when we threw stones, it's like I've always known who she was. His daughter. The pot of gold. Back in the pub on her birthday she was surrounded by people, the light was poor and she never looked at me, but this time she did, this time she looked right into me as though she knew.

Knew what, Nat? Knew the truth? Because you don't even know it yourself.

I know enough. I know how to keep them off the trail. I told them they were attacked by a mad man, that there was no point in reporting it or trying to follow it up. No one was hurt.

Not even Arch?

He'll mend. I made up a story. I borrowed your life.

Easy?

What?

To borrow someone else's life?

You'll never know. And I'm sure you wouldn't mind. I'll lend you mine some time if you want it. It's a means to an end.

What end, Nat?

Fame and fortune.

What else, Nat?

I said I was from Leominster. Had I run with the bulls, she asked, but that's Hereford. It was like she was testing me.

And you passed.

With flying colours.

So she's a fool.

I didn't say that. She's certainly no fool. She has this touch of red in her hair, even though it's black.

Which means?

Nothing. Or there is more to her than meets the eye.

I thought of him lifting our Jet. Just imagine it, Sam, hurling Jet into the water, walking away. Try and think how he might have felt, what he might have thought. It's impossible. Then I thought of all the other times he might have been watching, spying, waiting. I thought it would make my skin creep but it didn't. I looked at him and he smiled. He has these warm eyes, they're not always hard, something in them betrays him, even when he sets his jaw and grinds his teeth at the back, they betray him. So I tried to hate him. But I couldn't. I thought of the plan, I thought of me as bait and him as the catch and I felt sorry for him. Can you believe it? I don't think I have ever felt so sorry for a person. Not even Dad with his illness, not even you with your tubes. Don't ask why. It's because he doesn't know, I suppose, it's because he's so stupid and he thinks he's so clever. I asked him about the bracelet. He's a jeweler, right? Why shouldn't I? He walked straight into it. Yes, he'd made it himself, Nathaniel Clegg, master jeweler. What of, I asked, softening him up. Plant gold, he said. Tell me more, I said, what's plant gold? It's not the real thing, he said. One day he would get the real thing and make something special. I asked him what the bracelet meant, two dragons inter-twined, one sharp, the other smooth, what did he have in mind when he made this wonderful bracelet? He looked at the sky and the trees waiting to be betrayed or waiting for another voice to answer but when it didn't he smiled again and was about to shrug. I saved him. I'm too soft. Let me guess, I said, let me tell you what I see in it, let me tell you what my Dad taught me. I touched him then, for the first time. I took hold of his wrist and pulled the bracelet off. I imagined his pulse was racing, but so was mine so I couldn't tell for sure, but he was very quiet, so were Owen and Andrew, they seemed to sense something. Oh yes, I said, ever-wise, God you would have been proud of me, Sam, I didn't know I could be so full of bullshit. But then I realized I had him, he was hooked. There's two devils. I said. Ones enough for me, said Owen, but Clegg was quiet, the eyes trying to look dark. Like there's two devils in each of us. This one is ribbed and with scales, the other is smooth and curves. This one wants to make the world too hard, this one wants to make it too soft. Which one are you, I asked. I didn't wait for an answer. Tomorrow I'll find out. I'll ask him for his help. Tomorrow I'll play the maiden in distress. I've got him, Sam, he's helpless. I could spit anything into his throat and he would swallow it.

There are two devils, Agnes, as you well know. It's a question of balance, I told her. The hard and spikey one, I said, that's the Comfort Zone, that's life on-line, watched. The smooth and curved one, that's the Wildside. That's why we're here.

So why are you there, Nat?

That's what she asked.

And what did you tell her?

What do you think?

You ignored her

I tried to. But she kept looking, not asking, but looking. It's all to do with balance, I said. We have to find the balance. The Welshman got me off the hook. Quite right, he said, and a lifetimes work it is too!

A lifetime's work, Nat. Can you be that patient?

No need, Agnes, I've got them. I've got them in the palm of my hand. I can screw her any way I want, every way I want.

I'm sure you can, Nat. I never doubted it. Virgo has a black heart, right? Your kind of beauty.

FORTYSEVEN

Iron steps led down to a corridor from which several doors gave options. Clegg and Beth seemed to have been descending for minutes. The growing dark and the hollow thud of their echoed steps increased the sense of depth and isolation. They were entering a mountain, and in more ways than one. Slate quarries had cut half of it away two centuries ago, the old Ministry of Defense the rest. During the war with Germany the nation's works of art had been stored here for safety. The door at the far end of the corridor was open. Clegg thought he heard music but as he drew closer it transposed into something half human and half mechanical and was lost as a nurse bustled from the room, passed them with barely a nod and went about her business. There was to be no grand or formal reception, no red carpet or fanfare of trumpets. They had been met at the entrance and after a brief exchange of pleasantries were being led below ground by a bare-footed youth. One of several around the place, Clegg noticed, body guards by any other name. The expectation was painful, the growing weight of solid rock above their heads was no more oppressive than the weight threatening to crush Clegg from the inside-out. As a youngster he had worked ferrets. Their eager and liquid dive into dark places had always horrified him, as had their ability to get stuck, head first and fatally. Ferret-like, Clegg had now blundered into their tunnel and the sense of constriction made his throat tighten and his pulse race.

Beth, on the other hand, was putting on a complex act but barely knew it. She had followed her father's instructions by bringing Clegg here but was more confused and anxious than at any time since her forced entry into the undertaker's. There was still so much she dared not understand, but her need to impress Clegg, to place him rather than herself into the dunce's corner, was simple enough. She led the way, she assumed the knowledge, her shadow on the tunnel wall was as big as his. In an ideal world she would have taken his hand in order to comfort them both.

Clegg was on the cusp between ecstasy and panic. As far as he was concerned his wonderful charm and cunning had brought him to this point. He was being led to John Savage, to the great shining lie at the heart of it all. Beyond the final door might be the answer to questions he had never even dreamed of asking.

`Come in please, both of you.` Clegg was not surprised to see the priestess who had presided over the bizarre healing of Llanidloes. It was appropriate that she should be here, proving a link between different expressions of the same madness. He found something overwhelmingly familiar about her, like a favorite newsreader or the checkout woman at the local shop, something everyday and ordinary but very reassuring. `My name is Madeline.` she said, her voice gentle but earthy. Clegg wondered what Arch would have made of this, what lewd and irreverent comments he would have laced the meeting with. She offered Clegg her hand and gestured him through the doorway into a large, high ceilinged room lit discreetly and in which a strong smell of something medicinal and unpleasant struggled against decent wax, wood and fabric.

Poor Arch, thought Clegg. The ribs were only bruised, not broken, he was not far away and still had his part to play in the greater scheme of things but he should really have been here to see this, after all, it was Arch's inspired ramblings that had put Clegg on the trail. He thought of his friend's theory. Arch had been explained it to him again the night before whilst pleading his case for gate-crashing today's party. Lots of Arthurs, or different people with the same title at different times, each fighting for freedom, each an outsider come from nowhere, each with a mysterious voice whispering in their ear. Whatever, as Arch might have said.

Today's Arthur, as invented by tabloid mythology or devious Comfort Zone policing, Arch's main man, his Holiness John Savage was to one side of the room, prostrate. The trappings of court and heraldry were sparse. Perhaps Arch was in the right place after all, because this could only ever be a huge anti-climax. Savage rose awkwardly as Clegg and Beth entered, took a few faltering steps and then stopped, gaining support from a table piled high with books and papers. His face, though ravaged by weariness and age, held illness at bay for the moment. In there, somewhere deep, perhaps somewhere desperate, lurked a spirit so indomitable that even his parchment skin and blood-drained eyes lit up in a generous smile.

`Mr.Clegg,` he said, warmly, coughing slightly after the effort but soon composing himself. `Mr.Clegg. Might I call you Nathaniel? Would you mind? It is wonderful to see you. Wonderful. Beth told me how you helped them. It was a frightening experience for Beth and her companions. Heavens only knows how it would have ended if you hadn't been there. You were under no obligation, no obligation at all. You really are very kind.`

Cut the crap, Clegg wanted to say, afraid that it was becoming too easy. You've got me dangling on a string. Who the hell are you? What do you want? Shall we both come clean? But none of this came further than his abdomen in which a stone-like feeling had settled mid-way between excitement and fear. I know you, he thought. I have always known you, but only by your absence. The whole world knows you, somewhere deep down. `It was the least I could do, Mr.Savage. I am only glad I got there in time. But Beth said there might be something else, some way in which I could help.` He managed to keep his hands still through this, his voice steady, even slow.

The priestess intervened. `Please, Mr.Clegg, take a seat close to John. He shouldn't tire himself.` The four of them shuffled around the couch. John Savage lay, Clegg, Beth and the priestess drew up seats.

`You have come a long way, Mr.Clegg.` she continued, `Beth tells us you are a jeweler.` A pause. `Did you study under Agnes Trimble?`

Above Clegg's head rock-shifted, seismic cracks heaved open, revelation by the ton seemed ready to crush him. He had known there would be questions and statements he might not be able to place in any category, but such a question and so early in the proceedings alarmed him. `I believe I did.` he answered slowly, waiting for the catch, for the suffocating lurch of stone.

`I thought so. Beth described the bracelet. Agnes' style. Do you mind if I see it?`

Clegg handed the bracelet to the woman, wondering if it was about to betray or disguise his deceit. He would like to have been the only one bluffing, playing a game, but he felt certain that he was caught in someone else's reflected reflection.

`I believe Beth has explained something to you of her father's work.` Madeline inquired.

`I believe we should all be grateful for what Mr.Savage has made possible.` said Clegg playing the good citizen, words, to his amazement, oozing like honey.

`But you have not always lived on this side of the Line.` she stated, as though it made him instantly criminal.

`We all make our choices,` said Clegg, wondering what the hell he meant by that. He looked at their faces, allergic to any hint of zeal they might have shared but was surprised to see one and the same expression, knowing that in this at least they were equals. Weariness. They all looked tired and he felt suddenly weary of it himself, he wanted to flood daylight into a few dark corners and lay down certain lies that had become unbearably heavy, like the rock over-head, but knew he must keep up the act a while longer.

The others exchanged glances, conceding one to the other, not conspiring, but wondering how best to initiate Nathaniel Clegg into this most odd of mysteries.

`You have some experience of the other side, Mr.Clegg. Beth has explained why that could be so important to us?`

Clegg felt cheated that the questions were coming from the priestess and not from Savage. He looked from one to the other. `I am like Beth,` he said. `I have crossed over for reasons of my own. I have a past. Don't we all? Some things I have left behind for good, but others stay with me. I find it difficult to refuse a challenge.` He was pleased with the statement. It was honest and completely new to him.

`You understand what is at stake?` the priestess asked. `You understand that unless John secures the necessary changes in the System, unless he and his children can be united that all this could be destroyed.` Behind the generous nose and tired eyes was an enormous feminine strength. Clegg had found Agnes intimidating but this woman would have made the best of men impotent. `If they get hold of John, if they find out how he has penetrated the System and used it to defend this corner of the earth they would finish it off.` She made the words `penetrate` and `earth` sound sacred and exclusively female, something no less delicate and profound than `womb` or `labia`, words only a women could truly understand and which men in their poor ignorance could do little more than profane.

`Then that must be prevented.` said Clegg, flatly.

`We can give you assistance, Nathaniel, of course. We can help you from this side. It would not be possible otherwise.` Savage offered. `We are asking you to bring my son to me, to bring Sam out.`

Clegg struggled to remember what Danny had told him a lifetime ago. Sam was the son, two years older than Beth. He had tried to cross the Line, there had been an accident. `You want me to go back?` he asked slowly, feigning disbelief. `You must know that's not possible.`

`There are ways, Mr.Clegg.` the priestess said.

`And risks.` Savage added. `We can't pretend there aren't risks. We can give you an identity to go to, fictional shoes to wear. It involves back-dating a biography, inventing someone, if you like. We have access to the System and can do it. We have done it before.`

Clegg knew only too well the kind of thing they had done before. `So it's perfectly safe?` he asked, attempting irony.

`It means living a lie. Are you able to live a lie?` the priestess asked.

`Can I live a lie?` Clegg mused, staring her out, ignoring Beth and her father for the moment. His lies held up the roof, they were a skeleton of props holding back oblivion. `I'm a man like most others, Madeline. I can live a lie if the price is right.` He turned to Savage, certain he had scored some kind of point over the priestess. `Where is your son?`

Their hesitation should have made Clegg suspicious. Had he known how anxious they were to time their cast and to reel him in just-so he might have been able to appreciate their efforts. They knew that their next revelation might be their last.

`He is in a place north of Nottingham. It is an old stately home or mansion with a huge net-work of tunnels beneath it. Welbeck secure hospital.` John Savage said.

The props buckled and gave way. A billion tons of darkness rushed in on Clegg, intent on crushing him, of turning to dust and fossil his conceit and deception. The last few weeks had certainly brought their share of surprises. That cabbages could produce gold, or that water spirits could be bottled had been hard enough to take but Clegg knew with a cold certainty that he was entering a different league of revelation and exposure. All the rest was suddenly insignificant alongside this new reality, this new truth that threatened to choke him. It must be like this to pull on the ripcord and feel the parachute snag or tangle, to know that nothing can save you now, nothing whatsoever. He was at the point of saying that he had once worked at Welbeck, in security, when all this hit him, the realization that they had planned it from the start, that they had played him like a fish, from the badger sett to the mountain hideaway, everything, all of them, it was a massive sting, a huge conspiracy, he had been head-hunted in the most ruthless and cynical of manners. Beth was the bait. That's all she ever was. He looked at her almost with pity. How much of this had she known? Which was worse, to be the prey or the maggot on a hook? It was him they wanted all along. He looked from one face to the next, feeling strangely weak, not angry or ready to fight, but enfeebled. He had been stung. The great Nathaniel Clegg made a fool of, left floundering, captive. Architect of his own fate? Never. Every certainty of the last two months fell away and tried in vain to reform itself. Every conversation, meeting, chance encounter was born again, streaked through with the insane possibility that John Savage had planned it all, that John Savage had indeed used his daughter as bait to lure Clegg stared into the awful unknown. Beneath the crushing weight something survived, tapped hopefully in the dark, praying for rescue. Shock was receding. Anger seemed an obvious response, but in its place, to Clegg's relief, was admiration. He had said nothing. He hoped his face and silence had not betrayed his discovery. Playing dumb might still be to his advantage. The only consolation he could salvage was to deny them his knowledge and recognition.

`I plan a lot of things, Mr.Clegg, it's what I do best. But unlike some planners I am also quite good on detail. Both God and the devil are in the details I always find.`

`Meaning?`

`We have an identity for you to go to. And a job. The job will bring you into contact with Sam.` This was Beth speaking, completing the triangle around him. Whether she had known from the start was an open question. She certainly knew now. Her expression was suddenly less weary.

Why not? Clegg didn't need to think very hard to imagine their price and how it could be doubled by a simple betrayal. He had the lot of them, if they did but know it. They thought they had been so clever, so wise, such excellent planners, Clegg would show them, Clegg would have a surprise or two for them yet. Judas was not to be bought off so lightly. They wanted to use him to bring out Sam? Then he would bring out Sam, just far enough to trap them all. Wasn't it called playing one hand against the other? Child's play.

`I have my conditions.` said Clegg, wondering just how strong his negotiating position was, how many bare-footed body guards would be on hand if he refused to help. He had not really imagined it would be a question of simply throwing Savage over his shoulder and bundling him off in the back of Arch's charcoal burner but he had secretly hoped it might be.

`What are your conditions?` Savage asked, not even trying to hide his anxiety.

Clegg savored the moment, sensing it might be some time before he once again felt in control of matters. This was his way of burrowing to the surface, of escaping the suffocating gloom of ignorance. `I want to know why.` he said. `I want to understand. Why the secrecy? What's behind all this? This mountain, the guards, the need for a family reunion?` Your wife, he could have added, your daughter, this sacrifice. His pulse was racing, his breathing irregular. He recalled the exchanged glance in the market place when Beth's look in his direction had made him blush. She had known even then. And in Clun, from the pub down to the river side where he had seen her with her boy friend, had that been chance? It was Agnes who refused to believe in chance and Agnes who had taken him to Clun, Agnes who had found him strung up, directed him first towards Arch and then here. Have you studied under Agnes Trimble, the priestess had asked. The bastards. They knew more of Clegg's last six weeks than he knew himself. It was time to reclaim his own past. Beth was staring at him. At least here the light was dim, she could not confuse his change of colour for anything more than controlled anger. But he had stood his ground. By asking for an explanation he had at least stemmed the tide of revelations, given himself a brief respite from confusion. `There is a whole country out there split down the middle by your ideology and your secrets. I want to know how it works. Then I might help.`

They led Clegg and Beth through the far door, Savage supported by the priestess. It gave on to a balcony overlooking a small underground lake contained in a cave, the roof of which had been shaped to an almost perfect dome. Clegg felt himself shiver and wondered if he was the only one made uncomfortable by the surroundings. It reminded him of the planetarium he had visited as child, a similarity that was soon to increase. He looked at Beth and realized that she too was uninitiated, also eager to understand the strange science of her father's world.

`I call this the Hollow Mountain,` Savage explained, `Or the Crystal Cave. Ideally it would be ten times the size. The acoustics would be very different.`

Acoustics. John Savage's heresy. The world was created out of sound, music, harmony, not from the violence of a bang. In the beginning was the Word.

`The Hollow Mountain and the Crystal Cave,' he repeated, `In Arthurian legends there is always a mountain to which Arthur is taken to sleep, to wait for the call when the nation needs him, and the cave where Merlin consults with the spirit worlds.`

Arch's version of things had seemed garbled, crazed, but this was something else, this was almost too subtle for Clegg to grasp. The simple and absurd certainties of a game were preferable to the hint that there might, just might, be something sound and true in what John Savage was about to explain. Where are you Arch? thought Clegg. There is one of your kind here. You would love this. There were voices in your head but that was nothing compared to my game, Arch. This man really believes he is King Arthur. Now who or what is virtual?

`Of course they are only symbols,` Savage continued, as though reading Clegg's thoughts. `All symbols. The Hollow Mountain is the head, the skull, the dark and private place in which the initiate makes his plans. And the Crystal Cave is the power of thought, clairvoyant maybe, the brilliant glancing light of ideas and imaginations which arise inside the cave. Lovely symbols, that's all. It's a shame really. But we aren't completely out of touch with legend. We have found some ways of respecting them. Let me show you.` He walked stiffly over to the far side of the balcony where a security light lit a small array of scientific equipment including a computer screen. `You could cast me as the mad professor in a Bond movie, Mr.Clegg. Did you ever see any of those films? But I have no piranha to throw you to. I'm rather at your mercy, I'm afraid.`

Clegg followed Savage's gesture in the direction of the lake. As the mad scientist pressed a button a large silver globe emerged slowly from the water. It was supported on a smooth column of steel, like a head on a stiff body. On either side of the column, in perfect symmetry, were two strands of metal which curled outwards from the neck and down into the water. The whole construction was not unlike a stylized angel, with head, body and wings. It had stopped rising and the ripples were quieting down. Clegg looked at John Savage and was struck by the look almost of devotion on his weary face.

`The Lady of the Lake` Savage said. ` What else could we call her? Let me show you what she can do.` He pressed a second button and then gestured Clegg to join him. He had taken a small syringe from its wrapping and he pricked this into the ball of Clegg's thumb. He drew out a tiny amount of blood, handed Clegg a swab and then held it to a light. `To enter a computer you need a key, Nathaniel. All information, all knowledge, all actions and transactions over there in the Comfort Zone are there for you to watch and listen to and involve yourself in. If you have the key. Of course there is more than one. Entry level, security level, commercial level, co-ordination, they all have their keys and codes to help them play around with the details of your life, of everyone's life. But at the heart of it all is a level they cannot reach. A kind of Fort Knox. Did you see that Bond movie? One of the earliest. Rather good.`

`And you have the key?`

`I had the key. Sort of misplaced it. Things move on and I need to get back into Fort Knox before the opposition, to put it simply. They have started to guess how the key was made.`

`And how was it made?` asked Clegg, the tiny pipette of his own blood still between them.

`If I'm to play the mad scientist, Mr.Clegg, which it seems I must, then I might as well milk it for all it's worth, don't you think?`

Clegg was touched by the farce of it all. Anything less like a mad scientist it would have been harder to imagine. A sick man riddled with doubt and regret, perhaps, but mad, certainly not. John Savage's voice was weak, strangely honest, never evangelical.

`To start with the human skeleton, Mr.Clegg, the frame we hang ourselves upon.` he held his own arms out and smiled at the frailty of what age had left him with. `The skeleton is frozen music, of course. You could play an octave on a skeleton, though I wouldn't suggest you tell the neighbours. The notes of music are the skeleton, in a manner of speaking. And in between the notes are the intervals. Do you understand music, Mr.Clegg? A shame.` He meant it, too, not just because it interrupted his narrative but for Clegg's sake it seemed. `The intervals are the interesting part, you see. They give the piece its personality, its *feel*. The intervals of the human being are expressed in DNA, Mr.Clegg, part of your genes. But the notes and the intervals, the whole piece of music, they are more than the parts, Mr.Clegg. They are the work of the composer.`

`God?`

`Well actually, no. Though God might argue the point. You see, Mr.Clegg, we compose ourselves: notes, intervals, flesh, bones, genes and all. So back to the key, Mr.Clegg. You asked how it was made and you have probably guessed. By using DNA, my own. And that of all my children.`

With that he got to work. First the blood was placed in a minute centrifuge, no larger than a kitchen blender, where it was mixed with pure alcohol. The alcohol floated to the top forming a distinct layer above the bottom liquid, but where the two met a film of residue began to form. It was the work of two minutes at most. Savage drew a small amount of the residue off with a second pipette and this he now placed on a microscope slide and the slide he waved towards Clegg. `Your DNA,` he said. `Unique. Nothing quite like it. How is the old girl doing?`

The `Old Girl`, the Lady of the Lake, was vibrating steadily. She made no noise as yet but the water was rippling vigorously, making the light above their heads and on the ceiling shudder strangely.

`Machines,` said Clegg, finding his voice. `It's all machines to me. I thought your world was against machines?` Machine Man or Green Man as Arch had put it.

Savage was shaking his head. `A common error, Mr.Clegg. There are few things more beautiful than a well-made and well-designed machine. Some are quite exquisite. But only people who love the world should be entrusted with machines, Mr.Clegg. And most people have been taught not to love the world but to use her, to which end machines are terrible things. Show me a man who loves the world and I will trust him with every conceivable machine. For those who do not love the world, Mr.Clegg, I'm afraid it's back to the stone age for them, try again. Now watch.` he said, loving the moment, climbing above his illness. He placed the microscope slide inside a scanner. Within seconds an elaborate sequence of numbers stormed across the monitor, a blur to their eyes. When the sequence ended he pressed the enter key and Clegg took a step closer to the dawn of creation. His own. The Lady of the Lake, having listened via the computer to the secrets of Clegg's DNA was literally changing her tune. The vibration of the wings had subtly responded to the code which was now being expressed as light, wonderful rippling patterns beating across the dome of the cave. Clegg was captivated. The planetarium was coming alive. Instead of stars and galaxies his own private universe was being converted into silent fireworks. He needed no explanation or theory to be completely transfixed by the show.

`I'm impressed.` he muttered as light swarmed above his head and washed against the white walls of the cavern.

`This is nothing, Nathaniel, just a party trick. That's your bar-code on the ceiling, nothing more. The real treat is this.` He handed Clegg a head-set. `The myth of DNA is that the stuff makes us what we are. It's the other way around, Mr.Clegg. We create our own DNA before birth. And I know how. The universe didn't start with a big bang, it started with the Word, with sound, with resonance. We sing ourselves into creation, Nathaniel. We make the choices that modern science ascribes to chance. It may take a century or two for science to escape its blind alley, until then we must take good care of the truth.` John Savage smiled. Through the ruin of a face there was still a glimmer of light and humour.

`So that's the great secret.` Clegg repeated, almost for his own benefit.

`The secret is, Mr.Clegg, the Wildside is a symphony, each human is a song, they are dancing to my tune, and always have been. The System depends on our family's DNA.`

`Then its like the Holy Grail.` said Clegg, thinking how Agnes would have looked to hear him say such a thing. But he was in no mood for fantasy. Drawing close to the mystery only made him keener. `So does that make you Christ?` he asked, at last meeting Savage as an equal, at last rising to the challenge. For a moment it occurred to Clegg that this sick man so close to death had dreamed it all up, had invented this entire world. Perhaps his power of thought was enough to set wolves free in the mountains and bring knights on white chargers storming to the rescue. Perhaps Clegg had been thought into being, as surely as the rest of them, just like players in one of Arch's cyber games, all caught up in each others fantasy. Stranger still was the realization that he would not have minded. Let Savage do his worst, let him create a world of illusions, it could only be better than the real one. Meanwhile his question had hit the mark.

`It makes Christ of everyone, Mr. Clegg, everyone who chooses to be free. That's the magic of it all.`

It will take more than magic, Clegg was about to say, but he held his tongue. A flick of the switch had brought lights and sound together as the entire flooded cave hummed to the unique music that had created Nathaniel Clegg. He held his peace. And listened.

FORTYEIGHT

How nice it would have been to have sat them all at one table, thought Finn. A round table, surely. John Savage, his daughter, the crippled son, Owen, Agnes, Andrew, the Priestess, Arch, perhaps even the doctors Johnson and Khalil. Oh yes, and Clegg. Like the Knights of King Arthur, like the war cabinet and Churchill, like Christ and his disciples, forming the chalice, the Holy Grail in which their blood and their passion would unite to form a light and a strength to defend the freedom of others. Always twelve in the circle, supporting the thirteenth, and always great trials and strains and challenges for the twelve. And always one empty seat, the Seat Perilous, the one Judas had occupied, the one Galahad had filled, always an apparent traitor whose motives and intentions would give the story its unwanted twist. And behind them the shadows cast on the wall. Each could see the shadows cast by the other, but none could see their own.

What would they make of such an idea? John Savage would probably scoff, firm and polite but putting Finn in his place. Andrew and Owen might glow with pride. The priestess would devour the theory. Arch, Finn knew, would nod manically, all his ideas vindicated, the Game shifting between various dimensions of reality, each one accessible to Arch and Arch only. And Beth? She was the hardest to guess. Beth might take it in silently or spit it out with venom, there was no way of knowing with her. Perhaps it would depend on who presented the idea, whose handsome lips and slate-grey eyes packaged the improbable. Clegg she would listen to open-mouthed, Clegg she would nod at and smile for, as though he were the source of all wisdom and salvation. Which in a way he was. Yes, from Clegg she would accept anything.

Finn had met a man once who made a fortune selling emission rights that belonged to non-existent factories. They were supposedly in Norway, manufacturing household tat, but they had closed down years earlier, crushed by Chinese competition. They still had carbon rights, however, and carbon rights were money, then as now. In the end it hardly mattered that the factories were defunct and were emitting nothing into the atmosphere. The belief, supported by a legal anomaly and a bureaucratic error, was sufficient to fuel the bidding, tempt the money, make the sting. Perhaps, thought Finn, a little sadly, this whole myth and legend angle, the Wildside's Arthurian pedigree, perhaps it, too, was a non-existent factory, producing non-existent goods and emitting non-existent smoke. What mattered was that people believed in it, or tried to. What mattered was the shared deception. Far better than having nothing to share, surely?

Finn had left the rest by slipping into the shadows. Barefooted Finn who had made the background his very own and who should now have been feeling pleased that Clegg has been hooked or snared or landed but who found that other feelings, unwanted feelings, could be more powerful and more persistent. His training was rigorous and complete with nothing left out, which for a young man meant intimate and tender exploration of difficult facts. But you can discuss the theories of desire and the techniques used in countless cultures for burning it out of the body and thence the soul all you like, theory still needs the test of practice, which no teacher or tutor can simulate, no matter how loved they might be. Finn was still a novice and hopelessly unprepared for the effect Beth had had on him. Being forced to watch her from a distance of course made things more difficult and how gladly he would have traded places with Andrew or Owen who could admire her at close range. She was beautiful, but also resilient, unpredictable, sometimes joyous, horribly vulnerable and exposed to Clegg, who she appeared to worship, Clegg the clever, scripted to play the hero's role and win Beth's heart whilst Finn, backstage and unnoticed, could only agonize in silence. To be capable of bringing down a hare at full speed with a crossbow from a hundred yards in driving rain counts for less than nothing if you are too love-sick to eat the thing. That night in Clun when she had led his hands over her breasts and breathed into his neck he had been so frightened, so confused, yet grateful beyond words, yet ignorant of who to thank. Had he done right by Beth? Would she think badly of him? Was she offended? It would have been so easy, so wonderfully easy to take her, to make her his first.

This was Finn. But also genuinely concerned and not only for himself. The game they had elected to play was dangerous because Clegg was an unknown quantity. In pinning their hopes on his knowledge and greed they were riding a very dangerous dragon indeed and Finn had seen, because jealous eyes are not blind but finely tuned, that Beth was too close and too trusting and altogether too keen on Clegg for her own safety. That he was twice her age would count for nothing if he chose to use his luck and position. Finn's only hope was that Clegg might be so caught up in the intrigue and dishonesty of his motives that he would fail to notice how Beth hung on his every word and admired his every habit.

Finn had left Llanidloes reluctantly, wanting to share his concerns but terrified of being recognized as love-sick. He had travelled at a swift jog for two days eastward and rested up with friends, also bare-footed, before dropping down into the marshes below the Wyre Forest, closer to the Comfort Zone than he liked, closer to what he called the Land of the Dead, but still necessary to make his meeting with Dr.Johnson and the Boswell. He had wanted to divert south in order to consult with Agnes, but time would not allow, the expectation and hope now being that things would move quickly.

He had to admit that things had gone unexpectedly well, starting with his first meeting with Clegg at the badger sett. He had watched the men carefully for those four nights, studying their moves and habits, enjoying the way they annoyed each other. He had almost felt a sympathy for Clegg by the end of it. During the day he had even practised his aim from the tree, acting out the encounter, preparing for all eventualities. Confronting them on the track, forcing them to strip and remove their tags, that had been the most terrifying. They could have called his bluff so easily, forced his hand, exposed how raw and anxious he really was. But they had obeyed. They had become as meek as lambs as his certainty had grown by the second. He would always cherish the memory of Clegg and his friend stripped silver and shivering with cold and fear on the old railway line. Even the theft of their boat engine and the trail of clues via Machine Head on Malvern market had worked perfectly, despite all the risks. It was no different to fishing in the end. You cast your bait on the water, you found the likeliest pools, you bided your time.

But following Beth had almost undone him. They had enjoyed their share of luck, but was it not said that John Savage could manipulate even luck as surely as he could manipulate the Comfort Zone and its System? But not even John Savage could have known how complete his daughter's hold on Finn would have become after such a short time. She had known straight away, she said, but so had Finn, from the Boswell onwards. Now his motives were complicated by his own wants and wishes. Beth had become precious to him, suspended beyond his reach for now but tantalizingly in view. But was she still precious to the plan? And, the harshest question of all, would her father find her expendable? Rumour had it that he had cast off his wife, Beth's mother, years ago, to serve his ends. If Beth was no longer needed then her safety would be of secondary importance to them all. And where did that leave Finn? She had risked everything to cross the Line. What would he risk for her? And would they be tribe of two when choices had to be made?

Finn looked across the valley, south towards Bredon, west into the Malverns. Literature: Hardy's *Tess* and the idealized west. `The atmosphere beneath was langrous, while the horizon beyond is deepest ultramarine.` Long may it stay so, Finn thought. `The prospect is a broad rich mass of grass and trees, mantling minor hills and dales within the major.` But for how much longer? Comfort Zone ambitions were not just a threat to the Wildside, to landscape, birds and animals, to sentiment, they were a threat to Finn's soul, to what made him unique, gave him strength, fed him like a mother. There was nothing he would not do to save it all from tarmac and corruption, from the kind of filth Clegg represented, even if the myths, like non-existent factories, were a means to an end and nothing more.

Finn's rendezvous with the doctor went as planned. Johnson had made the necessary contacts amongst the barge community at Stourport. Nobody is better placed to gain trust than a doctor, and everybody likes to tell him their secrets.

So it was that Dr.Johnson introduced Finn to two young Dutch immigrants, in the quiet of his barge lounge one late evening in the early summer. That they were smugglers went without saying. That they wanted money but could be relied on went with the accent. When your country had been washed away or buried under silt your roots find a footing in all that is best and worst in your threatened culture.

`We can bring anyone out, for a price, sure, but it needs time and you have to know this is different and dangerous.' Which would put up the price, no doubt. The one called Cornelius was speaking. It was his boat they were placing at risk and having only one eye gave added weight to his talk of danger. He and his brother Nico lived life on the edge, thriving on the razor-sharp tensions of No-Man's Land, the perpetual back alleyway of the modern world.

Nico took up the story. `Last year we was back and forward all night, sure, but each year is different, you know, and maybe tighter. What worked then won't work now, no guarantees, okay? Bringing out someone who don't want to come? That's kidnap. That's very different. Can you afford it?'

Finn reached into his bag and took out the cigar box. `There is more where this came from.` he said. `Take this for now, as a sign of good will, one more for each of you when it's done.'

The brothers held the jewelry reverentially. Nico, ever practical, took a tiny electronic scale from his coat pocket. Jewelry was common currency.

Cornelius smiled as he produced a bottle of jenever and four glasses, including Dr.Johnson in the conspiracy. `To Midsummer's Day,' he said, raising a toast, `and to your man Shakespeare.`

FORTYNINE

`I don't like Mr.Clegg.` Andrew muttered. `I don't like him very much at all.` he was confiding in Owen as they rode in a long, broad valley in the shadow of dull green mountains.

`Don't trust him, is it?` Owen asked, impressed by his brother's instincts.

`No, I don't trust him. Shall I tell Beth?'

`Its not that simple, Andy, old boy. Beth has to make her own mind up. Anyway, Mr.Clegg can help us, like he helped us when that man attacked us.`

`Not really,` said Andrew. `That man was Mr.Clegg's friend.`

`You've got that one wrong, Andy.`

`I've not got that one wrong, Owen. They were friends in that town, they were talking the day before that man attacked us.`

Owen said nothing. Andrew rarely got such things wrong. He observed carefully at all times simply because he rarely made any judgements as to what he was seeing. Today was exceptional. Today he had gone beyond observation to something a little more disturbing. It was neither possible nor necessary to explain everything to Andrew, indeed there were things Owen did not understand himself. It was true that just as they were wondering how to tempt Clegg to reveal himself the matter was taken out of their hands. Of course Andrew was right. Clegg had staged the whole thing in order to get close to Beth and thence to her father but now that the plan revolved around Clegg there was no choice but to trust the outsider. Having no obvious alternative did not make it any easier.

`I'm going to tell Beth.` Andrew repeated, `tell her not to trust him.`

`You tell her, Andy my old fruit, but don't expect that to change very much.` The two brothers looked back along the track. Clegg and Beth were bringing up the rear, Beth talking, Clegg listening. Owen noticed how easily Clegg directed his horse, never more than one hand on the rein, a regular cowboy, yet until yesterday he appeared to have been without one. Of course Owen had noticed how struck the girl was with the hero of the moment. He could understand it, but like Andrew it also made him uneasy. He also felt responsible for the little group now that he understood more of their task and in the master scheme of things he had a definite role to play. It had all been agreed late last night in conference with John Savage. Beth and Clegg were making for the border. Arrangements had been made to get Clegg back across the Line whilst Owen and Andrew would start moving the balloon over land because their responsibility was to get Savage to the rendezvous point. There was no doubt that Clegg faced a difficult and dangerous task. And Andrew was probably right. What if Clegg was a step ahead of them all, intent not on bringing Sam out but in luring John Savage into danger? Clegg's choice of rendezvous had been agreed to. Stratford. Owen had tried to persuade Savage from travelling, insisting that there was no real need, but they knew that Clegg would not deliver Sam unless the boy's father was within reach. It was worrying, even without Andrew's suspicions and sulk. Owen knew that the latter was never without reason and often led to the unexpected.

That night they made camp at the watershed of two valleys above the line of mist which had been forming these last few mornings. They gathered wood, Owen lit a fire and Andrew offered to cook. He had a pack of green bacon and two jars of dried mushrooms that he soaked in beer for half an hour before frying. As he worked on the food he began to sing to himself, tunelessly but unconscious of the others. When a sulk turned to song it usually meant that something had been resolved, or was about to be. Perhaps Andrew had a plan now that everyone else seemed to.

It threatened to be a perfect night, one that made Clegg wish for Agnes to share it with. A large white owl, corpse-silent, gave them close inspection. Bats of all shapes and sizes, like black shooting stars, buzzed the insects and the fire's sparks. A vixen, called from far away, disturbed by their smell and anxious for her teenage cubs, now roaming at will. Clegg watched the fire and its effect on their faces. Owen and Andrew, for all their differences, actually looked like brothers in the sharp contrast of red and black. Beth was more intense but calmer than all of them. She could have been anything between twelve and twenty in this light, very beautiful and very fragile. Looking at her made Clegg feel strangely sad. Her innocence was there for him to crush, like a flower screwed up in the hand. Her life force still believed in itself, had yet to be dulled by the reality of life. Why had it survived when Bonny's so obviously had not? The men in this drama were world weary and worldly wise, they already knew betrayal in at least one of its several forms, but in matters of trust and faith Beth appeared as pure as the driven snow, a virgin in such things. Clegg wondered if he would be doing the world a service by screwing her illusions. He was skilled at penetrating anything and everything vaguely sacred, so why not Beth Savage? In the meantime he had to remind himself of her material worth, of what he might buy by selling her innocence.

Clegg caught Beth's eye accidentally. She smiled and looked away at which Clegg looked upwards following the sparks until his eyes readjusted to the stars where there were no borders to cross, only lines imagined into place to help explain away their profusion. The game he had played with his mother came back to him. To see shapes or faces or animals in the stars. As a child he had seen hundreds: beetles, wasps, lions, elephants. With a wonderful disregard for zodiacal wisdom he had peopled the sky with a zoo all of his own, all the creatures entwined into one childish story with no start or finish or logic. They were all gone now. He was expected to see the sky in a certain way and did so. Invisible lines of cultural habit divided the mass for him just as lines and cables and wires divided the night sky of a town or city.

Beth studied Clegg with big eyes as he lay back to watch the stars. Andrew was playing with the embers. Owen was whittling at a piece of goat's horn to make a walking stick handle. The brothers had not eaten mushrooms. They had been offered only to Clegg and herself and now she understood why. She was scared, then thrilled, then angry, three moods within as many seconds, but then strangely confident in her ability to remain within herself whilst soaring above them all. Had Clegg realized? She thought not. In this she was about to prove older and wiser and one step ahead of her superman. She squinted to make a blur of him and watched, smiling, as he dissolved into flame and sparks which rose up as a huge black residue, a shadow against the dark, writhing in fire below but sucked into the cosmos above. Poor Clegg, she thought, torn in two. She felt a sudden wave of pity for the man. She saw him now very clearly, one part consumed and tormented into ash, the other part reaching for the unreachable heights above their heads. She felt a cool curiosity to know which of the two Cleggs would prevail and what might be left of him at the end of it. And did she appear the same to him? No. She had no doubts. Nothing in Clegg's diet or distorted chemistry could make her dissolve or resolve and torment in the same way he was doing. Let him stare all he wanted, she thought, I, Beth Savage, will remain seated by the fire, rock solid, perfectly poised between heaven and earth.

Against her better judgement Beth rose from the fire side and started walking to the cairn at the centre of the field, certain that Clegg would follow, just as Jet had always followed, as though on an invisible string. At first she was unsure of her legs and their ability to carry her but no sooner had she thought to give up than she found herself sitting on the cairn, looking across the valley, Clegg next to her.

`What did you make of my father? she asked.

`He is very ill, Beth.`

`He has good reason to be.` she blurted out, shocking Clegg with her tone. `He's an idealist.`

`I'm sure.` was all Clegg could manage. That ideals made you an ill was a simple enough concept but not one he had expected to hear from Beth.

`I mean, that's why he's still alive.` she added, as though reading his thoughts. `Without his ideals he would have given up long ago.` There was a suitable pause. `Could you kill for your ideals, Mr.Clegg?`

`I'm not sure I have any.`

`That's honest of you. I don't think you're always honest. With yourself I mean.`

`What makes you say that?`

But Beth ignored him. Her head was spinning with the mushrooms and space had expanded strangely around her. She could feel Clegg's breath on her neck but it felt as though he was on the other side of the field. `He killed my mother.` she said. She was shocked, not by the words or their content but by the fact that they had leapt out unbidden, but before she could soften them she had moved on. `Can you see the dragon?' she asked. Everything in her field of vision was swirling and giddy but it didn't matter because she remained static. She pointed to where smoke and sparks merged with the stars.

`I can see the dragon.` answered Clegg, trying to point but getting no co-operation from his out-stretched hand. `I don't believe you. I don't believe he killed her.`

`You're just saying that to please me.` she answered to the sky. `He could have saved her. He didn't.`

`Perhaps he had his reasons. How did he do it?`

Beth wondered why she should tell him, why it could possibly matter. She would never have troubled Owen with the story but here she was confiding in Clegg the gate-crasher. `By the time I was born most cities had rebuilt themselves. They just moved a bit inland and up hill and filled all the land behind them, isn't that how it was?`

`I suppose so. I didn't pay much attention to geography lessons.`

`But you played on building sites?`

`I tried to.`

`There you are, then. Just after I was born there was a plan for a new city in the Lake District. Do you remember that? You must do. It looked beautiful on paper.`

Clegg was struck by the ridiculous thought that Beth, too, would look beautiful on paper. He imagined her mapped out like an architect's drawing, proportions and curves just so. The next moment she had emerged from the drawing board, a grid of lines rising from the page. But no drawing could map the intense anger around her eyes, he thought, nor the soft smile about her lips, no drawing could show the sheen of red through the black.

`Lake-side homes for the rich,` she continued, `water buses, cable cars to the high-up developments. Six million people would have been housed in the most beautiful city in Europe, they said, perhaps even the world. The problem was that the plan came from the Comfort Zone and the Lake District was on the Wildside. In those days the Line was different. You must know, you must have been a teenager around then.` She looked at him differently, frown and smile balanced, trying to imagine Clegg the teenager, allowing him a past, even a childhood. It was almost as though she shook her head before speaking. Clegg noticed her tongue dart across her lips and knew she had a power over him that was dangerous to them both.

`There were rows and arguments and threats and violent protests but it was decided to go ahead. From what I understand of it the Department of the Environment was the bit of government that decided. The DoE. They made the decision to go ahead with it. You can imagine the kind of money that was involved. And the politics. It meant calling the Wildside's bluff, pushing surveillance into rural areas. Dad stuffed them. He completely stitched them up.`

Call my bluff, he thought, stitch me up, stuff me, whichever way you want. It's in my DNA. I sang you into being. You're a song to get my mouth around. Once upon a time, he remembered, a family walked across a park, a father and his two children. Once upon a time a gang of youths with nothing better to do, hurled stones at the huddled threesome. A prelude. Or a false note?

`The day after the decision was announced the DoE disappeared. Every record, every data-base, every file, past and present, they just ceased to exist. Even pension records for ex-employees, all vanished from one moment to the next. They couldn't even get inside their officers because the doors wouldn't open. Brilliant! He could do that sort of thing, you know. He still can, in fact, that's why they're so scared of him. Computer access codes, tax records, invoicing systems, the lot. They said it was the biggest single act of computer terrorism ever carried out and it was certainly the most effective. Terrorism. They called him a terrorist, you know. Wanted the Swedes to strip him of the Nobel thing. If you want to know how effective he was just go to the Lake District. It's still there, you see. I haven't been but people say its more lovely than ever. It was his declaration of war. There was no doubt who had done it because Dad was the only person alive who knew how. To make matters worse he was the only man alive who could prove or demonstrate who had done it and he was the only man alive who could undo it, who could bring the DoE back to life so he had them, didn't he? He really had them stitched up.`

She was touching him. Smooth brown hands with hard little nails rested on his arm. He imagined each finger having a life and a will of its own, exploring his body.

`He still has big ambitions.` she said.

`Like what?`

`To plant more trees.

Clegg was not sure he had heard it right. `To plant...but surely.` The sense of an old man planting trees was beyond him. It was like making jewelry to give away. He dismissed both ideas with a shake of the head. `You said he killed your mother,` he managed to say, changing the subject. `what's this got to do with her?`

`There are two dragons up there.` she said, pointing to the stars. `Like on your bracelet.`

` I wish they would stay still.` Clegg said.

`They never stay still. That one's going to eat the other one.` It didn't matter which one or where you drew the imaginary lines. Beth was deep inside Clegg's unconscious and her own. The Line was down, they were swarming across, first one way, then the next. `Which one are you?` she asked, listening to her voice as though in a recording. She was aware of wanting to ask him something else but could not remember what. She wanted to be reminded, she wanted a memo, a single word to prompt her, certain that the right question would unlock all she and Clegg needed to know, now and forever.

`That one.` he answered instantly. `The one on the left.` He pointed to his right. He was light years away. He was on his mother's lap, shivering and happy, he was suckling pure gold from Agnes' breasts, he was on the hook cast by Andrew's mushrooms, stoned and high on thirty years of untruth.

`Dad told me that people wish disasters on themselves. Do you believe that, Mr.Clegg? Do you believe that? Floods. It was greed that made them happen. If your body is ill you get a fever to make you better. Isn't that how it works? People in America and Europe used to spend as much on disaster films and disaster books than they did on helping the victims of the real thing.`

She looked directly at him and realized how close they were sitting. Clegg could see the feint down of her cheek, she could see the sharp bristles around his jaw. He realized he was waiting for the tongue to end the sentence, to run along the soft line of her lips.

`They love it.` he said, `War, floods, famine, they can't get enough.`

`And you?` she asked, taking the dragon by the tale. `Do you long for it, Mr.Clegg, do you adore it and lust after it? Do you need disaster to make sense of things?` As she spoke she lowered herself to the floor, her back to the cairn. Clegg slid next to her and was not surprised when she nestled her head against his chest and accepted his arm around her shoulder. He was warm even through his clothes, and offered a kind of strained comfort. Something was burning him up from within and she needed it for the moment to stave off the chill.

`I don't know the details of all that happened,` she said, suddenly back with her mother and the Lake District city. `We had to move house. Dad had to stop work. The newspapers tore him apart. I only remember that Mum was taken ill, suddenly. One newspaper called him Doctor Frankenstein, apparently, said he had created a monster and that the monster was out of control. It was too late to destroy the monster because it ran everyone's life, but it was not too late to bring the mad Doctor to account, to prevent him from releasing such chaos on the world again.`

`For some he was a hero.` Clegg stated softly, memories suddenly reforming themselves.

`How do you know that?`

`Because I do remember. I remember this bit. For some he was a hero. On the Wildside and in those parts of the country which still had to choose which side of the Line they would finish up on, he was a hero. A kind of born-again saviour.`

`The sleeper awoken.`

`That kind of thing. The protector for all time of British people and British freedoms. King Arthur.`

`But Mum was dying. They black-mailed him. Give us back the DoE, they said, give us back our city in the Lake District and you can have your wife back. But he didn't. He let her die. Ideals you see.`

Clegg was distracted by the feel of her pulse at the temple against himself. It was racing, as was his own.

Beth suddenly remembered what she wanted to ask, the question that would unlock both their secrets. `That's it.` she said, excited. `That's the question. What do you want? Why are you helping us? What makes you tick, Mr.Clegg?`

`Lies.` he said, despite himself, `Lies make me tick, Beth. Lies turn me on.` He was not shocked by his own honesty. He could almost hear the first of the thirty pieces of silver falling to the ground, taking root, blossom turning to fruit in the form of Beth's warm body. The fruit of such a betrayal would be sweet indeed, he thought.

`Strange.` she said, and laughed, but whether she was laughing at him or her own response was unclear. Suddenly she drew back and looked with great sadness and sympathy as though seeing the root and cause of Clegg's torment. `You haven't got any children, have you? You don't have children. You wouldn't say that if you did. You would hate lies if you had children, I know you would.`

`I have a step son.`

`Do you lie to him?`

`No.`

`Well then.`

`Well then what?`

`You couldn't lie to him, could you.`

`No, not really, not a real lie.`

`Then lies don't make you tick. Lies are a substitute for...`

`For what?`

`Do you believe in love?` she asked.

`I don't believe in talking about it.`

`Some people think it's just a tool to get what you want.`

`They might be right.`

`And they might be wrong. If you loved somebody would you let them die for your ideals?`

`If I loved somebody, and if I had ideals...` he said hesitantly, but Beth cut him off.

`You can't lie to some one you love.` she said. `It's one of those laws. It all makes sense. That's the amazing thing. Its all held together by wonderful laws. It's just that we can't see them. We can't hear the music.`

Yes, thought Clegg, it all made sense. The Hollow Mountain, the music of the spheres, Arch with his wraps and quest for King Arthur. Well Clegg had found him hadn't he? Myth and legend were dead and buried, just like Savage's wife, sacrificed for something simpler. Clegg should get the reward, the millions in useless gold. And then what? What made him tick beyond the gold, beyond the thrill of winning? King Arthur was a mad scientist in a Bond movie, King Arthur could suck your blood and spread you across the ceiling in wave after wave of glorious light. King Arthur's daughter had down on her cheeks and could make you blush in a public place. King Arthur's daughter turned him on more than lies could ever do. But if I have sung myself into being, Clegg asked himself, shaped my own DNA, prepared my life in advance, then why am I sitting here on a bare hilltop, arm round a sixteen year old girl, head spinning and two dragons waiting to claim the dregs?

When she looked at Clegg she felt the power that Finn had made her doubt. It ran hot in each limb and muscle, each gesture she made, each brush of her hand against Clegg's body. Yes, she would use him. She would use him as countless boys and men had used her in the past, to grow unbeatable. But this time her power lay in not conceding. By denying Clegg she would help the cleansing that would prepare her for Finn, besides which, incest was not to her liking.

She was perfectly safe. Andrew watched from a distance as they both drifted towards sleep. Which particular imp had suggested this scheme he couldn't say, but it had worked. Andrew knew that in someway Clegg had been exposed, found out, if only by Beth. But Andrew knew just a little bit more, for with the others, including Beth, all soundly asleep he was the only one who savoured the unmistakable, gentle and perhaps rather beautiful sound of Nathaniel Clegg quietly sobbing.

FIFTY

`Spare your sympathy for me, Watson, not Clegg.`

`Sympathy, Sir?`

`Sympathy, Watson? God forbid. Requires too much RAM I suppose. Let me remind you. Midsummer's Day is approaching. Midsummer's Day is on hand. Midsummer's Day is upon us. Sympathy, why that now?`

`Why sympathy, Sir?`

`Midsummer's Day, Watson. We know what that means do we not.`

`I will not be available during the Midsummer period, Sir.` Watson replied, apologetically it almost seemed. `Normal service will be resumed at 6.00a.m. of the 22nd of June.`

`I wouldn't bank on it, Watson.`

`Bank on it, Sir?`

Sir David got up from his empty desk and strolled to the window. The word in the corridors was that it might be his last Midsummer. The word in the corridors was one of hushed concern, but then it had been for over a decade.

On a good day Sir David could look out across a glittering landscape of greed. His view allowed the lost city of London to glint back hopelessly from beneath its silt and reeds. Old monuments, preserved on reinforced footings, sheltered the swarms of leisure boats. Nelson's feet were washed clean by the tide and his head was decked not with pigeon shit but the oiled paste of sea-gulls. Vast tributes to the folly of carbon consumption. Who could have guessed fifty years ago that it would have come to this? Was there any stage in the past when it could have been halted? Sir David had once visited a museum village in the States, set up over a century earlier by the great Henry Ford. Ford had indulged his love of nostalgia by creating a small Utopia, the idealized frontier town with moral decency soaked into each of its white picket fences. And no cars. Ford had excluded the automobile from his Utopia.

Nowadays the village was ringed by car parks. Somewhere along the line each and every individual had started to believe that they were the centre of the universe, that they had the right to instant ease, entertainment, access and bliss without any responsibility. Now look at them, grid-locked from dawn to dusk, from birth to death, clogged in their own freedom, each the centre of a universe grown cramped and sordid.

He looked at the shelf above his desk on which an old carriage clock stood proudly. It was beautiful, it was gold and it was engraved with a message from the past. Savage had given him the clock many years ago, Savage had made his intention clear even then. It was a quote from Alexander Pope. Savage, as Sir David was fond of joking, always was an erudite bastard.

`Lo! Thy dread empire, chaos! is restored:
Light dies before thy uncreating word:
Thy hand, great Anarch! lets the curtains fall
And universal darkness buries all.`

`Great Anarch indeed. Very clever, John, a perfect description of your contribution to the universal darkness of Midsummer's Day.` Sir David muttered. The longest day of the year and the longest night all rolled into one. Every year without fail Midsummer's Day became an orgy of riot, looting, street-crime and marital infidelity. Every year, without fail, the Great Anarch would remind his great rival that the System was only a flawed substitute for God. Every year without fail the System would crash in unpredictable ways and unleash millions from their invisible and deeply resented electronic tethers. Every year Sir David's department promised to limit the damage and prevent major disruption. Every year they failed to keep the promise.

The Wildside's statement was simple. Disruption to the System was in direct proportion to border violations and westward drifting air-pollution. Clean up your greedy little world and leave us in peace, was the message, otherwise your disciplined and order-loving people, finding themselves free of tags, monitors, control and surveillance will be free for the day to behave like animals released from their cages. If you want to build your lives around these machines and sustain your morals thanks to their watchfulness then live, briefly, with the consequences.

Sir David knew well enough that the disruption went far beyond the one day. Whole patterns of consumption were determined by what might be stolen on Midsummer's day, a whole industry of prediction, prevention and insurance flourished in the months and weeks either side of the event. Insurance policies for the one day, where available, were literally as expensive as all the other 364 together. Covet your neighbour's wife? For the entire year her every move would have been under surveillance, her every conversation with the milkman timed. For one day the collective chastity belt would be removed. For one day the curtain would fall on every indiscretion. And nor was it confined to the poor, the unlettered, those who have never heard of Alexander Pope. Respectable white-collared workers encouraged by the greed of their children and perhaps their own childhood memories would approach the year's shortest night with the same carefree abandon their grandparents once reserved for Halloween or Bonfire Night. Looting of every kind would be rife. Old scores would be settled. Unwanted pregnancies, all to be aborted, flushed down the toilet, would peak in March unless the clinics worked overtime in July and August.

Why? Sir David had his theory, but not one to be shared with Watson. Perhaps the inner landscape was to blame, the bleak shopping precinct landscape where everything must be available to everyone right now and at a discount. No deposit, no interest, no payment, arrears to be collected on Midsummer's Day, blame a million Henry Fords, all of them desperately searching for a parking place.

`What will it be this year, John?` Sir David asked himself absently. `What do you think, Watson, any theories?`

Of course the machine had theories based on statistics and precedent. Last year all pension records for the armed services had been deleted, lost forever. The year before vast sums of money had jumped from the accounts of the good and mighty to those of the unsung. Robin Hood could have done no better. At least this year the annual rush of capital to foreign banks had been sensibly regulated, even encouraged. The slow task of converting computer records back into hard copy was underway in ever more government departments and there was always the hope that simple and crude blackmail, or better still a timely arrest, would put an end to the chaos once and for all.

Sir David Armstrong looked from the clock to the orderly world he helped control and allowed himself a smile. No crime, no social unrest, no terrorism or kidnapping. Everyone forced to do the good. Complete acceptance of poverty, unemployment and inequality to an extent tyrants had only dreamt of in the past. But how boring. How unbelievably, sickeningly boring. The average young adult watched over one thousand films a year, more than three a day, the average young child spent four and a half hours a day inside a virtual reality kiosk. The average marriage lasted three and a half years. The boredom was unbelievable, the hunger for distraction was insatiable, the epidemic of suicides and mental illness quite explicable. Thank God Sir David had his old friend to entertain him, to distract him from the world's emptiness.

How might it appear ten days from now when Midsummer was upon them? The glow of fires from the city centre riots would warm the night. Teenage gangs, let loose, would release a year's supply of frustration and anger. Shops and services would board themselves up, bury their heads in the sand of complacency. Welbeck Secure Hospital might be a good place to be that day. At least it had its own generator and nor was there a Casualty Department to be cluttered with the unclean human debris of it all.

Oh no. Sir David was forgetting. This year all hospitals would close their casualty departments for twenty-four hours. You would be on your own out there this year as never before.

Or perhaps not. Perhaps things were shifting and shaking at last. The tantalizing message from Mr.Clegg had excited Sir David. There was a logic to events that was just beyond his grasp and this he enjoyed, like a game of chess. After Clegg's message they had been met only with silence and had put in half a dozen MSA, miniature surveillance aircraft, each one the size of a dragonfly, each one with smart cameras and each one hideously expensive. Five had failed to produce anything, but the sixth had blundered across Arch the Game-player. It was via Arch's palm-top that the message had been sent but the low-quality pictures were of Arch, alone, travelling in an absurd looking vehicle to the back of which was fixed a scrambling bike, the one Clegg had stolen. The obvious conclusion was that Clegg was no longer in the frame. But Sir David suspected otherwise.

Dr.Khalil's office was one small corner of the vast underground ballroom that had once accommodated more than two thousand guests. For months after his arrival he had marvelled at the model railway that was now used to bring medicines from the pharmacist's lab to the ward trolleys and he even wondered if such a system was common to all European hospitals. But now his sense of wonder had been replaced by a grim realization. This was no typical hospital in which he had found employment and here were no typical patients, even allowing for the variety usually found amongst the criminally insane. It was no great secret that any restoration of the monarchy above ground would first require the release of Welbeck`s most securely held and most heavily sedated patients. Less well known was that a silent war between Comfort Zone and Wildside had raged in these wards and corridors for over thirty years, and never more intensely than during these last twelve months.

Dr. Khalil was anxious. The 3.30 from photocopying had derailed outside the stock room. Always a bad omen. Even worse was that Armstrong's visit was the second in three weeks. At least this time he was alone. That awful policewoman with the hawk-like eyes and the high-heeled voice was missing.

`Is your family happy?` the good Sir David asked, genuinely curious. He had been watching the trains with mild amusement and they had put him in a good mood. To find such playfulness in a place so awful was strangely comforting.

`Oh yes, sir, very happy, very happy indeed.`

Their temporary permission to remain had been converted to permanent only that week. The doctor's was still pending.

`I'm pleased,` said Sir David, wondering how many more displaced water rats would wash up on his particular shore. `Yours won't be long now. Bureaucratic delay. You understand the kind of thing.`

They entered Sam's room. Although Sir David had braced himself for the usual choir of demons and the awful frailty of the youth he was forced to gasp at what actually confronted him. This ghost he had never met before and yet he had always known it and more intimately by far than the rest. Its presence was huge, like a tidal wave of grief, its gesture was one of awful admonition, its expression one of profound sadness and defeat. Sir David almost staggered backwards out of the room in order to be free of the thing but he knew it would follow him down every remaining corridor of his life now that it had been released from its bottle. He swallowed hard and clung to Khalil's words as though to a lifeline.

`Of course, Sir. Bureaucratic delay.`

`It should be through in about ten days.` he mumbled.

`Ten days, Sir. That will be marvelous.`

`Won't it just. Marvelous. There is just one thing,`

`Yes, Sir.`

Sir David stared at the tragic monster as he spoke, transfixed by its sadness. `How is the old sense organ, doctor?`

The two men had seated themselves on opposite sides of the patient. Khalil tried to ignore Sir David's discomfort although the change in mood was palpable. `Sir?`

`The sense organ, doctor. Religion.`

`Sir, I'm not sure…`

`Deaf and blind, watching opera, can you imagine? Incapable of smell in a rose garden. Tasteless with a gourmet meal. No sense of touch whilst in bed with a beautiful woman, numb to it all. I understand it now, Khalil, I really do. And I'll tell you another thing. If we don't develop your religion sense organ, doctor, others will take its place. Can you imagine that? I hope not, I really do hope you have no idea what I'm saying. It's enough to make any man an atheist. The boy.` his voice dropped slightly, `How is he progressing?`

`Progressing, Sir?`

`Yes, Doctor. Progressing.`

Khalil quickly recalled the rules. `He is stable, Sir.`

`Stable. Wonderful. I think perhaps he is a sense organ himself. Do you ever get the feeling he knows what is going on around him? Everything.`

They looked at Sam. `Sir.` Khalil whispered, `I have never doubted it.`

Sunlight and dust performed their act, a ticking in the water pipes went about its business. To his relief the awful ghost evaporated. `Which makes two of us.` Sir David said, very quietly, `Two of us.` He cleared his throat, shifted in his chair, raised his voice a notch. `I knew his mother, you know?`

`Sir?`

`The boy. I knew his mother. She was the only woman I have ever loved.` He was enjoying this. He had never told anybody, and now he had told a virtual stranger, a man whose existence depended on his own whim and fancy, a man who would never ever repeat any of this.

`Sir?`

`We live in interesting times, Doctor Khalil. Very interesting times. Have you ever thought what it must be like on the other side of the Line?`

`I understand it is very dangerous, Sir, that people live like animals.`

`Like in the camps?`

`Just so, Sir. Like one very big camp.`

Before Sir David could respond to this the gentle vibration in his breast pocket alerted him to Watson's agitation. The machine was instructed to disturb him only for very specific and very limited reasons. Sir David connected the ear-piece, apologized to Khalil and spoke to the tiny microphone in his lapel. `Yes, Watson, has the Prime Minister been shot?`

`Sir, there appears to be a message from Mr.Clegg.`

Sir David smiled. As he had thought, the man was still alive and kicking.

`Although it comes from Arch's machine.`

Then it was suspect, but no less interesting for all that. `What does it say?`

`It does not actually say anything. It is a ticket.`

`A ticket? What for?`

`For a play. At Stratford.`

`What play, and when?`

`*The Tempest*, by William Shakespeare. To be performed on Midsummer's Day.`

`Then let the curtain fall,` Sir David muttered, speaking neither to Watson nor Khalil, gazing at Sam's shrunken form, `Let the universal darkness bury all!`

FIFTYONE

Clegg was surprised with himself. In the middle of all this it was not flight he craved but to talk with Agnes, he wanted to share the joke with her, to see what her shrewd angle on things would make of the twists and turns that had brought him to this point, because in the end she was more right than she could possibly have known. It was indeed a Quest for the Grail, as she had insisted all along, but a Grail filled with fragile and very human blood, its divine power completely man-made.

Clegg was alone and looking down into the valley. If there is one day when spring and summer meet then this was it. The greens were still tipped with the red that would leach away after St.John's and birds now sang for the sake of it. The great oak trees wore their lightest greens and seemed dusted with lemon. If he could have flown above it, taken wing to free himself of the earth he might have become part of its festival, but his feet were still firmly in the mud of his previous life. With a quick switch he could see it all as bleak and hopeless, in the perpetual grey of November, a battleground in which birds and animals fought eternal trench warfare, in which isolated farms hid isolated farmers, suicidal, whiskey-breathed, hunched over fiddled accounts or crude magazines in damp kitchens, bones of their fathers and grandfathers buried under muck heaps which never got smaller no matter how much they were spread.

Clegg fingered the bracelet and not for the first time today he forgave the Wildside its strange ways. He had much to think about. He had taken command on the afternoon of his initiation in the Hollow Mountain. Initiation. That had been John Savage's word. Some people prepare all their lives, he had said, some people devote themselves to spiritual discipline and rigorous training to do what Clegg had done and was now to complete in such a short time. He had spoken of death and rebirth, of trial by fire, air and water, of crossing fearsome thresholds. It had not all been gibberish, but now

Clegg could recall hardly a single word of it. Only the practical details had stuck, and fiercely. Clegg was trained for this kind of thing. Cross-over, rendezvous, communications, fall-back, safe-houses, these were the artifacts of faith he was most comfortable with.

He was discreet in his use of authority amongst the others, surprisingly confident, and an easy man to follow. After all, he was taking the risks, not them, and although each would do their bit he would ultimately make spectators of them. For these reasons there were few arguments and fewer questions when he asked for a day's grace. He would rejoin them at Clun Castle, he informed them. From there he and Beth would carry on to the east whilst the others went south to start moving the balloon. He had loose ends to tie up, he said, unfinished business. Part of it was secret liaison with Arch, easy and practical, part was a meeting with Agnes, complex and impossible to justify.

Clegg left on horse back mid-morning. Arch, by arrangement, was only five miles away, shadowing their progress and on call. He was enjoying the Game as never before but was desperate for the return of his beloved pen and nail combination and its access to worlds unreal. Clegg left him the horse and together they unloaded the scrambler from the back of the charcoal-burner. Following Owen's directions it would take him less then six hours to reach Agnes' reassuring world of cabbages and cheese, avoiding the Arkites unpleasant little province, but just as he was taking his farewells of Arch he had second thoughts. Owen's horse, always eager for exercise, looked at him balefully. The high forks and aggressive cut of the scrambler's mudguard by contrast were horribly impersonal. He returned the bike to Arch, shrugged an apology and continued on his way by horse. A slower journey would give him time to think, time to chew over the endless possibilities.

Yes, he had thought beyond the abduction. His motive from the start had depended on a clear expectation of the future and the pleasures money would buy. To reinforce the picture he had spent the money a dozen times over and also written himself absurdly into a very high-powered script. Clegg as the governor general of the theme park they would make of all this, selling off rights to fishing, hunting, timber; marketing choice building plots on the slopes of Snowdon or the ridge of Wenlock edge or carved out of these forests. Roads would have to be built, marshes drained, cables laid, boom towns built for the grunts who would cut down the trees and slice open the hills. What had taken fifty years in Amazonia would be completed here in five, the natives similarly wiped out or resettled. There was scope for several cities of several millions and vast fortunes to be made as all this was laid to rest forever under tarmac. Why not with Clegg at the helm? Why not make that the condition of handing over John Savage? It hadn't been done since the time of Cortez or Pizzaro. It was time to revive an old tradition. Stupid, he reminded himself. There were already plans and had been for decades. The Lake District city Beth had talked about was only one of them. Space meant people, people meant money. Within two or three years there would not be a tree left standing, a hill not flattened, a mountain not blasted. He could almost hear the contractors gunning their engines at the border, ready to rain down digger, dynamite and chain-saw on the last of wild Britain.

Or perhaps the Savage family would somehow slip through his fingers and it would all survive a little longer and to somebody else would fall the pleasures and rewards of bursting this stupid balloon. But dwelling on the consequences of failure was not in Clegg`s nature. The only thing he now doubted was what, exactly, would constitute success?

`Why did you give me this?` he asked her. They were sitting above the farmhouse waiting for the night to resolve out of dusk, just as he had hoped they might. She had not been surprised to see him, but certainly pleased. They had embraced without awkwardness, eaten together with Ralph and then drifted up here, taking sleeping bags and a flask of coffee.

Clegg was holding the bracelet up to the sky, remembering what Owen and Beth had said about the thing, watching the last light fall dull as lead on his hands yet still drawing a feint fire from the gold.

`To corrupt you,` she said, `I've told you its what I'm about, corrupting people. You should know that by now.` She was lying back as though tempting him to join her, but he was still absorbed with the bracelet.

`A girl told me about these two dragons, two parts of us all.`

`Clever girl. Not the one you were hunting?`

`It's her father I want, and `hunting` isn't the right word.`

`It sounds just fine to me, Nat. Can you think of a better one? I thought not. Go ahead, though I don't see how you can make a story out of an innocent bracelet.`

`Its not innocent,` Clegg reminded her, `Its corrupt, remember? So why did you give this piece to me and not another.`

`Chance?`

He shook his head. No, that wouldn't do. He was owed an explanation.

`All right,` she said, sitting up, taking the thing. `This dragon is you. This dragon is me.` His was sharp and angular, hers the sensuous one.

`As simple as that? And together they make a work of art, is that it?'

`Is anything as simple as that?` she asked. `You've lived long enough to know better, surely.`

`Oh yes, surely. But just one more question. How did you come to end up like this one, and how did I come to end up like that one?`

`Choices.`

`Carry on.`

`Choices you've made and choices that were made for you.`

`I make my own choices.`

`So why are you here? What kind of a choice was that?`

`There is something I need you to explain.` he announced. `Something that keeps coming back.`

Agnes was alert to his sudden change of mood.

`I'll try.` she said.

`It's this Grail thing. The stuff in the kitchen, the quote. I want to understand it. I want to understand your myth. Its what makes you tick, right?` He remembered Beth's question and his own answer. `Its what turns you on. I want to know about it.`

`You do?` her surprise was tender, not patronizing.

`Yes I do. Why not? If it's important to you then I want to know about it. Its kind of all things to all men, I know that much. That leaves it nice and vague, but what does it mean to you? I want to know.` He almost said `need`, he almost allowed himself the word that over twenty years of male conditioning had put at the exclusive use of his body. I need food. I need sex. I need a good time. Now he needed to know why meeting those needs was never enough, always left him dissatisfied. `Explain. Please.`

She was slow to answer. She was seeing him through different eyes, as though for the first time. She tried. She began with the big canvas, telling how there was a great battle between God and Lucifer and how a jewel from God's crown was lost and fell to earth. In time it was made into a chalice, she said, a beautiful cup, the Holy Grail. Whoever drank from the Grail was healed of their sickness, physical or otherwise. Whoever drank from the Grail drank the blood of God, even before the Last Supper. But even as she told this she knew he wanted more, that things would have to get more specific. She could sense well enough his need to enter deeply once he had taken the plunge. After the crucifixion the Grail disappeared.` she told him. `Joseph of Arimathea, the man who claimed Christ's body from the cross, he had the Grail safely. He understood its importance. He escaped with it to Europe and eventually England, to Glastonbury.`

The Wildside, he thought, that made sense. There was still an island there in the marshes that people went to as a kind of shrine. But where was Mary Magdalene in all this? he wondered, recalling her father's words, and how well did she know her Judas? Was she part of the not-so-bitter fruit? How did all these strange mythologies mesh together, because they did, of that he had no doubt. The whole web of strange symbols and double meanings had him gagging for what Arch called tabloid air, the simple uncomplicated bigotry of the consumer. He frowned, holding on to something familiar. A good woman, Agnes amongst them, was shaped like a Grail. Between the thighs and the waist was the chalice formed to receive a man's offering. He could hold and handle that.

But of course she meant something more. `Its not a physical thing. What really passed from Heaven to King Solomon, to the Essenes, to the hands of Christ, to Pilate, to Joseph of Arimathea and to some wet and green corner of England wasn't a cup or chalice or precious stone. It was something far more important. Something to kill and to persecute for. It was wisdom, the knowledge that two thousand years of Churchianity has tried to hide.`

Wisdom. It was a bit of a let down. It was not something you could easily market or willingly die for. But it was `churchianity` he queried.

`One of my father's favourite words.` she said.

`And what's the truth they've tried to hide?`

`A simple one. People have always worshipped the sun in one way or another. Two thousand years ago the Sun God came to earth in the body of a man. Its blood seeped into the earth. From that moment the earth became God. It was all foretold but most people still missed it. God is no longer in the sky, behind a veil, any more than he is in a church behind clouds of incense. He is here beneath our feet. Or she. Either way we are its children. Now the Grail is inside each one of us. It is the human heart. You find it only when you work selflessly for others, when you give everything you have to lift your brother out of the ditch. You only find it through your own blood, your own passion, your own sacrifice.`

For a second she was beautiful, inner fire and outer form meeting perfectly. Hers was a chalice he could offer to. Whenever they talked the vision of his fever came back, her on top and in control. Perhaps that was what stopped him from making a move, from initiating what they might both have wanted. Was that why he had come here, or was it to be preached at? It was becoming a habit. He did not need reminding that the last time they had sat here she had made him an offer and crowned him as king. He leant over and kissed her on the mouth. She neither responded nor withdrew. `So why is this the Land of the Grail?` he asked, weighing up her reaction.

`That's a mistake we have to live with.` she sighed, but the smile not far away. `This is no more the Land of the Grail than some inner city high-rise. But the people who created the Wildside believed that the earth is God. That is not a bad place to start.`

`So how do you search for the Grail?` he asked.

She laughed but then became serious. She reached out and touched him on the cheek, as though thanking him for the kiss but not yet inviting a second. `Once upon a time,` she began, dramatically, but then became serious, almost apologetic, as though she had betrayed something tender in Clegg's question by making fun of it.

How sad her voice sounds, thought Clegg. What does she have to be so sad about? She knows more than is good for her. Just like Beth who seemed wise beyond her years. Agnes was twice Beth's age and twice as wise. Stick to jewelry. Stick to cheese.

She told him as briefly as she could about Parzival, about how they were all naive fools, blundering into the truth and not recognizing it. `He failed his real test,` Agnes said. `The real test of whether you are a man is not in battle or between some woman's thighs, its when you are faced with someone else's suffering. A coward turns and runs. A seeker after the Grail stays and tries to help the one who suffers. You know what Parzival had to do? He came to the castle of the Fisher King. The poor man was in agony from a wound in the groin. All Parzival had to do was ask the question, one simple question.`

`Which was?`

`What ails thee? That's all he had to ask to free the King of his pain. He didn't. He didn't ask. It's all about asking questions, see.`

`Why didn't he ask?`

She laughed, releasing some of the tension held in the story. `Because he was a selfish, arrogant, egotistical bastard!`

`So what next?` Clegg asked, not sure if he meant in the legend or here and now.

She laughed again and in one smooth movement rolled from next to him, pushed him to the ground, gathered up her skirt and straddled him. Looking down into the shadows of his face she saw confusion and was glad. `It all depends.` she said. `You hung your friend Arch up and played twenty questions. So why does he get all the fun? I don't need to talk philosophy all the time. I'll ask the questions. If you give the right answers, who knows? If you give the wrong ones you can forget it. A deal?` She bent down and returned his kiss.

`Its a deal.` Clegg tried hard not to stammer.

`First question. Why don't you bring your step-son to see all this like you said you would?`

`I can't. He's not mine to bring. I don't own him.`

She nodded approval at the answer and reached behind her head to release a single clip. The long brown hair fell invitingly around her face and down to Clegg's chest.

`Second question. Why don't you have children of your own?`

`Because I've been careful?`

She shook her head, acknowledging the question in his voice and giving him a second chance.

`Because I've been lucky?`

Another shake

`Because I've been afraid.`

No question mark this time and from Agnes an enthusiastic nod. She slowly undid the four buttons of her blouse and removed it. `What would you teach him, if you had a son and you brought him here, what would you teach him?`

`To search for the Grail.` he answered without any hesitation.

Agnes nodded again and unclipped the strap of her bra. She allowed Clegg's hands to meet her breasts as she leaned towards him. `A good answer, Nat. Keep up the good work. Though it came a bit too easily.` she spoke softly, kissing him on the forehead this time. `Why do you want to take the girl and her father back?`

Clegg struggled with the truth. Money was not in it anymore and to lie was not an option. Agnes would know, Agnes would see right through him. But to tell the truth might be to cross the Line never to return. It threatened the wrong kind of exposure. `It's my only way back.` he said.

She clutched his hands and pulled them away from her body. `Why do you want to take the girl and her father back?` she repeated, this time almost viscously.

He looked at her breasts, they had responded to his touch and tempted him to truth. The line between game and deadly serious was shifting. `Because I hate them.` he said, his voice catching.

She had reached for a buckle at the side of her skirt which she slid down and away from her ankles. She eased herself to one side of Clegg and placed a hand on the rim of her pants. `And why do you hate them?`

`Because I'm jealous.` Clegg said, amazed by the truth when it came, as aroused by the revelation as by Agnes removing her everything and reaching for his buttons. `I'm jealous, that's why I hate them.` He repeated it with vigour and enjoyed the effect it had on him.

`And why are you jealous of them?` she asked when they were both naked. She drew back slightly to look at him, her smile glancing deftly over his taut body. Like in the fever she again straddled him, took the lead, but this time her touch was not imagined and Clegg's delirium was replaced by a different kind of reality.

`Because they belong.` he said, smiling as she lowered herself on to him neatly.

`And why don't you belong?` she asked, starting to breathe deeply, establishing a rhythm that pleased her. But the answer, if it came, was lost in the noise of their love making.

Later, as they huddled together for warmth and watched for shooting stars Clegg broke the spell. `Now can I ask.` he said, `Just one?`

`You've earned the right.`

But the question when it came was not the one she had expected. `Why do old men plant trees?`

By the time she had found an answer Clegg was already asleep.

FIFTYTWO

Owen, Andrew and Beth travelled in near silence for the best part of two days, each chewing on their own thoughts. They had the option of the train but Owen favoured the slower route. He wanted to give Beth time. For what, he could not have said. They were to meet Clegg's contact and put in place the next part of the plan. Like blind men feeling the elephant, as Owen put it, each had hold of a different part and a different idea of the whole. Amazingly, despite his state of health, no one doubted that John Savage at least had the complete picture.

Owen dared to wonder in silence whether there might be a bigger drama acting itself out, one of which not even Savage was fully aware. It made him concerned for Beth and inclined him towards fathering her, which he knew she would resent. At least in the evenings they had time to watch the flames rise up and to talk vaguely of things that troubled them.

One night Beth spoke of details, as she called them, but not details in the usual sense, not of precisely what must happen, when and how, but of details that lingered long after the action had spent itself. Some came to her in the shadows and of these she said nothing, of how dry lips stuck together with the smell of cigarettes remained, even though the taste of saliva spat into your throat did not, of how men, even young ones, when they rode on you for their pleasure seemed to gather age and weariness around the eyes and were made older by the act, not younger. And details that would not come back, no matter how she tried, like the touch of her mother's hands and the smile Sam kept only for her. `Like when you mount a horse,` she said, needing to share some, `when you have one foot in the stirrup and push yourself up. There's a second, just a split second when you think you are going to fly and leave the horse behind, like the horse is just a stepping stone to something far freer, and when you plonk down in the saddle there is always just the slightest hint of disappointment and let down. Oh, its a horse, I'm riding. On the earth. I'm not flying, not yet. Isn't there? Don't you know that moment?`

Strangely he didn't, and nor did Andrew, but the next night she spoke of another detail, one he could not deny. `The tiredness in Dad's eyes,` she said, `That look of being worn down to the bone, it's not the cancer, you know. It's not the fact of him dying slowly, its always been there, always. All my life, anyway.` She looked to Owen to deny it. He tugged at his beard but could not help nodding in agreement.

`Do you think there was ever a time when he was free of it?` she asked. But knowing the answer she moved on. `I hope when he dies that the look will leave him and when we see him for the last time he'll be free of it.`

When Owen tried to lighten things up he was pleased to see that Beth could respond and was not, as he had feared, descending into some kind of gloom. Mention of Finn had a particular effect, he noticed, seeming to make her alert. He told her his story of the bare-footed novices, how they had cost him a lot of money and inconvenience once. Clause ten of the constitution, he explained, the twenty mile rule. Electricity could not be transported more than twenty miles from its source of generation, a law designed to encourage lots of small-scale power sources, usually from water, wind or sun. Owen had bent the rules, colluded with a friend whose generator had spare capacity in the wet months. He put in a cable, a few miles over the twenty, and the bare-foots, or the trolls as he called them, knew it just by the shape of the buds in plants above the cable run, just by the way the bloody buds did or did not twist a certain way.

`Things are never as they appear.` Andrew said, by way of profound conclusion to his brother's story.

`I don't envy them their bare feet.` said Beth.

Owen and Andrew thought about that, with Andrew looking long and hard at Beth.` But the rest?` he said.

`The rest?`

`Yes. The rest. You could be like Finn and have all the rest.` he said, grasping for what might cheer her up. `You could learn to track and hunt and to ride a horse and use the crossbow and tell stories by the fire and make medicines from the hedgerow and navigate by the stars and swim all day.` The list came in such a glorious rush that Owen and Beth could only laugh.

`Can he do all that?` she asked, sure that in Andrew's eyes Finn could walk on water if necessary, wondering where admiration spilled over into envy. There was no doubt she felt both.

`Lets just hope he can do what your father has asked of him.` said Owen.

`That goes for all of us.` said Beth.

They fell quiet again. The night sounds and the hiss of the fire did its best to reassure them. Beth's thought went from the night of the mushrooms to Clegg's first meeting with her father. She saw no point in hiding anything from her two travelling companions. `Watching Dad talk to Clegg was very funny.` she said. `I wish you had seen it, Owen. They tried so hard to understand each other but they were both so busy standing their own ground. It was as if they were from different planets.` Yet very close, she might have added. Owen would understand her being jealous of Finn, but surely not of Clegg.

`So Clegg will get your brother out of there.` said Andrew.

`In slow motion.` she answered. Another of Dad's initiation things. Clegg did it the quick way Dad says. Can be dangerous the quick way, Sam's is the slow and careful way.`

`It'll be slow alright,` Owen agreed. `Can't get much slower than a barge and a hot-air balloon. Just pray the wind is right, mind, because we are going to need it, and just pray that Clegg keeps his cool, and Finn, and all the others, otherwise we'll none of us come out of this particular tunnel.`

The following day any misgivings they still felt were multiplied several-fold. Arch arrived. The bleached dread locks and lensed eyes peered crazily from the turret of the charcoal burner as he approached them at the agreed rendezvous point.

`Clegg trusts him.` Owen reminded Beth as they took in his appearance and manner, but how comforting that might have been was debatable as Arch eyed them each in turn, scripting them into his own unique version of reality.

`Arch's pleasure.` he said, climbing down to shake their hands, `Arch's your man, and Nathaniel of course. Arch and Nathaniel are definitely your men. Especially yours,` he whispered to Beth, `especially Arch. And what have we here?` he said, studying Andrew. `A chosen one. Chromosome Charlie.`

Beth put her hand on Owen's arm to restrain him.

`One more or less,` said Andrew, `I won't hold it against you.`

Arch began to leak laughter, at first quietly, under pressure, but then with a roar as though a valve had finally blown. He amazed them all by hugging Andrew. `I like it man, I like it. I want one for Christmas. I want you for Christmas. You and me are a team,` he said, taking Andrew by the arm. `What do you think of that?`

`Am I on your team or are you on mine?` Andrew grinned, stumbling over the sounds.

`Hey, we're on Clegg's team. We're on the great Nathaniel Clegg's team, okay?`

That seemed to satisfy Andrew for now. `Because Clegg can fly.` he said.

`Sure he can fly, Andy, Clegg can walk through walls, Clegg can walk on milk.`

But Andrew just groaned as though at a bad joke. `No he can't. But he can fly. Look.` He pointed through the trees to the edge of the Long Mynd, to where Clegg's ace was hidden.

At last Arch fell silent. If only for that the helicopter was a huge blessing.

FIFTYTTHREE

Jo's school was sponsored this week by a fast-food outlet. There was something unnerving about the sight of seven hundred children all in smog masks all converging on the same building, all decked out in matching baseball caps and sweat shirts, all advertising the same flavour of crap. Clegg was not sure he had made Jo out. At that age they can grow quickly and the dash from the car to the entrance took only moments but on the second time of watching he saw Jo emerge, talk to friends, climb in the car, crawl away into the line of traffic. So what? Come away with Cleggy, Jo. Leave your mum and friends and fast food certainties, come and whistle spirits into bottles. Clegg wanted to show him to Agnes and to Beth. I make sense, look. I've got a step-son, someone I could never lie to.

`Excuse me, Sir. Mr.Woolard. We have no record of you as a parent of the school.`

It took some seconds before the security guard's warning registered with Clegg. His ankle tag proclaimed him to the world as Derek Woolard, funeral manager. It had given him credit in all the shops he had so far entered and access to the brighter side of town. It had given him a small flat in a large block only a mile from the funeral parlour and six miles from Welbeck. But it did not, he was now discovering, give him the right to watch school children from a park bench half a mile from the school in question. Mistake number two. Although low down on the list he would by now, however half-heartedly, have been recorded as a suspected paedophile. No self-respecting school had less than a dozen security men processing movements in and around its area. No self-respecting parent would entrust their child to a school that offered less.

`Day-dreaming,` said Clegg, standing up, nodding awkwardly, feeling uncannily as he imagined a genuine nonse would feel if apprehended. Stupid mistake. There was no prospect of contacting Jo or his mum, no real point to the exercise.

Mistake number one had been the night before. He had gone to the Pig Trough. He dared not contact Danny directly but entertained the vague hope that his brother might be there. And what if he had been? Danny would have freaked. Danny would have panicked, gone up in smoke, endangered the whole enterprise. But Clegg's need to be amongst vaguely familiar surroundings had got the better of him. He had parked Derek Woolard on a pig and watched the night perform its absurd rituals around him. He had left a message behind the bar for Danny. A big risk, but necessary. He then walked home in a sullen mood only to find that the Pig Trough's junk mail had preceded him. Even at two in the morning somebody, somewhere had registered the fact that Derek Woolard, funeral manager had made his first ever visit to the Pig Trough and might be in need of a membership form and the addresses of twenty affiliated night-spots in the region.

Clegg had to keep his head down. Clegg had to learn patience and court boredom. He could not afford to draw attention to himself or his false identity. He must be as grey-faced and as anonymous as the people who shared his flat block or shuffled past him in the streets. He must follow his instructions to the letter if he stood any chance of success.

A week after his rebirth as Derek Woolard Clegg returned to the Pig Trough. The night had cut its throat again, clots of neon flooded the gutters but only Clegg noticed, only Clegg seemed to care as he entered the warehouse with the hunched up figures, shook off the wet, stomped rain from his shoes and entered the night club intent and purposeful, the slate-grey eyes all-seeing. Derek Woolard, on his second visit, having declined membership, asked for his tag to be fitted to Bill, but Bill had been claimed, unusually, and Clegg knew that Danny has got the message and was waiting for him in the blue room, backed by synthesized music, secure behind a whiskey.

Danny hardly knew whether to rise, to walk out, to touch his brother, which way to turn. `Don't tell me,` he began, hushed and anxious, `Nat, don't even tell me, I don't want to know, I just don't want to know. Where the fuck...?`

Clegg settled himself in the corner, took an orange juice, patted his brother on the back, a mix of warm and patronizing. `Don't over do it.` he muttered.

`Nat. Nat. Where the hell... I mean they told us you were dead, we didn't believe it of course, but they wrote you off. The flying club had a memorial...`

`That's nice of them.` said Clegg. `I wish I could have been there. I'm sure they found plenty to say.`

`And Jenny phoned me. She was cut up, Nat, I mean it. She thinks it's for real. You know, she dreamed of you the night you went down, she told me. Can you believe it?`

`Take a breath.` said Clegg. `Feel. Its me, okay. I bet you shit yourself when you got my message?` he smiled at the thought.

`You did it, Nat! You did it. You've been and you got back.' Danny was loosening up, `John Savage stuff. Is that it?`

`First things first, Dan. How is Bonny?`

It was as though Danny had not heard. `Did you find him, Nat, is that what this is all about?`

`How's Bonny?`

`Because if it is...`

`How's Bonny?` He slapped the tabletop. A few eyes turned their way but lost interest when no fight or argument developed.

Danny shrank into himself. The well-cut jacket suddenly hung on an uncertain frame, the salesman's gloss fell from his face. `She's been cutting herself, Nat. Self-mutilation. Cutting herself with knives, razors, scissors, anything, they even do it with grass, you know, blades of grass, they slice up their fingers with the stuff when they can't get a knife. Not just Bonny. They're all doing it. All her friends. A whole year of them at school. It's the age, they said. Nat, you should see them. Beautiful girls, bright girls, and its not just their wrists. Their faces, their cheeks. They look like fucking tribes women, Zulu or something.`

`What's her story?`

`Pain. They say they want pain. They can't get it any other way. Wrapped in cotton wool, Nat, they have it too good.`

Danny drowned his whisky and ordered another. After a silence of some minutes he was calm again, Clegg patiently waiting. `This is about you, Nat. You want something, I can see it in your face.`

`I want a lot of things, Dan, but I don't expect them from you. You're right. It's John Savage stuff. I've got him. Almost. I've got him eating out of my hand, walking into a trap, whatever,`

`How did you find him? Where is he?`

`Don't ask, Dan, it's too long. Anyway the deal isn't cut. There is still stuff to do. He's coming to Stratford for Midsummer. The son is the bait. You know, the one hit by the lorry?`

`I thought he was dead.`

`He's in a hospital close to here. That's not the point. I'm to get him out, shift him to Stratford, the son I mean, slowly but surely. Daddy Savage is nine-tenths dead, he's on his way out, wants to see his son one last time, that kind of thing.`

`I've got the picture.'

`No you haven't. You think you have but you've only got a part of it. Like the blind men and the elephant.`

`The what?`

`It doesn't matter. Savage will be in Stratford on Midsummer's Day.`

`Nat, I don't do Midsummer's Day, I can't, you know that. All we can guarantee for Midsummer's Day is rain. You're on your own if you're thinking of using Midsummer.'

`I'm on my own, Dan, I know that, but that's not what I'm asking. I'm setting things up, right? Now. Tonight.`

`Tonight?`

`Why not? You're ready.` he tapped his brother's breast pocket to confirm that the palm-top, his office, was at hand. `What does this number mean to you?`

Clegg had memorized it. He wrote it out in full on the back of a beer mat. Danny squinted at it for a while. Whatever secrets the number held were not immediately obvious. `It could be anything,` he said. `Customs, army, security services.`

`It's not army?`

Danny took out his palm top and tapped in the first three numbers. `No, it's not army.` he said, slightly disappointed. `Its some kind of game.`

`I know its some kind of game, Dan. But who makes the rules up?`

Danny punched in the next three numbers and then vanished for a time into his machine. He emerged with a satisfied look. `Its a game, but its run by the security services. It was launched two years ago. Restricted access.`

`How restricted?`

`Subterranean.`

`Which means what?`

`I'm not sure it means anything, Nat. I'm out of my depth. There are rumours, that's all.`

`What rumours?`

`That the air-waves are full, or not secure. The ether's corrupt.`

`Tell me something new.`

`The future's underground. Through the earth. It's still experimental but I doubt if anyone will stop them. They've got these huge steel blades sunk into the earth, twenty feet across, one hundred feet down. Bigger ones are planned. The air is so full of wavelengths they've started to get in each other's way, create harmonic feed-back, that kind of thing. These new wave-lengths push out through the bed rock.`

`Into the Wildside?`

`Why not?`

`Can you access it?`

`I can get in through air-waves, but I can't pull anything out. It's one way.`

`That suits me. Try these last three numbers as access code.`

`I'm not sure I want...`

`I'm not sure I'm giving you the choice, Dan. Just do it. Pretend the future of civilization as we know it might just depend on it. I've used it before. I need to send another message.`

`They can trace the entry point back to my machine.`

`How long would that take?'

`Quicker than it would take you to hide under the table.`

`Then use this one.` Clegg took Arch's machine from his pocket.

Danny opened it up and smiled. `No problem,` he said, `this machine has rights of access. What's the message?`

`Can you delay it? Can you put the message in it and get it to send at a later time?`

`Of course.`

`Put it on delay. Here's the message.`

Clegg wrote it on the same beer mat.

`Sir David Armstrong.` Danny gasped as he read the text.

`Tap it in and forget it.` said Clegg. Danny was eager to do both.

`Now what?`

`Fix it for sending in a week's time. The day before Midsummer.`

`Done.`

Clegg stood up to leave. Derek Woolard was a sober worker with no history of late nights.

`It'll be okay, Dan, I promise.` Clegg said, wanting to touch his brother but not knowing how. `Give my love to Bonny.` But Clegg could only watch in horror as his brother's smile became a mask and his nod turned slowly to a shake, a very forced and repetitive shake, woodenly from side to side, as the tears began to stream down his strained face.

`I'd love to, Nat, I'd love to, its just...`

Bonny, like the night, like the world they inhabited, had bled away into the gutter only a week before.

FIFTYFOUR

`It's my last tour of inspection, Sam!` John Savage said, as they lifted him into the basket. `One last look before it's all gone.`

The priestess and nurse exchanged glances. Caring for his spiritual and physical well being respectively they often disputed his dosage of morphine. But today the priestess would prevail. It was that kind of journey. If he wanted to talk to his absent son, so be it.

`Before *you* are all gone, John.` the priestess said, `This will still be here.`

`Will it? Are you sure?`

`People can't live without beauty, John.`

But he shook his head. It was a sentiment he agreed with, an idea that had inspired his disrupted life, but one that the Comfort Zone obliged him to question.

`You enjoy it, John. You've always enjoyed everything as though it were the last time.` she assured him.

`Have I, Madeline? I've tried to. It might always be the last time, and there was never any harm in having fun!`

`Never was and never will be.` she agreed, `Especially when your body's a bit suspect but your friends offer to float you across mountains and valleys.`

They had wedged the mad scientist in with cushions and wrapped him with a quilt. The balloon's crew, Owen's brother Dai and his twin sons, were checking valves and leads.

`Is it safe for me, lads?`

Jamie and David both looked his way but were unsure what to say. They were still in awe at the sequence of events that had led them from the boar hunt to this moment.

`Safest way to travel, Mr.Savage. So I'm told.` one of them answered.

`We've never been up before.` the other added, receiving a poke in the ribs from his father.

`Safe and peaceful, Mr.Savage.` Dai Morgan assured his passenger. He was an expert even if his sons were new to the trade.

`I might just fall out and die.` Savage joked. `It would save a lot of trouble. What do you think nurse? Are you scared?`

The girl, she could barely have been in her twenties, blushed. `I don't want you to die, Mr.Savage.` she mumbled.

`No, but I do!` he shouted above the blast of the burner. `Then I can fly every day.`

Dai nodded to those on the ground who in turn took their farewells of Savage. A girl of Beth's age, one of his nurses, was crying, not expecting to see her mentor again. The bare-footed youths seemed even more intense and sober than usual, standing awkwardly back from the balloon. There was a release of ropes, a blast of the burner, a half-hearted cheer and a great slow-motion awkwardness as the balloon rose surely upwards.

The perfect sky, the slightest of breezes, the sea behind them, gentle against the mountain, a single bone of beach to the south west and a slight haze in the distance where Ireland might have been. John Savage shook his head in disbelief.

`Is this your first time, John?` the priestess asked.

At first she thought he had not heard the question. They all felt the altitude shift in their ears and each burn of flame made them shudder slightly. John Savage was frowning, struggling for an honest answer. `I've been doing it all my life,` he said, softly, `floating above it all, looking down from somewhere high up and removed, getting annoyed with people who had their feet stuck in mud.`

`Rather than their head in the clouds?`

`Exactly.` he smiled. `We need each other, I suppose, dreamers and realists. Yes, it is my first time.` His voice trailed off. The priestess thought it best to leave him in peace. After a while she was aware of a gentle muttered commentary addressed to no one in particular, though twice she heard Sam's name mentioned, as though he were describing it to his son. They looked down at the hulking mountains and watched the shadow of the balloon scud like a cloud, effortlessly over crag and bog and through a farm's back yard. If death was indeed like this then who could doubt its attraction?

Their journey had started at the foot of Cader Idris to where John Savage's people had delivered him the day before. Tal-y-Llyn, Corris, the old slate quarries, the ragged forests of Dyfi, all these drifted silently below as the eagle of the balloon looked hungrily to the east, towards Garreg Hir above Carno where Betty Morgan would be waiting to signal them past and help from the ground if needed, which it would not be with the sky and weather so perfect, and thence to Town Hill and a clear view of their destination.

It was beyond Garreg Hir, with Betty's waving figure receding in the distance, that they entered a state of grace. Cader was far behind, the fears and risks still some way ahead and the views at their most perfect.

Savage was not looking down anymore. He was looking at the sky and for now at least his expression was almost as serene as it would be in the coffin. The nurse had her eyes closed and her face turned to the sun. It was as near silent as they would manage and into this no one was inclined to speak. Things looked so different from up here, things looked timeless and decent. In the end it was the great man himself who broke the silence. `Do you know how it all started, Sam, do you? How we came to be here, all our hopes in a balloon?`

The priestess moved closer to him. `Tell him, John. I'm sure he can hear.`

He nodded at that and smiled slightly. `Oh, he could always hear, Madeline. He could hear things before they were said. He always knew things ahead of the rest of us.`

`So how did it start?` she asked him. `How do we come to be here, all our hopes in a balloon?`

`For me. I can only say how it started for me. We all need beauty, isn't that what you said? Lets hope you're right, Madeline, lets hope they don't franchise beauty. I was eight or nine.` he continued after a long pause, `We lived on a farm. I grew up on a farm. But we lost it. It doesn't matter how but it was to do with money. Of course. So my family was forced to move from the farm where I grew up into the centre of Nottingham. Do you know Nottingham, Madeline? Of course you don't. You don't know any cities. Sam does. Sam knows what I'm talking about. Not much beauty there, Madeline, a few old buildings, some caves, a cemetery, one or two hard-working trees. Not much to inspire a young boy. It was November and misty. In my memory Nottingham is always November and misty. After the first excitement of moving and unloading boxes and furniture they let me look around the streets. I didn't know what I was looking for at the time but I suppose it was for trees and fields. I knew it deep down. But all I saw were roads and traffic and buildings. But then I found it, you see. It was at the end of a busy road behind our new home. There was a traffic island and beyond that island, half in the mist, was a big area of grass. I'd found it, without even knowing what I was looking for. The beginnings of a field, of open country, my own private Wildside. That's what I thought. I went back the next day. I can't tell you how excited I was. You know me, Madeline, you can imagine. I had sandwiches and a flask, I had binoculars, even a torch. But I'm afraid the mist had cleared, and any illusions with it. Across the busy road and the traffic island was the grass strip I had seen the day before but it was just the start of a grass verge to another road, another estate, another mass of houses. I felt something die inside me. I can still remember exactly how it felt. I felt like a prisoner trapped in a windowless cell. Can you imagine? I think you probably can. To be so close to a dream but then find it was a nightmare all the time. The dream was my hot air balloon. It was my escape.`

`You wanted your children to be free.` Madeline whispered.

`First I wanted *me* to be free. I was as selfish as the next man. But it's true. I wanted my children to be free. And then I wanted everyone else's children to be free.` he sighed. `Perhaps that was my big mistake.`

`Who says it was a mistake?`

`My wife. My daughter. Probably my son. How is that to start with?`

`Do they say that?`

`They don't say anything, Madeline. Two of them can't and the third one thinks it.`

But the priestess would allow him no self-pity. She smiled and touched him kindly on the shoulder. `It's very reassuring,` she said, almost whispering, `to know that even the great John Savage can be so terribly wrong about his own children!`

He said nothing for a time but continued to look eastward. He started to shake his head slowly but Madeline waited. `Nathaniel thought I was against machines,` he said at last. `If only it were that simple.` Another pause. `But they are waiting. I can almost see them, I can almost hear them.`

`Who is waiting, John?`

But he answered with another question. `Do you know what the world is for, Madeline?`

`You're about to tell me, John.`

`Everything, the whole cosmos, right down to each plant and stone? It's for us each to find our destiny. And live it. But so often we can't.`

`Can't what?`

`Find it. Or live it. If things get stuck, if things freeze over, if the machines win, Madeline, then it will be impossible for anyone to find their destiny. It needs to move and shift, all the time, the more the better. What is the opposite of initiation?` he asked, moving on before she could react. `I'll tell you. It's distraction. And when their machines have destroyed all the beauty, wiped out the opposition so to speak, paved the fields, felled the trees, then the second wave moves in, the distraction machines. What diggers and bulldozers do on the outside the second wave does from within. There'll be no more finding your destiny then, Madeline, just a living death. Was I wrong to fight that?`

But this time Madeline chose not to answer. `I can hear them too,` she said, `the machines, first to destroy, then to distract. You're right John, they are waiting and they always will be. That's why we have to fight them.`

`Oh we'll fight them, Madeline,` he answered with a sigh, `we'll fight them. Every inch of the way.`

FIFTYFIVE

Ashburn's funeral parlour backed on to the canal and had a problem with damp. Because the canal carried commerce to the Wildside there was no access for maintenance on that side of the building and the Chesterfield canal had been slowly finding its way into the building's basement over the years. Here Clegg was set to work, sanding, waxing and polishing funeral caskets, one of six employees who kept themselves to themselves, none knowing just who was and who was not involved in the company's lucrative but criminally insane side-line. Clegg knew to take his orders from Mr.Ashburn himself, but in a paranoid need-to-know environment nobody was about to take Clegg to one side and put him in the picture. That suited Clegg. A mood of mutual mistrust made him feel comfortable, it brought back memories of virtually everything he had experienced, from school through to the army.

It was not until day ten, a week and a half after his arrival, that the mood changed. Mr.Ashburn, a quiet, grey man called out to him in the basement. `Mr.Woolard. Could you drive out with Harry to Welbeck. He'll need a hand.` No explanation, no notes or whispered orders, rather a deliberate advertising of intent. Clegg was reassured. Perhaps he was amongst professionals after all.

Nor did Harry break the spell. He was a youth in his twenties who had exchanged no more than a dozen words with Clegg over tea and the newspaper. Now they drove together through the South Yorkshire conurbation, picking up the road that would lead them to Welbeck High Security hospital.

Harry broke the ice. `You got plans for Midsummer, Mr.Woolard?` he asked in the mongrel language of the erst-while East End crossed with Australian Suburb-Speak. He didn't wait for an answer. `Me and some of the lads is goin down Hillsborough. Gonna torch the ground. We owe them for last year.`

Harry inhabited a world in which grudges were held over for 364 days of the year and acted out ruthlessly on the 365th.

`I've got no plans.` Clegg muttered. `I'll keep my head down.`

`Sad git.` said Harry, `Its a long wait. Last year we did this shopping mall. Brute stuff, man, we creamed them, TV's, videos, the works. You can still see them in the canal. It was the best yet. Then with the girls down behind the station. Shag City, man, there was more than enough to go around and twice over. Married most of them, if I know my tail from my ass. You should get out more, Mr. Woolard. take your chances.`

Clegg switched off. He had left the once-a-year excitement of Midsummer's Day behind in a previous lifetime. It was no different to Arch's game, perhaps a little more violent. It was a mindless way of channeling mindless energy and dangerous frustration. They came to a stretch of motorway. The car was automatically `stacked` in an endless convoy, speed and distance controlled by unseen lasers. Harry took his opportunity. He drew a scruffy brown envelope from an inside pocket and handed it to Clegg. `Don't know what it ses, don't want to know.`

Clegg read it, again surprised at his own surprise. He had been waiting for contact, they were journeying to Welbeck and yet even now he was caught off guard. At the next service station he signalled to turn off, following the instructions of the letter. He parked on the edge of the coach bay. Several coaches had released their loads to the toilets and tea-rooms and the area was busy with pedestrians stretching their legs. `Take a break,` he said to Harry. `Over there.` He pointed to a catering outlet with seats clearly visible through the plate glass. He checked the letter once more. `Seat 72. We'll be back before they close.`

Harry climbed out. `They never close.` he said just before disappearing. `So it might be a long wait.`

Clegg watched him pick his way through the crowds, enter the restaurant, load up a tray with tea and cakes and then seek out seat 72. Its occupant rose as Harry approached, left the restaurant at a casual pace and then walked towards Clegg. He climbed into the passenger seat. Clegg handed him the letter as he drew the car out of the service area and back onto the motorway. He looked at the new-comer's feet. Trainers. The laces were new and Clegg asked himself if that was on oversight or deliberate and what it said about his own state of anxiety that he should register such details.

`You expected me to have bare feet?` Finn asked.

`I've given up expecting anything.` Clegg said, turning to take in his passenger's appearance. He approved. They had prepared well, but how the two of them would fare at the hospital was another matter. Crossbows would be of limited use.

`How long have you been over?` Clegg asked, certain that he would be spared the details.

`Since yesterday.`

Another long silence. Welbeck was only twenty miles away but the stack had reduced everyone' speed to just under ten miles and hour.

`Is this your first time?` Clegg realized too late how stupid the question could have sounded, a clumsy variation on `Do you come here often?` but Finn heard nothing comical in the question.

`First and last.` he said.

Clegg felt strangely defensive of his world at this hint of criticism. First and last, get me out quickly, was that what he meant? Of course it was. Clegg smiled. It seemed almost cruel to expose Finn the wood-elf to the real world, but perhaps there was wisdom in the pairing because now Clegg was more at ease, master in his own back-yard. It would encourage him to take command. Secretly he had been hoping for some super under-cover agent to make himself known and to take him by the hand, but it was not going to be like that. It was going to be the blind confidently leading the blind.

Their route took them from the motorway, through suburbs of small terraced houses and finally towards a huge security gate, razor wire bristling at all angles as much for psychological effect as for practical security, as Clegg well knew. They were waved casually through on the production of a pass. Ashburn's were frequent processors of Welbeck's dead. But Clegg only grew more alert. It was always easier to get into places like this than it was to get out.

Now Clegg and Finn were complete equals. They were equally dependant on the instructions in the letter, they were equally as vulnerable and at risk to capture and prosecution, they were equally afraid. The advantage Clegg had enjoyed of having previously worked at Welbeck he had long since shared with John Savagege and the fruit's of his experience were here in the maps they were to work from.

They parked the van in the allocated bay and climbed out. It was a cluttered area which held dustbins and a skip to the left and this parking space, reserved for the mortician's visits, to the right. Clegg unlocked the back, glanced up at the security cameras and pictured for himself the small control room in which a score of monitors were presently being watched by four very indifferent operatives. A couple of unconcerned rats watched them from beneath the skip. It had always been the policy to feed and poison the tribe of rats in monthly rotation. It kept them away from the body bags or the temptations of infiltrating the hospital's warren of tunnels.

Clegg had forgotten how oppressive the atmosphere of the place was. Even as an insider there was something about the damp grey tunnels and the endless miles of silent, sterilized corridor that ate away at any hope or optimism. As security men they had referred to it as the Lubjanca, in memory of the great Russian institution they professed to emulate. If the Lubjanca was Stalin and the K.G.B. and Soviet oppression all condensed down then Welbeck was a distilled version of the Comfort Zone; smooth sliding doors, polite cameras, a sickly smell of chemicals and expensive polish. Perhaps the rats had good reason to keep out. Perhaps it was more than the easy pickings that left them satisfied with the entrance and exit areas. Perhaps they knew something the paid staff tried to ignore. But a ferret would have gone all the way,

Clegg thought. A ferret would have squirmed its tidy little head and shoulders into the very bowels of the place.

`Never fly without a reserve parachute.` Clegg found himself muttering to Finn as they walked from the van towards the tunnel entrance.

Finn looked at him curiously but said nothing and Clegg realized that now was not the time to elaborate. He meant, have an escape plan, have a story, make something up now, not later. `If they catch us down here they really will make sure we never get out so don't be shy about telling lies.` he said, acutely aware of being dependent on Savage's manipulation of the System. The placing of a false identity into such a high security context was a tremendous feat and an enormous risk. Clegg had scripted any number of excuses and interrogation covers for the event of being exposed and apprehended, but none sounded convincing, not even the truth, not even the statement that he was taking these huge personal risks in order to tempt John Savage close to the border and to use the boy as bait before grabbing Savage. That this was deep penetration behind enemy lines could not be denied. The only doubt centred on who or what was now the enemy. At least Judas had had clear objectives, Clegg thought as he padded down the tunnel next to Finn. At least Judas had had the noose handy in his pocket for when it all went wrong. He asked himself why it mattered. If they were caught, thrown into one of these cells for the next thirty years, would it matter, and why? Clegg thought of the light and air of the Wildside, he thought of the oppressive and endless trees, those wonderful trees. Finn would surely waste away quickly, but Clegg, with less to miss, less to pine for, might fare better, might be quite familiar with the confines of a cell. He wondered what that said about his life.

They reached room 301. Finn nodded and continued on his way. Clegg watched him disappear in the direction of the mortuary and pinched himself mentally. Less than three months ago Finn had blasted Jacobs' dogs out of the air, stolen their out-board, lured

Clegg steadily westward. And he had seen Finn in Clun, with Beth, love-birds in the shadow of the castle, jumpy as hell. You should have taken her then, Clegg thought to himself, you might not get a second chance. He entered the room and was confronted by a spare, dark-skinned man whose expression of terror should already have alerted even the most indolent of guards. But there was no camera inside the room. Clegg double-checked before looking at the doctor, hoping for guidance.

`The neck` Khalil began, `Did they warn you about the neck? We can't risk the wrong movements. You will have to use a secure trolley with padding and straps, and you certainly mustn't lift him by yourself. Beneath the trolley are the medicines and feed for the first few days. Any more would look suspicious.`

The letter certainly had warned him about the neck and about Khalil's likely state of anxiety as well as the risks the doctor was taking. `His family will owe you for this, ` Clegg muttered, thinking that here was another dam holding back another complex life story.

`Nobody will be in my debt.` said Khalil `I have worse things to answer for than saving the life of someone I have abused. All I ask is that you forget me and my part in this. I must cling to the hope that no one will apportion blame to me. It must look like a job from the outside. Even conversations like this...`

Finn entered before Khalil could finish. He had been to the mortuary, shown Harry's credentials and been entrusted with this, a trolley on which a pathetically small body bag tried vainly to make some impression on the white acres of plastic around it. Clegg looked to Khalil. The doctor would now have to arrange the corpse on the empty bed, complete with pipes and monitors and he wondered how John Savage's secret army had prepared itself for that little trick. Finn provided the answer. He handed the doctor a disc which the latter inserted into the monitor. As they cautiously removed the one body and replaced it with the other the monitor continued to tell its stable story despite being out of touch with any kind of organic matter.

They nodded to Khalil, glad that words were unsafe because there really was nothing, absolutely nothing to say. Finn and Clegg directed the trolley through the doors, along the corridor and thence to the tunnel, every hundred meters they had previously travelled now doubled in apparent length. At the exit, beneath the security camera, Finn surprised Clegg by starting to whistle nonchalantly. It angered Clegg, not because it was unwise or badly done but because Clegg was the professional, not Finn, and Clegg should have been providing the finishing touches, not the wood elf. Clegg glared at Finn but otherwise held his peace, marvelling at his accomplice's ability to deliver the unexpected. The whistling stopped as they slid Sam's body, still strapped to the trolley bed, into the back of their van. Clegg comforted himself with the thought that he and Finn could at least keep moving, hopefully far away from this grey life-sucking hole, whereas Khalil was confined, Khalil was ministering to a corpse in a glorified prison cell. As usual, thought Clegg, no medals for the real hero, and for once he was not thinking of himself.

They approached the exit at a crawl. Not too eager, thought Clegg. He lowered his window and fumbled for the appropriate paper-work, hoping for the gate to open and the guard to nod them through. The gate stayed shut. The nod when it came was like a kiss of death.

`Nat! Nat Clegg! I thought I recognized you.`

Clegg waited for his life to flash before his eyes but nothing came, only disbelief. `Bob Green. How are you doing?` Clegg asked, wishing the man dead, a million miles away, off duty. Somewhere, probably in the control booth, Clegg's false tag was proclaiming him as Derek Woolard whilst out here an ex-colleague with a possibly lethal memory for faces and names was shaping up for small talk. Again the doubt, the lethargy of approaching defeat. Did it matter? Let the guard sound the alarms. Then what? It mattered, but why? The avoidance of pain? The pride of doing a job well? The good things still out there, Agnes on top of him, her cheese on his bread?

`How long have you been in this business?` the guard asked, nodding to the vehicle.

`Too long, Bob, too long, you know how it is.`

`Don't I just. Not seen you on this run before.`

`First time they've trusted me. You remember me, Bob, always likely to bend the rules.`

`That why they kicked you out?`

`Something like that`

`How's Jenny?`

Was there nothing this man forgot? How long before he recalled the stories of Clegg's disappearance? `Past tense, Bob. People move on.`

Bob Green didn't. `Bet you miss the old place, Cleggy. Five-a-side team isn't what it was since you left.`

`Er, excuse me.` It was Finn, leaning across Clegg to peer through the side window. `The smell's getting to me in here. This thing might be hazardous.` he gestured to the back of the van, sharing his fake irritation between Clegg and the guard. `Can we get a move on?`

Clegg shrugged at his former colleague as if to say there was nothing to be done about his partner's impatience. `I'll catch up with you next time, Bob.`

`Okay, Nat. Take care.`

Clegg closed the window, the gate opened and they drew slowly through.

`Fifty-fifty.` muttered Clegg.

`Fifty-fifty what?`

`The chances he looks at his screen, sees it wasn't me.`

`How will we know?`

`If we reach that lamp-post he didn't check.`

They passed the lamp-post. And the next. And the next.

`You did well.` said Finn.

Clegg reached across in one sudden and fluent movement. The anger contained so carefully these last weeks lashed out at the unsuspecting Finn. With one hand on the wheel and his eyes still coldly on the road Clegg forced Finn's head down onto the gear stick with a sharp thud on the bridge of the nose. It was too sudden for Finn to react with more than a grunt. Pain and blood were instant. Clegg threw Finn back against the side window. `Patronize me and your head goes through the fucking windscreen.` he snapped, his voice like a shard of glass. There was a silence. Seconds turned into minutes. At last Clegg sighed. He looked at Finn's shocked expression and thought again of the doctor, still inside, waiting to be caught. `Okay.` he sighed, `We both did well. Now lets get you back to table seventy two. We don't want your herb tea to go cold.`

FIFTYSIX

Khalil was not arrested for another four days. At three in the morning. That is when the next world war will start. Responses are dull, witnesses are few and in the approach to Midsummer's Day there will be no newspaper to report the deed. One police car and a van, unmarked. A modest display of flashing lights but a correct reserve of noise and sirens, space left for the blackbirds, still sleeping.

Not only Khalil was arrested, but his entire family, all eight of them, his wife and six sons, extracted from the high-rise they had fought so hard to belong to.

And then the lines. Thousands of lines, like a spider's web but chaotic, rival networks each ruled by a different geometry. Train lines, land lines, power lines, invisible wavelengths, roads in all directions, canals, cables, networks of people, families, colleagues, domino players, brass-band members, football supporters, millions of layers webbed together by shared interests, mutual distates, traditional habits, motives as complex as the mesh itself. The lines had always been there, parallel universes barely touching, more varied than any science-fiction writer could ever dream up. Only a fool could claim to control it, could assume to have it all at his finger tips.

The Khalil family travelled in the van, escorted by the car, along lines of tarmac as messages, both false and true, raced along cables beneath them and above them, as other lines of tarmac took their loads to different meetings and conclusions at the prompt of different messages, false and true, as the canal they crossed in a second carried its own life story and secrets just like the train that sped over them. There was no controlling genius to brood over it all, only Savage's single squirt of electronic miss-information clearing a path through the spider's jungle. The vehicles left Sheffield behind and headed for the umbilical tunnel to Manchester. The tunnel, once for trains, was now at the exclusive use of the Comfort Zone security forces as it cut its way beneath the Wildside's Pennine region. Somewhere between Hathersage and Edale the police vehicles broke all laws, of either side, swerved from the official route and climbed the Derbyshire Hills towards Buxton. By six in the morning Khalil and his family were entrusted to another web of lines, these for trains, by means of which they were taken south towards Shrewsbury port. By noon the stolen police vehicles had been compressed into tidy little cubes. An old pleasure steamer headed south with the family, its lines cut briefly ino the shallow waters of the Severn. By mid-afternoon Cornelius and Nico, their duties fulfilled, sat back and relaxed, happy to leave the explaining to Doctor Johnson.

`There really was no choice, Mrs.Khalil, no choice at all. You husband is a very brave man. He risked his life in order to save the boy. We had a debt to repay. The boy's father, John Savage, he had a debt to repay. We couldn't rescue Sam and then see you all punished, deported at very least.`

Mrs.Khalil was still tearful. Her husband had been even more discreet than anyone could have hoped for and had not even confided in her. She was in a state of shock, angry but with no obvious target for her feelings, relieved because the arrest had been false, scared because her knowledge of the Wildside was limited to tabloid scare-rumours. She needed placating, comforting, reassuring. She needed a woman's touch, and Doctor Johnson knew it. He beckoned to Betty Morgan who was making yet another pot of tea.

Betty took the hint. `You should be proud of your husband,` she said, trying a different angle. `Not many men would have taken the risks he did in order to save a stranger.`

`It was the honourable thing.` Johnson added, remembering vaguely that honour was held in high regard in other parts of the world.

`My husband has always been a man of honour.` she reminded them. `I think he would not have been linked with the boy's disappearance.` she suggested, ever practical.

`They could not have done it without my co-operation.` Khalil conceded. `I even think they half suspected me already.`

`There is no doubt about it.` Betty said. `As soon as they realize that Sam is no longer there they will arrest whoever was directly involved in his care. Outsiders might have managed the change-over, but only an insider could have ignored it for several days.`

`You all deserve better than that,` Doctor Johnson offered, `We would have been letting you down. Sir David has used your fear to keep Sam in a coma. When he no longer needed you he would have dumped you.`

`Our resident's status had been made permanent,` Mrs. Khalil reminded them, `by Sir David himself.`

`Not mine,` added Khalil, `not yet. He was blackmailing me. I think. It was never obvious what he meant or what he felt.`

`Perhaps he didn't have any feelings.` Johnson suggested.

`Oh he had feelings,` Khalil protested, `But they were too complex for me to understand.`

His wife shook her head, still trying to see a pattern to it all. Until this morning Sir David had been the good guy, the man whose influence had earned them a toe-hold of stability. Now he was the evil manipulator, a man who had required her husband to keep an innocent boy imprisoned by medicine. And what did that make her husband? He might have done the right thing now, but what did that make of his actions over the last twelve months?

`Anyway,` said one of the sons, philosophically, `nothing is permanent these days. Am I right?` Nobody disagreed. `Then what next?` he asked. `What plans have you made for us? You were clever enough to bring us out, you must be clever enough to help us on our way.`

`Over here you will have choices,` Johnson said, `You can settle where you want. Your father can work anywhere, from home, from a boat. You will be given horses, taught to ride. Or boats. You might want to settle by the water.`

`From a balloon!' Khalil suggested, managing the first joke of the conversation. `I could be the world's first balloon doctor!`

The balloon was in a field half a mile away, half inflated, Andrew and Owen were checking it over for the next stage in the plan.

`Who made the basket and where?` one of the sons asked. Doctor Johnson guessed Bristol, a specialist basket-maker.

`It was our trade` the son explained, `for generations, before the marshes were drowned in our home country.`

`And it could be again,` said Betty. `We can help you to settle and to start afresh.`

They had reached this point in the conversation several times before but it had never quite satisfied them. It was Dr.Khalil who moved things along.

`We had no choice,` he said. `Just as I had no choice, first to poison the boy, then to agree to your proposals for his rescue, just as we had no choice on where we lived, just as we had no choices in the camps. If you tell me you have brought us to a place where choices are possible then I say I am very grateful, I say we will be in your debt for the rest of our lives, for their rest of our children's lives, and for the rest of our grandchildren's lives.` His sons were nodding. His wife looked on impressed by her husband's sudden eloquence. `What do you want me to do now?` he asked. `You said that Armstrong is still a danger. You said that the boy is still in need of help.`

`He is being transported by canal. The timing is very critical and the canals are very slow, but by now he should have arrived.` Betty said.

`Why did you not bring him out like you did us?`

`On your advice. A nurse is with him. It is a very safe way to travel.` Johnson explained.

`Is he conscious?` Khalil asked.

`We have no news from the barge or the nurse. Is it possible by now?`

`Very possible. I stopped administering the sedatives one week ago. They are cumulative and will take a long time to work their way out of his system, but by now, after seven days, it is possible. Will I be allowed to attend to him, after all I have done?`

`We want him back, doctor.` Betty said softly. `You kept him in a coma for a very long time. Perhaps its only right that you should be there when he...arrives back.`

The doctor thought about this. `I would be honoured.` he finally said. `After all, I certainly owe the young man an apology.`

FIFTYSEVEN

Welcome to Stratford, the home of theatre. That's what it says on the sign. `Welcome to Stratford`, it says, `the home of theatre.` yet next to the sign at the water's edge where the well-to-do will arrive for the opening night there stands a gallows from which hang three corpses. Smuggling, like the smell of boats, the call of gulls and the deception of grease paint is in the town's blood. Two men and one woman twist like lanterns in the early morning light though there hardly seems breeze enough to prompt their little dance. Perhaps some unfinished business still itches in their bones. Perhaps some alien virus was spat into their throats at a tender age. Ignore them Clegg. They have crossed the wrong line for the wrong reason.

And this is the theatre, home of the Shakespeare Company, once Royal but no longer. The new theatre built in the old style, walls of rammed earth, turf roof, solar panels doubling as windows, a concourse of huge paving stones decked with dramatic statues of granite and wood. Only the experts dislike it. Steps from its entrance lead down to the water, water that extends 30 miles to the west in an unbroken sheet of slate grey. You could take a boat to Malvern or Shrewsbury or Bristol, would politics allow. You could cruise amongst reed and sand bank dense with waders and geese or even glimpse a flamingo if you were very fortunate. You could stare down on the drowned spires of Evesham and the sunken shires of middle-England, you could imagine the sad lowing of submarine cattle or the vicar's last call to evensong before the floodgates broke. You could slip from one world to the next in a single twist of the throttle.

Some of today's guests will come from the Comfort Zone, officially, welcomed at the border where they will leave their cars and be transferred to plush electric trams or even to ornate horse-drawn coaches in which they will ride like latter-day royalty to the opening night. Others will come from across the Severn, drawn not only by the spectacle of theatre but by the grim fascination involved in rubbing shoulders with aliens from another world. Some will come to do deals and arrange trade, both official and otherwise, some will come to meet old friends and relatives and to discuss old times. Some have come to pick pockets or trade gossip and have no ambition to sit in the stalls and watch the play. Still others are here for theatre pure and simple, to see their two world's parodied in the Shakespeare play that most exposes their extreme choices.

In the east, at the border, at Checkpoint Charlie as it is jokingly called, though nobody can remember quite why, the powers-that-be have reinforced their monitors and electronic surveillance with so-called Hard Security, real men with real guns and plastic lapel badges. It is their good old-fashioned job to inspect the passes of those wishing to spend Midsummer's Day in the badlands of Stratford.

Lists have been drawn up long since, permissions given or denied, security checks run in advance. After the great day all the to-ing and fro-ing will be entered manually into the System, to nibble away at its infuriating blind spot and to track down any who have abused the freedom granted by the year's one day of chaos.

Nathaniel Clegg, alias Derek Woolard, collected Finn from an agreed street corner, a simple unmonitored rendezvous, like in the good old days, and together they drove to the storage shed which backed onto the Stratford Canal and to which Sam Savage had been delivered. The biggest risk was now physical. Gangs, opportunist criminals, street riots, all were possibilities but by avoiding the town centres and shopping malls they had a good chance of proceeding quietly with their business.

Alive or dead? And did it matter? Again Clegg found it the most difficult question to answer. He had done his part. If the journey by undertaker's barge had proven too much then so what? He could still claim his reward from Savage and then betray him to Sir David, he could still win twice over, all ends up. What did it matter if one of the pawns had faded away in the meantime?

Inside the storage shed the nurse and two assistants had prepared the vehicle. It was electric, which would avoid any cross-border arguments and its back was stuffed full of flowers and bouquets. Beneath the flowers, hidden from view, was the same trolley Clegg had wheeled down the cloying corridors of Welbeck four days earlier and on the trolley was the same half-alive body they had taken all these risks for. Clegg took the ignition keys and nodded but said nothing before climbing into the vehicle next to Finn.

They left the industrial area and found their way to the main road. Joy-riders would be a danger on the motorway but this route offered a degree of safety.

`You don't trust me, do you?` Clegg asked, not looking at Finn as he spoke. A gang had gathered in a car-park on the far side of the road and was doing battle with a group of police but Clegg eased past the disturbance without a second look.

`I've got no choice.` Finn said.

Clegg recalled his conversation with Arch, when he had him strung up on a noose. Perhaps Finn's contempt and distaste for Clegg was comparable to how Clegg had felt that day.

`You should know me quite well by now.` Clegg mused.

`Why?`

`The badger sett. Malvern market probably. Breathing down my neck all the time weren't you?`

`Not quite. Whenever I could.`

`And you've got the bloody cheek to mistrust *me*.`

`We've got a job to do.`

`We certainly have, and wont she just love us for it?`

`She?`

`Beth. The other half of your tribe of two.`

Finn was stung by this intrusion into his private world and by the reminder that Clegg had spied on them in the shadows of Clun castle and strung his crossbow in a tree. He was also stung by the way in which desire had disturbed his own ability to watch and listen and skulk.

`She's a nice girl.` said Clegg, suggestively. `Old enough.`

`What do you mean?` Finn asked helplessly.

Clegg laughed. `You know what I mean! You should have done her when you had the chance. She wanted you to, disappointed if you ask me. That kind always expects to serve. Now it might be too late.`

`What do you mean?`

`I mean you missed your chance. She's closing off to things like that. She's like a wound that's started to heal. You can't just come and go inside her anymore.`

`I don't know what you're talking about, and anyway…`

`Oh you know what I'm talking about, choir boy. And don't forget you weren't watching her all the time. You weren't with us ten days ago on a hill top in Wales. A nice girl. Old enough, like I said.`

Finn counted to ten as his training had taught him. He tried to picture Beth withered by old age and eaten by maggots in order to nip desire and jealousy in the bud. It didn't work. `You leave her alone.` he said, sounding lame.

`Its a bit late for that.` Clegg chuckled. `You should have got in there while you still had the chance. Down by the river, May Day. I wouldn't have disturbed you. I might have watched to pick up a few tips, but I wouldn't have disturbed you. A tribe of two for God's sake!`

`Shut up!`

`We're doing a job.` Clegg reminded him. The traffic lights ahead were not working and caution was needed. `Do you hate me?` he asked.

`I'm beginning to.` Finn answered.

`That's good. That's very good. Because we've got a job to do and we've got to do it properly, right? We're a good team. Hate me all you like, it might help.`

`What do you mean by that?`

But Clegg didn't answer. They were approaching Check-Point Charlie's hard security. This time Clegg was relaxed. There was no one from the past to recognize him, the paper work was in order and the entry was straight-forwards. The mood on the other side changed. Anarchy here had a different quality. It was like before a big football match, opposing supporters mixing, a false joviality, an excessive show of good will, whilst beneath the surface a tribal tension was ready to stir the loins. Signs directed them clearly, first towards the theatre and then towards its service entrance.

`Would you like to hit me?` Clegg asked, picking up the conversation just as the theatre came into view.

`Don't be stupid.` Finn answered, confused by Clegg and by his own feelings.

`Of course you would. For everything I stand for. You know which side I belong on. You know what I'm really like. And perhaps I got to Beth before you did. How is that for motive?` A long silence. Clegg reversed the vehicle into the unloading bay. `Listen carefully,` his tone had changed. `I want you to hit me. Nice and hard. Put everything into it you've got. All that hate you pretend isn't there. Hit me for Beth's sake. Tonight. I'll tell you when, and I might even tell you why. Don't look so worried, you'll enjoy it!'

FIFTYEIGHT

`You have done well,` Sir David said, rising from his place to greet Clegg formally. The two men shook hands, quickly taking in the nuances of each other's appearance. Sir David was expensively dressed, the top civil servant on display. Clegg, a low-grade funeral director, had been clothed for less than the price of the other man's shoe laces.

Clegg looked around the restaurant. It was the right choice. They were above the concourse of the theatre. Their reserved table looked down onto the waterfront where the well-to-do were arriving for the play. There was a slight breeze from the east, Clegg noted, though not cold.

`What will you have?` Sir David asked, gesturing to the menu.

Clegg shook his head. Food was not upper most in his thoughts.

`Oh come, surely. At least a drink. It's a celebration, after all.` Clegg asked for water. Sir David was half way through a bottle of red wine, his party already under way. `So how did you do it?` he asked, dabbing the corners of his mouth with a napkin after each sip. `We have been trying for a long time, you know.`

`Why do you want to know?` asked Clegg. `It's done. That's all you need to know. You've got your man, assuming...`

`Oh yes,` Sir David nodded eagerly, `Of course, please, examine.`

There were two small and identical brief-cases parked next to the table leg. Clegg lifted them on to the table one at a time. Sir David slipped him a piece of paper on which two serial numbers were printed, one for the combination of each case. He checked the first. Gold ingots. He checked the second. Gold ingots. He returned them to the ground and drank his water.

`So now what?` asked Clegg.

But Sir David was distracted by the view or some distant and disturbing thoughts. `Who could have foretold even fifty years ago that it would have come to this?` he asked, waving towards the concourse steps and the open water. `But then who could have stood any where in Europe at any time and said with any accuracy how things would be fifty years into the future? Nobody I have ever met, Mr.Clegg. Nobody. Reassuring really that the future is so unpredictable. Don't you think?`

Clegg grunted.

`Do you know anything about self-mutilation?` Sir David asked, smiling at the effect his words had on Clegg.

`Why do you ask that?`

`Europe, Mr.Clegg. Self-mutilation. You must have thought of it, surely? Never has a continent shown such enthusiasm for self-mutilation, never has a continent tried so consistently to slit its own wrists in the tepid waters of greed and apathy. Wouldn't you agree?`

But Clegg was in no mood for philosophy. `I asked, what next?` he repeated.

`You're clean.` said Sir David, getting to the point. `Assuming everything goes to plan. You can go where you like, do what you want. A fresh start. The System can be very forgiving, you know. Run along and spend your money. Foreign travel, exotic beaches, tame women, the lot.`

`I didn't mean me,` said Clegg, not even trying to hide his contempt. `I meant you. What happens now you've got Savage?`

`Ah! Curiosity. A healthy trait I'm told. It didn't do the cat very much good, Mr.Clegg, now did it?`

`Then I'll have to guess.` said Clegg, `You'll take him up to Welbeck. Probably the girl as well. Then you'll have all three of them. You'll pump him full of drugs, wake the boy up, frighten the girl, persuade a few secrets from them, then fuck the Wildside.`

Sir David was nodding. `I couldn't have put it better myself, Mr.Clegg. But it's all a bit predictable don't you think? It's all a bit obvious. I might be old but I'm not boring. John always taught me to go for the unexpected. It's what makes life worth living.`

`You don't know do you?` said Clegg. `You don't know what you're going to do with them.`

Sir David shrugged but was nodding. `Ask the boy.` he said with unexpected force, `ask the bloody boy in the hospital bed.` He made himself relax, shook his head by way of dismissing the thought and then tried a question. `What would you do in my position?`

`Apologize.` said Clegg without a moment's hesitation.

Sir David, rather than taking offence, looked quite serious. `Thankyou, Mr.Clegg. I will take your advice. I will apologize. It will be good for my religious sense-organ.`

`And then take a long holiday.`

But Sir David smiled at that. `Is Arch dead?` he asked.

`Arch sends his love,` said Clegg, nodding to the two cases.

`Ah! You're in it together. How touching. One for him, one for you. Does he trust you?`

`He doesn't have any choice.` Clegg said, paraphrasing Finn. There was a long silence. He was staring at Sir David, aware that the older man was growing more uncomfortable by the minute. It's what makes life worth living, he had said, the unpredictable. Like Bonny. `The Arthur thing,` Clegg said, `Arch's game, but also the book and the newspapers, that was your idea wasn't it?`

Sir David looked fondly at Clegg. In another life he might have taken to the lad, trained him up, given him a worthwhile apprenticeship. The smooth domed head shone back strip lighting, the wary eyes reflected a hint of pride. `Of course. I had the book ghosted, that goes without saying. It's no secret. I leant on the papers. It was great fun at the time, I can tell you. Great fun. John was furious. I was not in the least surprised that people picked up the idea. I suppose it was the earliest version of the Game we eventually floated. It worked.`

`Have you ever thought it might be true?`

`What might be true?`

`The Arthur thing. John Savage, freedom, all that stuff.`

Sir David leaned forwards and gave Clegg a confiding look. `My dear boy, please give me some credit. Within weeks the book was forgotten and the papers had moved on to other things. John himself never read it, he was too angry. No, make no mistake, the only person who ever really believed, perhaps the only person who *still* believes it is yours truly.`

Clegg resented this man's continued ability to surprise him. He shook his head, drew back from the table, feeling too close to Sir David. `What do you really want?` Clegg asked, `I mean *really*.`

There was no hesitation. `I want it to end.` said Sir David, sighing, `Demons. You'll understand when you get to my age. It's been enough to be honest with you.`

`You wanted his wife didn't you?`

`Once upon a time.`

Something in the quiet of his voice alerted Clegg. Alarm bells rang. The ground shifted very slightly. `You never married.`

A shake of Sir David's head.

`It was her or nothing wasn't it?.`

A shrug.

`And the boy?`

`The boy?`

`Sam. The stretcher case. He's yours isn't he? You got in there first. He's not Savage's son, he's yours. And nobody knows.` Clegg whistled softly under his breath. `That's why you're haunted by demons.`

`I'll let you into a secret,` Sir David said, leaning forwards. `If you have any sense you'll put it to good use, Mr.Clegg. Once upon a time, in Emma Savage's bed, I fell in love. Are you listening carefully? With a man. I fell in love with a man. I had never met him before but I'd always known him. It was me. Or a variant of me. Somebody I could have been if she had allowed it. I had never met him before and have never done so since but although he died with her it's his ghost that haunts me, not Emma's or Sam's. His ghost. The most terrifying demon you could ever wish for, Mr.Clegg.`

`I'll take your word for it.`

`You'll do more than that.` Sir David snapped, suddenly urgent and threatening. `You'll meet him, face to face. And you might as well know before it comes to that just why he's so terrifying. You can't guess can you? You can't even begin to. It's because he loves me. No matter what a bastard I am and no matter how many people like you and Sam I crush the demon still loves me.` Sensing Clegg's incomprehension Sir David took a slow drink, leaned back in his chair and waited for Clegg to breath normally. `And I'll let you into another secret, Mr.Clegg. When we used Emma as bait John took it, the bait I mean. He was quite ready to betray the Wildside in order to save her. That's true love for you.`

`That's not what the girl thinks.`

`Oh? So what does the girl think?`

`She thinks her father let her mother die.`

Sir David was shaking his head, drumming his fingers on the table. `Wrong. He stuck by his wife, even though...`

`Even though you were in her bed...`

`You have a way with words, Mr.Clegg. I'm not sure why I'm telling you all this.`

`Guilt?`

Sir David laughed. `Its a pleasure doing business with you, Mr.Clegg. It's a shame we can't work together in the future.

`Tragic.`

`Do you like Shakespeare, Mr.Clegg?`

`I've never tried it.`

`You should, Mr.Clegg, you really should. You know Shakespeare used drugs to pull back the veil between this world and the next? *Midsummer Night's Dream.* Right up your street, Mr.Clegg, a fable for our time. Portia places faery potion in Titania's eyes, you see, she knew exactly the power of certain plants, when distilled and refined, of course, to transport their users into other worlds, other worlds often more compelling and certainly more desirable than this one, Mr.Clegg.`

Clegg thought of Andrew and his gently fried mushrooms.

`The trick is to cross the line in full consciousness, Mr.Clegg, to travel where Shakespeare sent Titania in full awareness and possession of your faculties. Very few can do so. It takes years of training and devoted practice, so they tell me. It is the realm of monks and hermits, of mystics and initiates.`

`Why are you telling me this?`

`Perhaps I'm rambling, Mr.Clegg, or perhaps my old friend John Savage had the skills of the mystic. He could lift back the veil without drugs and potions. That's what made him so great. Inspiration, they called it. You know, I sometimes think he knew exactly what we were all thinking, sometimes before we did ourselves.`

`So he's a clever man.`

`No! You've missed the point, Mr.Clegg. Everyone is clever nowadays, absolutely everyone. No, he was far more dangerous than that, Mr.Clegg. He was invincible not because he was clever, but because-he-was-moral.` He set the final word between them like a block of marble: pure, immutable; carve of it what you will. He sighed, looked around the restaurant, fiddled with his tie. He now seemed much more at ease. `Tonight it's *The Tempest*, it's one of Shakespeare's best. Its about a magician and his daughter exiled to an improbable island. Remind you of anything? One of the characters looks in the mirror and gets a nasty shock.`

`Indeed.`

But Sir David had finished for now. He took one last look at Clegg, nodding to himself perhaps with approval at the man who had contacted him via Arch's world in order to bring about this exchange. `If we meet again, Mr.Clegg I want you to tell me what it was like.`

`The play?`

`No. Looking in the mirror.`

FIFTYNINE

The Wildside. For every man a thousand choices. For every woman a thousand motives. For every child a thousand mysteries. Great oaks older than the nation's soul; sunken lanes dense and dripping with ferns and bracken; boulders hewn and worshiped by a dozen tribes across as many centuries. Blotched lichen on bleached stone, spotted orchids in dappled meadow, striped damsel fly beneath spangled ash and willow. Herds of deer, skeins of geese, gangs of wild boar and the smell of woodsmoke, horse's flank and crushed bracken acrid in the thousand different types of warm damp. Slabs of rock and earth crumbled like mature cheese, wrapped in dense layers of green, as many greens as there are eyes to watch, as many nuances of light as there are minutes to the day and days to the year. Old forests and new, ancient hedgerow and juvenile, tree become copse, copse become wood, wood become chase. Hills, endless hills with secret folds, each with its own primeval name and untold history, each with long buried bones of nation-shapers and its half-forgotten myth and legend of boggart and fairy glamour. Man-made scars healed and opened a dozen times, each time the absolving green irrepressible, its appetite vast and all-consuming, no sin too great for its power of forgiveness, Magdalene the sacred whore comforting each wound. As many secrets as there are shrines, as many paths of initiation as there are blossoms on the hawthorn.

And the Comfort Zone. For every man a concrete box, for every woman a shopping precinct, for every child a free plastic toy. Endless cars and lorries, wall-to-wall motorway, 284 TV channels, 57 flavours of condom, 187 Bonnys dredged daily from the tepid bath water of despair, a thousand shades of shit in which to dredge for silver fruit.

But did it matter, Clegg asked himself, did it really matter at the end of the day? And if the answer, God forbid, was 'Yes' then what could he, Nathaniel Clegg, tomorrow's Judas, do about any of it? He watched, against his better judgement, as the concourse emptied towards the stalls and gallery. As usual excluded from the warmth and anticipation, as usual the unwanted gate-crasher even if it was his own party. He saw Beth in a borrowed dress, hiding her discomfort, he saw her weary father and his quiet retainers. The magician and his daughter exiled to a fantastic island. A play he never would see, a mirror he did not care to look in. Tonight called for presence of mind, a cool head, years of training and a wind from the east.

And again the lines. Thousands of lines, like a spider's web but chaotic, rival networks each ruled by a different geometry. Life lines, destiny lines, family lines, invisible wavelengths of choice and motive, people in all directions, networks of people, strangers, friends, colleagues, actors, lighting technicians, cloak room attendants, Sir David's heavies, Clegg's confusion, Finn's jealousy, millions of layers webbed together by shared interests, mutual distastes, traditional habits, motives as complex as the mesh itself. The lines have always been there, parallel universes barely touching, gossamer blown like candy-floss more varied than any science-fiction writer could ever dream up. And whether it matters or not there was no escaping it. You could smash through it with anger and violence but only create an ever more complex and beautiful web than existed before. Only a fool could claim to control it, could assume to have it all at his finger tips. Only a fool could hope to escape it, to fly above it on wafer thin wings of delusion.

Of course there could be no incident in the theatre itself. Sir David Armstrong and his people were effectively guests in a foreign country and etiquette had to be observed, but in truth they could have stopped the play mid-scene and made a great and public spectacle of the arrest, fearless of reprisals and there were those who urged such action on their boss and were privately dismayed by his lack of urgency. All in good time, was all he would say, never rush the end-play. Certainly not. The crowds would thin. Savage and his daughter would be taken quietly, `escorted` might be the professional word, via the service lift and thence to Sir David's waiting boat. Their own, to where they expected Clegg to deliver his charge, was moored only twenty yards away, but for those few paces they would be surrendering themselves quite freely and ignorant of the treachery Clegg had made possible. Sir David waited, staring at Watson's face on the screen, scripting the alternative endings, trying to outguess for one last time, his old friend and rival. Only one thing was certain. It would not proceed as planned. But where and how the surprises would be sprung, there was the excitement.

`It's Mr.Clegg,` the police officer said, bursting in on his superior's reverie, `something appears to have gone wrong.`

What a surprise, Sir David almost said. Would we want it any other way? `Oh?` he queried, wondering how he was supposed to react. `Have you lost him?`

`No, Sir, that's just it, we've found him.`

`Well that is just wonderful then. But could you explain the use of the word `found`, ? Could you explain how you find what has not been lost? And if you've found him why is there a problem? Could you also explain that one?`

`It's odd, Sir, something doesn't add up. We found him in the bushes. Somebody had jumped him, taken the gold. Clegg was tied up and half conscious.`

This was an interesting development. Sir David wondered if he had over-estimated Clegg. His suspicious mind immediately thought of Arch, the criminal under-class eagerly cutting its own throat, betraying Clegg for a double dose of the gold, but just at that moment a second officer arrived on the scene.

`A message, Sir, from Welbeck.` he handed the note and retreated. It was from D.I.Jones. Sam Savage. He was not in Welbeck hospital. To judge by the body posing in his bed he had been removed a week ago. Khalil had disappeared. Please advise.

Although Sir David had long since lost any desire to be in control of events he did not like to be made a complete fool of. Yes, it was enjoyable to watch the chaos break around him, like waves on the beach, and far more entertaining to react and respond than it was to direct events from on high but this latest development almost took his breath away. After all, wasn't he supposed to win? Confusion and admiration competed with the fear of defeat. Things might be running away from him. Wonderful! What a climax his friend John had orchestrated.

`It may be one of our own men, Sir.` the officer said, reminding his superior of the assault on Clegg. `We may have a man out there who was aware of the financial consideration involved.`

`You mean the gold.` Sir David corrected softly, `I am the one who speaks in riddles. You stick to plain English. The gold has gone and you think one of our people has walked off with it? Wouldn't that be a bit obvious? What a simple universe some people inhabit. Take care of Mr.Clegg would you?`

`He's being brought here now, Sir.`

`Why? If the man is in distress he will need medical assistance.`

`Sir. Mr. Clegg says he knows where they are.`

A shiver of dreadful anticipation toyed with Sir David's spine but with it also the thrill of the inevitable. When you backed an outsider on a hunch and it came storming home you felt briefly immortal. He had the feeling that in this he could not lose. Whatever the outcome, whoever died, whatever prevailed, he would allow himself to enjoy it either way. `Where *who* are?` he asked, already knowing the answer.

`The Savages, Sir,` the briefest of pauses, `they're not in the theatre.`

`They are not in the theatre?`

`Sir, they appear to have given us the slip.`

Sir David was caught between disbelief and anger. `What do you mean they've given you the slip? A girl and a sick old man! Bounded off into the woods have they? Turned themselves invisible?` He stepped out of the boat and up onto the walkway, uncomfortable at being peered down on.

The officers instinctively stepped back to leave him a sphere of importance. `Sir, when the play was over they entered the lift according to the plan. When it arrived at the bottom it was empty.`

`Well if it was empty they must have got out on an intervening floor.` Sir David suggested.

`There is no intervening floor, Sir,` one of the officers mumbled. `It's the first thing we checked.`

`Then they must be in the cellar or on the roof.`

`There is no cellar, Sir.`

`Which leaves?`

But before Sir David's inferiors could respond to his hints and promptings a new voice cut through the darkness. `It's too late. You're all too late.` It was Clegg. He was being supported roughly on either side by police officers. His face looked grim and angry even without the welt above his eye and the matted blood in his hair. Somebody had hit him very hard, and more than once. `It's too late,` he repeated. `They've stuffed you. They've made fools of you all.` He spat, half out of contempt, half to clear his mouth which was filling with blood again. `They've got the boy. They've got everything they want. You might not be able to apologize after all.` he hissed, drawing close to Sir David and shrugging off his minders.

On cue, as usual, the roar of the hydrogen burner turned their attention upwards. Still briefly in the floodlights of the theatre the great eagle-headed balloon was visible in all its glory. Sir David, Clegg, the attendant police, spectators all, looked stupidly towards the quiet glory of the thing, a huge statement of certainty above their heads. They watched almost in reverence as it vanished into the waiting dark.

Sir David looked up and gasped. He fought hard to suppress a smile and found himself strangely sharing in the triumph of those who were drifting away westwards above his head. There should have been applause, all those on the ground who were chasing their tales should now applaud even in defeat. Sir David wanted to cheer them on, to propose a toast, to follow gloriously on wings. `What next?` he said, turning to Clegg.

`It's all right,` said Clegg, with massive authority as Sir David appeared to falter. `Let them go.` He measured his next words very carefully, relishing the small and intimate audience all desperate for some magic solution, staking all on one last throw. `I know exactly where they're going. I know what their game is. I can bring them back. And my gold. But this time...` and his concluding words he virtually spat into Sir David's rather surprised face, `this time, you incompetent bastard, just leave it all to me.`

SIXTY

The brain is never more than half alive, they say, the brain is always close in nature to the cold and lifeless tomb in which it lies, almost dormant. No other organ of the body is less served with blood, no other part of the body is more removed from the activity of its host. The brain does not even think, the one task we assume it to be consummate at, the brain is incapable of creativity or imagination, logic or sequence, insight or intuition. Oh no, thoughts are out there, out there in the world, like the air we breathe, common property. You can be brain-dead in the terminology of modern science, kept alive by machines and drugs, but you still breathe the air, you still think the thoughts which live in the world's unconscious. Perhaps more than those who are still confined to within their own skulls, locked away inside their Hollow Mountains. The brain is a wonderful mirror, a skilled reflector of World Thought. But the brain does not think, no more than Africa migrates to meet the swallows, no more than the symphony hides inside the cello. The brain is dead. Long live the brain.

And from its mortuary world the brain has spawned dead off-spring, tiny tentacles of death, tiny vacuums of negation, minute cancers which unite in one vast illness, and like all great healers John Savage knows you must fight like with like. Inside his Hollow Mountain is a computer. The machine he despises more than the cancer in his own body is the machine that keeps his hopes alive. It has taken the offered blood of all his children and passed the blood's secrets to the oscillator, the Lady of the Lake and she has converted them into vibrations and thence to sound and it is this sound which activates the computer's major function and this sound which gives John Savage and his small crew of helpers unlimited access to the System. Like x-rays or Ultra Sound they can pass through its clumsy programmes, they can read, cut-out, scramble and implant at will, they can toy with a technology which by comparison with their own is almost Neolithic in its crudeness. They are Beings of Light, or at least of sound, and they can move unhindered through the silent darkness of The System. At Savage's direction these beings have taken his children's blood and found, somewhere between the notes and intervals, somewhere just beyond the weaving of genes and DNA in the realm of pure creation, of pure origins, a key. Not quite the Grail mystery that Agnes wove into her life, but close enough with its chalice of blood, its all-mighty powers and its mystical appeal to tread close on the heels of the occult past to which she subscribes. The human spirit would always prevail above the evil of computer technology, Savage once told a lecture audience, though it may take a thousand years to win through.

But there is still one thing beyond the capabilities of the System, of John Savage's Beings of Light, even of the cyberspace version of Merlin the wizard whispering in King Arthur's ear, and that is the riddle of motive. Motives can be the most complex mess of worms on the planet. Ask Clegg. Ask Sir David. They both know.

Clegg has placed Sir David and his other officers in a police half-track which has been ferried across the water and in contravention of all agreements and protocols has burned its furious path along lanes and remnant roads and even, at one point, a railway line, to reach the Long Mynd, a place much loved of errant hunters and abandoned helicopters. None amongst the dazed police have thought to ask how Clegg could possibly have known where the balloon might fetch up. Their knowledge of such technicalities makes of Clegg an expert, whilst his trust in Owen's handling of the balloon and basket gives him the conviction to bluff his way through the dark night and grey morning. It is still an enormous relief, however, as he climbs the top of the Mynd, to see the stage set as per directions. A mile away, huddled bleakly around the mobile but false charcoal burner stand Owen, Beth, Andrew and Arch. Khalil, the hospital trolley and its fragile load are already inside the strange vehicle. On the ground, next to them, stands the balloon basket and burner, but the balloon itself remains rolled up. The wind that had served them so well the night before now kisses them, like Judas, on the wrong cheek. It has turned through 180 degrees and offers them no way home. Savage has indeed arranged things right into the detail. The fact that they would have taken their stand here even in the most perfect of ballooning weather is a fact the excited police fraternity will be spared.

`We've got them.` D.I.Jones, proclaims. She is newly arrived from Welbeck, fanatic with the will to incarcerate.

But Sir is silent. Sir is in awe. He almost wants to wink at Clegg, to be admitted into this wonderful conceit. `Stay here.` he says, `Mr.Clegg and I will go ahead.`

`Sir, is that wise?.` But he waves the objections aside. He and Clegg climb out and begin the slow walk towards the charcoal burner and balloon. He waits until they are out of earshot but does not turn to Clegg or break his stride.

`Brilliant,` he mutters. `Absolutely brilliant. You and he make a great team.`

`You want it to finish,` said Clegg, `That's what you told me.`

`Oh, Mr.Clegg, you have no idea. Lines and shadows. Demons and ghosts. The weariness of Emma's face. I do. I do want it to finish.`

`Then you have to do what I tell you. Can you manage that?`

`I will certainly try, Mr.Clegg.`

`Then I want you to promise me something.`

`More gold, Mr.Clegg? You surprise me.`

Clegg did not even bother to waste his contempt. `Something worth more than gold.` he stated. `Now shut up and listen.` For the next five minutes, in the great buffeting silence of the Long Mynd, Sir David did just that.

This is the Last Supper, Clegg thinks, the Last Supper and Crucifixion all rolled into one. Disciples, soldiers, martyrs and villains. And Judas. Feet washed, noose at the ready. Thank God Agnes is not here to watch, Clegg thinks, dumbly. How would he explain to her? How would he justify what not even he can fully comprehend? Oh yes, and the resurrection. He had forgotten that. Someone, somewhere, might still step forwards to roll away the stone from the tomb that Clegg had helped dig. Bring on Arch, wraps and manic grin, bring on the Knights of King Arthur, Churchill's spitfire pilots, Queen Elisabeth stirring her sea-captains to great feats of folly and bravery, all to save the last freedoms of this sceptered isle. Sound track by Elgar, panoramic shots of faces against great swathes of landscape. Shit coated in candy.

But the final act needs no directing. John Savage, supported by Beth and a walking stick, walks as surely as he can towards the old enemy. Sir David needs no support. He times his approach to meet them half way. There is even a bench at the ready with views down into the Stretton valley for the two men to admire as they speak.

One sick, the other possessed. Beth finds it difficult to watch. She shows contempt on behalf of them all as Sir David greets her. To his credit he begins with the right question.

`How is your brother, Beth?`

It is the question her father did not ask. `It doesn't matter, does it?` Beth answers.

Sir David looks slightly hurt for a moment, as though he had expected respect and civility from one so young. Then a smile creeps up on one side of his face.

`No, it doesn't really matter, Beth. It does rather look as though the game is over. I hope you enjoyed your time here, Beth. It will be something to look back on if you have the chance to grow old. As for you John, you've had your fun, wouldn't you agree? Most boys make do with a toy train-set, you had half a country to play around with! Its time to get back to reality.`

But Savage is not ready to speak. There is no contempt or malice or even anger in him towards Sir David, only an ever growing love for the world of green and trees that he has surrounded himself with. Having sat, having patted Beth on the knee to quieten her, having acknowledged the skylark on the edge of the Mynd he turns warmly to Sir David. `Oh yes,` he answers. `Reality. I just about remember that, David. I'm surprised you do.`

Was this how it would end, playing with words? Beth had imagined it differently, but of course her father knows his old rival far better than she does. He knows that Sir David's curiosity will need satisfaction sooner rather than later, and why not now in the intimacy of these empty spaces? He owes him that much, surely.

`You can bring Sam back,` says Sir David. `You know I always wanted to. I have kept a close watch on him, John, I give you my word. Its only a drug.`

Like Andrew's mushrooms, like Portia's fairy potion, access to another world, one Sam was ready to finish with.

`Not even Khalil knows about it. He'll be back, you'll all be together again. But we will want some information first.` As he speaks Sir David takes a small palm-top from his pocket and places it on the bench between them. At the press of a button Watson's face appears and floats around the screen. Sir David glances at Clegg.

`Not quite.` Clegg says, startling Beth. `Their mother won't be there. They wont all be together, will they? Is someone going to bring her back as well?`

Beth glares at Clegg. What did this have to do with him? Why was he taking her confidences and playing them back in front of these two men? He was invading her family and anywhere else she would have turned on him with fury but for now she bit her tongue.

`I think we've been here before, John. Perhaps Beth hasn't. I know I offered and you accepted back then. This time its different. This time I will deliver.`

`What are you talking about?` Beth asks, alert to every tone and nuance, `What do you mean you offered?`

Sir David does a strange thing. It may be out of character but it is certainly very deliberate. He knows exactly what he is doing. He is honouring his promise to Clegg. He is returning John Savage to his daughter. `I killed your mother, Beth. Did you ever doubt it? Your father was willing to betray the Wildside just to save her life, even though...`

`Don't lie for Beth's sake.` Savage says. `She can think of me what she will, but never as a liar. I killed her. I take responsibility.`

Sir David looks confused and starts to shake his head but Beth speaks out and silences them both. `Two old fools.` she says. `Look at you. Arguing over who did what thirteen years ago. You still haven't realized have you? You think everyone is there to be shunted around in your game? You think everyone is just sitting around waiting at your beck and call. Have you ever thought that Mum made her own choice? You're not the only ones with ideals and beliefs, you know. Perhaps Mum loved you both, if that helps. But she loved the Wildside even more. The best choices tear you in two. You should both know that by now.` With that she turns and walks away, back to the charcoal burner, the three men put resolutely in their place.

Clegg watches her, no less shocked than the two old fools on the bench. Her words are indelible. He knows that nothing anyone now does or says will erase them from his hearing. He starts to follow her but then remembers a vital detail. He gestures to Sir David and the machine next to him. Sir David nods. He speaks to the computer, looking at Savage as he does so. `Please record everything we say, Watson, to be transmitted in, what, ten minutes?.`

`Certainly, Sir. Any reference?`

He should have thought of that, some grand symbolic file reference for them to ponder over in the debriefing rooms of history, but for once Sir David's imagination fails him. `No reference, Watson.`

Savage looks on quizzically, chewing over Beth's words but also wondering and half guessing why Sir David is so keen to record and send and for it to be known that he is doing so. `So why should this time be any different, David?` he sighs, ` What has changed, not you, surely?`

But Sir David is unable to answer, or too clever. He looks at his old friend and something passes between them that no outsider can detect. It is John Savage who continues, comprehension now complete. `I'll give you the information,` he says, `more than you could possibly have hoped for, enough to de-bug your System, to call our bluff, to roll up the Wildside, to send in the machines. But I think you've guessed most of it by now.`

`I think so.` Sir David nods, speaking to the computer. `It needs all of you, doesn't it? Sam's blood wasn't enough. Nor is it just the DNA`

No, Sir David, not the DNA. In the beginning was something far more wonderful and far more complex than you and your kind can ever comprehend. From the frozen harmony of the skeleton into world-shattering, world-shaping power. Ask Clegg, he has heard it, your right hand man has been corrupted by the heresy, he has listened to the Creative Word, the symphony, the orchestra of resonance, each note shaping a different from, each form dancing to a different tune. Explain that to a gene-manipulator, explain that to a society which would have aborted Andrew in the womb. Explain that to the likes of D.I.Jones who need to measure and number, for whom music is no more than maths out of control. Now is not the time. John Savage knows his ideas will need a century or two of darkness to incubate them. But he does have something to say, before it is too late. There is something Sir David wants the computer to know before the play can move on.

`You need us all, dear David, you have done since they were born. All of my children. I adapted the codes to include their blood. And yes, you're half right. It is DNA and sound. You blow on the right combination of paper and comb and seventy million people dance to your tune.`

Sir David always loved John Savage's images, he savoured them like a connoisseur would savour a wine, rolling them around his own unfulfilled imagination. `They have to dance to somebody's tune, John.` he answers, replying in kind.

`What about their own?`

But Sir David is shaking his head sadly. `You know better than that, John, they don't want to anymore, not on my side of the Line. They're quite happy to leave it all to the beloved System.`

`So now what?`

`Oh, John, now what! You wouldn't believe the things they have planned, wonderful things, John, wonderful things. Your System was just the beginning. Once they have complete control they can confine it to the history books. Your name will live on, John, of course, you need have no worries on that score. I have always insisted that credit be given to those who deserve it. But tell me, look at all that, what do you see? Tell me like you did in the good old days, you used to put it so splendidly.` He gestures to the rolling views which extend as far as the eye can see, the hills, trees and valleys of Shropshire.

It only takes Savage a moment to get Sir David's drift. `You know what I see,` he answers, `I see a living thing. I see the Grail. I see you and I as drops of Christ's blood in the Grail. Don't mock me, David. It does not become you to mock me.`

`I'm not mocking, John.` his voice betrays genuine dismay, `I am not mocking you, I swear. We have known each other too long for that. It's just that your way has lost. Theirs has won. That's all there is to it. You see the earth as the Grail, that's your choice. They see something else. They see a machine with a magnetic field which can be programmed quite simply, they see a vast mother-board waiting for its instructions. They are close to being able to programme the whole earth, John, the greatest computer conceivable, you and I as synapses, not drops of blood. Radio, images, computers, human thinking, all tied into one wonderful System, the air alive with it, the very earth shaking in sympathy. Machine Man has won, John. Destruction and distraction all rolled into one.`

The centuries of darkness are almost tangible as Sir David describes the vision, not his own, but `theirs`. Had Savage managed to delay it by a decade or two? Was that what this was all about?

`But what about us?` John Savage asks, `what about the people who want a choice, who want to be free to make mistakes?`

Sir David looks him in the eye again, a little sadly. `Don't be so silly!` he starts to laugh, `Don't be so bloody silly!` and he throws his head back so that his laughter reaches to left and right, to the two groups waiting and watching, so that his laughter can echo in the earth's empty chalice.

John Savage has the presence of mind to wait before placing a hand on Sir David's arm. `All right`, he says, `but listen, I haven't got much longer to live, and as for Sam...`

`I've told you, we can bring him back.`

`To like he was before? He was always in the shadows, David, you know that, he was always on the outside looking in. Just be careful with us, David, that's all I ask. Not for old time's sake, I'm not that stupid, but for your sake. If anything happens to us before you've processed our DNA then it's lost forever. You can scrap the System, but not before you've lost control of it and your people.`

`Don't worry, John, you've made it very clear. Watson, has Mr.Savage made the position clear?`

`Your voices are recorded accurately.` Watson replies, `to be transmitted in ten minutes.`

`In that case, Hal, my old friend John and I are just going for a short journey.` He rises from the bench and takes his former colleague by the arm, leaving Watson to repeat its desperate refrain in its synthetic east-coast accent.

`I wouldn't do that if I were you, Dave.`

SIXTYONE

Few things can rival the silence of a helicopter suddenly shut down. A bomb is followed by screams and sirens, but a helicopter dumps dead air for miles around and leaves a vacuum that nothing is keen to fill. John Savage and Sir David watch from a short distance as Clegg leaves the motor to idle, climbs from behind the controls and gestures towards Beth and Owen. The charcoal burner is one hundred yards away, Sir David's minders are a mile away, straining anxiously to watch what their boss intends. There is no certainty that they do not have binoculars trained on the helicopter, which is why Clegg insists on the full charade. First Arch brings the charcoal burner closer but still on the blind side. Next the stretcher bed is lifted into the helicopter in full view of the police. Sir David, Beth and her father duck beneath its idling blades to join Clegg and Sam's stretcher. Sir David even allows himself a wave back to his colleagues. Clegg closes the door and for a few brief seconds they are all together, inside the grey-green egg of metal, enclosed by its secure frame. Almost straight away Clegg gestures to the door on the blind side, away from the watchers and adjacent to Arch. Sir David slides it open. Wind and air rush in as Owen and Andrew pass Sam's stretcher through the helicopter and back out into the charcoal burner, where it came from only moments before. Owen gestures Beth to follow. In a flash she realizes what is about to happen. Her father's eyes will be at peace at last, something she has always wanted, but she will not see it. Sir David will apologize as she knows he should but she will not hear it. Clegg will try to give her the dragon bracelet as a parting gift but she will not accept it. She is in no mood for Hollywood candy, has no stomach for farce. The stakes are too high. Soon Watson will broadcast the truth, tell his minders that everyone who is anyone is now inside this machine and must be safely handled, that the future undoing of the Wildside folly begins with this helicopter load of DNA. `Don't worry,` she says, `I'm not going to try and stop you, don't think I am.` with that she climbs out of the far door without a backwards glance and within seconds she is stowed safely in the charcoal-burner, next to the stretcher, imagining the bracelet, imagining her father's eyes, glad she has escaped them.

In the relative quiet and vague light of the vehicle she looks at Andrew, Owen, Arch's dread-locks, Sam's body. She hesitates. Strings and shadows are confused at such times, motive becomes unclear, but to some prompting she cannot understand she takes Sam's hand, clenched like a claw, and softly eases it open. The shred of balloon, the crumpled mess of a once beautiful feather, both drop to the floor. She peers through the tiny window as the helicopter blades, almost above them, pound into action. Arch has reached for the feather. He stares at it for a moment, smoothes the barbs, places it behind her ear and then slams down the pedal and draws the vehicle away.

Detective Inspector Alice Jones and the uniformed officers watch with satisfaction as the grey-green snub-nosed beast lifts into the air, swings low and heavy over their huddle and then heads out above Stretton towards Wenlock Edge. Within the hour it will have disgorged its load into the damp tunnels of Welbeck. They do not worry about the charcoal burner making its hasty exit down the Mynd's western slope, away to the Wildside's deep bosom. They do not see the covey of grouse cringing in the heather close to their feet and static with fear. They do not see the osprey drop to its nest beside the lake on the escarpment edge, nor the bare-footed youth, a tree or two to its left, who can see them to his right and the helicopter rising ahead.

It is not the time for crossbows, dear Finn. They have their time and place as you well know, but this is not it. Do not reach for a crossbow when the sky is about to fall in. Nor is it time for jealousy. The low long ache for Beth, for the wholeness she offers, her soft answers to your harsh questions, her explanation of all the mysteries, now is not the time. Now is the time for Clegg's style of discipline. He has prepared you well.

Finn reaches for the remote control in his pocket and simply presses a button. That it should come to this. Once Arthur led chain-clad troops on horse back into screaming battle, pilots in planes of canvas and wood roared above southern England, sea captains launched their cannon and their men across the crowded narrows of the English Channel. Now Finn presses a single button. He closes his eyes to the explosion and tries to imagine the faces of the watching police, their arrogant and triumphant expressions run away like hot wax as the precious cargo in its grey-green snub-nosed coffin bursts into violent and lurid oranges and reds, as the noise thuds out across a score of valleys, as any illusions of victory shatter into a million grey-green shards of metal. Another vacuum of silence into which nothing will enter.

SIXTYTWO

Dear Sam,

I know you can't hear me. I can't post this and you wouldn't be able to read it but it doesn't matter, I'm going to write it anyway, I'm going to write just one last time and then burn it, I'm going to send the smoke and ashes into the air like we used to do for Father Christmas.

We kept our promise, Sam. I hope Clegg realized that. We kept our promise to fix things for him, to get him across the Line, even though I made it under duress, even though it took so many years. Did he know, when he sat me in the toilet and gobbed into my throat, did he know back then that he was my brother, or at least half brother, that we were flesh and blood? Is that why he was so angry, so bitter, so ready to hurt? Or did he only know, really know, for the first time, when he met Dad in the Crystal Cave?

I would love to ask these questions but never will. What is the point? Things move on and change before you know it. Like with Mum. At least we know the truth of that, at least Dad was returned to us before he died.

In place of all the questions, Sam, I will give you one last thought, one last image from beyond the heat-haze of the motorway. It belongs to Stratford, the home of theatre. A dull yellow light echoes off the water and a cold wind chases theatre-goers from their boats and trams into the warm welcome of the concourse. A group of girls giggles in some foreign language at the sight of the legendary bare-footed youths who mingle with the crowd. Drinks are ordered to be taken in the scramble of the interval and others admire the photographs and landscape paintings which decorate the walls and celebrate the beauty of the Wildside, the Land of the Grail, the place where healing is found through landscape.

How nice it would be to people today's audience with familiar faces. I would love to do that for you, Sam, I would love to *do that for you more than you can ever imagine. Me next to Finn, perhaps, hand-in-hand, eager for the play. Dr.Khalil`s wife with the priestess, now close friends. Andrew and Arch trading views from their different planets. Owen, calm and thoughtful, fresh from the funeral of his old friend John Savage on the hospice island of Bredon. Clegg listening to Ralph Bailey's latest theory. And you of course, Sam. You contracted like the rest of us to the confines of your mended brain. No more flights of fancy, Sam, no more secret short-cuts to the minds and motives of others.*

But it is not to be.

Only Agnes of this audience would be familiar to you, Sam. Only Agnes, who knows where motive met with history to preserve for a while longer the fragile freedom of at least some of this country's people. How much of all the theory she subscribes to, whether Arthur awoke on our behalf and defied the awful odds set against him, we will never know. Agnes knows many other truths. Not in her brain but intuitively, in the lovely warmth of her loins, where Clegg's unborn child, Dad's only grandchild, waits for its inheritance, carries its key to the secrets of the Hollow Mountain. Agnes will be the alchemist again, transforming Clegg's past inside her womb. Step-son Jo, niece Bonny, both out of reach. But he will have a child of his own. And he will never tell it a single lie nor break any promise.

But there is one thing she does not know and never will, though I think we know the answer, Sam, you and I both. Was Clegg, like Judas, the unspeakable traitor? Or was Clegg, like Judas, the unsung hero, the saviour, the one whose sacrifice would make possible a thousand Easters? The fruit of betrayal, after all, is not always bitter.

Was Clegg's deal with Finn as she suspected, as she hoped? It was Finn who had delivered the gold to her, real gold, still in Sir David's brief case. With such gold she could make real beauty to corrupt the souls of the blighted. Had Finn stolen the gold?

Reclaimed it in all the confusion? Or had Clegg known all along, as the accompanying note had suggested?

'Dear Agnes, I know why old men plant trees.' the note said, *'In the meantime, may this help you find your Grail as you helped me find mine.'*